WHATEVER FOR HIRE

a Magical Romantic Comedy (with a body count)

RJ BLAIN

WHATEVER FOR HIRE
A MAGICAL ROMANTIC COMEDY (WITH A BODY COUNT)

Warning: This novel contains excessive humor, action, excitement, adventure, magic, romance, and bodies. Proceed with caution.

Fetching a cat out of a tree should've been a quick, easy fifty bucks in Kanika's pocket. Instead, following one stray thought, the devil pays her a visit and leaves her with a debt to repay.

Owing the devil a favor is bad enough, but her life is turned upside down when it's time to pay the piper. First, she doesn't want the world's sexiest firefighting, kitten-rescuing Scot as an unwilling companion. Since that wasn't bad enough, she doesn't know who wants him dead or why, but there's no way in hell she's going to let someone mar his perfection.

Add in the fact the devil wants an heir, and there's only one thing she knows for certain: she's in for one hell of a job.

Cover Design by Rebecca Frank (Bewitching Book Covers)

Dedication

Amy, thanks for dancing in the flames with me on this book. I needed a good partner for it. P.S.: I'm not sorry about that pun.

To my readers, thanks for sticking through this crazy ride with me. I hope you have as much fun with this story as I have.

I never should've named my
mercenary gig Whatever for Hire.

I NEVER SHOULD'VE NAMED my mercenary gig Whatever for Hire. People took the name too literally, which explained why I was stuck in a tree fetching a cat. If I'd been thinking, I would've refused Miss Angorra's fifty dollars, leaving her precious kitty Mistoffelees to fend for herself. Instead of taking her money, I should've told her to learn how to spell before hightailing it out of town. Mephistopheles really didn't like when people screwed with his name. Call him the devil, call him Satan, or call him Lucifer; he didn't care as long as you spelled his name right. Nothing pissed off the Lord of Hell quite as much as someone calling him Satin.

It happened. I'd witnessed when an idiot thought it'd be funny to invoke Satan's name as graffiti. It hadn't ended well for him. Mephistopheles had appeared, wrapped the poor sod up in satin, and lit him on fire, screaming something in German about the importance of education. I had watched the whole episode with my mouth gaping open like an idiot.

I'd learned an important lesson that day: forget summoning circles. If I wanted a quick chat with the devil, all I needed to do was get some glitter and write his name in it—spelled incorrectly. He'd light my ass on fire, but he'd probably let me live to tell the tale so others would learn from my mistake.

For some reason I couldn't fathom, the devil liked me.

Mistoffelees mewed, and I was willing to bet my soul the eight-pound ball of white fluff was scolding me for not getting her out of the tree faster. Cats: couldn't live with them, and no, no matter what people liked to say, I could easily live without them.

"Oh, Mistoffelees," Miss Angorra wailed. "Come home to Mommy."

The cat hissed, and I didn't blame her one bit. No sane being wanted to be named—incorrectly—after the devil. It courted trouble.

"All right, kitty. We can do this the hard way or the easy way. Pick."

Mistoffelees climbed higher into the sap-oozing pine. Why make it easy for me to pocket some change for once in my life? Asshole cat. "I'll get glitter, and so help me, kitty,

I'll write your name in it. And when the devil shows up, I'm going to blame you. Sure, he might kill me over it, but it might be worth it. Must you start shit?"

With a defiant flick of her tail, Mistoffelees climbed higher. Yep. Kitty was starting shit just because she could. How repulsively cat-like of her. "Come on, Mistoffelees. Not today. Please, not today. Let's cut a deal. Take a rain check on tree climbing, and I'll get you some treats. I'll give you a five percent cut, paid out in treats, if you come down from there right now."

Mistoffelees rejected my generous offer and ascended to parts of the pine I couldn't reach, at least not while human. Damn it. I didn't want to strip and shift. The resulting disaster involving two cats stuck in a tree would either make me a laughingstock or a prime target for Miss Angorra, who probably hoarded cats while deluding herself into believing they liked her.

Maybe if I had better control over my shifts, things wouldn't be so bad. I could always shift, but I played Russian roulette with the results. I blamed my father's side of the family for that; Ruska Roma to the core, he'd wandered his way to Egypt, seduced my mother, and wandered off to wherever it was gypsies roamed after making their conquests.

More often than not, I ended up a sex

kitten with killer six-inch heels, gypsy bells, a deep diving, too-tight blouse, and a satin sari skirt that accommodated my furry tail. On a good day, I got wings to go with my feline head, perfect ears, human body, and clawed hands. Well, as close to a human body as someone with silky black fur got. My mother might've even approved. What self-respecting Egyptian woman wouldn't want to be the spitting image of Bastet but better dressed?

Me, apparently.

I wasn't a very good Egyptian *or* Ruska Roma; coming to America as an abandoned infant had ensured that.

To add insult to injury, when my shifts went wrong, they went really wrong. The real Bastet could kick my ass in a fight; my big, bad lioness warrior form weighed in at fifteen whole pounds. A Maine Coon could beat the shit out of me, and the average dog viewed me as a snack.

No, if I shifted, I wanted my sphinx form. First, I could fly. Second, I could fly. Hell, did the rest even matter?

I could *fly*.

On the plus side, weighing six hundred pounds came in useful at times, as did my enhanced hearing, eyesight, senses of smell and taste, and my beautiful black fur and ivory wings. But when I boiled it down? If I had to go through the hassle of shifting, I wanted to touch the sky, flying as high as possible because I could.

I blamed the cat in me.

I hated cats sometimes.

"Don't make me do this," I begged.

Mistoffelees hissed at me and disappeared higher up the pine. Yep, the damned cat was going to make me do it. Closing my eyes, I sighed and contemplated summoning His Most Indignant Majesty, Lord Satin of Hell. Shit, Satan. Lord Satan of Hell. It didn't count if I didn't write it down, did it?

Then again, death was a far better fate than endless humiliation. Regretting the day I'd founded Whatever for Hire, I stripped.

FEW THINGS SUCKED MORE than trying to navigate pine branches while rocking glittery red heels. I'd lucked out though; they were only three inches tall. I shifted with relative ease, and my magic dressed me in a satin sari skirt to match my shoes, but instead of adhering to the glitter motif, I wore a cascading silver coin belt, the kind belly dancers attached to their costumes. As if my belt jingling wasn't bad enough, I had bells tied around my wrists and ankles. Adding to my woes, my red satin blouse was decorated with even more coins, drawing unwanted attention to my cleavage.

Damn it, why couldn't sex kitten me have reasonable breasts? My usual C cup was bad enough, but I really didn't need the headache of dealing with double Ds. I wanted my smaller, almost manageable breasts back. Flattening my ears, I lifted my head and hissed at Mistoffelees.

The cat hissed back.

"Oh my word!" Miss Angorra squealed from below. "Well, I never."

If the woman even thought about uttering a single word from the musical she'd thieved her cat's name from, I'd catch Mistoffelees just so I could throw her at her owner. Alternatively, I'd find a more dignified human to care for her. If the cat insisted on evading me, she wouldn't like her express trip out of the tree.

"You wouldn't actually do that," the silky, satiny, and sexily smooth voice of His Most Indignant Majesty cooed in my ear.

Then the bastard yanked my tail.

I roared. Mistoffelees yowled. For the first time in my life, I witnessed a cat faint. If I'd been alone, Miss Angorra's beloved feline would've splattered on the ground fifty feet below. Satan plucked the falling furball out of the air, and I glimpsed a glimmer of gold out of the corner of my eye. A moment later, I wore the feline draped across the back of my neck.

Since pulling my tail wasn't enough to please the devil, he squeezed my ass.

I mule kicked, and the devil grunted. When I wasn't incinerated along with the tree and the cat, I kicked him again to make sure Mephistopheles kept his distance. "It's my lucky day. Lord Satin of Hell has visited me."

Today was going to be the day my mouth would finally get me killed, but at least I'd go out with a bang. As far as obituaries went, death by Satan's hand would turn heads.

"You know, I have a fondness for cats. They're delightfully rebellious creatures. Only a cat could get away with calling *me* Satin. Well, and my wife. My wife calls me whatever she wants, and I'm supposed to shut up and like it. I'm absolutely positive this'll shock you, but I don't listen very well. Maybe that's why I like cats. We have a lot in common."

"Tell you what, Lord Satin of Hell. You stop groping my ass and run on home, and I won't tell your wife on you." I thought the arrangement was a good one; I lived, his wife was none the wiser about Satan's demonic and completely expected behavior, and he returned to Hell where he belonged. It didn't matter I hadn't known Mephistopheles was married. I seized the advantage. I was willing to bet his wife was one hell of a woman who'd kick his ass for showing affection to any ass but hers.

"That she is, and right you are," the devil agreed. "Let's bargain, cupcake. My wife'll string me up by my wings if she finds out I couldn't resist that satin-clad tail you're packing. You're going to make a man real happy one day, little lady. You should be proud of that tail of yours. It's top grade. Anyway, if you don't want me smiting you for calling me Satin, you'll do me a favor."

There was no way in hell—Hell, even, or anywhere else for that matter—I'd do Satan a favor. I'd rather die first. Death would give my soul a chance to go somewhere other than hell. I didn't want to become Satan's eternal toy. "I don't do favors, Beetlebub."

"Beelzebub," he snarled.

"So sorry, Manifesto."

"Mephisto!"

"Damn it. I'm sorry, Lucy." Since I was going to die anyway, I'd get in a few last jabs first. "If you want me to work for you, you need to pay me. None of this favors bullshit. Fair pay and right of refusal. Refusal means I can say no if I don't like the job, for those of us who are contractually impaired. By us, I mean you."

"Do you remember what happened the last time a mortal called me Satin, cupcake?"

"Sure. You wrapped him in satin and lit him on fire. That charming memory is the whole damned reason you're here. Jesus. A girl slips once and look what happens—all hell breaks loose. All I wanted was to fetch a damned cat out of a tree."

"You have no idea what self-preservation is, do you? I'll buy you a dictionary for Christmas so you can look it up."

"How sweet. Satan observes his rival's birthday. That's so civilized. Anyway, I'm up a tree arguing with the ass-groping devil. What do you think? If you want a favor, pay me a fair wage for the work. There are easier ways to hire me than harassing me in a tree, by the way. You could call me. Try it sometime. I answer my phone."

I always answered my phone. I couldn't afford Caller ID.

"How is it you survived to thirty-seven?" Lord Satin of Hell sighed.

"Hell if I know. Frankly, I'm surprised I made it past birth. I'm pretty sure if my mother had had anything to say about it, she would've drowned me the instant I drew my first breath. It's the whole resenting having slept with a gypsy thing. Long story." I turned my attention back to my work, which involved an unconscious cat draped across the back of my neck. How was I supposed to get her down without dropping her?

Maybe I'd done a shitty job of naming my business, but I was a grand champion of improvisation. First, I needed my jeans. With my jeans, I could get us both out of the tree alive. "Hey, Lord Satan of Hell, Your Most Magnificent and Sulfury Majesty, please pass me my pants."

The invisible bastard pressed me against the tree trunk, making it pretty clear Her Royal Hellish Majesty was a really lucky lady. Since it counted as rude to yell at him for doing what I had asked, I kept my mouth shut.

Satan gave me my pants, and since I wasn't going anywhere with the devil pinning me to a tree, I tied the legs together to fashion an impromptu cat carrier. Grabbing the white feline by her scruff, I stuffed her in my jeans, made sure she wouldn't fall, and slung her under my arm. "Thanks, Satin."

"So, about that favor."

"Pay me."

"Now look here, Kanika!"

"No. Pay me." I eased away from the Lord of Hell with Mistoffelees contained in her jeans prison, her little nose peeking out of the denim. "I didn't summon you. I didn't ask for your help. You saved the cat of your own volition. I demanded, you obeyed, so I'm under no obligation to do anything for you."

It sucked to be the devil, but I'd seen him

bargain before. I was a lot of things, but I wasn't usually stupid. Usually. I had my moments, but when it came to the devil, I needed to play it smart or I'd end up dead. Enslaved for the rest of eternity was also a possibility, one I hoped to avoid. I eased my foot onto the branch beneath me, tested my weight, and when it held, I worked my way down and out of Satan's reach.

If he wanted me, he'd have to chase me, and Mephistopheles was a lot of things, but he had a severe case of lazy when it came to mortals beneath his notice.

"Kanika."

I hesitated. "What?"

"That branch is going to break."

Since when did the devil give away anything for free, including advice? Startled, I jerked my head up. A faint golden shimmer betrayed the Lord of Hell's approach. A moment later, he took Miss Angorra's cat. "Hey, what do you think you're doing?"

The devil laughed. The branch broke beneath my heels, and I fell from my lofty perch with an undignified yowl.

MOST CATS LAND on their feet. I belly flopped, thoroughly tenderized after smacking into every branch on the way down. The Lord of Hell laughed in my ear, set Mistoffelees on my back, and whispered, "I'll call you, cupcake."

"Please don't," I groaned. "Ever." I shouldn't have wasted my breath. The devil was already gone.

"Mistoffelees!" Miss Angorra wailed, scooping her cat off my back. The animal hissed her displeasure. "My darling angel."

I suspected the woman had more issues than a posse of psychiatrists could handle. I shuddered, wheezing as my chest and ribs protested their close introduction with the hard-packed ground. Would my insurance cover injuries sustained while retrieving a cat out of a tree? Probably not. "That'll be fifty dollars, please."

While I liked cash, I preferred when my clients handed it to me rather than dumping it on the ground in the general vicinity of my outstretched hand. She did get points for prompt payment, though.

"Oh, don't forget your things, cupcake." My clothes, wallet, and cell phone material-ized beside me. "You might want to get your ribs looked at. One's close to poking a hole in something rather important to you mortal types."

"Thanks, Satin. Appreciated. You're just swell."

"It'd be a pity if you died before you're useful to me. You know how it goes."

"Sure. I get it. You're still paying me."

"What a bother. Very well. Your hospital fees—all of them for the next six months— will be your retainer. A hundred an hour for your work, including travel time. You can even keep your precious right of refusal if you absolutely must. Final offer. I suggest you take it. You'll appreciate the retainer, trust me. Since I'm such a generous soul, our arrangement will be effective starting now."

"You have a soul?"

The devil sighed. "My wife told you to say that, didn't she?"

Did I know the devil's wife? Huh. If I did, I'd have to have a long talk with her about better leashing her wayward husband so he wouldn't bother me as much. "Your wife's probably crying into her beer because she has to put up with you for the rest of eternity."

"Well, she's the one who agreed to marry me. The other bachelorettes wisely ran away. Do we have a deal, Kanika? Also, you need a last name. You also need a middle name. A good Russian girl like you has three names. You have one. Get on the ball. Three names, Kanika—pick two, any two, but give yourself a proper name."

"No, Satin. I'm not picking extra names be-

cause your delicate sensibilities are offended."
Even if he wanted me to name myself in the
Egyptian way, following my mother's culture
and traditions, I didn't exist, not on paper, not to
my so-called family. Names were inherited by
the legitimate. The Egyptian government often
refused to issue birth certificates to children
without fathers officially heading the family. I
suspected the judgment my mother had faced
because of her pregnancy had led her to ship me
off to America to live with my aunt, who disliked me almost as much as my mother did.

According to my aunt, Egyptians valued
marriage above all else. For them, family was
a serious affair. For me, it meant a living
nightmare. At least in America, I had a birth
certificate, although I legally only had one
name. I liked it that way, although it made
people uncomfortable when they learned I
lacked a surname.

"I wasn't asking you to name yourself in
the Egyptian tradition, Kanika, but even if I
did, I'd only ask you to go back a couple of
generations. Or even one. I'd accept one.
Couldn't you take your mother's family's
name? I thought the Russian way would be
easier for you. You'd be properly American."
The Lord of Hell hummed. "We *are* in America, right?"

I sighed. Why, exactly, would I want to
take my mother's family's name? The devil

needed a reality check—or a swift kick in the ass. If I met his wife, I'd have to suggest she act on my behalf. "We're in Tennessee. Yes, Tennessee is in America."

"Ah, good. It's annoying when I get turned around, think I'm in America but found my way to Argentina instead. Anyway, do we have a deal, Kanika?"

"I'm going to regret this, aren't I?"

"Of course you will. I'm the devil."

For a hundred an hour plus hospital expenses, I could live with a few—even many—regrets. "Sure, Satin. We have a deal."

"Damned cats," the devil muttered, then he left with a faint pop and a golden flash of light. I lifted my head to discover Miss Angorra had wandered away, probably headed home with her poor cat. The distant wail of a siren promised more suffering, but I'd endure as always. What else could I do?

I needed to work to eat, but I needed my ribs and my internal organs intact so I could work, so I waited patiently for the ambulance to arrive.

TWO

Ugh. I had the Lord of Hell as a
client.

THE DOCTOR and nurses at the hospital had no idea what to make of me and my almost human anatomy, although their fancy machines confirmed one of my ribs was perilously close to puncturing something important. Normal people called the organ a lung. While I refused to owe the devil for something freely given, I'd remember his help when he came hiring.

Like it or not, the first job he gave me I'd agree to do. That seemed fair to me.

The surgeons needed magic to fix my ribs, an expense my insurance company wouldn't cover. I couldn't afford the policy. True to his word, Satin authorized the hospital to bill him for my care. The doctor called him Mr. Santana, and when I laughed so hard I cried, he didn't understand what I found so funny. There was nothing Hispanic about the devil and his hell, although I supposed hundreds of years of religious migration ensured my un-wanted client had global notoriety.

Ugh. I had the Lord of Hell as a client.

Four hours later, following one surgery to return my ribs to their proper places and fuse my broken bones together, the hospital re-leased me. The incision, with the help of more magic and an ointment, would heal in a few days. Scowling at the towering stack of paperwork didn't make it go away, nor did it change my species entry. While 'mixed' for my race was accurate, why couldn't they have listed the correct species?

The hospital refused to acknowledge I was a sphinx. The doctor had tried to con-vince me there was no shame in being a ly-canthrope, especially since I had such a beautiful hybrid form. Infuriated, I'd insisted on a scan to check my lycanthropy virus lev-els, thus proving I wasn't one. No virus meant no lycanthropy, so they'd written panther shapeshifter as my species. Me? A *panther?*

Not even roaring or waving the tufted tip of my tail in their faces had convinced them I was a black lioness. How many times would I need to shift to prove the truth? My driver's license listed me as a humanoid, the nice way of saying I only *looked* human.

Damn it, I was a sphinx, a benevolent guardian and a treasure of Egypt, a stranger far from what should've been my desert home. When human, my skin was much paler than my aunt's brown, and my hair had come from my father. While many Egyptians had dark hair, my family's hair was a rich brown. Mine was as black as the night and prone to frizzing.

I loved my hair. Sometimes, I pretended I was Cleopatra with her glorious wig, ready to rule her empire. Unlike her, I didn't need a wig to pull off the look. All I had to do was trim my bangs and braid jewels into my hair.

In reality, I clung to what had been denied me because of old traditions and modern prejudices. Shoving the papers into a plastic bag with my jeans and shirt, I headed for freedom. There would be time for fury later, after I secured more work. A retainer fee of paid hospital bills wouldn't cover my hotel room or fill my belly. If matters became dire, I'd check out and shift, hunting to survive until my phone led me to more work. I had two weeks left on my prepaid hotel stay.

I wouldn't be forced to hunt as a miniature lion again if I had anything to say about it. I hated it. I hated questioning every decision I'd made since escaping my aunt's house at sixteen. No one, not even me, had known I was a sphinx, a good thing in my opinion. Tired of me wasting space and costing her money, my aunt declared I would marry an appropriately wealthy businessman so I could take his name and get out of her life.

Yeah, right.

My midnight escape had ultimately led to the discovery of my true self. Sphinx. Gypsy. I was both without truly being either. In true gypsy fashion, I roamed, though I did so out of necessity. One day I'd plant roots and build a home.

I'd make it happen one day. Sometimes, when I stayed in one place for more than a few weeks, I rented an apartment, testing the waters. It didn't happen often, but I liked the idea of permanency.

Permanency was a long ways away. Fifty extra bucks in my pocket wouldn't get me far. Nothing clarified my situation more than a good look at rock bottom. I reminded myself I liked my life when I wasn't acting like a broken record. Tightening my hold on my bag, I marched into the late afternoon light, striding towards the cab stand.

I liked my life. I liked my life. Damn it, I liked my life.

My phone rang and jarred me from my thoughts. I grimaced at the number of people passing me on the sidewalk but dug the device out of my blouse anyway. At least my gypsy magic accounted for my breasts and helpfully included a bra with my attire; one day, maybe my magic would acknowledge the usefulness of pockets. Without bothering to look at the display, which chronically reported 'unknown caller,' I answered, "Kanika, Whatever for Hire."

"Has anyone ever told you that's a ridiculous business name, cupcake?"

I would never again assume my day couldn't get any worse. "I see you found my number, Satin."

"Accept the job offer you'll receive in five minutes. My pay's on top of whatever deal you cut with the caller."

Excellent. I wouldn't have to wait to fulfill my moral obligation to play nice with the devil. "You got it, Lucy."

I loved hanging up on the devil, smiling as I returned my phone to my blouse. With laughter bubbling out of me, I spun, my bag whipping out while my sari skirt flared around my legs. If I allowed it, my father's blood would take control of my feet and transform my coins and bells into the sweetest music. I indulged on my way to the cab stand, not caring who watched or if they approved.

My dancing didn't hurt anyone.

When I arrived, I yanked open the back door of the first car in line and slid into the seat. "Garden View Hotel, please."

"You got it, lady. Sure don't see many lycanthropes out in the open round here."

"I don't have lycanthropy." The lingering wild joy of my short dance kept my voice pleasant. "I'm a sphinx."

"You sure don't look like no sphinx. You look like a gypsy cat goddess."

I almost smiled at that. "It's easier to get around this way."

Lie, lie, lie. As a sphinx, I could fly. It took work, but I could *fly*.

"I reckon you're right. Next stop, Garden View Hotel." He started the engine and pulled away from the stand.

"Great." I retrieved my phone and waited for the call Satan claimed would come. Right on schedule, my cell rang. "Kanika, Whatever for Hire. How can I help you?"

"Can you make someone disappear?"

If I hadn't promised myself I'd help the devil with the first job he threw my way, I would've hung up. Since starting my business, I'd done three assassinations, and I'd done them as a vigilante, refusing to accept pay for a murder. The men I'd killed, murderous assholes who'd escaped the law, needed to die. They hadn't escaped from me.

Well aware I had a witness listening to my every word, I answered, "For how long?"

"I don't want you to hurt him, cousin and all, but I need him out of town. He won't leave, not without a fight. So, I want you to relocate him for me. I'd do it, but he'll kick my ass if he gets his hands on me. The idiot won't hit girls, and your site said you're a girl."

My website said I was a woman of inde-terminate species, as I thought it was amusing to keep potential clients wondering. It landed me jobs, too—no one assumed I was a vanilla human, and that translated to competency for some reason.

Flattery often got me everywhere, and I planned on milking my new client for every-thing he was worth. "I have no idea why he'd do such a thing. You seem like a nice gen-tleman to me, concerned for your family. Please tell me more about your cousin."

"You'll do it?"

"If the price is right, I see no reason I can't help your cousin with his move." There. Un-less the driver was freakishly suspicious, he'd think I was helping someone move to a new home. "What's your name?"

"Bubba. Bubba Eugene Stewart, ma'am. My cousin's Malcolm Findlay Stewart. Uncle Boyd's a wee bit more of a traditionalist than my pa. Bottom line's this: he's just not doin' the Stewart name proud. Pa says my cousin needs a lickin'. Uncle Boyd thinks Mal hit his head a few too many times as a child. I think he needs some fresh air and some space. He's drivin' us all batty. We can offer ten thou for you to take him out west, find him a nice place near a lake, and dump him in. Fresh water, none of that salty nonsense, you hear?"

What on Earth? Why would I dump someone *in* a lake? Since I wasn't going to drown someone for ten thousand, I decided to take the vague approach. "Sure, I can find him a nice lodge near a lake for that much. Will he need help settling in?"

"I reckon not. You could just dump him in the water and bail; he'll be fine on his own. Little lady like you couldn't drown that rat even if you tried. Trust me. I've tried." Bubba sighed. "It's damned hard finding a lady merc willing to take a hike anywhere. They've all got themselves family and won't leave. Can't really blame them. You seem perfect for the job."

Me, little? In my heels while doing my Bastet impersonation, I towered over people. One day I'd measure myself, but I was over six feet. Fortunately for both of us, I didn't need to like my clients to do my job.

"I'm going to need more information from you, Bubba." The cab slowed, and I glanced out the window, startled to realize we'd already arrived at the hotel. How had so much time passed already? Damn it. I scrambled for cash, glancing at the meter. I owed eight, so I fished a ten out of the wallet tucked in my cleavage, handed it over, grabbed my bag, and headed for the lobby.

To my relief, no one was outside the lobby having a smoke break. I waited for the car to leave before asking, "How many people will be looking for him?" I loitered by the glass doors, something I commonly did when on the phone so the hotel staff wouldn't think twice about it.

A gusty sigh from Bubba warned me of trouble. "A few."

"Define a few."

"He runs a business in town. Them workers of his'll figure out he's gone pretty quick."

I'd have to find out which town and state, although judging from Bubba's thick accent, I wouldn't have to go far to fetch his cousin. "Ten grand's starting to sound like you're lowballin' me, Bubba. How long'll I have to get this job done, and how hard will they look for him?"

"I reckon they'll call the coppers pretty quick like. They like him over at the fire-house, and then them folks over at that in-vestment doohickey like his money, too. He's gotta go, ma'am. He's ruinin' our turf."

If Malcolm Findlay Stewart was hurting Bubba's turf anywhere near as much as Bubba hurt my head, no wonder the man wanted to get rid of his cousin. "Tell me about him. Any women? Lovers? Close family?"

"He's the black sheep of the family. We

like him, but we like him at a distance. No
ladies. He's into that equality bullshit and
only wants a high-class broad who matches
him, whatever the hell that means. He hasn't
found one. The ones with money aren't his
type, and the type he likes don't got enough
money or motivation to satisfy him. He likes
sayin' if he wanted arm candy, he'd hire himself a hooker, but he won't do that because
the hookers only want him for his money."

Ah. Malcolm was a wise, wise man. "In
short, he wants a go-getter, but a smart, ethical one."

"You know him, lady? That's the same
type of shit he says. If a broad wants to ride
him all night long, he should let her. Ain't that
what studs are for?"

Dear God, I'd found a man I hated more
than the devil. "If you say so. If you want me
to do this job, I'm going to need everything
you know about your cousin. Listen carefully,
because this is really important. I'm going to
need his height, his weight, rough body fat
ratio, and species metabolism level. If he's
ever gotten medication from a pharmacy, his
metabolism rating is on the bottle. Look for
MRL and a number. Better yet, get your
hands on one of his prescriptions and take a
picture of it for me. I'm also going to need an
idea of his diet and habits."

"What do you need all that for?"

I snorted, ignored his question, and replied, "I'm also going to need to know where he goes, who he's usually with, his work hours, a list of who he knows in law enforcement—anything you think might be useful. Too much information is better than not enough information. Once I have everything, I can plan his vacation."

With the important requests out of the way, I headed into the lobby, waving at the employees, who grinned at me. Since checking in almost three weeks ago, they'd grown accustomed to my furry forms—all of them. I'd even spent a few hours as a sphinx beside the pool between jobs.

It'd been too long since I'd indulged in carefree shifting, and I treated the hotel like a resort. I pressed the up button for the elevator and waited for the old, rickety thing to arrive. It would take a while; taking the stairs to the fifth floor would've been faster.

The silence on the phone dragged on, then Bubba sighed. "That's a lot of stuff you need."

"It's required. No exceptions, unless you want to be attending his funeral." I meant it, too. I could think of a few ways I could kidnap a man, but they were risky. The safest method involved the use of a potent drug, one the public wasn't supposed to know about. If I dosed Bubba's cousin appropriately, he'd be drowsy, functional, and pliant. I could tune his dose to the minute and make him completely obedient to my every command.

"I'll get it for you. This needs to be done fast."

The light for the elevator blinked, showing it was on the eighth floor and on its way down. I glared at the panel, tapping my foot while I thought through Bubba's opening offer of ten thousand dollars. The Lord of Hell wanted me on retainer and had shown up mere hours before Bubba's call. The six-month time frame stuck out to me. When it came to the devil, there was no such thing as a coincidence.

Mephistopheles answered summonings at his whim and his whim only. No matter how powerful a practitioner believed himself, Satan took orders from no one, not even God.

I'd met him in the flesh three times, although I'd tried to forget about our second meeting.

The elevator dinged and opened, and I stepped inside, tapping the button for the fifth floor. The door closed with a clunk, and the damned thing groaned its way up. "All right, Bubba. Here are my terms. I don't feel comfortable leaving your cousin alone, so if I'm doing this, I'm keeping him busy for six months, starting now. You'll pay me ten thousand up front. In addition, you'll pay me ten thousand per month while I'm keeping him company, to be paid on the first of every month, so seventy thousand total."

"That much?"

"If he wins fights against other men, he's going to be a handful, and even the most chivalrous of men make exceptions when it comes to punching women. This isn't going to be an easy job. Seventy thousand dollars, Bubba. Are you in or out?"

"In," he snapped.

"I have rules. You'll obey them. Understood?"

"What rules?"

For a change, the elevator wasted no time getting me to the fifth floor. I marched out, striding to my room, my heels clicking on the worn hardwood floors. "No one in your family hires anyone to interfere with him. If your family has already hired someone, sever their contract. I'm working a live job, and I mean to keep him breathing. No allies outside your family will interfere, either. I understand Malcolm has friends he can't control, but I won't tolerate anyone acting against him. For the next six months, he belongs to me. Understood?"

"What would happen if someone broke your rules?"

I smiled. Imitating Bastet involved

showing off a lot of sharp, pointy teeth. "They die. It won't be pretty, Bubba. I take my job seriously."

At my room, I dug my key card out of my wallet and swiped it, pushing inside when the light flashed from red to green. Piles of neatly folded sari took up way too much space, turning the once bland room into a riot of color. I'd have to do something about my clothing hoard again, damn it.

"You have a deal, ma'am. I'll call you with all that stuff you need tomorrow night. I'm texting you now. Reply with your banking details. I'll transfer the funds tomorrow."

I licked my lips. "Perfect, Mr. Stewart. I'll give you an email address you can use to send any necessary pictures or documents to. I look forward to doing business with you."

Not.

I hung up and tossed my phone on the bed, my gaze settling on my one splurge purchase, my laptop. Twenty-four hours wasn't a lot of time to prepare. I really should've charged Bubba Eugene Stewart a million. I'd earn every penny and then some by the time this gig was over, of that I was certain.

THREE

They could charm the skirt off a girl
faster than an incubus.

IF I EVER FIGURED OUT how to reliably shift
back to human, I'd be set. Having to strip before shifting annoyed me, but I hated the discomfort of wearing extra layers of clothes.
How many sari, bells, belts, and shoes did a
girl need? I took the lingerie happily, though.

That shit was expensive, and my magic
provided me with a bit of everything from
seductive lace to comfortable cotton. I tossed
most of the thongs, kept the boy shorts, and
decided on a case-by-case basis for the rest.
My shift went better than usual; I could work
with black, and the bra did nice things to my
breasts. For a rare, appreciated change, I got a
pair of traditional Ruska Roma slippers, comfortable on the feet, durable, and meant for
long travel.

I disliked omens, but I believed in them
enough not to ignore the blessing or the

warning. That was the problem with omens; they could go either way. The shoes meant change, and that was that. I believed change was coming my way. Bubba's call had made a mess of the few plans I'd had.

I'd done one kidnapping gig before, hired by a teen's parents to teach the girl why it wasn't wise to venture into the worst part of Detroit alone. One scare later, their daughter had learned a very valuable lesson about protecting herself. Her parents had paid me a thousand. I might've done it on the house if they hadn't been so eager to give me their cash for solving their problem.

So many things could go wrong during a kidnapping. Grabbing my target would be the easy part. Keeping him would be the problem. If I believed Bubba, I'd need a body of fresh water. Did it have to be a lake? I hoped not. Unless I carted him to northern Canada, lakes attracted people. If my target had aquatic talents, he'd cause me a lot of problems. The first thing I needed to do was figure out why Malcolm needed to be near water. How long could he be away from it? Would I need to stop along the way to expose him to his element?

Could he be a nymph? Despite legend and lore, there *were* male nymphs. They could charm the skirt off a girl faster than an incubus. I wouldn't mind being stuck with a male nymph for six months. I'd enjoy some of the best sex of my life without any risk of pregnancy.

Unlike incubi, nymphs weren't compatible with humans. They only looked human. Unless a fertile female nymph was around, the males fired blanks, and according to the male nymph I'd been lucky enough to net, there hadn't been a fertile female in over a thousand years.

He thought it would be a few more centuries before their breeding season began.

If Malcolm Findlay Stewart was a nymph, I'd need a net. When caught in a net, nymphs fulfilled any reasonable request. I doubted Malcolm was a nymph with his lack of ex-lovers; nymphs would sleep with anything, and they weren't picky about species or gender. However, it would explain Bubba's stud comment, although no self-respecting nymph called himself a stud.

According to the nymph I'd netted, they were gentlemen until the pants came off.

If I delved into the non-human pool, what sort of species would call themselves studs?

Incubi topped the list, followed by minotaurs, and I really, really hoped the Stewarts weren't a Greek minotaur clan. I'd spend the next six months keeping him out of my pants, although it'd simplify matters for me. A minotaur would pursue a female for months if he thought he might get a son out of the deal. Minotaurs were more aggressive than nymphs, though; they viewed reproduction as their sacred duty, and they'd impregnate any girl stupid enough to sleep with them.

Fortunately for women around the world, minotaurs were rare. Unlike what the myths implied, they played fair. They only bred with consenting females, although they didn't necessarily tell the girl she was consenting to more than just wild sex. I knew better.

Damn it, everything circled back to the Lord of Hell. Thanks to him, I knew minotaurs were real, although I never wanted to see the insides of one again. I'd caught a glimpse of the devil in his full glory that day.

I shied away from my memories of that image, but two things had stuck with me: he'd been as beautiful as he'd been terrible.

If I hunted a minotaur, somewhere remote would work, somewhere most wouldn't go for fear of death. I wouldn't lose a minotaur; they loved mazes almost as much as they desired a son. For the lost, there was no better guide. A windowless cellar at a farmhouse would work, especially if I could rig a pond for him. But why would a minotaur want water?

The requirement for water threw me off my game—and potentially eliminated minotaur as Malcolm's species.

"Who are you, Malcolm Findlay Stewart?" I muttered, turning my full attention to my computer.

The internet knew all, and if Malcolm was anywhere near as popular as his cousin thought, I'd find information on him. I sat at the desk, cracked my knuckles, and touched my fingers to the keyboard.

My phone rang.

"Really?" Muttering curses, I fetched the device. "Kanika, Whatever for Hire."

"You need Caller ID, cupcake."

"And I need a bonus three-month retainer to cover any injuries sustained as a result of the shit job you've saddled me with. We don't always get what we want, Satin."

"It's yours under one condition."

Alarm sirens blared in my head, and idiot cat I was, I couldn't help but ask, "What condition?"

"I have papers I want you to sign without reading."

"No." What sort of idiot signed a binding agreement with the devil without reading it first? Scratch that. What sort of idiot signed a binding agreement with the devil? "No."

"You said no twice. Once was sufficient."

"I wanted to make certain you heard me."

"Why not? It's a good deal for you."

I scowled and shook my head. I was willing to bet the devil was spying on me in some fashion. Displaying my middle finger in case he was watching, I took several breaths to calm my nerves. "Only an idiot signs papers without reading them, Lucy. Also, did you really have to use Santana as your surname? It's ridiculous. Have you even been to South America?"

"A time or two. And yes, I did. Would you prefer Mephistopheles?"

"As a matter of fact, yes, I would, Mr. Mephistopheles."

"Never was there ever—"

"Don't you dare finish that sentence. I'm not signing anything without reading it first."

"Are you sure about that, cupcake? In addition to the bonus three-month retainer, I'm willing to pay you half a million dollars in the form of a bank card you have permission to use, which will disintegrate after you've spent the money you're entitled to. I'll also allow you to ask me any questions you like, which I'll answer with complete honesty. I'm willing to have an angel verify the truth prior to you signing."

With half a million reasons to become an idiot, I thought about it. If I picked my questions carefully, I wouldn't have to read the document. I'd still be an idiot, but I'd be a rich idiot. With that much money, I could roam because I wanted to rather than because I had to.

I could find a permanent home for myself.

"Half a million dollars after taxes and no limit on the number of questions I can ask. If I don't like the answers, I'm not signing—and the *truth*. The complete truth. I'll be asking an angel to confirm the truth of every last one of your words, starting from the instant I answered the phone."

"Done. Ask your questions."

I'd start with the obvious. "Will I be signing over my soul in any fashion?"

"No. Your soul is safe. Signing won't influence your fate."

Huh. The devil hadn't tried to buy my soul? Interesting. "Will I come to any harm as a result of signing?"

"It's possible. You *are* signing a deal with the devil, cupcake. You want to ask if signing will earn you enemies. The answer is yes. Not signing will, too. You don't want me as an enemy."

That didn't sound good at all. "Will refusing to sign make you my enemy, Mr. Mephistopheles?"

"It would pain me, but it's possible. I'm betting on you. How many others can say they have the devil rooting for them?"

"You say that like it's a good thing. Honestly, I couldn't care less."

"You're cruel."

"Go cry yourself to sleep. I'm sure your

lovely wife will tuck you into bed and give you a teddy bear so you feel better. Why do you want me to sign this document?"

"I want to protect you and your interests."

The world crashed to a halt. Astonishment erased my thoughts and left me with a stunned nothingness, and my breath left me in a whoosh. The Lord of Hell wanted to protect *me*? Not even my aunt, my own flesh and blood, was willing to do that. She had fed and clothed me out of familial obligation, not for me. Never for me. We'd gotten to the point of mutual tolerance by the time she'd decided to sell me to an asshole, perverted business man, which had resulted in me jumping ship and swimming for shore. She had pitied me.

I didn't handle pity *or* slavery well.

Maybe one day, I'd suggest to Satin he take lessons from Isaac Asfour, the world's nastiest, sleaziest pervert. I still had nightmares of becoming the asshole's young bride. No distance would be far enough away from the likes of him and the other suitors my aunt had wanted to sell me to.

I hid my discomfort by blurting, "Are you crazy?"

The Lord of Hell laughed, a startlingly pleasant sound. "Sometimes. Is it so difficult for you to believe someone might want to protect you?"

"In a word, yes. Why would you of all people want to protect me?"

"That's a better question. I made a deal with someone. The price was to protect you. This is my way of meeting the requirements of that bargain."

"Why the fuck would anyone bargain with you over me? That's stupid."

The devil cracked up laughing, snorting several times before clearing his throat. "I'm not at liberty to say even if I knew why, which I don't. I don't care why people want to sell their souls to me. I'm the devil, after all."

Crap on a cracker. What had I gotten into all those years ago when I'd witnessed someone summon Satan by spelling his name wrong? "And you having me sign this paper is the best way for you to protect me?"

"Shockingly, yes. I don't normally give my prey such a good deal, but some souls are worth it. In a way, that one might've gotten the better end of the deal. It happens from time to time."

"And if I refuse?"

"Everyone loses, especially you."

Double crap on a cracker, I didn't like the sound of that at all. "Will signing financially fuck me over later?"

"No. It's entirely beneficial for you, even on a metaphysical level, which absolutely disgusts me. Your agreement benefits me in the deal for that other soul."

"Why's that soul so important to you?"

"That's another good question. Excellent. You're learning."

I was? I frowned but remained silent.

"It's simple. I'm Mephistopheles until the end of days. Did you know several have worn the mantle of God? The current one hasn't been around long. Don't tell him this, but I actually like him. As far as those who have held his portfolio go, he's a realist. Anyway, that soul will grant me something I currently lack. A freedom, if you will."

The devil lacked a freedom? Curiosity dug its cruel claws into me. "What freedom?"

He sighed, and I didn't like the way the sound made me feel. Why should I care about the devil's discomfort? "Until now, until the possibility of you signing, I've been unable to have a child. You signing will change that. That's what that soul gains me. I'm the only divine incapable of having a child. For that to change, you must willingly sign."

Something in my chest tightened. "You really can't have children?"

"Correct. I can't have children, not until you sign."

"And your child. What price will Earth pay for you having a child?" Would it change his hell or the heavens? I didn't care much if it did. Devils and angels could take care of themselves better than mere mortals.

"What an interesting question, but a wise one. It would make me happy. That would piss off the man upstairs. That's between just us, by the way. It doesn't leave his heavens or my hell. As for Earth? A child of mine is but a drop of water in the ocean. Nothing would change for Earth. That's the beauty of mortals. They make their own fate, and their choices are what shapes the Earth's future. Could my child change the world? Yes. Will my child change the world? Not even I know. The future is a fluid thing, and it's tiring contemplating all the possibilities. It's rare for there to be a fixed future. Mortals change things. That's their nature."

If Mephistopheles kept surprising me, I'd suffer a heart attack before I had a chance to sign the papers. "I could almost feel sorry for you."

"Don't. I'm an asshole, and we both know it, cupcake. Don't waste your energy feeling sorry for me. I *am* the devil. Worry about yourself. Do we have a deal?"

"Is there another question I should be asking?"

"There are two main questions and a few minor ones you should be asking, but only the first one actually matters."

"What questions should I ask you?"

Choking sounds came from the other end of the line, and the devil whimpered his laughter. "You're truly a jewel among mortals. You should ask me how long the contract is valid for. That's important. The rest are details."

"The devil's in the details," I reminded him.

"So I am. These details won't harm you. I have to keep the lawyers happy."

"Heaven forbid we distress the lawyers."

"Exactly. No one can whine—or flood your office with extraneous paperwork—quite like a lawyer. Well, are you going to ask me?"

"Fine. When does the contract expire?"

"It doesn't."

I frowned. "Will I ever find out what I'm signing?"

"Oh yes. You're going to find out, all right. I really want to see your face when you learn what I've done. It'll be beautiful."

That worried me a lot. "That doesn't sound good for me."

"Your expression will be priceless. I look forward to it. Do we have a deal?"

It turned out five hundred thousand dollars made me an idiot. "Heaven help me, I'll sign, but only after an angel has verified you've spoken the truth and nothing but the truth. If you told me a single lie, no deal."

"You won't regret your decision for long," the devil promised. "Expect company at dawn, cupcake."

Long after the Lord of Hell hung up on me, I stared at the wall with my phone still held to my ear. What had I gotten myself into?

Everyone made mistakes, but mine were worse than most. I couldn't tell what I'd missed—if I'd missed anything at all. Maybe I'd land on my feet instead of belly flopping and breaking most of my ribs again. Who was I kidding?

I'd just fucked myself over by making a deal with the devil, and I'd fucked up so spectacularly I didn't even know what I'd agreed to. No wonder greed counted as a deadly sin. Five hundred thousand had made me cast my common sense to the four winds.

At least I still had my soul. That counted for something, didn't it?

IF I WANTED to be awake for my dawn date with the devil, I'd need to pull an all-nighter, especially since I doubted I'd be able to sleep even if I tried. Despite knowing I courted trouble, there was too much to do if I wanted to pull off my job for Bubba Eugene. Worrying about signing the Lord of Hell's paperwork wouldn't help me kidnap Malcolm, although the extra money would make things easier.

Signing would ensure I'd have the funds needed to pull off the kidnapping. In the worst case, I could pin the job on Satin. That thought made me giggle.

Never had 'the devil made me do it' been truer. I'd savor the moment I whipped that line out in court. If I got caught, that's where I'd end up. When I made my declaration, it would be in the presence of an angel—an angel I could request thanks to having been born human despite my species shift during adolescence. In a perfect world, I'd escape into obscurity after unloading Bubba Eugene's infuriated cousin on his doorstep. While they fought, I'd take advantage of the excitement and run for the hills.

Every complicated job started with a plan. Plans tended to explode in my face, so I'd layer backup plans until they blended together and formed a convoluted entity. No matter what happened, I needed a way out for me and my target. Keeping my client's victim alive was my top priority.

Protection gigs sucked, especially when it involved protecting someone against their will. No matter what happened, I was screwed, and my success hinged on learning everything I could about my victim.

"Who are you, Malcolm? Why does your family want you gone?" I made myself comfortable in front of my laptop and tapped in my password. The instant I logged in, I changed my password to a variant of 'Satin sucks socks' for shits and giggles.

I'd invoke the devil's misspelled name every time I used my computer, and I'd do it with a smile. Once satisfied with my blasphemy, I went to work.

I started with a name search and was dismayed to learn Malcolm Findlay Stewart was a very common Scottish name. On second thought, I could work with a Scot. I didn't know a single woman who objected to the occasional objectification of a smoking, bare-chested Scot in a kilt.

Considering the little Bubba Eugene had told me, I tossed in fireman as a keyword to see if I could narrow the two million results to something a bit more manageable. I grinned. If Scots in kilts could make a woman's blood boil, what would a hunky fireman Scot do? Curiosity reared its ugly head and bit me in the ass, and unable to resist the lure, I checked the image results.

A half-naked man covered in soot holding an entire litter of disheveled, soaked kittens took the top spot.

"Holy abs," I whispered, licking my lips and swallowing so I wouldn't drool. It took far longer than I liked to realize the rest of his clothes were on the ground serving as a blanket for a bunch of sopping wet puppies. Clicking the image took me to an article about a fire at an animal shelter, declaring Malcolm Findlay Stewart a local hero for entering the collapsing building to rescue as many of the trapped animals as he could.

A second picture showed more of his face, which was bloodied from a cut near his hairline. Beneath the blood and soot, I thought he was blond or a pale ginger.

Meow.

If my job involved kidnapping him, I'd be a very happy kitty. I'd even hunt him as a feline, since I couldn't purr when human. Lionesses couldn't purr, either, but I'd do my best. On looks alone, he was worth purring over. Add in his dedication to rescuing kittens and puppies and I might not ever let him go if I got my hands on him.

I'd met too many pretty men who couldn't tie their shoelaces without help. This specific Malcolm Findlay Stewart jumped into burning buildings, and he didn't draw a line at only rescuing sentients. He risked his life for unwanted pets.

Could a more perfect man exist?

Since he was so easy on the eyes, I made a note to check if he'd modeled for any sexy fireman calendars. I bet they made him Mr.

July on virtue of him being too hot to handle. I needed every last calendar featuring him so I could properly indulge in my fledgling crush.

It took a lot of effort, but I dragged my attention back to work. The addition of fireman to my search had narrowed my pool down to several hundred men scattered across the United States. Creating a spreadsheet, I began the tedious task of listing them by name, state, and city. Once finished, I filtered by the states I believed might have men nicknamed Bubba. I refused to believe Bubba was my client's real name. Still, I checked his name, too, just in case a Bubba Eugene showed up on the same page as a Malcolm or Malcolm Findlay.

No such luck.

However, I did discover three Bubba Eugenes. Two lived in Virginia and one lived in Tennessee. I thought it safe to assume the cousins lived in the same state, thus limiting my pool of eligible Scots to six, and the rescuer of baby animals numbered among them.

I thanked God several times for the hope I might get my filthy paws on a Scottish firefighter worthy of a second look, and not just because he—them, all six of them—looked like escapees from the high heavens. Their abs alone made my mouth water. I suspected their presence was responsible for elevating the state's temperature by a few degrees. The men could easily explain a few things about the state's weather, too. I bet Mother Nature summoned storms most nights to cool her jets.

Since they all shared the same name, I went with the sexy fireman calendar theme and assigned them a month. The hottest one, Sir Kitten and Puppy Rescuer Supreme, retained his title as Mr. July. August went to a ginger with a beard. I liked beards; they reminded me of whiskers, and I liked August because of its instability. While he wasn't quite as devastatingly handsome as Mr. July, August still smoldered.

Who was I kidding? If one of them was Bubba Eugene's cousin, I'd have my work cut out for me. Not only would I need to keep him alive, I'd have to make sure not a single inch of his perfection was marred while in my care.

The title of January went to an ice god with the palest blue eyes I'd ever seen. May went to the oddball elf-thin Scot with a smile so bright it needed to be classified as a dangerous weapon. October went to a rugged man who, according to an article I'd found, enjoyed rock climbing in the high peaks.

I figured his big hands could crush stone to powder with ease. However handsome, of the six, he was the one I didn't want to get

into a fight with. Even in my feline forms, I
suspected he could smash me to pulp.

The last of the men—and my most realistic option—lived within twenty miles of
Tennessee's Bubba Eugene Stewart. Something about the Scot's dark eyes worried me,
cold despite his otherwise pleasant expression. I named him February because of my
dislike for that month, when it felt like spring
would never come. With my luck, I'd be stuck
with February, and no matter how handsome
he was, eyes like his worried me.

They were the eyes of someone who'd
enjoy skinning me for my pelt.

Mr. February enjoyed showing off his
body—all of it—on social media. Maybe his
eyes creeped me out, but I could lose hours
admiring the rest of him. At twenty-four, he
was younger than I liked, which did a good
job of cooling my jets and convincing me
maybe I should work rather than lick my
chops and think of the many ways I could
enjoy him for dessert. His public profiles reported he worked at a car dealership, which
fit some of Bubba Eugene's vague descriptions. Twenty minutes into my browsing, I
discovered links to his online dating profiles.

I clicked.

Big mistake.

If the pictures of him showing off his
prowess with his equally pretty boyfriends

were any indication, he had a very active and public sex life—so public he used his exploits to attract new men to his bed. To add to the chaos, he was openly engaged to two of his lovers.

Damn. I needed half his luck. I scratched the man off my list of candidates, filing away his profile information in case I needed to drag my client over coals for lying to me. If Mr. February was Bubba Eugene's cousin, Bubba was going to end up with a really rude wakeup call in the form of my foot up his ass.

I hated when my clients lied to me.

It took less than ten minutes to eliminate Mr. October from my list; he was married with children. Mr. May was engaged. Mr. August went through women almost as fast as I collected saris, leaving me with Mr. January and Mr. July as my viable options. Both were volunteer firefighters and led private enough lives. I couldn't find them on social media; they only showed up as mentions in rare articles detailing their acts of heroism in the face of fire—literal fire.

Deleting Findlay from my searches helped; I scored a hit on Mr. January.

He deserved a very successful career as a fashion model. Was he my target? Did models make enough to be involved with investments? I had no idea.

Models were way out of my league, and

not because of my looks. I had the exotic market nailed down, and men liked that well enough, but when it came to public events, I became a liability. When courting wealthy companies, the rich and famous wanted pretty but generic American girls hanging off their arms.

If Mr. January was my target, I wouldn't have to guess his measurements. His modeling agency included everything from his species to his metabolism rating. With a rating of ninety-five percent human, it was no wonder they showed off his private information. I'd never met such a pure human before. I'd heard of them, but they were going extinct. Within a hundred years, humanity would only exist because so many different species liked sleeping together, resulting in what the CDC classified as a human but wasn't, not really.

Even then, hybrid children weren't human, not really. To make matters worse for humanity, people like me existed, non-humans who'd been born human to human parents but changed during puberty into something else, further diluting the gene pool. When the magic failed again, people like me would die out or go into hibernation until the magic returned and rewrote what it meant to be human.

Cultural divides would ultimately reset

humanity back to its state before magic had bloomed and taken over Earth. If I endured beyond magic's recession, my exotic appearance would sink my ship in European-pale America.

I struggled enough as it was; I didn't need my odd skin color and foreign appearance becoming the primary focuses of discrimination and prejudice. It was hard enough convincing people I was a sphinx. If prejudice turned skin deep, I'd be in trouble.

Shaking my head, I forced my attention back to my work. No matter how many different ways I scoured the internet for Mr. January and Mr. July, I couldn't eliminate either one of them as a possibility. I couldn't figure out why anyone would want them to disappear. Neither had a single scandal sullying their name. At first blush, they were truly beautiful and perfect in all ways.

Leaning back in my chair, I scowled at my laptop. If either one suggested I should hop into bed with him, I'd do it without hesitation, and not just because it had been way too long since I'd dived between the sheets with someone. Despite my father's nature and my wandering feet, I liked the illusion of security and permanency. Maybe one day I'd find a lycanthrope to share the rest of my life with, which would solve my relationship woes. A lycanthrope wouldn't leave me—he couldn't.

The virus wouldn't let him, not until death did we part. I supposed I'd be influenced by his virus, too, despite my immunity to lycanthropy.

Magic worked in mysterious ways.

My single status boiled down to my ignorance. I had no idea how long sphinxes lived, and I didn't want to commit to a lycanthrope when it was entirely possible I'd drop dead from old age within a year. No one knew anything of substance about sphinxes, not even the CDC. Unlike lycanthropes, who had lived in secrecy between the magic surges, sphinxes existed only in mythology, and thousands of years separated me from my predecessors.

At least I'd been spared becoming a research subject of the CDC. I'd been born human, thus entitled to the same protections other humans enjoyed despite my change in species categorization.

I sighed, wrinkled my nose, and closed my browser so I wouldn't have to look at either Scottish dream come true. According to my laptop's clock, I had an hour to blow before the devil came calling, further entangling himself in my affairs.

What did the devil want with me, anyway?

I sucked in a breath. What use did an almost pure vanilla human have for fresh water beyond drinking it? A body of fresh water had been critical to Bubba Eugene. Mysterious Mr. July could be anything, just like me. I only looked human. My DNA had been rewritten during adolescence, so much so I'd be surprised if a scan found any actual human in me at all.

Could Malcolm be someone like me?

I'd never actually met anyone else born a human and later twisted into a non-human, although I'd heard rumors about them. Most of my papers declared my species was human despite my protests. While the idea of kidnapping someone still didn't sit well with me, the silver linings I found made the job a lot easier to stomach.

I wanted to know more. I wanted to know why. I wanted to discover the truth about Bubba Eugene's cousin.

Hopefully, curiosity wouldn't get this cat killed.

THE FIRST LIGHT of dawn peeked through the curtains. Ten seconds later, someone knocked on my door. Since Lord Satin of Hell—

"Satan!" the devil snarled.

—would just pop in if alone, I assumed he had angelic company ensuring his good behavior. While I had no problem courting death at the devil's hands, angels scared me.

Their lack of a head freaked me out every time. Bracing for the inevitable, I unlocked and opened the door.

Two angels waited in the hall, and the devil himself lurked behind them, an ebony beauty in a designer suit. He might've even succeeded at playing human if he hadn't sheathed himself in fire and given himself a spade tail, leathery wings, and a pair of ram horns. The tousled hair was a nice touch.

Despite his efforts, the devil had nothing on Scottish firemen. "Well color me amazed and sign me up for a cruise to Scotland," I muttered, shaking my head and retreating into my hotel room. "Come on in. Don't mind the mess, please."

Sane sentients didn't invite the Lord of Hell into their home, however temporary a home my hotel room was, but I supposed pulling an all-nighter stalking Scottish studs disqualified me by default and classified me as a little crazy.

"A little?" Satin blurted.

"Shut it, Lucy." Heading to my chair, I flopped onto it and closed my laptop's lid so they'd have to invest effort if they wanted to meddle in my affairs.

The angels hesitated but strode into my room. It unnerved me that creatures without eyes could watch me, but I could feel their attention on me, scrutinizing and judging. With the exception of their wings, they were identical. One had blue bands on his feathers while the other's were scarlet.

"You call Mephistopheles 'Lucy?'" the scarlet-banded angel spluttered.

It creeped me out that I could tell which one of them was talking. Damn it. How could an entity speak without a head? To add to the confusion, the angel sounded male despite lacking obvious genitals.

If I focused on the angel's shocked splutter, I could ground myself—and find a sick sort of amusement in the situation. I'd astonished an *angel*. "I like calling him Satin, too. Drives him wild. I really don't know why I'm not dead yet. Last guy to call him Satin got wrapped in a fortune's worth of fabric and lit on fire. I must be lucky."

"Or he wants your soul and doesn't have it yet."

"Wait. I'm not headed straight to hell yet? Now I'm really impressed. I'm Kanika. Make yourselves comfortable."

"Michael," the blue-banded angel replied.

"Gabriel."

My mouth dropped open. Angels *couldn't* lie. They could twist words and omit the truth, but no falsehood ever left their nonexistent lips. Two archangels stood in my hotel room while the Lord of Hell, the devil himself, examined my pile of sari on the floor. A single angel could smite an entire city.

Michael alone could herald in the end of days.

If I ran for the balcony and shifted, could I outrun the apocalypse?

"No," Michael replied, stepping to my bed, twisting around so he could keep tabs on Satan. "Don't fear, Kanika. It's a lot of work ushering in an apocalypse. I'd like to be home in time for breakfast."

"Of course." Right. Archangels needed breakfast, too. "It'd be rude of me to keep you from your breakfast. Let's get down to business. How does this work?"

Gabriel stretched out his right hand, and a black briefcase materialized in a flash of golden light. Gripping the handle, he set it on the bed. "You'll ask Mephistopheles your questions. He'll answer them. We'll confirm the truth. Should you be satisfied, you'll sign the papers. You won't be able to read the script, which will be covered as a precaution. The documents are written in Angelic and Demonic. An English translation will be made available upon Satan's approval." The archangel paused. "Few mortals dare to accuse the Lord of Lies of actually lying."

"They're stupid, then. So, Satin. Stop playing with my sari and start talking. Was every word you said on the phone with me true, in spirit and in content? In short, are you trying to trick me?"

The angels' laughter chimed, and I held my breath until the sound faded.

"You're wise," Michael complimented.

Huh. An archangel, one of the direct servants of *God*, thought I was wise? There certainly was nothing wise about even considering signing a deal with the devil.

"Don't think too hard about it," the devil advised. "You'll just give yourself a headache. Every word I spoke to you was the truth in all ways."

"He speaks the truth," the angels declared, and their proclamation shook the hotel.

All right. Since when did the Lord of Hell play fair? "You're really not trying to trick me?"

"I'm not trying to trick you. You blind signing these documents is nothing more than a passing amusement, a game of wits and will, one that won't directly harm you. We've spoken of made enemies, of course, a factor beyond my complete control."

"And that's the truth?"

Michael laughed and stretched his wings, smacking the Lord of Hell with one. "He speaks the truth."

Satan grunted and shoved the archangel's wing out of his face. "Feathered menace."

While uncertain of the consequences of keeping my word, I nodded. "I'll sign."

Neither angel attempted to change my mind, which startled me. Gabriel used my bed as a table, opening his briefcase while the Lord of Hell crossed his arms over his chest and watched. The inside glowed with a soothing, golden light.

Curiosity dug its sharp claws deep into me. Muttering a curse that made both angels twitch, I fought the desire to ask one of the many questions rattling around in my head. As the silence lengthened, I fidgeted before finally blurting, "I thought archangels lived to thwart the devil."

Everyone laughed, and Michael whacked Satan with his wing again. "However much fun it is to annoy our brother, no. That's not how it works. We're like any other family. So, while we can't quite seem to keep the same father over the years, we are the originals. He has his role. We have ours. This? This is a game we've never played before, a future without a past reflecting it. In our way, we're rather like cats. Curious. Inquisitive. This is new to us. New is rare. I look forward to watching this new future unfold, so much so I won't even peek. That would ruin the fun."

"This is just a game to you."

"A rare one, one we can participate in without worrying for the fate of your soul.

There's nothing for us to protest. Even the devil can do good in the world, and I rather enjoy when he gets ulcers over it."

I waved bye-bye to another misconception about angels. "You have a bit of a mean streak, Michael."

"I prefer to think of it as a rivalry with my wayward kin with a dash of brotherly love mixed in."

"I'm still older than you," the Lord of Hell muttered.

"And I thank Our Heavenly Father for that each and every day."

While Gabriel prepared the papers, Satan glared at Michael, who didn't seem to care he'd incurred his brother's wrath. I smelled sulfur and hoped the stench wouldn't linger. Any other time, the silence would've bothered me, but the trio fascinated me too much for me to disturb the quiet. They seemed so at ease with each other, as though my hotel room had become a safe territory for old friends meeting in secret rather than a neutral meeting place for ancient enemies destined to battle over the final destination of souls.

Was that what it meant to be family? I wondered if I'd ever find out for myself.

Mephistopheles, the Lord of Hell, the devil of the Christian Bible, and the Prime Evil, flashed a grin at me and winked. "You'll find out soon enough, I'm sure. It's human nature to unravel the secrets of the universe, after all. Sign, cupcake. You gave your word."

Without a real reason to say no, I nodded. "Give me a pen and show me where to sign."

Two archangels and the devil produced a pen, and I laughed at the absurdity of them pulling writing implements out of thin air. Choices, choices. Which pen would I choose?

I picked the devil's. His wasn't made of pure light, which I assumed dramatically lowered my chances of the damned thing smiting me before I finished scribbling my signature on the pages. Gabriel stacked the sheets on the briefcase, and curtaining bands of blue, gold, and black covered the text I wasn't allowed to read.

Kanika felt like a lonely name, but I signed it faithfully all the same.

Something about my thoughts amused the three immortals, and I scowled at their laughter. What assholes.

They laughed harder.

FOUR

No riddles today—at least not the
kind that'll get you eaten for a wrong
answer.

INSTEAD OF SLEEPING like a sane woman, I
took the devil's money out for a test drive. I
needed a few things to pull off my plans—
okay, a lot of things, and many of them I
couldn't get in Bristol, Tennessee. A car
topped my list. Armed with my new debit
card, I purchased a prepaid credit card, hit a
rental place, and picked a classy but common
SUV with tinted windows. It'd be the first of
many; I'd switch vehicles as I went, eating
extra charges along the way. As long as my
name wasn't spread around, I'd be able to al-
ternate forms to keep any pursuers off my
tail.

With transportation arranged, I was ready
to leave town and start the heavy lifting. I
needed weapons, the kind the government
didn't want people like me to have. Returning
to my hotel, I detoured to the front desk to

add parking fees to my bill before retreating to my room.

Even if I had to transform a hundred times, I needed to go as a sphinx. Preparations were necessary to account for my lack of hands. My wallet and phone went into a small duffle bag sitting on the bed with the straps dangling over the edge, which would allow me to slip it over my head without my claws tearing holes through the canvas. I wished I could go in another form so I could drive my rental, but my black-market contact wouldn't deal with me unless I was a sphinx. He didn't know me in my other forms, and I didn't have the weeks necessary to convince him I wasn't an FBI mole attempting to bust his operations. I also didn't want to sit in some alley shedding sari, hoping I'd become a sphinx instead of a human or a sex kitten.

It didn't hurt I'd be able to hide my trail while I was a sphinx. Only people who'd met me knew my species; I made a point of maintaining secrecy on my website. The few who had posted information about me neglected to include pictures. Descriptions ranged from an unusually pale African American woman to a cat lycanthrope. One had even listed me as some sort of oversized faery specializing in illusionary magic.

Few wanted to spend time getting to know me, and most went with the illusion theory, which made it easy to move around undetected. Even when I tried to tell the truth, no one believed me. They needed to see my sphinx form before they accepted the truth. Gorgons, faeries of all sorts, and even centaurs enjoyed the benefit of the doubt.

I'd be fighting to prove my species until the day I died.

It took three tries to become a sphinx. I supposed my heightened annoyance somehow helped. I wasted almost an hour preening in front of the mirror, shaking my head so the silver and gemstone beads decorating my many braids tinkled. In Ancient Egypt, the style had been reserved for the highest of nobility.

Someone like Cleopatra would've worn her hair like mine, and she would've also worn an usekh similar to mine. Fashioned of silver and turquoise, the collar clung to my throat and draped over where my skin transitioned to fur, disguising where woman and beast merged.

Despite popular belief, the lack of gold set me apart in a good way, and if I had lived in the days of pharaohs, I would've ranked among them. Gold had been plentiful when the pyramids had risen from the sands.

Silver came from distant shores, so expensive only the wealthiest could afford it.

When I shifted back to human, my hair

would frizz from my many braids, requiring a
lot of conditioner and a straightening iron to
fix. The usekh would chafe if I wore it for too
long. In the end, I found it all worthwhile.

I could fly.

Satisfied I would confuse anyone who
might pursue me, I slipped my head through
the strap of my bag, slinked to the balcony
door, and pawed it open while cursing my
lack of hands. To fit through the door, I had
to stretch my wings vertically, a painful stunt
on a good day, no matter how many stylized
pictures depicted sphinxes in the position.

If I ever met the jerk who'd come up with
the pose, I'd rip him apart with my claws and
eat his entrails, imitating my Greek brethren.

The distant thunderheads promised a late
afternoon storm, and I hoped it would stick
around for my night flight back to the hotel. I
enjoyed flirting with the elements and riding
the gusting winds, and I appreciated the challenge of rain weighing down my feathers.

I jumped, cleared the rail, and took flight.
I dipped down before surging upwards,
stretching my wings to catch a thermal to the
thin clouds above. On my trip to Gatlinburg,
I'd consider the difficulties the black-market
operator would inevitably subject me to before selling me his wares. While I'd wandered
across most of the United States, I'd only in-
filtrated one black market in Tennessee. I'd

struggled to earn Hagnar's trust, and I wondered how he'd react to my unexpected arrival; it had been several years since my last
visit, and I wasn't even sure if the gun shop
fronting his operation remained.

I'd find out soon enough.

Flying was tiring, and while it would have
taken twice as long to drive, I regretted not
having my rental. I longed for a nap. Then
again, after several hours of driving, I
would've been just as tired.

Fortunately, my luck held out; I found the
store where I remembered, tucked down a
side street in the city's downtown core. A lit
open sign welcomed me, and I rose on my
hind paws so I could push my way inside.
Hagnar leaned against one of his glass coun-
ters, his eyebrows rising at my entrance. His
two customers, middle-aged men in ragged
jeans and stained t-shirts, gaped at me. Narrowing my eyes, I stared until both men decided they valued their lives more than they
wanted to buy Hagnar's guns. They shuffled
outside and didn't look back.

"They would've bought something if not
for you."

I liked the man and his gruff ways. I
thought he was meaner than the devil and as
wicked as sin, which added to the feeling I
toyed with a lit stick of dynamite whenever I
paid him a visit. Laws meant nothing to him,

and he worshipped at the altar of the almighty dollar. "I'll buy far more than them, I'll pay you better for it, and if someone asks you, you can be honest when you say survived a sphinx paying you a visit. No riddles today—at least not the kind that'll get you eaten for a wrong answer."

I'd be surprised if Hagnar knew the differences between Greek sphinxes and Egyptian ones. Most didn't. Egyptian sphinxes had a bad rep due to our Greek brethren, but fear served me when I donned my beloved wings.

"You always ask for interesting things, lady sphinx. Kanika. It means black in Egyptian, doesn't it? Is that your real name, or one you chose because of your fur?"

"And ruin the mystery? Don't be ridiculous." I made a show of rearing so I could get a better look at him. The years hadn't changed him. Even the wrinkles etched into his sun-worn face were exactly as I remembered.

Interesting.

"What do you need today?"

"I was hoping we could talk in the back." I'd graduated from annoying passwords and key phrases after my third visit, something I appreciated. He'd likely test me in some fashion, but I no longer needed to earn my right to see his office. My third visit to the old man had cost me two weeks on a scavenger hunt across Gatlinburg, ferreting out clues so he'd let me access his wares.

For someone who worshipped money, he made it awfully hard for me to spend mine.

Hagnar grunted. "Need to lock up."

While I waited, I admired the guns in his cabinets. I found three I liked, and with five hundred thousand to spend, I'd take them all. The Desert Eagle amused me, the Beretta would serve as my main weapon, accurate and reliable, and the cute little handgun with sparkly blue grips matched my favorite pair of heels. I'd let Hagnar talk me into extras, too.

A woman could never have too many guns.

I could've spent another hour browsing the weapon selection, but Hagnar marched across the shop to the back door and barked, "Come."

I followed, careful to avoid banging into anything, a challenge when maneuvering hundreds of pounds of bulk and wings through confined spaces. Once again, I needed to stretch my wings straight over my back to squeeze through the doorway. At first glance, his office was uninteresting, sparsely furnished with a metal desk and a few plastic chairs for the rare times he brought customers to the back. I shuffled out of the way and waited for the man to reveal his secrets.

The floor mat hid the first secret. When Hagnar stepped on it with one hand pressed to the wall, the wooden floor descended several inches, clicked, and slid away to reveal a staircase. Once and only once, he'd let me try to open it, proving there was more to the lock than knowing where to stand and what to touch.

I'd been unconscious for almost twelve hours before Hagnar had managed to wake me up, and he'd enjoyed a good laugh at my expense. Some lessons I'd never forget, and Hagnar's I remembered better than most. Look but don't touch was my motto when it came to him and his lair.

The man grunted his satisfaction and lowered his hand from the wall. "New tricks, so don't touch unless told."

Yeah, right. He'd have to bribe me if he wanted me to touch anything even with his permission. When he tricked someone, he tossed their ashes out with the trash. I'd seen him kill once, and I wanted to avoid becoming an addition to his bucket list. He engraved the names of those he had murdered on the metal bucket he used to dispose of their bodies. I couldn't judge; I'd made a deal with the devil and planned to spend his cash —now mine—to kidnap a far better person than I'd ever be.

Guilt had a way of rearing its ugly head

and nibbling on me at the worst times. I got the feeling I'd be courting remorse for the next six months.

Hagnar headed down the staircase, which was illuminated with wall-mounted lamps. Since my last visit, six fresh black smears marked the pale stone steps, and I dodged them as well as the faded, older stains. "I see you've been busy."

"The devil went down to Georgia, and business has been booming ever since."

I lifted my head, sucking in a breath. "Please tell me you're pulling my tail and yanking my chain at the same time."

"Afraid not, darlin'. He's gone and made himself a nest there, and the local demons are vying for his favor, so hunters are on the move. Some are saying the devil's looking for new fodder for his army. Others claim he's about to pick himself a prince so he can begin the final war with the high heavens. I'm rather partial to the idea he's bored and wants to stir things up because he can. So, if you're looking for demon-hunting gear, I've got slim pickings. Don't involve yourself with any devils."

Too late. "How much is that little tip going to cost me?"

"It's all rumor, so nothing. No one's confirmed anything except a few notable demons and devils close to the devil have been spotted in Georgia. Since the bit about demon hunters might affect your purchases, that's fair game."

"How much for a full data dump on the Georgia situation?" With the devil actively interfering in my affairs, I was ready to bet the information would be worth more to me than the money I'd spend getting it.

"A thousand. You're not the first to ask, and you can walk out with it today. I'll even be a gentleman and toss in the memory stick for free."

Whoever had struck the first deal for the information hadn't been wise enough to seal Hagnar's lips, and I wasn't going to look a gift horse in the mouth. "Deal. Any exclusive tidbits you can toss me?"

"I might know a thing or two if the price is right."

"Think about it. I'll need a lot from you today, if you're selling what I'm buying."

Hagnar chuckled. "When am I not?"

I could think of a few times he had refused to sell to me, and they almost always involved someone else getting to the man first. The rest of the time, someone had tried to make off with his stock without paying for it, putting him in a mood so foul he refused to sell to anyone. The six new smears further exposed his lie, but I wouldn't question him about it.

I didn't want to become smear number seven. Whatever Hagnar was, he wasn't human, or he had a magic rating so ridiculously high he could join the divines and their flock of immortal kin. Either meant trouble for me if I crossed him. Wings, a few hundred pounds of bulk, and claws couldn't win against someone capable of reducing bone and teeth to ash.

Flesh burned readily enough, but the rest? No, it took flames hotter than what mere mortals could hope to produce. A phoenix could reduce a human to cinder.

I knew of no other species outside of the burning pits of hell who could.

At least I could say with some confidence Hagnar *wasn't* the devil's kin. Satan left his mark on anyone he ventured near, and a devil—and some breeds of demons—could identify those who'd been in the presence of their unholy patron. The first time I'd met His Most Majestic Pain in My Ass, I'd crossed paths with an incubus several days later.

The incubus had known, and he'd stalked me for almost a week before the devil's scent had worn off. There were worse things in life than having an incubus around after dark, much worse things. It was his fault I'd started thinking of myself as a sex kitten when in my Bastet form.

Good memories were worth cherishing, and he'd done wonders for my self-esteem.

We descended several stories, my claws tapping on the stone. It would take fifteen to twenty minutes to reach the entrance to his primary and secondary warehouses, and on the way, I spotted fifteen more smears Hagnar hadn't bothered scrubbing off the floor yet.

That, too, I didn't question. On the grand scale of exotics, I ranked a mere three or four out of ten, and I only ranked myself so high due to my free lifetime supply of matching bras and panties. Those things weren't cheap, and when I added in my shoe collection, I was a sphinx of good fortune.

"All right. You win the contest of silent wills today. What do you need from me?"

Had we been competing? I cracked a grin at my accidental victory and made a note to woolgather later. "Weapons, mostly. I'll need blow darts or a tranq gun and some restraints, including soft, light rope, handcuffs, and a suppression cuff if you have one. I'd also like a signal jammer and a whistler for one vehicle, one of your encrypted laptops with tracking prevention, nationwide cell tower taps if you've got them, and that's just for starters."

"I can't help you with the tower taps; the FBI figured out how to reverse them, so they're the equivalent of wearing a bullseye nowadays. I can hook you up with some burner phones; we'll talk about the specifics later. Since when have you worked live relocations?"

Live relocation was such a pretty name for kidnapping. "Is that what it's called these days?"

"Among the more civilized of us, yes. You'll want a dose of influencer. You know your target's age, weight, gender, height, and species?"

"He's a man, but otherwise unknown across the board. I'll be getting his vitals tonight. I can work the dose, I just need enough of it. I want to keep him long term."

"Are you hunting yourself a lover, sphinx?"

Why not? If I was taking Mr. July or Mr. January, I'd dream about being his lover for however long I held him captive. I wouldn't touch the man, as it wasn't professional, but I'd love the view while he was in my care. "Sure. He's pretty, so I might not object to keeping him."

Hagnar chuckled and shook his head. "This isn't your expertise, girl. You're courting trouble."

"I wouldn't be working this job unless I needed to. I'll pay for advice, and I'll also pay the tip needed so this conversation never happened. If anyone asks, you were helping me pick a new handgun, and you had a new model you wanted to show me. You never sold me anything except that Desert Eagle upstairs, a Beretta, and that glitter gun in your display case, all legal acquisitions because I called in asking you to run my record —and you'll run it to confirm my legal status. You'll also run a check for my concealed carry status. More importantly, should a situation occur where your silence would harm more than help, you'll talk to someone you trust will have *my* interests at heart if you believe it will make the difference in a life-threatening situation."

"My silence is going to cost you ten thousand with those terms."

"Sold."

"In advance."

I lifted my chin and sniffed. "My wallet is in my bag. Use the black debit card."

"You can pay for it with the rest of your purchases." Partway down the hall, more new smears stained the stone. Hagnar halted and pressed his hands to the wall, which melted away to reveal a tiled foyer barely large enough for both of us. Looks deceived, and I wondered how many people had found the small room and believed it was an antechamber rather than an elevator.

Unfortunately, Hagnar hadn't seen any

need to install wide doors, requiring me to contort my wings to squeeze through. I crammed against the wall so the black market operator could enter without having to crawl over me to reach the steel door on the far side.

Hagnar touched the door, the wall clicked, and we descended deep into the Earth.

THE FIRST TIME I'd purchased illegal merchandise from Hagnar, he'd locked me in his office for five hours. I considered myself lucky he'd warned me to go to the bathroom first. I'd heard rumors some hadn't been so fortunate. With nothing to do and little room to run, I'd settled in to wait and done what cats did best. I'd taken a nap.

The second time, he'd shown me the tunnel and locked me in the hallway while he went into the warehouse, once again leaving me to wait and stay out of trouble. He'd given me a ten foot section of the corridor to move around in and threatened death if I wandered. Some of the smears were likely from those who'd failed Hagnar's second test. The third time, after he'd sent me on a wild goose chase across town for a week, he'd taken me to the second floor to a miniature version of his main warehouse.

With hundreds of millions worth of illegal merchandise in the second-floor warehouse, it didn't surprise me people risked death to steal from Hagnar's operations. If I was going to risk my life, I'd do it for more than just money.

A hot Scottish fireman counted, although I'd need to keep our relationship to look but don't touch, unless the Scot had a kink for sleeping with his less-than-human kidnapper.

No, I'd have to keep my lust leashed and remain professional. Some lines I wouldn't cross, and assaulting my hostage was one of them.

Unless I wanted an awkward conversation with Hagnar, I needed to get my head back in the game, stand still, and wait patiently. When it came to the long elevator ride, which I estimated at taking around ten minutes, he liked peace and quiet. If he wanted to talk, he would. If he did, I'd listen, since the man never talked without a reason. Maybe my willingness to leave the silence undisturbed had ultimately earned me the right to visit his main warehouse.

It alone was a mystery I wanted to solve, and while I'd learned some about the vast caverns beneath the Earth, I'd only scratched the surface. Before Hagnar had moved in, it had belonged to a gorgon clan foolish enough to share space with a dragon. The dragon still slept, and Hagnar refused to tell me what had happened to the gorgons. I yearned for a closer look at the living, breathing ebony serpent studded with glittering gems.

The glimpse I'd captured would never be enough, and I wouldn't ruin my chance to see the coiled beast in all its glory.

"Ten dollars for my advice," Hagnar announced, removing his hands from the steel door. The elevator halted, and several clicks and thuds offered hope it wouldn't plummet to the main warehouse below. The small warehouse only took a few seconds to reach, the equivalent of a floor below the hallway, and I guessed we'd been in the elevator for maybe two or three minutes, nowhere near long enough to reach the main warehouse.

To cover my unease at the unexpected change to our routine, I barked a laugh. "Add two zeroes, then you'll be closer to what your advice is actually worth."

"This is why I like dealing with you. You understand the value of things. No, today, my advice comes at the cost of the memory stick containing the information. Consider the advice a token of our good business dealings. You value me and my craft. I value your discretion and money. It's a good deal for both of us."

"Ten dollars it is, then."

When Hagnar smiled, I worried, and the

man's good humor tempted me to climb the walls to see if I could bust through the top of the elevator into the relative safety of the shaft. He rapped his knuckle against the metal door, and it clicked before popping open. Cold but clean air blasted into my face. The light failed to penetrate beyond the doorway.

"I'd say hold my hand for this, but as you lack hands, I'll touch your shoulder to guide you. You must trust me. You'll be in the dark for a while."

"Well, this is new."

Ugh. I sounded like Michael, Archangel of the High Heavens. It didn't matter if Hagnar showed me something new. Ah hell, who was I kidding? When Hagnar showed me something new, good things happened.

"To you, yes. Not for me. Try not to panic. The air will be cold, damp, and uncomfortable. It'll be warmer once we reach our destination. If you have electronics with you, I'll need to protect them."

"My phone and wallet are in my bag."

"I'll charge you standard book rate for the magic required, added to your bill."

I liked no-brainer offers. Standard book rate guaranteed a fair cost as determined by law, laws created by a coalition of labor unions, the United States government, and the CDC. "Deal."

It took Hagnar less than a minute to work his magic, which boded well for Satin's bank account.

"Walk with me."

I obeyed, bracing for the disorientation of blindness. Hagnar set his hand on my shoulder, his touch gentle, the faintest of pressure against my fur, giving me directions on where to walk and when to turn. The cold air swept into my lungs and numbed me from the inside, and I recognized the sensation from the few times I'd been sedated. Although I was worried, I kept walking, placing my paws with care and unsheathing my claws for better purchase on the floor. Each step, I tested the floor before shifting my weight.

My caution made for slow going, but since Hagnar didn't complain about our pace, I kept to my wobbly plod. The numbness and chill intensified the longer I remained in the darkness, worrying me yet crippling my ability to do anything about it. I hated swaying, and I needed to use my claws to keep from falling.

"Almost there," Hagnar promised. "I know it's smothering."

It amazed me the man could sound so pleasant. Where had the gruff Hagnar I knew gone? "Drugged," I slurred. I wrinkled my nose and tried again. "You drugged me."

"It's so nice when my hard work is recognized. It's temporary; it'll wear off a few minutes after we leave this area. Can't make it easy for you to find your way back here without me, after all."

"This isn't your main warehouse. Not deep enough." Talking helped, and the more I spoke, the easier it became to make my tongue do what I wanted. It also helped me concentrate and coordinate my paws so I didn't stagger as much.

"And this is why I take the precautions I do. You're right. We're about to turn right. Step carefully, as there's a ledge. I recommend against falling, although you won't hurt for long if you tumble over the side."

I took extra care with my steps trying to find the edge of the floor so I could avoid it. To my paws, the floor felt like stone. "You're a man of many surprises."

"I've lived as long as I have because of my precautions. You're among the more trustworthy to see my caves, so instead of dragging your unconscious body through my maze, you're blessed. I'm letting you walk."

"I think I'm blessed because you don't want to drag six hundred plus pounds of sphinx through your maze."

"That, too."

After having seen a minotaur in both forms, I eliminated the possibility of Hagnar being one; minotaurs did a poor job at playing human. "You're not a minotaur. What are you?"

"Why don't you think I'm a minotaur?" he demanded, and while his gruff tone had returned, his voice lacked the sharper edge of actual anger.

Did Hagnar really think he could play me? "You're too human, too good at playing human," I slurred. Concentrating on my breathing, I willed my tongue to cooperate. "Haven't asked if I'm fertile, not once. Haven't sniffed me or snorted in my face, either. I'm an exotic. Minotaurs love exotic. You would've been itching to breed with me the moment you saw me."

"You're a sphinx. Exotic or not, you don't have the right number of legs and arms! You're not a minotaur's usual fare."

"I'm a female. You're not a minotaur. Minotaurs view species differences as challenges to overcome. Anyway, if you were a minotaur, you'd lose me in your maze at least once for the fun of it, you wouldn't sedate anyone who wandered into your lair, and you'd lure those you wanted to get rid of here so you could watch them starve to death. When they got nice and desiccated, you'd eat them. You'd also take the least direct path. Did I mention you wouldn't sedate anyone? Your labyrinth would dip into the deepest pits of the devil's hell and rise into the peaks of the high heavens for no reason other than you felt like being elaborate. No, you're not a minotaur."

"I should hire you the next time I require minotaur lore. I'm even going to give you a discount on today's transaction for helping me see the error of my ways. I'd like my maze to better mimic a minotaur's. How'd you learn so much about them?"

"Saw one's insides, thought I should learn a bit more about them."

"Huh. You don't seem like the type to disembowel your prey."

"I didn't do it, I just watched." Only an idiot got in the way of the devil in the middle of a maiming. I shuddered, shook my head, and tried unsuccessfully to forget the memory of the bat-winged monster sheathed in flame turning a minotaur inside out.

"We're about to leave the darkness—two of your steps. Close your eyes; it's bright. The air's warm, too. Some find this unpleasant. Try not to faint. It'd be a hassle to drag you the rest of the way."

"More smothering," I muttered but closed my eyes as directed. After a steadying breath, I stepped into the light.

FIVE

It's nice to see history hasn't been
completely forgotten.

A JUNGLE PARADISE dipped into a valley and
disappeared beneath a canopy of trees and
thick foliage. Birdsong broke the quiet, although I saw none of the birds responsible in
the light of a golden crystal floating near the
carved stone ceiling above.

A ziggurat rose from the cavern's heart, its
pale stone gleaming. I'd seen something like it
before, and I stared until realization struck
me. If I restored the temple at Machu Picchu
to its former glory, I'd likely end up with a
similar temple. My mouth dropped open, and
after a long, stunned silence, I spluttered,
"Machu Picchu. There's something like this at
Machu Picchu."

Hagnar laughed. "*Inti Watana*. You know it
as the Temple of the Sun. It isn't the same, but
yes. You tread the right path. The few others
I've brought here didn't bother to guess at all.

It's nice to see history hasn't been completely forgotten."

True to the man's warning, the cavern's heat roasted me while the damp air sought to drown me for daring to breathe. The sedatives didn't help, leaving me panting. My face sweated while the humidity clung to my fur and made my feathers stick together.

"You weren't kidding. It's hot in here." I kept my tone light, careful to avoid whining too much. Hagnar would forgive a little whining, especially since he was to blame for my discomfort. I liked it hot, but I liked it *dry*, and I didn't understand how everything could feel so wet without rain being involved. "There are so many trees. What is this place?"

"My home. I've judged you and found you worthy. Here you'll find everything you need and so much more. Now, follow. By the time we reach the valley floor, you'll feel more like yourself. It's cooler below. I'd like to make it inside before it rains."

To reach the jungle, we had to traverse a staircase carved into the stone, which meandered around ancient stalagmites. At first, I paid no attention to the common cave structures, but then a glint of red caught my eye, and I halted, twisting around to locate the source. A red crystal lurked beneath the pale stone. "Hagnar? Are there gems in these rocks?"

The man chuckled. "Yes, there are. Pretty, isn't it?"

"Is that normal?"

"No. Once upon a time, magic pooled in this cavern. It's in everything." He pointed up at the floating crystal above. "That's natural."

I sucked in a breath and stared into the light, my eyes wide. "That's *natural*?"

"A relic from when the magic flowed beneath the Earth, waiting for the next surge so it could return to the surface. I believe it's a node."

"A node?"

"A theoretical source of magic. As I rather like my home, I haven't invited anyone to have a closer look at it."

"Smart."

True to Hagnar's word, by the time we descended into the valley, the sedative's influence eased. I went from numb to energized, and I fluttered my wings, itching to take to the air. I remained grounded, although it took a great deal of effort to tear my attention away from the cavern's ceiling and back to the stone path we walked. Flowers of all shapes, sizes, and colors lined the path, and I slowed to sniff them all, marveling at the variety of scents.

One of them took offense to my curiosity and bit my nose. I yelped, slashing out with a forepaw. After a brief but fierce disagreement with the flower, I wore the crimson blossom tucked behind my ear, preening over my conquest.

"That was rare," Hagnar complained.

"If it hadn't bitten me, I wouldn't have claimed it as a trophy."

"Please try to avoid destroying my home."

I flashed Hagnar a smile, showing off my teeth. While my face mostly looked human, I had pronounced incisors. "I was generously helping you with your landscaping. You seem to have an aggressive species in your lovely garden. How long have you been growing this jungle?"

I was no expert on trees, unless it involved getting stuck in them, but they seemed old— very, very old.

"A thousand years or so. This place reminds me of home. Everything you see here, I've built with my own hands. Every bird, every plant, every animal living here descends from the ones I brought when I left my ancestral home."

I halted. Hagnar had been working on his valley for a *thousand* years? I struggled with that, choosing to shrug and not think about it too hard. With negotiations in progress, I didn't need the sort of headache I'd earn contemplating the man's age. "Why bring me here?"

"We have more in common than you

think, and you interest me. I need no other reason why. I needed to come here for the drug you require anyway. This is where I make it. We'll have to go to the main warehouse after, but there is a way down from here."

"This is incredible. It really is." I could understand why Hagnar killed to protect his operation. The government's inevitable interest in the floating crystal would ruin his home. Add in the jungle, the drug I planned to use on Malcolm Findlay Stewart, and Hagnar's wealth and illegal property, and people would start wars to possess it. "You've made something truly amazing here."

Moss-burdened vines crossed the path, forcing me to scramble beneath, stretching and flattening my wings. Hagnar chuckled at my contortions, ducking beneath the foliage with practiced ease. Beyond, the jungle retreated, and a mowed lawn surrounded the ziggurat's base. The front door made me laugh; I'd seen the same one at a hardware store for a hundred dollars, as cheap as it got. Inside, instead of Incan grandeur, the place reminded me of a cheap motel. The paint, which has been used to hide the evidence of mold, peeled away from the drywall in layers, evidence he'd surrendered to the mold's inevitable presence in his home.

I blamed the jungle's humidity, a formidable foe of any homeowner.

Hagnar crossed the barren entry to a closed door, a more expensive storm door with glass panes, opened it, and waited for me to follow. "What can you tell me of your prey?"

"His family wants him out of the way but not killed—at least not by me. I'm not convinced they don't want him dead and are positioning to get rid of him permanently. Since I wouldn't put it past my client to backstab my new and unwilling friend, I want him coherent enough to defend himself if necessary. I'm anticipating he'll have a six month stay with me. The client's paying a low upfront payment and additional funds each month, which makes me think there will be trouble. Altogether, it's a lot of money, but I doubt he means to pay it all. Maybe I'm being paranoid, but I don't think my client really wants his cousin to live. Why else tell me to dump him somewhere and leave him?"

It took an unpleasant stretch of my wings and a bit of squeezing to fit through the door, which led to a wood-paneled office, one cooled with an air conditioner and boasting a dehumidifier.

Hagnar hummed, nodded, and closed the door behind me. "Tell me the details of the deal from the very beginning, but so far, I'm

Whatever for Hire   89

agreeing with your assessment. You may be in over your head."

"I'm willing to bet my client's counting on that. One person pulling off a kidnapping isn't easy, not when the target is a full-grown man."

While Hagnar circled around his desk to sit, I stretched out with a groan, positioning so I could enjoy the cool breeze. Starting from the moment I'd gotten the order to accept the next contract, I detailed my conversations with Bubba Eugene Stewart, leaving out their names. After I paid him for his silence, I'd consider discussing the Stewart family and possibly digging for additional information on them. I doubted Hagnar could find out anything I hadn't on the internet, but I'd pay dearly for what he could find out.

If I had reason to believe someone in the Stewart family used Hagnar's services, things would've been different. I would've been able to bribe Hagnar into giving me information, unless they had paid for his silence. Most didn't.

When I finished, he nodded. "Seems fishy to me. All right. I do agree with your base tactic. A conscious capture is best. If you have the twenty thousand, I have a suppressor bracelet that can rein in most talents, no matter their strength. Someone strong enough and determined enough can bust through, but most can't. It would be keyed to you, and you would wear a matching bracelet. It won't suppress your magic; it'll let you control the matching bracelet, so you can give your prisoner access to his magic at your whim. If he does have magic, he'll be able to use it. However, it comes at a price beyond the payment of cash."

I worried, as twenty thousand seemed cheap to me for such a potent tool. "What price?"

Hagnar's smile transformed my worry into full-fledged anxiety. "You'll be attuned to him. His emotions, good or bad, will feed back through the bracelets. You'll know if he's sick or injured. You'll feel his pain as if it is your own. If he has a lot of magic, he might even be able to sense things from you. If he breaks through the bracelet's suppression, you'll be hit with the backlash. It's dangerous magic. Short term, these side effects aren't bad. I can't tell you what will happen if you wear it for six months. It's dangerous, untested magic."

Great. I'd be playing Russian roulette with the most potent weapon in my arsenal. "Backlash? What do you mean by backlash?"

"All the magic he uses to break the suppressor will hit the matching bracelet, which means it'll hit you. It could be lethal. It all depends on the type of magic he uses, what he's trying to do when he breaks the bracelet, and his talent rating. At the very least, it'll hurt. But for what you need, it's the safest option—for him. For you? It's a very dangerous gamble."

Well, I appreciated the main perk of dealing with the devil: health insurance. "I have a good health insurance policy for this job."

"Good. You'll need it if he breaks the suppressor, assuming you make it to the hospital at all."

I appreciated Hagnar's candor about the situation almost as much as my new health insurance policy. "I have the twenty thousand. I'd prefer it if no one gets killed. I'm treating this as a protection gig, and the body I'm protecting is completely unwilling. If this *is* a set-up to get him killed, I want the best odds to thwart my client and fuck up his plans."

To make matters worse, I had a double dose of paranoia to work with. I could easily believe the devil would double cross me. He was the Lord of Lies, after all.

"You have a good reputation on the small jobs. The big ones are a different story, but you're smart about protection work. Maybe your client is counting on your tendency to shy away from the heavy lifting."

"There's just one of me. That's why I'm not a big job girl."

"You're also not the type to kidnap people, either. That might work to your advantage, assuming you have a professional game plan. You will. I find these sorts of jobs entertaining and complex."

"How much is your wisdom going to cost me?"

"A thousand if you spend below fifty thousand, on the house if you spend more."

Considering I was already at thirty thousand and counting, I'd be walking away with free advice. "How much is the influencer going to run me?"

"Thirty darts, the appropriate gun, and ten vials is going to ding you five grand. For an extra thousand, I'll give you two extra vials and syringes for them. I'll make sure to label them carefully; they're made differently and have different dosages. There'll be a reference chart for both types. At twenty-times human metabolism, the batch should last you a little longer than a month."

"Perfect. I need a six-month supply. My current plan is to rotate through prepaid credit cards to pay for car rentals, which I'll change in each state at least twice, swapping companies and using after-hour return services. That way, I can book several days for the rental and return them early to throw potential pursuers off my trail."

"I can make fake identification cards for you."

I shook my head, and the beads in my hair tinkled. "No, I appreciate it, but it's better that I don't. I'm not used to acting out fake identities. All I'll do is get busted if I try it. Realistically, I need to avoid detection altogether and stay off law enforcement's radar."

"Can a sphinx even drive a car?"

Laughter burst out of me at the doubt in Hagnar's tone. "I have my ways."

"A humanoid form?"

"Yes."

"Let me see what I have to work with. You might need body armor."

I thought it through and realized my best hope was for him to kit me like I was going into a firefight, and not the type involving hot Scots in fire-retardant gear. Rising to my paws, I stepped away from his desk and shifted. I expected my human form but ended up imitating Bastet in her full Egyptian glory. Instead of my usual gypsy dancer attire, white linen clung to my every curve, accented with silver, turquoise, and cerulean jewelry. My hair remained the same, and a turquoise and silver usekh clung to my throat and draped down my chest and shoulders.

Hagnar's eyes widened. "You're Bastet."

"No, I just look like her. I'm a sphinx."

"You'll leave a trail looking like that. Everyone will remember you."

I sighed. "If you think this is bad, when I'm human, I look like Cleopatra."

My gypsy attire and Russian heritage would help protect me, even from Hagnar. I told the truth yet lied by omission at the same time. The devil and his two archangel brothers were obviously a bad influence on me.

"Not *the* sphinx, not Bastet, but an embodiment of Egypt. Fascinating. I'd thought personifications had died out long ago."

"Personifications?"

"Every culture has a personality. Thousands of years ago, when it was believed magic had existed as it does today, sometimes someone would be born the ultimate example of their culture. They usually took the form of one of their gods or spiritual entities. In Egypt, it's believed the pharaohs are those entities. Myth and legend have to come from *somewhere*."

I didn't feel like I personified Egypt, a place I'd never been, a home I'd never visited. "This information remains with you alone."

"I gave you my word in exchange for your money. Our bargain still stands."

If it meant saving my life, Hagnar would tell my secrets, but it wasn't much of a secret.

I'd struggled for years trying to get people to believe the truth. If anything, if Hagnar had to speak, his word would validate my existence. Everything came at a price, even something as simple as my peace of mind. Pulling out my wallet, I handed over my new debit card. "Let's process that payment then, shall we?"

Hagnar took my card but set it on my desk. "I'll start the inventory and pull together the total amount owed. It's easier to run the payment at one time. You've provided enough of your secrets to serve as collateral. Do you trust me to supply you for your venture?"

"Please do, but justify and explain the expenses. I want to know what I'll be working with, plus I'll need lessons on how to use any new equipment."

"Deal. Sit. The real work is about to begin."

MY PHONE RANG HALFWAY through inventorying, and Hagnar gestured for me to answer while he kept working. It amazed me he had reception so deep underground. "Kanika, Whatever for Hire."

"I have the information you need," Bubba Eugene announced.

"Good. Email it to me. Have you deposited my funds?" Without the deposit, I'd be spending a great deal of money without someone to kidnap, which would sour my day.

"I'll email you with the confirmation."

"Were you able to get all the information I requested?"

"Yes."

It amazed me how one little word could contain so many lies. The trick would be separating the truth from the lies. "Good. I'll review the email and contact you if there are any issues."

I expected a lot of issues. Until I reviewed the information, I wouldn't be able to guess if he was lying, which I anticipated, but I feared the lies involved my target's vital statistics, which would make my task of drugging him dangerous—and potentially lethal. If Bubba Eugene wanted his cousin dead, after my warnings, that'd be the way to go about it. Listing the wrong metabolism and weight could turn a kidnapping into an assassination.

I'd have to do my own research and confirm everything I could about Malcolm before I made my hit.

"When can you grab him?"

"You'll know when he disappears." I hung up on my client and checked the call time.

"Twenty seconds. Is that long enough to do a trace?"

"Traces are instantaneous if you have access to the towers," Hagnar replied. "On that call, you're covered; I mask signals to here. It'll register as an unknown location. I recommend you use burner phones once you're on the move. Dump them after each use. I can give you a few—two hundred a phone. I recommend you take twelve; that's all I've got set up right now. Once you've burned them all, you can get cheap phones without a contract and pay for minutes individually. It's expensive, but it works."

"I'll take them, and add fifty per phone to keep those extra secret. If someone needs to reach me in a life-or-death situation, you text the burners with the number I need to call."

"You've improved at this game. Done. I'll teach you a trick to better hide your location once you've used the phones. Keep them off until you make a call, then dump them in someone's car or some other vehicle on the move. Putting them in a box and shipping them somewhere by courier is a good way to get a lot of movement. They'll go on a wild goose chase tracking the phone. For a thousand, I'll give you a special phone. It's so old it doesn't have GPS technology. It barely works, and it's only compatible with one cell network. Reception's terrible, the battery life is shit, but if you're in a big city, it should work."

What was an extra thousand when it came to buying a little extra security? Nothing. "I'll take it."

"I recommend you keep that one off unless you need it. While it lacks GPS technology, if they have the number, they can still track you to the tower you're using for the call. That'll give them a rough idea of your location."

"Better than nothing. How much for you to charge my phone and send it on a trip somewhere? Maybe New York City?"

"Why there?"

"There's reason I might go there. It's as good a place as any." While my aunt wouldn't appreciate someone sniffing around her house looking for me, she'd be telling the truth when she claimed she knew nothing about me. I doubted the woman even knew I'd become a mercenary.

"Fifty dollars, and that includes cleaning off finger prints, removing any DNA evidence, and postage."

"Add it," I ordered. "Got a laptop handy?"

"The one you want is in the main warehouse. All location services are permanently disabled on the machine; the chips enabling GPS were removed, and the wireless chip is custom made. It'll get you on the internet, plus it'll help cover your tracks. Don't ask about the technology that does it; I'm not at liberty to say. The laptop is new enough to do anything you might need, it's fast, and it's encrypted. If you type in the password incorrectly five times, the entire machine will be erased and then destroyed. I recommend you give it space, as approximately twenty seconds after the fifth wrong password is input, a small explosive inside the machine will detonate and blow apart the insides. No one will be getting any data off it. It'll become a very expensive paperweight. It'll cost you five thousand."

I liked the sound of that. "You have yourself a very nice sales pitch there. What's my total bill so far?"

"Seventy-six all in."

Ouch. I hoped my sexy Scot was worth his price tag. "How much else do you want to add?"

"Maybe a few thousand. Eighty's a safe bet. The good news is this: you'll be as protected as I can make you."

While foolish, I believed him. "Sounds good. Finish my inventory and pack this up."

"You're going to need a vehicle. I'll loan you my SUV tonight and have someone pick it up tomorrow, you just tell me where you'll leave it. I'll give you a magnetic holder for the keys, just stash it beneath the car somewhere difficult to spot."

"Kingsport." I was staying in Bristol, but I'd ditch the emptied SUV there and fly back to my hotel where my rental waited. If he was tracking his car, I'd be making stops in several other towns and cities the same length of time I would stay in Bristol unloading.

Trust only went so far when it came to black market operators.

My phone rang. Grumbling a curse, I answered, "Kanika, Whatever for Hire."

"Must you insist on using that wretched company name, cupcake?"

"Ah. It's Satin. How nice of you to call. My evening wouldn't be complete without you bothering me. What do you need?"

"I wanted to find out when you'd really be putting your bank card to use rather than doing a tiny test transaction to make sure it worked. I'd like to confirm there are no issues with payments beyond the basics."

Of course Lord Satin of Hell would think a five-hundred-dollar purchase classified as basic. "Don't worry. I'll be charging eighty thousand in a few minutes. I went shopping. I love shopping sometimes."

"What are you buying for that much? A new car?"

"I've never had my own car before," I admitted. I spoke the truth, too.

"Hmm. It's your money, cupcake." The devil hung up.

"It'd help if you stayed on the line while I processed the payment, asshole," I muttered.

"Seventy-nine thousand, three hundred and twenty-two dollars even," Hagnar announced.

"Charge it." There was no turning back, not with so much invested already. It wouldn't be the first time I'd taken on a losing proposition. I'd landed on my feet then.

I'd land on my feet again, somehow.

SIX

Catching Malcolm would be the problem.

IT TOOK several hours to gather what I needed, and I held off on checking my email until I returned to my hotel room. Before I investigated my target, I needed rest. I stayed awake long enough to lock my balcony window and door.

Eight hours of sleep did me a world of good.

One pizza delivery later, I booted my new laptop to get a better look at my victim-to-be. Fortune smiled on me; Bubba Eugene Stewart had taken me seriously, sending over a lot of information. Unfortunately, I couldn't trust it.

I doubted glorious, muscularly sexy Mr. July was a slick six feet even, weighed a hundred and ninety pounds, and had human-standard metabolism. Not even most humans had human standard; magic had a tendency to fiddle with its host, turning practitioners and the talented into something a little more —and a little less—than human.

If Bubba Eugene thought his falsified information on his cousin would lead to Malcolm's death, I'd enjoy surprising him. As long as I didn't give Mr. July a lethal dose, he'd burn it off faster and keep me on my toes. Keeping my victim alive was my top priority. To accomplish my goal, I needed to thwart my client at every turn.

Blackmailing a client wasn't my usual style, but with so much at stake and the devil's interest in the matter, I needed every advantage possible. If Bubba Eugene attempted to double-cross me, I'd recruit an unexpected ally: Malcolm Findlay Stewart.

According to Bubba Eugene's intel, Mr. July did business as Malcolm Montgomery, and a single search confirmed I had reason to worry; I'd been hired to kidnap a millionaire investor and businessman, one with a reputation for fair business dealings with everyone except his competition.

It didn't take long to figure out why Bubba Eugene wanted his cousin gone. He wanted to operate a business on M. Montgomery Enterprises' turf. I rolled my eyes at the pettiness of the situation.

Why did money always have to make a mess of things? With Bubba Eugene's motive exposed, once I got my hands on Malcolm, I'd work around his business responsibilities. Spiting Bubba Eugene and getting paid for it —by him—seemed like my sort of fun.

Catching Malcolm would be the problem. A man worth millions wouldn't be easy to grab. He likely had some sort of bodyguard, which would cause me problems. I muttered curses and regretted having ditched my phone.

Then again, if I called Bubba Eugene and tore into him for shortchanging me so badly, I'd blow my opportunity for some payback. I clacked my teeth and returned to my email, reviewing what I'd been sent. With the exception of my target's true vital statistics and value, Bubba Eugene had provided a fairly comprehensive schedule of Malcolm's behavior and general activities.

Kidnapping him would only be the first of my problems. I needed to find a way to contain a man who liked to be kept busy. Great. Intellectual types needed a lot of stimuli or they started trouble. Books might keep him occupied for a few minutes.

If he had a taste for revenge, I'd be set. I'd just tip him off to Bubba Eugene's activities and watch the problem resolve itself, maneuvering Malcolm so I got paid and his cousin took the fall later. I'd have to think about it later, after I put together a plan to capture him and make him mine.

Taking him at his home wouldn't work; a man with Malcolm's wealth would have an alarm system at the minimum. If Bubba Eugene's information was accurate, the only potential openings occurred when he drove to and from work. To help with my efforts, my client had included a photograph of Malcolm's car, a rather lovely Jaguar.

Meow.

The man was hot enough to melt metal, and his car came a close second. Too bad I couldn't get away with taking both.

A quick check of Malcolm's address revealed he lived off the beaten path. With a little luck, I could kidnap him between his home and the highway, which would allow me to ditch his Jaguar, pack him into my rental, and be halfway to Arkansas before anyone realized he hadn't made it home.

My second option was to lure him to a karaoke bar, get him drunk, put on my best sex kitten act, and hope he took the bait. I'd give him a ride he'd never forget in more ways than one. Alas, when I pulled a Bastet, I was far too memorable.

Roadside kidnapping it was. If I got my tail in gear, I could get into position near Nashville in time to catch him on his way home from his late-night shift at the firehouse. If I got lucky and staged the scene just right, he'd be compelled to pull over. I'd pose for him, digging at the engine of my rental.

If he liked go-getters, I'd pretend to be one. I'd siphon gas out of the SUV, spill some beneath the undercarriage, and play one part ditz and one part mechanic. When he pulled over to help, it'd take my dart seconds to make him mine. To keep him safe, I'd use a low dose, timed to give me a few minutes to question him, get his real vital statistics, and inject him with the appropriate amount of influencer. Then I'd put the suppression bracelet on him, pack him in the SUV, ditch the Jaguar, refill the gas tank, and call it a day.

While a simple enough plan, a lot could go wrong. A lot would.

The devil wanted me involved. Bubba Eugene hoped for my failure. I hadn't even left my hotel yet, and I already expected trouble.

In my not-so-humble opinion, I was in for one hell of a job.

I ENJOYED DRIVING, something I rarely got to do. It was a miracle I had a license at all; most states preferred when their drivers had permanent addresses. Using a mail forwarding service as my residence wasn't exactly legal, but it got the job done. Using New York as my base of operations kept me too close to my aunt, but I had an easier time keeping my license up-to-date where I'd grown up.

Many believed I still lived with my aunt, and I bet she burned every single piece of my mail out of spite.

To keep my activities difficult to track, I needed a lot of prepaid credit cards, so I made a point of stopping at every town between Kingsport and Nashville. For the first few hours of my trip, I maintained my Cleopatra appearance, deliberately drawing attention to myself.

Ten minutes outside of Nashville, I found a quiet place to pull over and changed forms, delighted when I ended up as a sex kitten with wings. As though God—or the devil—smiled on me, I wasn't dressed as a gypsy, and my skimpy outfit would reduce most men to a drooling mess.

For a brief moment, I hoped Malcolm would be one of those men. Drugging him during post-sex bliss counted as too evil even for me. To add to my frustration, a little off-road action prior to dosing him would be my only chance to sleep with him. Kidnappings tended to dampen relationships for some reason, and professionalism ensured I wouldn't be jumping into bed with him.

Having a good roll in the hay with a

victim simply wasn't done, not by anyone with an iota of self-respect.

Professionalism wouldn't stop me from thinking about him naked, though. There were limits to how chaste I could be, especially when the subject of my fantasy was the perfect example of heaven on Earth. While I waited, I daydreamed about the man; I wouldn't get many chances later, that much was for certain.

I'd be sleeping with one eye open and testing the limits of my endurance. Even drugged, I couldn't afford to trust Malcolm. A smart man like him might find a loop hole in any order I gave him. I'd have to wait for him to sleep and beat him awake every morning. When the going got tough, I'd put everything on the line for someone who'd hate me within a few hours, assuming I pulled off the kidnapping.

So much could go wrong.

For my plan to work, I needed to find the perfect spot near Malcolm's home to stage my ambush. I waited until certain the man would be at work before heading towards his property. Midday, traffic was light, which boded well for my late-night adventure. At four in the morning, we'd be the only ones out and about—I hoped. A helpful farmer would ruin my plans, but I believed they'd rise with the sun several hours after I had my target in my custody.

It took me almost an hour to find a good spot. There was a wide shoulder and an overgrown access road less than a quarter of a mile away where I could dump the Jaguar without anyone realizing it was there. Someone would find it eventually, but I wouldn't leave anyone any clues.

I'd have Malcolm hide his vehicle.

Satisfied with my selection, I returned to Nashville to wait until it was time to put my plans into motion. I spent the day hiding out in an abandoned lot surrounded by weeping willows. The SUV's tight confines made my wings ache, but I didn't dare leave my vehicle. If someone did spot me, they wouldn't get a clear view of me. They'd see I was avian of some fashion, which would throw searchers off my trail once I left the area and shifted to human form.

As far as disguises went, it was dreadfully flimsy, but it was the best I could manage on such short notice.

I arrived at my ambush point twenty minutes before I expected Malcolm Findlay to show up, which gave me the time I needed to drain the tank, pop the hood, and poke around the engine armed with a flashlight and my tranquilizer gun. I'd loaded the first dart estimating my target's weight at two-twenty. If he *did* only weigh one-ninety with a human standard metabolism, I'd have my hands full, but he'd live. Hagnar's chart included a column for lethal dosages, and I stuck well below threshold.

I wouldn't do Bubba Eugene's job for him if he did want his cousin dead.

Within minutes of setting up my ambush, headlights illuminated the road and my SUV. I lashed my tail, hoping he knew enough about cats to recognize my agitation. The vehicle behind me slowed, and gravel crunched as it pulled off the road before coming to halt.

I either had Malcolm or a good Samaritan, and if I had a good Samaritan, I'd have more trouble than I wanted. I tightened my grip on my gun in my right hand and twisted to look over my shoulder, lowering my wing so it wouldn't obscure my view. Through the headlights, almost blinding in their intensity, I identified the vehicle as a sports car.

Bingo.

According to Bubba Eugene, Malcolm was six foot even, on par with sex kitten me without heels. I'd been lied to again, no doubt about it, unless I'd lost a few inches somewhere.

What a bastard.

"Everything all right, ma'am?" A hint of a southern drawl blended with a Scottish lilt, something I hadn't heard from his cousin.

Damn, the man sounded even sexier than he looked. How was that even fair?

Since shoot first and ask questions later applied, I fired, hitting him in his jeans-covered leg with my dart. "Sure is. Stay there," I ordered. I smiled, flashing a bit of fang. "Don't move and don't speak unless questioned. No magic, either."

Malcolm Findlay Stewart stiffened, and his eyes widened.

One day I'd have to give Hagnar a kiss he'd never forget for his help. The backstabbing-prone bastard always delivered on his promises, and his drug worked better than I had expected. Closing the distance between us, I pulled out the suppressor bracelet from my bra and clasped it around his left wrist.

"*Upally*," I murmured. I had no idea what the word meant, but Hagnar promised it would activate the bracelet's magic. The matching bracelet around my right wrist warmed. "Is your name Malcolm Findlay Stewart?"

"Yes," he growled through clenched teeth.

"Weight and metabolism?"

"Two-thirty and five above standard." Rage darkened his tone, and my bracelet's heat intensified.

I'd won the lottery; while I'd gotten his weight wrong, I'd dosed for six above, which would give me eight minutes before I needed to dose him again, plenty of time to have him ditch his car and return. "There's a side road behind my vehicle. Take your car, hide it in the woods, and return here within five minutes. Leave your electronics in the vehicle. Bring only your wallet with your driver's license, your insurance cards, bank cards, and your credit cards. The rest stays. Don't leave any notes, make any calls, or otherwise indicate there's a problem. Oh, and don't even think of hitting me or my SUV. Go."

He obeyed, and as he turned, his expression soured so much I had no doubt he hated me. While I waited for his return, I refilled the tank and started the engine. The SUV purred. Four minutes later, Malcolm marched towards me, and his fury once again heated my bracelet.

"Front passenger side," I ordered. Guilt took a few nibbles out of me for taking away someone's free will, but I shoved the feelings aside to deal with later. "It's really in your interest to cooperate. *I* want you alive. I've reason to believe others don't."

Malcolm moved with stiff reluctance. I was aware he didn't want to, but he couldn't fight the influence of Hagnar's drug, which I assumed was made more of magic than medicine.

I settled behind the wheel, muttering curses over my wings. Until I had Malcolm under my complete control, I couldn't afford to shift, no matter how badly I wanted to become either a human or my wingless sex kitten form.

If I could have spared even the five minutes, I would have taken to the skies. Damn it, I didn't want to kidnap a sinfully sexy man. I wanted to fly.

Malcolm glared at me from his seat, his arms crossed over his chest.

"Buckle up."

He obeyed, and his cheek twitched.

I turned on the overhead light, reached over, and opened the glove box, pulling out my box of syringes and vials of the drug, diluter, and extender. It took me a full minute to confirm the dosage against the chart; to play it safe, I'd start with twenty-four hours and work from there. "Keep still so I don't hurt you."

Well, by accident. I was pretty sure I battered the man's pride and dignity. I rolled up the sleeve of his soot-stained, denim shirt to reveal his tanned arms. Frowning at the evidence of him having recently fought a fire, I injected the clear liquid into his bicep. Returning the empty syringe to the box, I closed it before shoving it under my seat.

I buckled up, put the SUV in gear, and made my escape. One U-turn later, I began phase two of my plan.

Since when did things ever go right for me on the first try? Other people would've gloated over the triumph. I worried.

I MADE Malcolm stew in silence for twenty minutes to soften him up for the unpleasant discussion ahead of us. "Here are the rules, Mr. Stewart. I'm the only one you'll obey, period. If I give you an order, you do it. My job is to keep you alive. As such, I want you to protect yourself from anyone other than me. Unless I tell you otherwise, stay near me. The bracelet you're wearing suppresses magic. If you need to use magic to sustain your health, tell me."

"Sometimes," my unwilling companion admitted.

"You're fine for now?"

"Yes."

"Good. My name is Kanika. Bubba Eugene Stewart, or so he calls himself, hired me to get rid of you. According to the terms of our agreement, I believe he wants you gone on a more permanent basis. Since I'm not a damned assassin for hire, I have no intention of giving him what he wants. No matter what I named my business, I'm not in the business of killing people."

When I killed someone, I did it on the

house. It made my guilt a little easier to bear. While Whatever for Hire sometimes led to unwanted calls, I dealt with those with a curt refusal.

It took me a moment to realize I hadn't given him permission to speak. Damn it. "When we're alone, you can talk to me as normal. In public, you're to show no sign you're an unwilling participant in our road trip. If you behave, I might even let you drive."

"Since when did angels start kidnapping people?"

"Me? An angel?" I laughed so hard I hiccupped. "Wrong mythos. I'm no angel. Don't think I have a drop of angelic blood in me. Also, cat." I held the wheel with one hand and pointed at my face. "Black fur."

"I noticed. Are you a lycanthrope?"

"Not one of those, either. So, is Bubba Eugene the type to want you dead?"

"He'd throw a party over my grave given half a chance."

Why wasn't I surprised? Oh, right. Bubba Eugene oozed malice like a festering wound, transparent even over the phone. "I got that feeling. He tried to sell me a pretty story about how you're the family's black sheep. I figure you're just better at business than him and he's jealous."

"Bit of both."

"Is it true you have no lovers? Are you involved with anyone?"

"I have no lovers, nor am I involved with anyone."

Hot damn. I stole glances while checking my side mirror. Photographs didn't do the man justice, and the day-old stubble shadowing his jaw had to be some form of seductive magic.

Falling in lust with him was way too easy, but I had a cure for that: bad questions.

"Are you gay? Asexual?"

"Neither." He snorted. "Do I look gay to you?"

"You look like sex on a stick. I bet you could get anyone of any species to jump in bed with you with a single 'come hither' look."

He snorted again. "I'm straight. I experimented once. Didn't like it."

Hello. Now that was a statement begging me to ask so many questions. The cat in me took control of my tongue and growled, "I'm so tempted to ask."

Damn it, I wish I could purr.

While brief, he smiled. "Go ahead."

"How'd you experiment? What went wrong?"

"Threesome with two men. Turned out my girl just wanted to watch. Let's just say I regret everything, especially the girl."

If I had a hunk like Malcolm, I wouldn't share him with anyone. Then again, if I had a hunk like Malcolm, would I even let him out of the bedroom? Probably not. Her loss.

I would have changed so much if only I hadn't owed the damned devil a favor. Neglecting research before accepting the job from Bubba Eugene had been the second of my mistakes. My third had been insisting on having some morals during a job requiring me to throw most of them out the window.

Oh well. There wasn't anything I could do about it. "Well, never fear. I avoid mixing business and pleasure."

"This isn't one of those sex-trafficking grabs?"

I almost drove the SUV into a ditch, and I slammed the brakes to regain control of my nerves and the vehicle. "What? No!"

Several deep breaths later, I eased the rental back onto the road where it belonged.

"I'm strangely disappointed."

Maybe Bubba Eugene had more than financial reasons to want to get rid of his cousin. "Are you mentally ill?"

"No. I just like sex."

Malcolm liked sex but avoided it like the plague? Also, I couldn't afford to think about sex with him. If he asked, I'd be tempted to pull over, to hell with my morals.

It was going to be a very long trip.

"I'm going to stop for gas at the next station. No signaling for help in any fashion.
Play along. Pretend you're my boyfriend or
something. If anyone ask, we're skipping
town for a bit of fun."

Malcolm chuckled. "I can do that.

"Please do." I hesitated, wondering what
he thought was so funny about the situation.
"You get to pump the gas. No fucking up my
rental or driving off without me."

"Okay."

"No water or windshield wiper fluid in
my gas tank, either."

"I'm fairly certain that falls under not
fucking up your rental."

I sighed and regretted I hadn't spent more
time planning the kidnapping of Malcolm
Findlay Stewart. We hadn't been on the road
for long, and I was already in over my head.

TO KEEP anyone from tracking Malcolm by
his money, I took possession of his wallet and
gave him one of the prepaid cards I'd purchased on the way to Nashville. While he
pumped gas, I bought snacks and drinks for
the road before taking a few minutes in the
bathroom to splash cold water over my face.

No matter how bad my case of lust became, I wouldn't jump Malcolm. I wouldn't

sleep with him—or anyone—under the influence of drugs. I wouldn't sleep with him even if he wasn't on drugs, either. Kidnappings put dampers on relationships, and I wasn't interested in corrupting Mr. July, who was hotter than the devil, into suffering from a classic case of Stockholm Syndrome.

Some lines I refused to cross, and that was one of them.

I cursed my ethics, which were twisted on a good day, kicked the concrete foundation of the building hard enough my toes throbbed, and used the pain to get my head into the game and out of the gutter. With my chin lifted, I returned to the SUV and slid behind the wheel. Malcolm leaned his seat back, stretched out, and yawned. He feigned sleep, but I caught him watching me through his lashes.

I left him alone; there'd be time enough for mind games later. Leaving the gas station, I drove until I found a dirt road leading away from the highway. Pulling off, I parked far enough from the road no one would catch a peek of me shifting.

"Stay," I ordered.

Shifting took longer than normal; instead of the few seconds I'd grown accustomed to, it took me over a minute, and it hurt a lot more, too. I blamed the bracelet. Some good came of it, though. I ended up in my human form, but instead of my usual full gypsy attire, I wore a pair of jean shorts and a denim halter top barely able to contain my breasts. I hadn't escaped my heritage; a coin belt hung off my hips, and bells decorated my suppressor bracelet.

Best of all, I wore a pair of kickass combat boots.

I refused to think about omens involving combat boots. If I did, I'd jump at shadows and look for trouble. A good fight was the one I avoided, and I already had more problems than I knew what to do about. While I hoped to dodge any form of combat, I expected it. My three handguns wouldn't help much if I faced a real assassin or battle mercenaries, but I'd look good going down.

The pair of thigh holsters I added to the ensemble made my legs look fantastic. Killer, even.

I snorted. Armed and somewhat dangerous, I returned to my place behind the wheel. Malcolm gave up his act and watched me with open curiosity.

"Any habits I should know about, Mr. Stewart?"

"I get mean without coffee, I like beer, but none of that American swill they try to pass off as beer. I also eat a lot."

"You'd have to. Couldn't keep those nice muscles otherwise."

"There's going to be a manhunt for me."

"I know."

"I could help you get off lightly. Minimum charges."

"No can do."

"Why not?"

"I like breathing." I spoke the truth, too. The devil didn't like it when people tried to screw him over. "I accepted the job, so I'm going to do it. You're going to cooperate. I'm sorry about that. The not having a choice part that is."

"You realize I'm going to fight you every step of the way, right?"

I got back on the road and headed west. "I figured that out the moment I saw the picture of you and those kittens. Men who go into burning buildings to save kittens and puppies tend to be stubborn."

"I prefer courageous, steadfast, and heroic."

I preferred naked and on the bottom. In what had to classify as a miracle of the highest order, I didn't blurt that out. "Give me an idea of how screwed I am."

Oops. Fortunately for me, he had no idea that was a slip of the worst—and best—sort.

"In those shorts? Pull over and find out."

Or maybe he did. I flushed and added sex-deprived womanizer to my list of Malcolm's characteristics as a bonus entry on my growing list of regrets. Why hadn't I tried to sleep with him *before* starting my brand-new career as a kidnapper?

"I'm not sleeping with you, Scottish sex god or not. So, cut the innuendo. I'm not selling you into a sex-trafficking ring, either. And you know what? Just be quiet. I'm not interested."

I'd never told a worse lie in my life.

SEVEN

Liar, liar pants on became rather
literal.

LIAR, liar pants on became rather literal, much to my dismay. The cause of the accident remained a mystery. One minute I was minding my own business, carting Malcolm towards the west coast. The next, the damned SUV burned in a ditch, my backside roasting. To add to my woes, Malcolm was gone.

Had I ordered him out of the vehicle? I hoped so. With him out of the car, I could worry about my immediate problems.

The SUV was on fire, and I was stuck upside down in it. The seatbelt cut across my chest, my face throbbed, probably from a hard collision with the airbag. Next time someone sang the praises of airbags, I'd agree, but I'd also point out the damned things were torture devices.

The rental company wouldn't be happy

with me when I informed them about their SUV.

I shook my head, hissing at the intensifying heat. Worrying about my car woes would have to wait until I escaped. The first thing I needed to do was unbuckle my seat belt.

The strap hadn't caught fire, but it had gotten so hot it gave at my touch, scalding my fingertips. The plastic oozed, jamming the mechanism securing my belt. I took the hint; if I didn't get out fast, the damned thing would become a flaming restraint. I didn't need a lesson on what would happen next; I'd catch a serious case of dead.

Car fires happened, and I'd seen enough pictures of them to understand what I faced. Flesh didn't stand a chance in an inferno capable of melting plastic and metal.

My first instinct was to shift, but I feared panic shifting wouldn't help. Half the time it didn't. Logically, I understood my best chance was to stay human and wiggle out.

My body hadn't gotten the memo. Feathers and fur burned really well, but my sex kitten claws could do what my burnt fingertips couldn't. I clawed at the belt, put my inhuman strength to work, and tore through the torched material. I dropped, smacking into the SUV's battered roof.

I just loved when vehicles flipped. Air

flowed through the broken windshield and fed the flames, but the gap left in the glass was too small for me to squeeze through. I checked the driver's side door.

It resembled a crunched soda can, which left me with the open passenger door. I twisted to crawl through the opening, made it a few inches, and came to a halt. I coughed at the smoke and lifted my arm to cover my mouth and nose, discovering the stench of charred fur made breathing even harder.

First, I needed to escape. *Then* I could worry about my fur and feather problem.

A moment later, it occurred to me my legs weren't cooperating, and fear choked me even worse than the smoke. Through the gray haze filling the vehicle, I couldn't tell if I was pinned from the crash or paralyzed.

Either spelled death for me.

Panic shifting seemed wiser compared to waiting for my death. I snapped to human form, and without the fur and my wings buffering me from the heat, the pain intensified.

My new clothes also offered the flames a fresh source of fuel.

I fell into a cycle of agony; first, the pain of shifting stabbed deep, then the flames burned me and undid the little healing transformation provided. Stubborn pride joined forces with my refusal to die from something so mundane, and I groped for the one form that might save my ass.

When I finally exchanged hands for paws, the flames ate away at what remained of the vehicle, engulfing the passenger's side completely and leaving me with the windshield as my only viable route of escape. I wormed through the broken glass, which melted from the heat. Every step hurt, and my body throbbed. Pain stabbed deep to my bones, and even the tip of my tufted tail hurt.

The burning SUV offered plenty of light, illuminating the predawn gloom. Of Malcolm, I saw no sign. I limped to safety and turned, flinching as the fire consumed the vehicle. Mud filled the bottom of the ditch alongside the road, and I spotted tracks leading into the woods.

Had Malcolm gone into the woods? If so, why?

I gave the destroyed rental a look over, crawling forward enough to peek inside. Mud and water pooled on the roof, and I spotted the ruined leather of my wallet inside, still intact.

I couldn't afford to lose absolutely everything. Hissing my fury, I braved the flames to snag my wallet with a claw and drag it out so it wouldn't be burned to ash. I'd have to carry the damned thing in my mouth, but it beat the alternative.

A setback I could handle. Complete destruction of all of my plans, however, was a bit much even for me. Kissing most of my investment goodbye along with any chance of forcing Malcolm Findlay Stewart to cooperate with me, I grabbed my wallet with my teeth and picked it up.

Gas, mud, and melted plastic tasted terrible.

Shuddering, I turned away from the wreckage and followed the tracks into the forest at a slow, painful limp.

THE TRAIL MEANDERED through the woods, and I found Malcolm standing over a body with one of my guns, the Desert Eagle, in his hand. Had there been gunfire? I couldn't remember hearing anything other than the roaring of the flames, the crack-pop of plastic bursting, and the hiss of melting metal plopping into the mud.

Malcolm nudged the body with his toe. "Were you after me?"

The body groaned.

"Stop being a baby. I only hit you once. Well? Were you after me?"

I took shelter in the shadow of a tree, my filthy wallet still in my mouth, and eavesdropped on the rather interesting one-sided conversation.

Malcolm upgraded his nudging to a full kick, catching his victim in the ribs. "Next time, I kick below the belt. Who were you after?"

The next time I needed a little encouragement during an interrogation, I'd have to ask Malcolm. His expression remained so cold and neutral I wondered if he cared if he killed the man at his feet.

"Didn't know there'd be anyone else in the car. Ordered to get rid of the cat bitch."

"Cat bitch?" Malcolm chuckled, and the sound terrified me. "How crude. Why?"

"Don't know. Ordered to kill her, so I did."

Snorting, Malcolm shook his head. "The crash didn't kill her. She's unconscious, not dead."

"Is now. Did you think she'd be safe if you chased me? I'd already birthed the flames. You left her to burn to death, and she did. Guess it's a les—"

One bullet from my Desert Eagle put an end to the conversation. Magic could do a lot, but no one could survive a hole between the eyes.

Then the dead man's words filtered through the pain and shock. I could understand *Malcolm* being a target, but me? What the hell had I done to anyone to warrant an assassination?

I thought about it, sitting back on my haunches so I'd put less weight on my burned and blistered paws.

Being born counted as an offense, although my mother had solved her problems by shipping me to the United States. Had running away from my aunt's plans to marry me into money been sufficient for her to hire someone to kill me? I doubted it; my aunt didn't have a lot of money to waste, especially not on me.

Over the years, I'd stolen a lot of things from a lot of people, including a few priceless family heirlooms.

On second thought, it'd be easier to create a list of people I hadn't annoyed into wanting me dead. It'd be shorter.

A lot shorter.

No wonder the devil kept bothering me. My name and good didn't belong in the same sentence. My ethics stood on sandy shores, and a few nudges would knock it into the ocean. After I finished my obligation to the Lord of Lies, I'd take some time off and do a lot of thinking about the rest of my life.

Then again, I had to survive the next half year before I worried about my current trajectory straight to hell.

Since all clouds had a silver lining, I focused on the good news: I'd paid extra for full insurance on the rental, so I didn't need to worry about the repair—well, replacement —bill.

Malcolm straightened, inhaled, and spat curses, spinning on a heel and headed back to the trashed SUV. Flattening my ears, I waited for him to spot me.

He didn't.

Following his own trail, Malcolm marched, lengthening his stride until he verged on breaking into a jog. It hurt to walk, and I had to stop every few steps to catch my breath. I considered leaving my foul-tasting wallet behind, but I soldiered on. The thought of being left behind—or losing Malcolm and completely botching my job—spurred me into an unsteady lope.

The stench of scorched rubber and metal hung heavy in the air. At the tree line, Malcolm halted, his gaze locked on the wreckage. I stalked forward for a better look.

Between the crash and the flames, the SUV had been reduced to a charred husk.

"That mother fucking son of a bitch!"

Heat flared from my bracelet, penetrating through my burnt fur deep to my bones, and the man's rage strengthened with every passing moment. As a firefighter, I suspected he hated death from smoke and flame; the good ones did.

I could ease his anger. It wouldn't take much. I wobbled to him and dropped my wallet on his foot.

It turned out white men really could jump; Malcolm defied gravity and landed several feet away in a crouch. The whites of his eyes showed, and he sucked in a breath.

"You bitch!" Then he took a second look at me, his expression smoothed to an emotionless mask, and he rose to his feet, and closed the distance between us. "You're burned."

Of course I was. I'd been burned, but I would live. I nodded, braced for the misery of transformation, and shifted, not caring which form I got.

Nothing happened.

Things had somehow gone from bad to worse, and I yowled my dismay for the world to hear.

MALCOLM WAS DETERMINED to wait for the police to show up, and since I couldn't shift and order him to leave, I sulked in the deepest mud puddle I could find. Most cats hated water, but the muck soothed my burned pads and made the pain tolerable. From my spot, I got a good look inside my rental.

Nothing inside remained, and I supposed it was for the best. With one look at the illegal merchandise I'd been carrying, the cops would have a field day. I'd have an unfortunate number of questions to answer and a lengthy stay in prison ahead of me.

The only good news was the lack of evidence of my wrongdoing. Malcolm would obey me for at least another eighteen hours—maybe longer. As I couldn't remember the crash, my phones were destroyed, and Malcolm wasn't wearing a watch per my orders, I had no idea what time it was. The sun had risen, but it wasn't noon yet.

When the cops and firetruck finally showed up, Malcolm relaxed. Smiling, he waved down one of the firemen. "Samson!"

"Oy, Malcolm. This ain't your beaut. What's goin' on?" The firefighter slid down the muddy bank into the ditch, close enough to splash me with muck. I flattened my ears and hissed.

Either Samson didn't care he'd angered a lioness or hadn't noticed me, but he strolled to Malcolm and they clasped hands. Malcolm's smile widened into a grin. "Went on a ride with my new girlfriend and a pyro torched her rental. Possible ex-lover, as he really had it out for her." The man pointed at me, and I didn't like the glint in his eyes. "She's been burned. She's a shifter, and I think she's hurt badly enough she can't shift without help."

Samson frowned and twisted to look me over. "We're not geared for lycanthropes."

"She's not a lycanthrope. She's an actual shifter."

I needed to take lessons from Malcolm on misleading people and lying. If he kept it up, he'd be the one with his pants on fire.

"Huh. I never thought you'd get over Caitlin's stunt. She's a cat shifter? I guess that's one way to do it. Is she a beast in bed?"

With that one question, I remembered why I'd forgone men for the past few months. Inhaling, I roared at him for assuming girlfriend was another word for slut.

"I wouldn't know," Malcolm replied, ignoring me. "We're dating. That doesn't mean we're sleeping together."

Judging from his tone, he'd meant to include 'yet' in his statement.

"What's the point then?"

If I killed Malcolm and his friend, would it count as a provoked murder? With over fifty thousand down the drain, jail didn't seem like too bad of a deal. I'd be clothed, I'd have shelter, and I'd be fed healthy food three times a day without fail. Better yet, the devil wouldn't be able to visit me.

The good prisons had protections in place against teleportation of any sort.

Yep, I regretted everything.

"Samson, I'm in the middle of trying to skip town with her when I should be heading to work in a few hours. Can we get to filing the paperwork so I can get back to it? If possible, I'd like to keep this quiet. My plan is to take her to the hospital and resume skipping town."

"What about the pyro?"

Malcolm shrugged. "Killed him. It was him or me, and after he tried to murder my girl, I wasn't going to end up a victim, too. His body's in the woods; he tried to run after he came to make sure he'd killed us. Shot him with my girl's gun."

Calm as can be, Malcolm rooted through my wallet, pulling out permit after permit until locating the blue one for Tennessee. "She's an enthusiast. Lost her two other guns in the fire, unfortunately. I took this one since it was in reach. I couldn't get her out, not with a pyro on the loose. He tried to light me up."

One of the cops slid down the bank to join us, regarding the torched SUV with a frown. "Self-defense, open and close case. You're cursed, Mal. We already called for an ambulance, but it'll be twenty minutes until it can get here. Why don't you show us the body while we're waiting. You can tell me more about your lady, too."

"Her name's Kanika, and she's a queen of Egypt."

Next time I gave the man orders, I'd make sure I gave him a very short leash—or better instructions. Damn it, I only had myself to blame for the man's words, and I hated it.

"Pretty?" the cop asked, and his interest in my fake relationship with Malcolm unsettled me.

"Too strong to be pretty." Malcolm smirked and headed for the trees, leaving me behind and taking my wallet with him. "She has legs worth risking death over, though. They're about a mile long and curved in all the right places."

What a pig. Next time, I would remember innuendo didn't cover all things sexual.

"Oh-ho! Better than Caitlin's?" Samson crowed, hurrying to follow.

"So much better. I can understand why a pyro would burn with jealousy. There's no describing what she can do a mere man like myself. Anyway, the body's this way, but he may have smoldered by now. You know how it goes with pyros."

"Sure do," the cop replied. "Hey, Carlos! Keep an eye on his girl, would you?"

One of the firemen looking over my rental sighed and shook his head. "You three gossip worse than girls."

I had the feeling truer words had never
been spoken.

IT OCCURRED to me we should've been far
from where Malcolm worked or volunteered,
yet he seemed to know everyone. The ambulance arrived shortly before the trio returned
from their hike in the woods, and they confirmed my would-be killer's body had smoldered to ash.

Maybe Malcolm would be able to offer
the paramedics a clue; neither knew what to
do with me, and they argued over how to
treat my burns without catching lycanthropy.
Malcolm ran his hand through his hair and
scratched the back of his head. "Why not take
her to the hospital?"

"We don't treat pets," the younger one
snapped.

Burned paws or not, when I got a hold of
him, I'd leave him a few reminders that I was
not pet. Teeth bared and hissing, I lunged for
the paramedic. Malcolm caught me around
my belly and hauled me back with a grunt.
Since I couldn't hurt him without defeating
my purpose, I roared and thrashed, careful to
keep my claws sheathed.

"She's not a pet."

"Looks like a cat, sounds like a cat, that means she is—"

Rage blazed through me. If I couldn't rip the paramedic to shreds as a feline, I'd get satisfaction through any means possible. I exchanged charred fur for raw, red, and blistered skin. Malcolm's hold on me turned an already painful transformation into agony, and my fury extinguished under the onslaught of pain.

"—a very angry, naked, and badly burned woman," the paramedic concluded, his tone mild.

Naked? The shock of having, for the first time in my life, shifted without clothes momentarily distracted me from my burns. I was already grateful for my nudity; Malcolm's touch hurt enough without adding clothing to the mix. "I'm not a pet," I hissed through clenched teeth.

The paramedic ignored me, shaking his head. "We're not equipped to transport a lycanthrope, Mal."

"I'm not a damned lycanthrope, either!"

Malcolm tightened his hold on me, and tears blurred my vision. "She's a shifter, Rex. If you're too scared to touch her, I'll handle the work, just tell me what to do."

Like it or not, I was going on a ride in an ambulance, as Malcolm ignored my protests, yelps, and curses, dragging me out of the ditch as though I weighed no more than a feather to him. I found another silver lining in the shit storm I called my life; I was about to cost the devil a great deal of money.

Maybe that'd teach him a thing or two about involving himself in the affairs of un-lucky mortals like myself.

EIGHT

I would miss my hair.

UNDER NORMAL CIRCUMSTANCES, shifting altered every bit of my anatomy, right down to my nails. Only my eyebrows and eyelashes escaped the flames, and my burns ranged from red, raw skin to pale white blisters. Shifting had spared me from any actual charring. Several nurses under the supervision of two doctors applied salves. By the time they were finished bandaging me, I resembled a mummy.

I could deal with mimicking Bastet and Cleopatra, but mummies were an entirely different matter. They were the reason I refused any job dealing with Egyptian artifacts. Too many myths about mummies, especially those of pharaohs, existed for me to wave them away as superstition.

The last thing I needed was a curse added to the rest of my problems.

According to the triage nurse, shifting had

saved my life, lessened the severity of my burns, and would help mitigate scarring. It would take several years before the scars all faded. To make matters worse, my hair was gone, and unless I got really lucky or could pay absurd amounts for special treatment, it could be years before any of it grew back.

I could deal with burns.

I could deal with scars.

I would miss my hair, my one true vanity, a symbol of my heritage, and a badge of pride. I hadn't cut it since the day I left my aunt's home; she had hated long hair and had demanded I keep mine short. Would shifting help it grow back?

I'd never been bald before, and even when I transformed into a sphinx and adopted ancient Egyptian hair stylings, my hair grew back to its natural length when I returned to my human form.

Tears blurred my vision, and I clenched my teeth to hold them back. No matter how many times I called myself a sex kitten, I turned heads because I was exotic, not because I was beautiful. I'd turn a lot fewer heads if I ended up with half as many scars as the nurses claimed.

Crying wouldn't help. Revenge wouldn't, either, since the bastard responsible was dead. I couldn't even get the satisfaction of kicking his corpse. That left me with the pyro's boss. One way or another, I'd find them. When I did, they were going to die a slow, painful death for torching my hair.

While I stewed over my misfortune, the three nurses mummifying me tortured my tender skin, making it difficult to keep my tears at bay. A little old lady with too much spring in her step bounced to the examination table armed with a clipboard "Dear, there's an issue with your insurance."

"Now what?" I snapped, and then I grimaced at the waver in my voice and my shameful behavior. "I'm sorry. That was rude of me. What's wrong?"

"Don't worry your pretty head about it one bit, dear. You're hurting. I tell you, last time I got burned, I was a bear for a week." The nurse smiled at me and tapped her finger to her papers. "Says here we need to notify the main policy holder whenever you come in, but I think there's a mistake. It's not a valid number."

I could make a guess at the devil's number, and the nurse was right that it wouldn't be valid—not normally. "666-666-6666?"

Her eyes widened. "It's a real number?"

"Whatever you do, don't spell his name wrong. He *hates* that."

"There's also the issue of your relationship with the policy holder..."

"Take it up with him; I gave you all the paperwork I have." Of course, the paperwork I had was a single card and a policy number involving a lot of sixes. The devil needed to let go of his unhealthy obsession with the number. "I wish I could help you more than that, but everything else burned. I don't suppose there's a chance I can be discharged today, is there?"

I needed out of the hospital before something else went wrong—or Malcolm broke free of Hagnar's drug and ran for the hills.

The nurse sighed. "If the doctor approves. I'll go ask."

As soon as the woman left, my trio of torturers giggled, and Nurse Meredith flashed me a grin. "666-666-6666?"

"The number's owner has a wicked sense of humor."

The nurses snickered and returned to their mummification work. At least they hadn't embalmed me first. That really would've ruined my day.

WHILE I WAS HAVING a devil of day, miracles happened, too. Malcolm was waiting for me in one of the lounges, and several plastic bags littered the floor around his feet. "While you were being treated, I left long enough to get us some clothes and a rental. You should change. Wearing a hospital gown out of here's a little tackier than I can handle."

Rising to his feet, Malcolm snagged one of the bags and held it out. He pointed across the waiting room. "There's a bathroom over there."

It hurt to take the bag, but I held on, lifted my chin, and limped away, determined not to wince even once. I lasted two steps before I hissed at the throbbing pain in my feet. I set the bag in the sink so I wouldn't have to bend over more than necessary and dug through his purchases.

While Malcolm had talked a lot of shit about my legs to his friends, his clothing selection exposed the lie—or made him a lot better of a guy than I had initially thought. When the painkillers wore off—which would be within the hour—I would appreciate the loose, lightweight slacks and the thin, flowing blouse. I wasn't fond of the bright blues and greens, but I'd buy clothing for myself later. At the bottom of the bag, I found a pair of sandals with minimal straps, easy to put on and take off without hurting my feet even more.

I'd definitely appreciate that over the next few days.

When I returned to the waiting room, Malcolm looked me over and nodded. "You got lucky, you know."

No shit. Had I been a vanilla human, the forensics crew would be working to identify which bits of ash were mine. "You're remarkably helpful for someone who swore he'd thwart me at every turn."

"That was before a pyro tried to kill you. I prefer a challenge."

I canted my head to the side, wincing at the pressure of the bandages around my throat. "What does that have to do with anything? My death would benefit you." Out of the corner of my eye, I glanced at one of the waiting room's clocks. "In twelve hours, you won't have to obey me at all."

Malcolm scowled and lifted his left hand, displaying the suppressor bracelet. "The advantage still belongs to you. I need my magic, and you control the bracelet. I tried to take them off after the crash. I couldn't."

I upped the value of the bracelets to priceless. I'd really have to thank Hagnar for giving me such a great deal. I was still forcing Malcolm's cooperation, but he retained his free will. Holding him hostage wouldn't be easy, especially when I needed to deactivate the bracelet for the sake of his health. I'd cross that bridge when I reached it.

Even knowing I had some control over Malcolm, my situation wasn't good, no matter how I spun it. Some omens I couldn't ignore, and having my rental lit on fire counted. I should've taken more care—and paid attention to the combat boots. I had survived so far, but I worried about what tomorrow would bring.

A wise woman would have requested a wheel chair, but I chose to limp out of the hospital. Malcolm kept a few strides ahead of me, stopping to wait whenever I fell behind. Outside, he crossed the parking lot to a sporty red car, pulled keys out of his pocket, and disabled the alarm. I couldn't drive, not with my feet already throbbing from the relatively short walk.

In unspoken agreement, he slid behind the wheel while I eased into the car, hissing at the pressure against my burns. If I sat perfectly still, I could tolerate the discomfort. My seatbelt proved a problem, especially where the edge of the strap dug into my shoulder.

Malcolm fastened his seatbelt and started the engine. "Where are we headed?"

"West," I hissed through clenched teeth.

"Where west?"

"Just west." Until I had a chance to heal, it didn't matter. Walking had hurt, and just sitting in the car morphed my pain into nauseating misery. I controlled my breathing so I wouldn't throw up all over the leather interior. "Stop at the first decent pharmacy you find, please. Also, I'm not responsible for anything that happens to this car."

"Feeling sick?" Malcolm's expression softened. "Don't worry about it. I was aware of the risks when I picked the rental. I took a page out of your book and got full insurance on it just in case. I'll try to keep the ride smooth."

Why was he being nice to me? I hadn't done anything to earn courtesy from him. Still, if he could play nice, so could I. "Thanks. I'll chart a route for us after I get a new laptop. For now, just take us west."

"West it is."

My bracelet warmed around my wrist, and I frowned at the sensation. Instead of the searing discomfort of his rage, something gentle and soothing spread up my arm. Malcolm eased the car out of his spot, maneuvering around the shallow holes most would've driven over without a second thought.

A man capable of killing someone without remorse should've been the type to make me suffer for what I'd done to him. Had I kidnapped an onion disguised as a human? Each layer I uncovered made me want to peel away at him until I learned everything I could about him.

When we were on the road, Malcolm asked, "Why did that guy want you dead anyway?"

"I'd say your guess is as good as mine, but I've never seen him before."

Malcolm hummed. "Any guesses why?"

I took my time thinking about it. Why *would* someone want to kill me bad enough to hire a pyro to do it? Hagnar topped the list of possibilities despite having given his word. Blackmail and backstabbing was his bread and butter, and everybody had a price, especially him. With enough money, I bet he'd talk about my plans. Well, he wouldn't talk. He'd just leave the inventory of supplies I had purchased out where someone could find them, which wouldn't violate his oath of silence.

What I had purchased exposed my intentions.

"I could make a few guesses." For the moment, I'd eliminate Hagnar as a suspect, which left a disgruntled enemy. I had plenty of those thanks to the gigs I'd done over the years. "He was probably hired by someone I'd pissed off."

"And how many people might that be?"

I cracked a grin at Malcolm's annoyed tone. "In Tennessee?"

"That worries me for some reason."

I shrugged and flinched at the pressure of the bandages against my burns. The accursed seatbelt strap dug in deep, and my eyes watered. Closing my eyes, I concentrated on my breathing until the throbbing diminished to an ache. "Grudges happen in my line of business."

"Kidnappings do tend to upset people. Statistically, most victims of a kidnapping are killed if they aren't rescued within twenty-four to forty-eight hours."

"I already told you I don't intend to kill you. Anyway, I freelance, thank you very much."

"Interesting. So today you're a kidnapper. What were you before you picked yours truly as your target?"

"I didn't pick you, your cousin did. He just hired me to do it. You're not my type." I hoped my liar, liar pants on fire tendencies wouldn't lead to even more burns. I had enough of them already. "I'm also not your type, according to your cousin."

"I do tend to favor blondes, but I might make an exception this once. Nice attempt at dodging my question. What had you been doing before you kidnapped me?"

I grumbled curses over the reminder of my encounter with the devil. "Climbing a tree to fetch a cat."

"I've fetched more than a few cats out of trees. And before that?"

Even wrinkling my nose hurt. It'd been over a year since my last major job, and I'd done hundreds of small jobs to keep afloat, much to my disgust. "I do whatever people need. Unfortunately, that's why I gave myself the worst business name."

Malcolm chuckled. "What's your business name?"

"Whatever for Hire."

The stunned silence didn't last long before Malcolm laughed so hard he cried, which in turn forced him to pull over so he wouldn't wreck the car. Then he laughed some more, slumping over the steering wheel while beating his palm against the dashboard.

"It's not that funny."

Choking back his mirth, he replied, "It really is. My cousin hired a no-name mercenary with a ridiculous business name to kidnap *me*?"

Since killing Malcolm would violate my contract with his cousin—and ruin my reputation—I lifted my chin and crossed my arms over my chest, ignoring the pain. "I pulled it off, didn't I?"

That shut him up. People often laughed at my business name, but I hated it all the same. Once I finished the toughest job of my career without murdering the man I'd sworn to keep safe, I'd put some serious thought into a new business name, one less likely to land me in trouble.

IT TOOK Malcolm over an hour to find a pharmacy that met his standards. While I filled my prescriptions, he handled acquiring the rest of the things we'd need for our road trip.

The devil had a great prescription plan, and I spent five dollars on painkillers, special bandages, two jars of salve, an antibiotic, and a vitamin supplement. The supplement confused me, but I kept my mouth shut. Only an idiot questioned the devil when he was footing the medical bills.

While the pharmacist went through the mile-long list of warnings for my medications, I looked over my list of medical expenses. I found a perverse satisfaction over the cost of my care; my medications alone dinged the devil thousands. A wise woman didn't make a deal with the devil in the first place, but a smart one didn't look a demonic gift horse in the mouth. After I added in the hundred an hour he owed me, the fifty thousand in incinerated supplies didn't seem like a big deal.

I looked forward to the day I invoiced the devil for almost half a million dollars. The sum made the hassle of dealing with Malcolm worthwhile. Basking in the glow of costing the Lord of Hell so much money, I hummed a happy tune, handed over the money I owed the pharmacist, and smiled all the way to the door.

Malcolm intercepted me, grabbing my bag of medications and medical papers out of my hand. At a single glance at the invoice, he burst into laughter. "I need your healthcare plan."

I shot him a glare and snatched the documents out of his hand. "Aren't you a millionaire? You can afford any plan you want."

"I have a poor relationship with my insurance company."

Of course he did. I remembered the picture of him rescuing kittens and puppies. "That's because you run towards fires rather than away from them. Last I checked, insanity counts as a pre-existing condition."

"Point," he conceded.

I limped to the car while Malcolm followed, and he hovered close enough to catch me if I tripped. I suspected if I did fall, he'd be carting my unconscious body back to the hospital. To distract myself from my burns, I focused on work—and pondered how I'd keep Malcolm contained and cooperating. "Your cousin hired me to keep you in my custody for six months. He paid me ten thousand up front and is paying an additional ten thousand per month."

"You got ripped off."

No kidding. "I have supplementary income." Some things Malcolm didn't need to know, and the devil's involvement counted. "I don't like being put in a situation like this, so while I need to live up to the terms of my contract, nothing says I can't help you with your business dealings, assuming you can work remotely. Can you?"

"I can. My cousin's an idiot if he thinks getting rid of me will sink my company. All I need is a laptop and an internet connection."

"We'll stop somewhere and buy you a laptop and a cell with a data plan, neither of which you'll use to screw me over."

Malcolm chuckled, unlocked the car, and opened the back door, tossing his bag of purchases and my medications inside. "I needed a vacation anyway."

How wonderful. Why did I always find the crazy ones? "You're not supposed to like being kidnapped. You're supposed to be fighting me every step of the way. Aren't you super wealthy types supposed to be smart?"

"I've been bored. This is anything but boring. You're interesting, and while I'm a little annoyed my cousin went this far, I can appreciate the change of pace. I'm tired of the grind. It's usually the same old shit on a different day. I go to work. I volunteer at the firehouse. I go home. Bubba did me a favor without realizing it." Malcolm waited for me to buckle up before starting the car. "I'm particularly grateful you're not some muscle-bound freak. That'd make this trip a lot less pleasant."

"Normal people would say you have Stockholm Syndrome."

"I don't have Stockholm Syndrome. I just looked for ways this situation benefits me."

"I fail to see how any of this benefits you."

"I already told you I'm not bored."

Were all handsome men crazy, or was it just Malcolm? I'd already given my word, so like it or not, I was stuck with him for six months. I could handle six months, couldn't I? Between Malcolm and his cousin, I already had my plate full of trouble. Add in the devil, and I feared what tomorrow would bring.

NINE

Just don't spell it wrong; that's a
good way to piss him off.

BETWEEN MY BRUSH with death and the
painkillers, I wasn't capable of tying my shoes
let alone planning anything, so Malcolm
made hotel arrangements. Had I been coherent, I would've ordered him to take us to the
cheapest dive possible.

I accepted my idiocy with cheerful disgust. A hot as hell millionaire wasn't going to
pick a cheap dive. Oh, no. Only the nicest
hotel in Little Rock, Arkansas would do. A
bald mummy stuck out among the other
guests. I couldn't even call myself a bloody
crow to their swans. Crows had feathers. Ah-
ha! I was a molted parrot dunked in bleach
compared to their peacocks.

I assumed the well-dressed men and
women in the hotel lobby were wealthy,
which would explain their disgusted glares
and ill-concealed whispers. Within five min-

utes, I was primed to attempt murder with my bare hands since my Desert Eagle had been confiscated as evidence. The cops had claimed I'd get it back eventually. I expected they'd return it in a few years.

If I picked the right targets, I could kill most of the snobbish onlookers before someone stopped me. It was a win-win. I got rid of a bunch of obnoxious elitist pricks *and* I'd get to spend at least six months in prison. If I played my hand just right, Malcolm would face a guilty verdict, too. Prisons were safe. They were uncomfortable and boring, but prisons were safe. How had I never noticed the subtle benefits of incarceration before?

Alas, I hurt too much to indulge in murder, so I pretended I was alone in the lobby while Malcolm checked us in. Most women probably would've loved to be seen with such a handsome man in public, enjoying delusions of grandeur. Me? Not so much.

Delusions of normality were closer to my speed. Normal meant boring, which in turn meant safe, and I'd had my fill of excitement for a few months. I fixed my gaze on the far wall and waited.

And waited, and waited, and waited.

Staring at the wall only helped so much; a line grew behind us, and the other guests whispered to each other about us.

Malcolm planted his elbows on the mahogany counter, leaned forward, and hissed, "What do you mean my card's been declined?"

What could go wrong was going wrong, and we couldn't even manage to check into a hotel without trouble. Lovely. Stupendous. At least I could do something about the money situation, although I'd leave the worst sort of trail—one the devil could follow. I sighed, fished out my new debit card from my pocket, and slapped it in front of Malcolm. "Put it on this. We'll figure out what's wrong with your card in the room."

The hotel's desk jockey swiped my card, and a moment later, he sucked in a breath. "Ma'am, this account is flagged for use by the Mephistopheles family."

"And? Just don't spell it wrong; that's a good way to piss him off."

Malcolm narrowed his eyes and frowned. "What are you talking about?"

"Long story." Any other time, I would've flashed the hotel employee my best smile, but I'd figured my recent mummification would twist a normally pleasant expression into a horror show. "I've had a long day. Can we have our room key, please?"

"O-of course, Miss Mephistopheles."

I sighed at the misunderstanding but didn't correct him. Explaining how I lacked a surname, even when I went to the extremes

of whipping out my birth certificate and per-
mits, took too much time and effort. Two
minutes later, keys in hand, we retreated to
the elevators.

Malcolm pressed the up button and
arched a brow. "Miss Mephistopheles?"

How spectacular. If I didn't want Malcolm
breathing down my neck, I'd have to tell him
about the surname issue. "I don't have a last
name. Banks don't like people without last
names, so I'm often addressed by the last
name of the expense account's owner. This
just happens to be one of the more annoying
expense accounts."

"Someone has a lot of nerve using *that*
name on their bank account."

The elevator dinged open, and my worst
nightmare stood inside, doing a very bad job
at playing human. Surprise, surprise. If I ignored the devil, would he go away? Unlikely.
Biting back a groan, I stepped inside and held
the door for Malcolm. "Oh, look. It's Satin.
Why am I not surprised?"

"Kanika, I see you've embraced your heritage to a rather extreme degree," the Lord of
Hell replied, and the tip of his black tail
twitched.

Malcolm shot me a quizzical look, but I
waved him off, waited until he was inside the
elevator, and tapped the button for our floor.
"Don't you have better things to do, Satin?"

"But I came all this way just to see you."

"Normal people would call you a stalker."

"That's not very nice."

"I'm supposed to be nice to you? That wasn't a part of my contract."

The devil pouted. "Don't you love me anymore?"

"No. I'm not your mommy."

The Lord of Hell blinked, as did Malcolm. They stared, their lips parted, and I frowned at them in turn. "What?"

"You're not my mummy?"

Shit. I twitched. "If I tap my heels together three times, will your brothers show up and make you go away?"

"No one has tried that before. Give it your best shot."

If the devil's plan was to drive me insane, he was well on his way to succeeding. Clicking my heels while wearing sandals didn't work very well, and I wasn't surprised when no archangels appeared. I shrugged and stared at the elevator's floor display, willing the damned thing to move faster. "What do you want, Satin?"

"For you to stop calling me that."

"Oh, right. Sorry, Lucy."

The devil sighed. "Why are you doing such a good impersonation of a mummy?"

My mouth dropped open, and I blurted, "You mean you're not omniscient?"

"Do I look like Santa to you?"

I learned something new every day. "How'd you know about the job, then?"

"There might be some truth to your stalker theory. My wife tells me I have a bad meddling habit, too."

It occurred to me if the devil had been poking his nose where it didn't belong, *he* was the one to blame for my involvement with Malcolm Findlay Stewart and his cheapskate cousin. "Are you saying this is your fault?"

"Yes."

The devil was going to die, and I was going to be the one to kill him. With an inarticulate scream, I lunged for his throat. "You bastard!"

Malcolm dropped our bags and wrapped his arms around my waist, grunted, and hauled me back. "Not in public."

"You owe me fifty thousand, you piece of shit—"

The devil laughed, and then he disappeared, leaving me to claw at empty air while the faintest hint of brimstone lingered in his wake. I cursed him and Malcolm until the elevator dinged open, and when I didn't move, Malcolm shoved our bags out of the elevator with a foot and dragged me down the hallway, ignoring my struggles.

Once I finished killing the devil, Malcolm

would be next, and both of them deserved slow, painful deaths.

OUR SUITE WAS spacious enough to have a dedicated sitting room, but there was only one bed. Had I entered heaven or hell? Sharing a bed with Malcolm hadn't been part of my plan. Beds led to the sort of trouble I couldn't afford to have.

I glared at the fluffy comforter and plump pillows. Sharing a bed with him couldn't be *that* bad, could it? It wasn't like I was going to jump him. I could keep my hands to myself, and Malcolm didn't seem like the type to force himself on anyone.

Narrowing my eyes, I debated between retreating to the couch or staying in the bedroom.

I must have hesitated too much for Malcolm's liking, as he grabbed me by my waist and tossed me onto the bed. I landed hard and bounced on the mattress. The flash of pain was so intense I forgot about everything for a while. When I finally regained the semblance of coherency, Malcolm was stretched out beside me, watching me with a smirk. "Before you try to kill me for that stunt, you needed the rest, and it was the only way I could think of to guarantee you'd stay down for a while."

I groaned and lurched upright. It went better than expected. My skin felt too tight, but I no longer throbbed, not even where I touched the bed. "That wasn't nice."

"It really wasn't. The worst you might've done is pop a few blisters, and the salves they applied will help them heal faster. You got off lucky. You should've had third-degree burns from head to toe. Your worst are second-degree, and they're not that bad. They hurt like hell, but you'll heal. There's a good chance you'll have minimal scarring, too."

"I shifted," I admitted. "The seat belt was jammed, and my legs were trapped."

"I know. I was certain we'd need the jaws of life to get you out. I was debating trying to find help when the pyro arrived to finish the job. I swear on my honor I believed there was no risk of a fire. I'd never leave someone to die like that."

It was foolish of me, but I believed him. Then again, my trust in him made sense. Someone like him, who put his life on the line fighting fires, wouldn't leave anyone to face the flames alone. I respected him for his dedication, however much I disliked admitting it. "Thanks for that. I do wish you'd gotten something useful out of the pyro, like his boss's name."

"That occurred to me right after I pulled the trigger. Sorry about that. I don't get along with pyros."

"Obviously."

Malcolm stretched out, looking me over with a smile. "If I have to deal with being a hostage, I think it's fair you have to deal with sharing a bed with me. Please tell me you normally sleep naked."

Malcolm was going to drive me insane. "First, I'm not your type. Second, if you're trying to make me uncomfortable, it's not working. Third, I already told you I don't sleep with my clients *or* my victims."

"You don't know what my type is, if my goal was to make you uncomfortable, I have far more effective ways of doing it, and I think that should be negotiable. I have a habit of cuddling up to pretty women in my sleep. I wouldn't want you to get cold at night."

I eased my way out of bed, taking care to limit how much pain I inflicted on myself. "How long was I out?"

"About ten hours. I woke you up long enough for you to eat dinner and take your medicine, but you went right back to sleep." Malcolm frowned. "You don't remember that?"

I shook my head. While having a memory lapse worried me, I suffered from them sometimes, especially when really tired or woken up for a short period of time. "What time is it?"

"Six in the morning. It's time to change your bandages and apply the ointment. It's as good a time as any to hit the road."

Malcolm sounded way too awake and eager for my liking, and I hissed my annoyance, heading for the bathroom to begin the tedious process of removing my bandages. Before I could close the door, he stepped inside.

"I didn't invite you."

"I invited myself. You'll need help, especially with your back."

While true, I scowled at the implication I couldn't take care of myself. "Don't even think of trying anything."

"I prefer a challenge fairly won." His subtle smile promised trouble. He picked up one of the jars of ointment, opened it, and sniffed. "I really need your insurance policy. They gave you this and the rest of your medications for five dollars?"

"That's what the pharmacist charged me," I confirmed.

"Well, they gave you the good stuff. This'll not only lessen the pain, it'll help you heal faster, plus I'll be very surprised if you end up with any bad scars. Think you can undress without help?"

If I could have balled my hand into a fist

without it hurting like hell, I would've cleaned Malcolm's clock for asking. "I'll be fi—"

Malcolm poked me in the ribs, and when I blinked, I was on the floor with my head nestled on his lap.

"I barely touched you," he announced. "I thought I'd just point out you need help. Please believe me when I say I wasn't intending on making you black out again."

"You're a jerk." He was, too. He was a jerk for being right, for pressing my buttons, and most of all, for being far too nice for someone I'd kidnapped using a very illegal drug. Add in that I was holding his magic hostage, and he had every right to kill me and bury my body in a shallow grave.

"I am. It's a bad habit, as is cuddling up to pretty women in my sleep."

I clenched my teeth, braced for the worst, and lurched upright. "We went over this already. I'm not your type. You could have just waited the two minutes for me to try and fail miserably."

"But then I wouldn't have been in position to catch you. You might've hit your head on the floor or the vanity, and you don't need a concussion on top of everything else." With a smug smile, Malcolm grabbed hold of my shirt and pulled. I expected him to pull it over my head, flinching at the thought of raising my arms.

The fabric tore, and he repeated the process until scraps of cloth littered the floor.

"You ripped it," I blurted.

"Yes, I did."

"But why? That was a perfectly good shirt. What did it ever do to you?"

"Unless you want to be at this all morning, would you please sit still while I take care of these bandages? Your shirt was in the way, so I got rid of it."

"You have testosterone poisoning, don't you?"

He chuckled. "Maybe I was giving you a little demonstration of how strong and manly I am, entirely for your benefit."

"I'm not your type," I repeated. Maybe if I ignored him, he'd go away. I went to work removing the bandages, hissing at the pressure against my burns. As long as I controlled my breathing and avoided any sudden movements, I could handle the pain. While slow and tedious, I didn't need his help.

Or so I thought, but then I removed the first of the bandages and got a good look at my stomach and ribs. Some of the larger blisters had popped, I oozed in places I had no business oozing, and I'd never seen skin so raw and red in my life.

"What is my type, then?"

I kept quiet, mulling over Malcolm's type —or what Bubba Eugene thought Malcolm's type was. While I thought it through, I went to work removing my mummy costume.

After a few moments of confusion, we settled into a rhythm. I handled the front while he handled the back. We passed the strips of bandages to each other, revealing more and more of my battered, broken skin. Talking about Malcolm's interest in women seemed far better than thinking about how badly I'd been burned.

Taking a deep breath, I forced my hands to keep working, averting my eyes as much as possible from the splotches of blood and the greasy yellow smears courtesy of the hospital's initial treatment of my injuries.

"You're after a go-getter, someone who is on par with you, especially financially. You don't want a trust fund lady. You want someone who works hard without using her sex appeal to succeed. You're also looking for someone who doesn't actually need you or your money. I'm guessing you worked hard to build your empire, and you're not interested in a woman who'll suck the money out of you given half a day at the mall."

"Who told you that?"

"Your cousin."

"He would," Malcolm grumbled, taking the bandage out of my hand so he could work it around my back. He reached the end, balled it up, and tossed it into the nearby trashcan. "This might sting a little."

I tensed, closed my eyes, and waited. He pulled one of the bandages, and I yelped at the pressure along my back and right side. When he passed the strip to me, I cracked open my eyes and realized the hospital had used a self-adhering bandage to cover the gauze beneath.

Removing it hurt like hell, and I wasn't happy with what the gauze hid. I shuddered, averting my eyes, then on second thought, closed them. Some things I didn't need to see. Next time, I wanted the strong, manly fire-fighter with a shirt-ripping fetish showing off without burns being involved.

"Once we have the bandages off, if you can handle a shift, it'd be a good idea. It'll help you heal faster and close some of the open blisters. I doubt shifting will get rid of them, but I think you'll be more comfortable."

It was worth a try. I needed Malcolm's help to stand, and at his insistence, my only job was to remain still while he worked. I kept my eyes closed. It helped a little.

I didn't faint again, which I counted as a victory.

"All right. Try shifting."

Over the course of the next five minutes, I learned how to play a new game: one, two, three, floor. I managed to shift but, like in the hospital, no clothes made a magical appearance, for which I was grateful. I peeked at my arm, hissing at the absence of black fur. The burns seemed to have improved; I wasn't oozing anymore.

A single brush of my fingers against my scalp confirmed I had no hair. Since I couldn't play another round of one, two, three, floor while sprawled on the tiles, I shifted back to human. I trembled on the floor, panting in my effort to catch my breath. "That hurt."

"It helped, although not as much as I was hoping. This'll be the bad part. Let me know if you need me to stop. I'll start with your scalp and work my way down your back, which is where the worst of your burns are. The ointment will numb your skin in about half a minute, so sit tight."

"Do your worst." I hoped he did his worst in a hurry.

Malcolm popped the first jar open, and a moment later, he smeared a cool gel over my skin. It hurt, then it tingled, then I felt nothing at all, and I sighed my relief. "Magic?"

"More medicine than magic. The magic is what's numbing you so the medicine—and your body—can do the rest of the work. What was the deal with that incubus? Your boyfriend?"

His question startled me. He wanted to know if the devil was my *boyfriend*? "No!"

"Good. I'm not sure I can compete with an incubus."

With a little work, I bet I could list a hundred reasons why Bubba Eugene might want his cousin to disappear. "Are you trying to get me to kill you, too? If so, it might be working."

Malcolm laughed. "I'm trying to distract you from what I'm doing, actually."

He got full points; he was distracting me from the pain. Unfortunately, he was doing a stellar job of making me aware of his fingers stroking my neck and back as he applied the ointment. I needed a distraction from the distraction before I did something I regretted, like toss my few remaining morals to the four winds for a chance to drag him to bed, burns be damned. "Why aren't you in jail for killing that pyro? Everyone knows you did it. You confessed in front of a bunch of cops."

"I'm a licensed firefighter, that's why. My license includes the right to use lethal force on any pyro endangering public safety. It applies to all sentients, too, not just humans. The general rule is, if the victim is a species capable of learning a human language, I can go after the culprit however I feel necessary. Your burns and his flare-out confirmed I'd killed a pyro, and no one doubts the lethality of his attack. You're only alive because you're a shapeshifter. I might need to show up in court to confirm I knew he was a pyro before I pulled the trigger, but it'll be a five-minute session. The body smoldered fast, and I can verify under oath he intended to kill you."

I'd never realized there was more to being a firefighter than putting out fires. "And all firefighters have this license?"

"No. Most are volunteers or paid by the state to deal with emergencies. Usually, an on-duty cop patrol handles pyro incidents, but stations have one licensed person on all evening shifts, as most pyros work at night. I'm the one who keeps the pyro busy until the police arrive. It's only happened a few times while I was on shift. One was apprehended, the others were killed. Fortunately, there aren't a lot of firebugs out to kill people."

I snorted a laugh. "Firebugs?"

"Seems appropriate to me. They're pests, and once they turn their magic on others, they deserve to be splattered beneath my heel."

The suppressor heated against my skin, and the strength of Malcolm's hatred shocked me almost as much as the cool neutrality of his tone. Had I not felt the echo of his emotions through the bracelet, I wouldn't have guessed his true feelings. Unless I wanted to find out what happened if his loathing grew any more intense, I needed to change the subject and fast. "Riddle me this. From what I can tell, your cousin wants your turf—or you've taken over part of his. How far do you think he'll go to get rid of you?"

"He'd sell his soul to the devil if he had one."

If Bubba Eugene had sold his soul to the devil, it certainly would've explained a lot. "Why?"

"So many reasons, so little time." Malcolm hesitated, his fingertips resting against my shoulder. "I'm sorry he dragged you into this."

"You have it backwards again. I kidnapped you, not the other way around. You're supposed to be indignant over your capture. That's how these things usually work."

Chuckling softly, he resumed applying the ointment, working his way along my spine. "I'm not bored, and it isn't every day I get to run my hands all over a pretty woman."

"You're into bald, blistered chicks? That is not what your cousin told me you were into."

"And here I thought we'd already established that my cousin is an idiot. Blisters heal and hair grows back. I'm a patient man."

I definitely needed to turn the conversation in another direction—any other direction. "Humor me. Why might your cousin want to get rid of you?"

"When I was five, I tied his shoelaces to

Dad's boat while we were on the pier. It was my turn to go water skiing. That started it, I think."

Just what I needed, men with old school-yard grudges complicating my life. "You've been harassing him all your life, haven't you?"

"He retaliated with itching powder in my shoes."

"How mature."

"Since I couldn't let him have the last say, I stole his clothes whenever he went skinny dipping. I thought I was doing him a favor, giving him a chance to show off for the girls. It's not my fault the girls didn't appreciate his physique."

Despite fearing the answer, I asked, "What else did you do?"

"I pixie dusted his graduation; he was the valedictorian. He giggled through his whole speech and took his gown off. Apparently, he wasn't aware those gowns weren't to be treated like kilts."

Had I been Bubba Eugene that day, Malcolm would've died before the sun set. "I didn't expect your cousin to be smarter than you."

"I graduated two years before him. Skipped grades to do it. I was the valedictorian for my year, and I dodged all of his pranks. I also made sure to wear clothes under my gown."

"There has to be more to it than a few harmless pranks."

"Well, one time I gave him a basket of rabid raccoons. We both ended up needing treatment after that one. That prank backfired on me just a little."

With the invention of neutralizer, rabies faced extinction. "How the hell did you find rabid raccoons?"

"It wasn't easy. He should appreciate how much work, effort, and money I've put into tormenting him. I could've just used healthy coons instead. No, I went all in and found rabid ones."

"Please tell me the rabid raccoons are the worst of your pranks."

"I'd be lying if I told you that. Last year for his birthday, I gave him a new pair of cowboy boots. I creatively wrapped them."

Did I want to know? Probably not. I sighed. "How?"

"I asked a practitioner friend of mine to reinforce a steel box. I put the boots in the box, put the box in his car, and took his car to the junkyard to be crushed. Then I wrapped it in pretty paper and gave it to him. The boots weren't even scuffed. His car had seen better days."

"You're a sociopath, aren't you?"

"Why would you think that?"

"I have only one thing to say to you: if this

whole kidnapping incident is part of a prank war, no one will find your bodies for a long time."

Malcolm laughed so hard he hiccupped and couldn't continue applying the ointment. I twisted, hissed at the pain, and snatched the jar. No matter what, I wouldn't kill anyone today. I would control my temper. It would test my patience, but I wouldn't murder Malcolm, no matter how satisfying I believed it would be. "Please go away. Do us both a favor and order breakfast or something. I'm going to finish dealing with my burns, and no, I do not need your help."

"But you want my help. Be honest, Kanika. You want me for my body."

I screamed my frustration and pointed at the bathroom door. "In your dreams. Get out!"

TEN

Isn't that a bit excessive?

IGNORING THE DOCTOR'S ORDERS, I bandaged the worst of my burns and otherwise let nature take its course. Malcolm's help would've simplified the task, but I refused to ask. Giving him extra ammunition was almost as bad as striking a deal with the devil.

I had to be running out of luck. The crash alone could've killed me, but if there hadn't been a pyromaniac out for my blood, I might've walked away with nothing more than a few bumps, bruises, and a limp.

It would batter my already damaged pride, but I'd try to be grateful for Malcolm's help. Like it or not, I owed him, which complicated matters for me. With a job to do, how could I balance my gratitude with necessity? No matter what I did, something would give. I'd either sacrifice my reputation and side with Malcolm, or I'd ruin my reputation and repay my life debt to him.

Except for the moment I had kidnapped
Malcolm, my plan had been a complete and
total failure. Until my burns healed, I needed
to rely on him for the little things, including
driving. In a dire situation, I could probably
drive, but my feet would hate me. Walking
hurt. The constant pressure on the gas pedal
would do me in—and forget it if I needed to
slam the brakes for any reason.

I shook my head, grumbled a few curses,
and went to work. By the time I finished with
the bandages and got dressed, room service
had arrived. Four covered platters waited on
the small table. "Isn't that a bit excessive?"

"Hardly. You need to eat a lot so you can
heal. I wasn't sure what you liked, so I got a
bit of everything."

Too tired and sore to argue with him, I
mumbled my thanks, grabbed one of the platters, and retreated to the couch. Sitting with
him would've been polite, but I couldn't bring
myself to share such close quarters with him
quite yet.

In a few hours, we'd be stuck in a car
together.

I peeked under the platter's lid to discover
a massive portion of bacon and eggs. Bacon
made everything seem a little better, and I
took my time savoring each bite. The eggs
didn't impress me, but they rarely did. I ate
them anyway. Malcolm was right about the

food; healing would take a lot out of me, and if I didn't stuff myself silly, I'd lose weight, a complication I didn't need.

Aware of Malcolm watching me, I returned the empty platter to the table and grabbed a second one.

He chuckled and pointed at the chair I stood beside. "You don't have to eat on the couch. I'm not going to bite."

Damn it. It was one thing to retreat but another to deliberately scorn him. I sat and kept most of my attention on my second breakfast, a stack of waffles covered in fresh fruit.

"You're not wearing your bandages."

"Really? I never would have guessed." Abandoning all pretenses of being polite, I went to work on making the rest of my breakfast disappear, refusing to stop until I scraped every last bit of maple syrup from my plate.

I felt Malcolm watching me, but I refused to meet his gaze. The silence persisted, and I fought the urge to fidget. When it became too much to bear, I growled, "What is it?"

"You're going to impair your healing if you don't use the bandages."

"I refuse to go out looking like a mummy again."

"You're going the zombie route, then? You'd make a good extra in a film. You really should wear the bandages. Without them, you'll hurt more, and you might get an infection."

"That's a risk I'm willing to take."

Malcolm sighed and shook his head. "Did you at least cover the burns on your back?"

"Yes."

"Has anyone ever told you you're a pain the ass?" Malcolm muttered.

"Not really." Most of the time, I limited my interactions with my clients to the necessities, and since I didn't tend to stick around in any one place for long, I had more enemies than I had friends. It didn't bother me much, except when someone like Malcolm came along and started asking questions.

Malcolm snagged the last covered platter and revealed a plate loaded with bacon. Taking a piece, he pointed it at me. "I have a proposition for you."

While tempted to steal his bacon, I took a piece of my own, chewed on it, and let him stew for a few minutes. "What sort of proposition?"

"One where we pay my cousin a visit and find out if he hired that pyro. If he wasn't involved, I propose we team up and find the bastard responsible. That'll let you keep your end of the contract with my cousin, I get to have a few words with him, and everyone's happy."

On the surface, his idea seemed like a good one; Bubba Eugene had told me to kidnap Malcolm and take him away. Nothing in our agreement barred me from bringing him back—or to his cousin—after I completed the first phase of the job. All I needed to do was keep him away from his usual haunts. "And I suppose you'll want me to remove the bracelet?"

"No. I'll ask you to deactivate it long enough for me to have words with my cousin, should I need any magic. While I don't like it, it's your insurance policy I'll behave. I'm willing to swear an oath to cooperate with you, but you'd be right to be wary." Malcolm smirked. "You might not even need it when I'm finished with him."

I shook my head. "There are more than a few problems with this."

"What?"

"I'll start with the obvious one. I kidnapped you. I'll get arrested."

"Oh, you might get arrested, but it won't be for kidnapping."

"What's that supposed to mean?"

"Cops are gossips. Word'll get around I was in an accident with a girl. They'll want to meet you, so they're going to come up with a bogus charge so they can get their hands on you for questioning. If you're really unlucky, they'll introduce you to my parents. Aren't you excited?" With his smirk still in place, he took another piece of bacon and pointed it at me. "You've made a big mistake."

Kidnapping Malcolm had been only one of many mistakes, and not even the first of them. "Specify. I can think of a few."

I had let him get away with pointing bacon at me once, but it wasn't happening twice. I snapped my teeth and snatched it out of his hand, chomping on it before he could try to take it back.

Laughing, he got a new piece. "You captured my attention. I warned you I like a challenge. Make no mistake, Kanika. I'm used to getting exactly what I want."

I snorted. "Too bad. I'm not a trophy, and you're just part of a bad job. Get used to disappointment, because that's all you're getting from me."

"We'll see."

AFTER WE FINISHED breakfast and checked out of the hotel, Malcolm called his cousin. The discussion only took a few minutes, and the pair declared a temporary truce and picked a neutral meeting ground in Memphis, Tennessee. The location worked well for me; Bubba Eugene couldn't accuse me of breaking our contract.

I hoped I was released from the job and paid my base fee. Between Malcolm driving me crazy and my failure to pull the job off despite my preparations, I wanted to be done with the whole thing. If Bubba Eugene had anything to do with the pyro, there'd be hell to pay, too—and I'd incorrectly invoke the devil's names as many times as necessary to force him to make an appearance.

I'd turn it into a game. How many times could I get away with it before he showed up and fried my ass? Did I want to find out? Not really, but I couldn't help but wonder.

The cat in me always wanted to test the limits, and the devil was the ultimate challenge.

Malcolm drove, an arrangement I liked since I still couldn't walk without limping. I doubted I could have handled the two-hour drive even if I wanted to, which I didn't.

I appreciated the quiet; Malcolm focused on the road while my thoughts wandered. If I got out of my contract with Bubba Eugene, where would I go next? I'd leave Tennessee. Tennessee was bad for my health. I'd also avoid Georgia, since wise women limited their interactions with the devil as much as possible.

Maybe I'd head to Europe and find a priest to perform an exorcism. Maybe I could get an audience with the Pope. Wasn't the

Catholic Church all about protecting the innocent from the devil's treachery? Then
again, I'd met the devil's brothers, and both
archangels seemed to like him. Go figure.

In any case, with my tentative plans ruined, release from my contract would be the
best thing for me. I could regroup, move on,
and look for new work—safer work. With the
devil's money lining my pockets, I could take
a few weeks to settle down somewhere and
heal without worry.

When we reached the hotel in Memphis, I
throbbed. I had no hope of hiding my limp,
and I wanted the strongest painkillers money
could buy along with a nap. I could take the
painkillers after I got something to eat, but
the nap would have to wait.

Malcolm parked the car and killed the engine. "All right. I'm going to need my magic
for this."

I spoke the word Hagnar had taught me
and reached over to unclasp the bracelet. "I
haven't had a chance to experiment with it, so
it's best if you're not wearing it."

"That wasn't our agreement."

"I'm not going to risk it. I don't know if
that limits how much you can use or not. If
you need your magic, I'd feel better if you
could access all of it." I spoke the truth, too. If
Malcolm made his escape, I could write the
entire job off and get out of the contract that

way, too. My reputation would nosedive, but I could deal with that. Time and effort would undo the damage eventually. "I'll feel better if you're not wearing it for this meeting. If you want to wear it after you talk with your cousin, that's your choice."

"Why?"

"I already told you. I haven't had a chance to experiment with the bracelet myself yet. I don't know what'll happen when you use your magic while wearing it." I shrugged and got out of the car. "Consider the scales balanced."

"I helped you, so you're helping me?"

"Close enough. Why don't you introduce me to your cousin? I can't promise I'll be polite, though."

"He wouldn't know how to be polite if you beat him with an etiquette book, so don't worry about it. Just try not to break his face. Faces are off limits."

"Fine. No faces."

Malcolm led me into the hotel's bar, and I had no trouble identifying Bubba Eugene. The pair were cut from the same cloth, looking more like brothers—or twins—than cousins. I hoped I never had to tell them apart if they both decided to wear the same clothes.

Bubba Eugene slid off his stool at the bar and strode to us. "Mal. You're late."

"Wasn't risking an accident speeding to

get here. The lady has had her fair share of trouble already thanks to you, Robert."

Bubba Eugene's first name was Robert? I bit back my laughter and smiled. Why would anyone choose to go by Bubba when he had a perfectly nice first name like Robert?

My client's gaze slid to me. "You're Kanika?"

"Yes."

"I expected more… hair."

If I murdered my client, how badly would my reputation suffer? I clenched my teeth and barely avoided balling my hands into fists. However satisfying it would be to snarl profanities at my client, I'd take the high road and keep my mouth shut.

Malcolm cleared his throat. "Were you responsible for the pyro, Bubba Eugene? If so, you better get on your hands and knees and start kissing her feet." Straightening his back, he shoved his hands into his pockets. "It's one thing to try to get rid of me, but she has nothing to do with our feud."

Bubba Eugene frowned, turning to his cousin. "Pyro? What pyro?"

"The one that crashed her rental and torched it while she was trapped inside. Before I killed him, he claimed he was after her, not me. So, I'll ask you one more time. Did you hire a pyro?"

"I'm an ass, but I'm not stupid, Mal. Only

someone suicidal would send a pyro after you."

"Not me. Her."

"Why would I kill someone I'm paying to get you out of my hair for a while? That's the classic definition of stupid."

"Anyone in our family?"

Bubba Eugene sighed and shook his head. "You're an annoying son of a bitch, but you're family. We don't torch family, nor do we torch the hired help. How did she do?"

"She's magnificent. Where'd you find her?"

I hated when people talked about me as though I wasn't standing with them. "He probably used the internet and found my website."

My client continued to ignore me, pulling out a phone from his pocket to check the screen. "An associate of mine recommended her. She's not known for big jobs, but she has a good reputation for the small ones. I figured you were keeping tabs on the specialists, so I needed a nobody."

"The specialists need to take lessons from her. That was the cleanest snatch I've ever witnessed, and she covered all her bases. If it hadn't been for that pyro, she would've had me clear across the country by now. Round is yours, Bubba Eugene. Care to explain what this is all about?"

"Payback for my car."

"You invested more than what the car is worth on this stunt."

"Worth it. I wanted a woman to best you. I thought it'd make your unexpected vacation a bit more memorable."

Malcolm sighed and looked me over. "Let's reschedule this for after we pin down who hired the pyro and deal with them. We got lucky. The crash alone could've been lethal."

For a moment, I thought Bubba Eugene was going to argue, but then he nodded. "Sure. It's no fun if it turns lethal, no matter how happy I'd be if you were finally out of my hair."

"You also owe her an extra fifty thousand."

My eyes widened. Why was Malcolm trying to meddle with my contract with his cousin? I'd paid the money out of pocket, expecting to do the job at a loss on the surface—at least until the devil's part of my pay hit the bank account. "That's—"

Malcolm covered my mouth with his hand, and he kept his touch so gentle it didn't hurt. "This is between me and Bubba Eugene, Kanika."

"Why?" Bubba Eugene demanded.

"That's my estimate on how much she invested to pull the job off. The pyro torched all her gear. Since you put her in this position, you'll compensate her for her losses. I'm willing to bet you also gave her bad intel, too."

"I lowballed it to keep you safe. I knew she was going to use some kind of sedative on you, and I didn't want any chance of overdose."

I'd end up thinking about his claim for a long time to come; I'd viewed the misinformation as a risk, not as an attempt to prevent an overdose. With Malcolm's hand still over my mouth, I kept my thoughts to myself.

"I appreciate that. I really do. What do you want? This is obviously more than just a prank to get back at me over your car. A prank would be having your girl grab me, steal my clothes, and leave me on the highway. This? This isn't a prank. You wanted me out of the way for six months."

Wrinkling his nose, Bubba Eugene turned his head and refused to look either one of us in the eyes. "Fine. Dad's tired of you. He wanted to hire an assassin. I suggested the kidnapping as an alternative to save the family name from shame."

"That doesn't surprise me. Uncle Edwin has hated me from the day I was born. All right. Tell him this: if I find out the pyro was his doing, I'm going to show him I know a lot more about the family business than he'll like. Clear?"

Bubba Eugene relaxed, and he grinned. "Perfectly. What about the chick?"

Why did they insist on talking about me as though I wasn't there? It made me want to kick them both so hard they'd wake up next week.

"What about her? I'm taking her home and caring for her until those burns heal. Count yourself lucky, Robert. If she'd been killed, I'd be the last man standing in this fight. Make sure Uncle Edwin knows that."

"I told him this was a bad idea."

"No, the bad idea was shortchanging the hired help. Send her the money—and make your dad foot the bill."

"That's just mean, Mal. Dad doesn't have the money."

"Then he shouldn't throw stones at me, not when he's in a glass house. Oh, and Bubba Eugene?"

"What now?"

"I meant what I said. The woman's off limits. She gets hurt again, and he'll get the blood feud he's been itching for. Got it?"

"Got it. Since I came all this way, wanna go have a beer?"

"No, but thanks. Another time. I'm driving. Take care of yourself, Bubba Eugene, and stop letting your dad talk you into stupid shit."

"You, too. Watch your back. I was in it for the fun and games, but he means business."

"So do I."

"DO you really believe your uncle would murder me for a chance to kill you?" I'd seen enough shit in my life to understand there were those who'd do far more due to a grudge. "It seems a little farfetched."

"He wouldn't hesitate. He doesn't like black sheep like me in the family. That said, he hates pyros even more than I do. That's part of why he hates me; I can legally kill pyros. He can't. He tried to get licensed, but he's too fanatical and too fast on the draw. Most of my family is. I'm too moderate, which pisses them off." Malcolm strolled to his rental and unlocked it before opening the passenger door for me. "None of my family will intentionally hurt you, not after what I told my cousin."

"Why? It doesn't make any sense to me." I limped to the car and slid inside, hissing at the pressure against my blistered legs. After the initial contact, the pain mellowed to a tolerable, dull ache.

Malcolm leaned against the vehicle and watched me. "The Stewart line doesn't have any women. There hasn't been a single daughter born into the family for at least three hundred years. My threat will remind them of that."

I sucked in a breath. "No daughters? That's insane. Why? How is that even possible? Is it some form of magic? A curse?"

While I didn't deal with curses—or unload them on the unsuspecting—my research on my gypsy heritage suggested gypsies could, and often did, curse their enemies.

"Yes, it's because of our family's magic. Stewart men are either really picky about their women or sluts. Unfortunately for our family, the ones who are more promiscuous have a difficult time siring children at all, so they hope each generation has at least one of the pickier men. Unfortunately for me, I'm in that category. They'll jump to some conclusions, but that's fine. It'll protect you if they think I'm interested in continuing the family name."

I tensed and struggled to keep my expression neutral. "But I'm not your type."

Malcolm snorted. "That doesn't matter to my family. The next generation is what they're worried about. Don't worry. I have no intentions of serving as breeding stock to satisfy their dated traditions."

"But they'll think I'm your girlfriend."

"Correct. They will." Malcolm slid behind the wheel, shut his door a little harder than necessary, and started the engine. "As such, I have a proposal for you."

"It better not be a wedding proposal," I warned, grabbing my seatbelt and buckling in. The strap hurt, but I'd deal with the pain over the consequences of not having it if we ended up in another accident.

"Bubba Eugene lied to us. I'm a bit of a truth seer if I work at it; that's why I wanted access to my magic, so I could tell if he was lying to us or not. He should've known I'd be watching him. He could do it, too, if he had the patience to learn the trick. Anyway, when he lies, his heart rate and temperature rise. I can feel that when I'm using my magic and paying attention. His dad wasn't the one who wanted to hire an assassin. I can't tell who, not without doing some digging, but someone in the family wants me dead."

"And the lie couldn't have been the part about the assassin?"

With a scowl, Malcolm backed the car out of his spot. Within five minutes, we were on the highway headed towards Nashville. "It's possible."

"What's your proposal?"

"I want your help digging into my family's affairs. If they think you're dating me, they'll start vying for your attention. Continuing the family line trumps all else for them, and let's just say my cousin attracts the ladies but can't get them to stick around."

"You and your cousin are it?"

"Not exactly. We're just the right age to have kids. I have uncles."

"I still think Bubba Eugene has it out for you. Anyway, I specified in the contract no one in your family—or anyone associated with your family—could make a run at you. I don't do assassinations, nor do I involve myself with any contract I feel is an assassination attempt."

"Contracts are a pretty big deal with my family. They would abide by Bubba Eugene's agreement. That supports the idea my uncle might hire someone to kill you hoping to kill me at the same time, though."

I scowled and stared out the window, watching the trees go by. "Did he lie about anything else?"

"Yeah. The money. Uncle Edwin's rich, unless he did something stupid. God knows that's possible. My cousin registered as toeing the line between the truth and a lie, so perhaps my uncle's funds aren't easily accessible right now. That's a possibility."

I had the feeling the entire Stewart family was shrouded in a mire of possibilities, which meant nothing but trouble for me. "So, what does your proposal entail?"

"I want you to do some espionage for me.

I'll arrange for you to get work in one of my family's businesses—not mine. I don't hire family, and I won't date someone who works for one of my businesses. That's part of what my family hates about me. My business is thriving, and they can't get involved since I don't employ family members. Anyway, if my family believes I'm interested in you, they'll hire you just for the chance to try to turn you against me. Since I'm picky, they'll assume you're from a good bloodline. Bubba Eugene will help when he fusses over how tough you are. Add in that you survived a pyro's attack, and you'll be in a good position to dig around and find out what's going on in my family. They won't talk to me. If you play your cards right, they'll talk to you."

Me, a corporate spy? I mulled over the idea of having a stable job instead of picking up freelance work whenever I could find it. "I've never done a corporate espionage job before," I admitted. If he wanted me to build a resume, I'd be screwed. I'd learned the hard way no one wanted a woman who hadn't graduated from high school. Diplomas and degrees opened doors.

My failure to graduate closed them.

"Good. Bubba Eugene would've done his homework before hiring you, so he'll know that."

I wondered if his homework included my

school records. I hoped not. "I wouldn't ad-
vertise if I'd done that sort of job."

"Even better." Malcolm drummed his fingers against the wheel and made a thoughtful
noise in his throat. "I meant it when I said
you're staying at my place until those burns
heal. If you accept the job, I'll buy everything
you need as part of your fee. I'll also replace
anything you need that was torched."

I knew he meant well, but it hurt my pride
all the same. "Everything I owned was in the
SUV. I'm a drifter."

Most of my clients eventually found out I
wandered. Often, they found my lifestyle
pitiful at best. A few longed for the road, too,
and those were the rare jobs I truly enjoyed.
Money paid the bills, but an escape from the
prejudice and judgment of society was far
more valuable than cash.

Malcolm spat curses and became my first
client to express anger over my circumstances and misfortune. "That asshole
torched all your belongings?"

"I didn't have much. I'm a drifter. I only
take what I can carry in a bag. It's not a big
deal. I didn't lose anything I can't replace." I
meant it, too. Sure, I'd lost a few pairs of
shoes I liked, but I wasn't attached to any of
it. Losing the work on my laptop would
annoy me for a while, but it didn't contain
anything I couldn't replace.

Clients came to me, not the other way around.

"It's my fault he managed to set the fire in the first place. I'll replace your things. That's the least I can do."

"I can afford to—"

"I'll take care of it. If I'd been paying attention, you wouldn't have gotten burned in the first place. Consider it a part of your payment for the job. I'll pay you a fair hourly rate and cover all of your expenses."

I frowned. It wasn't charity if I worked for it, which I could accept despite my dislike of accepting anything from Malcolm. "What counts as a fair hourly wage?"

"Twenty-five an hour from me, so that's on top of whatever my family decides to pay you. Just be careful with my uncle. He's a skinflint and a slave driver. Unfortunately, he's got the most connected company in our family; I'm the only one who doesn't work with him in one capacity or another."

I could live on twenty-five an hour without breaking a sweat. "For how long?"

"However long is needed to find out what's going on, and why my family seems so eager to get rid of me."

"I'll think about it."

Malcolm nodded, and we remained silent for the rest of the drive to Nashville.

ELEVEN

Death was too good a fate for
Malcolm Findlay Stewart.

MALCOLM'S CAR was where he'd dumped it,
and he insisted I drive it to the rental place. I
suspected insanity had something to do with
his decision to give me his keys. Fortunately
for me, his car came equipped with a dual-
transmission system, as I wouldn't have
gotten it onto the road without stalling
otherwise.

I had no doubt he found my ignorance entertaining, as he let me stew for a good ten
minutes before he offered enlightenment on
how to operate his precious baby. It would
serve him right if I crashed it.

In what had to classify as a miracle, I
made it to the rental place without incident,
and to add insult to injury, Malcolm walked
around his car to make certain I hadn't
scratched it.

"I know how to drive," I snapped.

"Like a little old lady afraid of the speed limit."

Death was too good a fate for Malcolm Findlay Stewart, and I needed to invest a great deal of time plotting his demise. I tossed his keys to him, grunted, and limped towards the front door. I guessed money had something to do with his general cooperation, as I still had his wallet. When I stepped into the building, the overly tanned brunette behind the desk frowned, her gaze sweeping over me.

Damned pyro. "Never seen burns before?" Somehow, I kept my tone mild despite my urge to snap at her.

"Not like that I haven't. Shouldn't you be in the hospital? Why'd they let you out? Those look awful."

"She's stubborn, that's why." Malcolm eased by me, careful to avoid brushing even his clothes against me. I handed his wallet over so he could pay for the rental. "I got the car I rented in Arkansas, so I'll need to pay the return fee."

The girl's eyes widened. "Mr. Montgomery!"

Just how many people did Malcolm know? I sighed and considered retreating to the relative safety of his car. If I had my way, I'd return to the peace and quiet of being a nobody; on a good day, the only people who noticed me were those who wanted to hire me for a job.

Malcolm smiled at the girl, and I suspected she'd be a puddle of goo at his feet within five minutes.

"I need to do a walk around, Mr. Montgomery. Do you need someone to take you home?"

She sounded like she wanted to be the one to take him home and have him for dessert, not that I blamed her. Had I met him under other circumstances, I probably would've fallen prey to his animal magnetism as well, and that was before accounting for his tendency to run into fires to rescue kittens and puppies.

"You should blame his ass. It's truly a nice specimen," the devil whispered in my ear.

I screamed, jumped, and whirled around, my heart pounding a frantic beat in my throat. Unlike his unwanted appearance in the hotel elevator, the Lord of Hell did a much better job of playing incubus than a human, and he no longer had horns peeking out of his ruffled hair.

Sucking in short breaths, I recovered enough to squeak, "You!"

"Me," he confirmed with a wink. "You're looking better today. Good."

Malcolm spun, his eyes narrowing when

he caught sight of the devil. "You're a stalker, aren't you?"

"Don't get your panties in a bunch. I'm here on business." The devil pulled out an envelope from the inner pocket of his jacket. "This is for you, cupcake."

I scowled but took it. "Dare I ask?"

"Pay day."

Ah, there were no stronger magic words or better music to my ears. Too many clients tried to get out of paying what they owed me. "You mean I won't have to chase you with an invoice? How nice."

"I even gave you a bonus. Also, I included the name and number of a practitioner who can help restore your hair to its proper glory. Go see him a week after the burns have healed. I can't promise there won't be streaks, but it's better than being bald, right?"

Was I supposed to thank god or the devil? Screw it, I'd be grateful to them both. "Thanks."

The Lord of Lies nodded and turned his gaze to Malcolm. "I'm expecting good things from you, son. Don't disappoint me. I get mean when little upstarts like you disappoint me. Also, your idea has merit, but you're barking up the wrong tree. Think it through and try again. I'll give you a hint since you're out of the loop and I'm such a nice guy. You want to get involved with what's going down in Georgia."

Malcolm relaxed his posture although his eyes remained narrowed. "Georgia, is it?"

"Lovely place this time of year, especially around Savannah. Good luck keeping the girl out of trouble. You'll need it. Oh, and one last thing. Kanika, replace your phone. It's so troublesome having to make personal visits all the time. I might have another job for you."

The devil's words filled me with dread. I'd survived a pyro determined to torch me. What else would happen because of Satin's involvement in my life? I didn't want to know, but I feared I'd find out. "I can't express how positively thrilled I am, Satin. So thrilled."

"But you should be. Anyone who can survive a full-out assault by a pyro is tough enough to keep around. Excellent job, by the way. You're surpassing my expectations already."

I only had one way to stack the cards in my favor when playing with a hand the devil dealt: bluff. "If you're the one responsible for that pyro, I'll make your death so horrific your successor will use your maimed carcass as an example for future generations." I smiled my sweetest smile. "Do we have an understanding, Lucy?"

Malcolm took a step to the side, shoved

his hands in his pockets, and watched me like he expected me to bite, which tempted me to snap my teeth at him to find out what he'd do. I suppressed the urge and kept smiling at the devil.

Satin sighed. "I had nothing to do with your accident or the pyromaniac. However, I'm viewing your survival as your job interview. Well done. You have passed with flying colors. I was right to pick you. Thank you for confirming it so early in our relationship."

That didn't sound good at all. It sounded so not good I took a page out of Malcolm's book and eased away from the Lord of Lies in case he decided to shed his guise as an incubus and reveal his true nature. He grinned at me, showing off his pearly, pointy whites.

The point went to him, and I grumbled, "Why me? Couldn't you have picked a normal girl? What did I do to deserve your attention?"

He laughed, the sound far sweeter than I expected from the devil. "I owed someone a debt. No matter what, I always keep my end of a bargain, even until the end of days if need be. I'm afraid you're stuck with me, cupcake."

Dipping into a deep, mocking bow, the Lord of Lies vanished, and brimstone stank up the lobby. I coughed, blinked, and retreated outside, cursing the devil every step of the way.

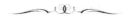

MALCOLM STARED AT ME, his eyes wide, his face pale, and his entire body tense. "You're friends with a devil? Why are you friends with a devil? That was a devil, Kanika."

I found his reaction to a devil intriguing. If *a* devil threw Malcolm for a loop, *the* devil would probably break him. If he paid attention, he'd figure out the truth on his own. What other devil would get so pissy over someone calling him Satin? Then again, I toed a dangerous line with the Lord of Lies.

If he got tired of me, he'd turn me inside out and leave my body for someone to find. If I really annoyed him, he'd take out anyone near me, too. I needed to be more careful, especially around Malcolm. I needed him to figure out the devil's identity without my help.

Lifting my chin, I stared into Malcolm's eyes. "I'm not friends with him. He's a client, and I don't discriminate against species. If the client has a job and is willing to pay me a fair wage for the work, I take the job. He paid well for my work."

Malcolm scowled, and the sense of apprehension fled from the man, much to my relief. "You seemed pretty friendly with him to me."

"He just paid me. Of course I'm going to be friendly with him."

"If that's all it takes to make you friendly, I'll cut you a check."

I raised my eyebrows. "Not a chance in hell, Malcolm."

"Toss me a bone here. Aren't you supposed to be my girlfriend?"

With the rental girl slobbering all over Malcolm's car, did he really think I'd fall for that? "I bet she'd volunteer in a hurry."

"She's in love with money and fast cars. Sure, she'd volunteer, but it wouldn't work out."

Right. Bubba Eugene had made it clear Malcolm was as picky as they came, and the instant the girl expressed interest in his money, he ran for the hills. "Yet you want to pay me to like you. How about no? I don't think so. It's bad enough your family already thinks you have a thing for me. At the rate you Stewarts want to throw money at me, you're going to have to put me on the payroll."

"That's not necessarily a bad thing."

Maybe I had been playing games with the devil, but at least I'd been playing against someone with a full deck. Had Malcolm hit his head during the crash? I hadn't been in any condition to think about how badly he'd been hurt—if he'd been hurt. He looked as though he'd emerged from the accident un-scathed, but I was learning not to trust my eyes when it came to him. All that pretty flesh hid a tricky man. If he wanted to tango, I'd treat him just like I did the devil. "I'm going to assume that's only because you're a picky Stewart man."

Malcolm grimaced, and I smiled my satis-faction at his discomfort. "There is that, yes. I won't lie to you. After Caitlin, my family as-sumed I wouldn't be continuing the family line."

Curses were serious business, and so were bad omens; if I'd paid attention to the ones I'd spotted while shapeshifting, I might've avoided so many burns. "What did your family do to get cursed?"

His jaw twitched. "I never said we were cursed."

"You're absolutely terrible at lying." I crossed my arms over my chest and huffed, shaking my head at his folly. "No girls, low fertility rate, pretty men, and a dying family line. That sounds like a curse to me."

"All right. Fine. You're right. I don't know what happened. I hadn't been born yet, and I don't think my father had been born yet, either."

"Well, I'd hope not. That would make you

an active immortal from pre-emergence, and that's just bad news. I try to avoid the active immortals." In truth, I was doing a horrible job at it since the devil insisted on paying me personal visits. I'd had a run-in with a pre-emergence minotaur who had wanted to breed with me, and I'd had a close encounter with two phoenixes once. To most, ten miles didn't count as *close*, but when demonic hell birds lit everything on fire while heading to the mountains of New York to roost, I thought I was justified in my claim.

"I take it you're not a fan of immortals."

"Not really. Pre-emergence immortals are usually talented at killing people like me. I like breathing."

"Not all immortals from before the emergence are lethal, Kanika."

"They're still dangerous."

Malcolm sighed. "I'm from a dormant line."

Oops. In the grand scheme of things, dormant lines were one step below pre-emergence immortals, carrying a history of magic within their heritage, which they fought to preserve through the centuries. The curse made a lot more sense, too.

In all likelihood, the Stewart family had been cursed before magic had faded away from the world during the prior emergence hundreds upon hundreds of years ago. While

I'd heard of dormant lines through folklore, myth, and rumor, I'd never met someone who openly admitted to belonging to one. Then again, he was Scottish.

The Scottish had a monopoly on dormant lines, potent folklore, real myths, and magic aplenty. With such a rich history filled with monsters and mayhem, it made sense some of their traditions and folklore were founded on more than hearsay. "I see."

If he expected an apology from me, he'd be waiting a long time. No, being from a dormant line made him even more dangerous, right along with the rest of his family. Great. I'd jumped headlong into another fire, and if I wasn't careful, I'd get burned again.

"I'll give you a better rundown of the situation at my house. It might help with the job if you go in with a better idea of what to expect. If the new information changes things for you, I'm also willing to renegotiate your price. We'll swing by a few stores and replace your phone and laptop on the way to my house, too. As I promised, I'll pay for them both."

I nodded. Within ten minutes, after Malcolm managed to convince the sales girl he really needed to leave, we were on the road. He hummed a merry tune while I questioned my sanity. How had I gone from kidnapper to the fake girlfriend of a Scottish hunk from a cursed dormant family line?

When all else failed, blaming the devil seemed like a good idea. He always made a nuisance of himself, especially when it came to the details, showing up at the worst possible time. If I prayed for salvation, would one of his brothers show up?

Then again, did I really want an archangel showing up? What would happen if I tossed a pair of them into the mix? Ah, right. Trouble. Instead of praying, I stared out the window and mourned for the loss of my quiet albeit difficult life.

I EXPECTED a man of Malcolm's wealth to live in a mansion. Had I not known better, I would've believed an average family owned the ranch, which was large enough to accommodate several children but small enough to classify as sane and reasonable. It bothered me, as the home gave the illusion of a family I knew he lacked.

On the surface, the property spoke of wealth and welcome, but beneath the thin veneer, loneliness lingered.

One look at his home and a little knowledge of his circumstances exposed broken dreams, and I had the feeling her name had been Caitlin. I feared I understood why his cop and firefighter friends had found me interesting.

Men. Why couldn't they be a little more honest about their feelings? In the time it took Malcolm to park in his two-car garage, I found new respect for Bubba Eugene. Maybe the issue of children in a dying family line motivated Malcolm's cousin, but if Malcolm needed a little shove to get over an old flame, I could respect the odd tactic.

However, being used as lady bait annoyed the hell out of me.

Determined to remain civil, I unbuckled my seatbelt and forced a smile. "Nice place. I was expecting a lot bigger with extra security."

"Looks are deceiving. My house may not be large, but I have a nice alarm system. Bigger isn't always better."

No kidding. Instead of succumbing to the temptation of cracking the obvious joke, I got out of his car, marveled at how empty the man's garage was, and wondered what sort of car the girl of his dreams would drive. If he had half as much money as I thought he did, I expected another sporty vehicle would take the spot.

If I were to park a car there, it'd be a truck, something I could get good and muddy. If I wanted something fast and pretty, I'd drive his—or get a rental.

Probably a rental.

I shook my head at my folly, swore to rein in my delusions of grandeur, and prove poor drifters like me could be good house guests. I blinked. Wait. Did I classify as poor with more than four hundred thousand in the bank? While the bank account belonged to the devil, it was my money to spend.

Huh. Later, after I took a well-earned nap, I'd have to put some thought into that. First, I needed to get a better handle on the Stewart family situation. "Do you have any ideas about what's going on with your family? What were you wanting to tell me?"

"It's not a whole lot. Caitlin and I were essentially part of an arranged marriage. I cancelled it. That did not go over well with my family. Beyond the usual bullshit, there's not a whole lot to tell. It was supposed to be love at first sight, an alliance between my family and hers, but she blew it. I was very clear on how she blew it, too. She proved she couldn't keep to look but don't touch, and I'm, as you like to say, picky."

The implications of his words sank in, making his situation even worse. His resentment became a lot clearer, if I tried to put myself in his shoes for a moment.

Malcolm had gotten burned in the worst

way possible. No wonder his friends had found me interesting. If he was half as sensitive as I suspected, they must have come to the conclusion I meant far more to him than I actually did.

Damn it.

"All right. If you think of anything important, tell me. Important things include any actions Caitlin's family might take against you."

"They won't; the Stewart family isn't worth their time unless it involves a marriage. I could see them trying to push the wedding forward, but they'd lose a lot of honor if something happened to me and it was traced back to them. Tit for tat. What's the deal with that devil? I didn't think they came out during the day like that. What species was he? There's no way he was an incubus, else he would've been after the sales girl. The wrong vibe. And anyway, most incubi are demons rather than devils."

Huh. I hadn't known there was a significant difference between demons and devils. "Sorry to break it to you, but I think you know more than I do. He just cuts the checks." Since he'd been fair with me, I'd play it fair with him, too. I ignored the blow to my pride and continued, "I didn't even think there were differences between demons and devils."

"In application, there isn't. They all serve the Lord of Hell. Demons are born on Earth, devils are born in hell. Devils don't like coming to Earth unless necessary, a bit like angels. Devils are usually more powerful than demons, and demons are more numerous. That's the only real difference."

"I didn't know that. How could you tell he wasn't a demon?"

"The brimstone stink and teleportation. Some demons learn to teleport, but no demon stinks of brimstone, and that devil friend of yours reeked of it."

It occurred to me that if Malcolm knew so much about demons and devils, he might have a clue on how to get rid of them. I held my breath, hoping against hope he knew a trick or two. "I don't suppose you have a recipe for devil repellent, do you?"

"Don't make any deals with a devil, and you should be fine. They're only interested if they think they can get something out of you. Just tell him no and walk away. He'll get tired of you eventually and go away. Devils prefer easy, profitable prey. If walk away, you're not easy. You might be profitable, but most won't bother when there are easier low-lying fruit around."

I doubted that trick would work on the devil, but determined to remain civil, polite,

and a little friendly, I bobbed my head to acknowledge him. "I'll try that. Thanks."

A tired smile made a brief appearance before Malcolm cleared his throat, straightened,
and retrieved the bags with my medications,
then grabbed my new phone and laptop from
the trunk, both of which had been heinously
expensive. "You're probably tired, so why
don't I show you around so you can tend to
your burns and get some rest? The painkillers
have to be wearing off by now. I have some
work to do, but I'll wake you for dinner."

The dismissal in his tone annoyed and
confused me, especially after his gentle smile.
I nodded and headed for the door. If I wanted
to get through the next few days—or weeks—
I needed to be sharp, which meant a nap was
in order along with a dose of the best
painkillers and ointments the devil's money
could buy.

TWELVE

How very trusting of you.

THE DEVIL'S call woke me, and I was tempted to fling my new phone across the room just to watch it shatter into a million pieces. Snarling over my disturbed nap, I grabbed my cell, swiped my finger across the screen, and snapped, "Kanika."

"Enjoy your nap?"

I needed to do some research on how to kill the devil. Only death would do. "I was until you woke me."

Instead of being properly cowed by my wrath, the Lord of Lies, Head Honcho of Hell, and Most Royal Pain in my Ass laughed. "Have you checked the envelope I gave you yet?"

His tone made it clear the smug bastard knew I hadn't. "No, Lucille. I was napping."

"How very trusting of you."

I would take my time plotting the devil's demise, and I would delay his execution until

I found ways to make him suffer first. "Is there a reason you're bothering me?"

"Yes."

I waited. When Satin remained silent, I grunted, rolled out of bed, and limped towards the guest bathroom. "What do you want?"

"I would like you to meddle in the affairs of the Stewart family on my behalf. I've an interest in them, particularly in Edwin Stewart."

Edwin? Which one was Edwin? Bubba Eugene was a Robert, so I eliminated him from my list. Oh, right. Bubba Eugene's father was Edwin. "I think you just like giving me more money for doing something I've already agreed to do."

"Ah, but you haven't taken your Stewart's job yet, cupcake. It's unconfirmed. Until the bargain is made, it doesn't count."

The devil was in the details. I grunted again, set the phone on the vanity, and splashed water on my face to help wake me up. I let Satin stew for a few minutes while I tried to convince my eyelids to remain open. After minimal success, I grabbed my phone, held it to my ear, and sighed. "I wasn't aware he was mine."

"That's because I hadn't given you the good news yet. I'm giving him to you. All children should have a pet, and I've decided he's yours to play with however you please."

I probably did count as a child to the devil, although I found his determination to slate Malcolm as my property disturbing. Maybe if I ignored him and his special brand of crazy, he would act in a sane and reasonable manner. I gave it a one in a million chance at best. "What do you actually want me to do?"

"I have an interest in the Stewart family. First, I want blackmail material on the older generation. Second, I want intel on the younglings. Your Stewart, as I have so graciously bequeathed him to you, is off my radar—for now. Should he displease you, I'll set my sights on him, never fear."

I feared for my sanity. How was I supposed to protect an innocent bystander from the devil? That I considered Malcolm an innocent bystander disturbed me almost as much as His Most Royal Pain in the Ass's insistence he could bequeath a man to me because he felt like it. "I'll keep that in mind."

"Please do. Now, listen up. The one who calls himself Bubba Eugene is of particular importance. I want everything you can get on him. If he takes a piss the same time every day, I want to know. No detail is insignificant. Profile him down to the number of hairs sticking out of his nose if you must."

The last thing I wanted was to get intimate with Bubba Eugene, especially close enough to count any of his hairs. "Why?"

"He's a reincarnation. While he's a member of the Stewart family, he's far older than he looks. In short, he has something I want, and I want every advantage so that when I bargain with him, he'll do what I need. Also, as part of your duties, I want you to play bodyguard for your Stewart. It'll be easy enough. Pretend you're interested in him. That should minimize your work. If he's demonstrating a desire to keep you company, the rest of his family will leave you both alone. Malcolm is their last chance to keep the family name alive, and they know it."

Ah-ha. "So, they are really cursed."

"They are. Good work figuring that out."

I huffed. "It was pretty obvious. Men that pretty shouldn't have any problems finding women willing to marry them—or at least sleep with them. Why are you interested in the family? Is it only because of what you want from Bubba Eugene?"

"Now you're asking good questions. Let's make a wager."

"No. Only an idiot wagers with the devil."

He laughed.

I scowled, as I meant every word. Accepting a job from him had caused me enough problems—and resulted in the loss of my hair, probable scarring, and a newfound dislike of fire. "I'm serious."

"I know you are. That's what makes it so amusing. I solemnly swear I won't trick you. I want to see you work. This will be a friendly wager."

Listening to his proposal couldn't hurt, could it? If I liked what I heard, I could always demand another session with an archangel or two. If Satin consented to the presence of an archangel confirming the truth of his words, I'd think about it. I couldn't see a reason not to if I could confirm I wasn't going to become his victim thanks to some wager.

Well, as long as I ignored the obvious. Bargains and wagers with the devil couldn't end well, could they?

I mulled it over for a few minutes, sat on the bed, and grumbled a few curses. "All right. I'll hear you out."

"Good girl. I bet you won't learn the Stewart family's secret."

The devil truly was a bastard, challenging me on the two things sphinxes loved more than anything else: riddles and secrets. I had no doubt he knew I came with a species disadvantage. "What are we wagering?"

"If I win, you must obey one order from me. I'll swear you'll come to no harm from my command, nor will your soul be jeopardized in any fashion. You'll have a right of refusal as well, but only if one of my pesky brothers confirms the legitimacy of your refusal."

My eyebrows took a hike up to my hairline. What Satin proposed would make the wager ironclad; the archangels would readily confirm every last word he said as truth—and turn those same tables around on me, too. "And if I win?"

"I'll break the Stewart family's curse on your behalf."

Curses were serious business; the older they were, the harder they were to break—and the more likely they were to backfire. I'd done just enough reading about curses and gypsies to understand when a gypsy bestowed a true curse, they had no intentions of unraveling what they'd done.

Egyptian curses weren't much different, although their curses were handled by mummies and sacred guardians, often under the sigil of a scarab.

In truth, if I learned the art of curses, I'd probably make potent ones, which frightened me enough to ensure I avoided learning how they were inflicted on someone.

What interested me was his side of the wager. "How does breaking their curse benefit me?"

"It doesn't, not directly."

Ah-ha. The devil was in the damned details, and I'd end up doing a lot of work for him while I'd only get something questionably beneficial in return. "I'd be an idiot if I accepted that wager, Satin. First, you'd be reaping all the rewards on that one, as you want me to poke my nose in their affairs. If I find out their secret, you'll find out their secret, and that's profitable for you."

"See? I told you I'd picked well when I'd picked you. Very well. I'll break the curse and pay you a hundred grand on top of your other fees for your investigative work should you uncover the Stewart family's secret. You're such a mercenary."

"Well, yes. I am. And you swear your request will bring no harm to me?" A girl had to cover her bases—and try to avoid a second close brush with death.

"I swear. Should you be endangered in any fashion, it won't be through any fault or intention of mine. View this as a friendly bet between friends."

Damn the devil and his money, bribing me into considering things only the insane should consider. Still, an extra hundred thousand in my bank account meant I could do what I loved doing without worrying where I'd find my next meal. I'd drift, but I'd drift on a full stomach and have the freedom to cherry pick future work. "How long do I have to figure out their secret?"

"Let's call it three months. That should give you some time to earn their trust."

"Do I get any hints?"

"Of course not. It wouldn't be a fun wager if I made it easy on you—and yes, I already know this secret. I'm just choosing to pay you due to the extra work involved in learning it." The Lord of Lies chuckled. "Do we have a deal?"

Damn it, damn it, damn it. "Why do I have the feeling I'll regret this?"

"I'd say you're smart, but you're striking a deal with me again. Ah, I'm feeling nice today, so I'll give you a clue to send you in the right direction. Remember what I told your Stewart earlier today. It might prove useful to you. So, do we have a deal?"

I was such a fool. "We have a deal."

"Excellent. I'll be in touch." Satin hung up, and I glowered at the darkened display for a long time, wondering why I'd even consider taking unnecessary risks to help a family I didn't even like in the first place. Then again, it made some sense. I was a sucker for pun-ishment with a troublesome altruistic side a mile wide. I needed to take my twisted ethics for a long walk off a short pier. For the mo-ment, I'd repay Malcolm's generosity the only what I knew how, through hard work and effort.

If I broke his family's curse, I'd give him the chance to have what he wanted most, then his home wouldn't feel so empty and lonely.

I SPENT the next week in a drugged stupor, although I appreciated having a sexy fireman as a bodyguard. It occurred to me someone—likely the sexy fireman—had slipped a sedative in among my painkillers. I should've gotten upset over it, but turnabout *was* fair play, so I didn't complain. Dodging the worst of the healing process made me more inclined to ignore his subterfuge. My blisters healed, what hadn't blistered peeled, and I itched when I wasn't busy dozing on Malcolm's couch, in his guest room, or in his bed.

The 'in his bed' part led to a few awkward moments, especially when I'd woken up in the middle of the night, gotten lost in my dazed stupor, and did what any sane cat did, seeking out the warmest body to cuddle with.

Since his body was the only one in the house, I had volunteered him. How could he blame me? I needed to keep warm.

If he hadn't drugged me stupid, I wouldn't have crawled into bed with him in the middle of the night. To be fair, I had stolen the blankets, leeched onto him, and refused to let go, which had resulted in an eventful morning.

Malcolm was a very strong and sexy fireman, and I'd ended up on the floor before he comprehended who had joined him in bed. Unfortunately for him, I'd taken him with me, as a wise cat didn't readily relinquish their prey.

I regretted that I couldn't remember the incident, although Malcolm made a point of reminding me of it every single morning.

Men. Climb into one's bed while under the influence of drugs, and a girl got a reputation.

Twice, however, meant I had a bed-invading habit. The third time, it meant a problem, but after the fourth, he accepted the inevitable. I stopped counting after five and enjoyed most of my mornings with Malcolm stretched out beside me, awake with his arms crossed over his chest while I clung to him, my nose pressed to his wonderfully muscular stomach.

Not only had I invaded his bed, I'd managed to take up the vast majority of it, too. Oops.

"Hi," I mumbled, and since I'd already made a mess of yet another morning, I slithered over him and oozed to the floor, reaching in the direction of his private bathroom, too sleepy to traverse the distance. "Too far. Make it be closer."

"You crawled into my bed again."

"Your furnace is obviously broken. I got cold. You can't blame me. You're the one who keeps slipping me sleeping pills. You only have yourself to blame for this." I stretched towards the bathroom door, pleased my healing burns no longer hurt. Even better, I only itched a little. I still didn't have any hair, but in a few days, I could think about meeting the devil's practitioner. Until then, I'd have to deal with being bald. "You should be happy I don't have to wash my hair."

"I'm not happy your hair was ruined."

I grunted, drummed my fingers on the sun-warmed hardwood floor, and debated if it was worth the effort to reach the bathroom. While it probably wasn't, I grunted again and began the slow crawl to his big bathtub, where I'd catch another nap while enjoying the jets.

Maybe some cats didn't like water, but I liked bubbles. They kept me amused when I wasn't enjoying a good snooze.

"You're going to run up my water bill again, aren't you?"

Grunting needed to become a recognized part of the English language. I almost made it to the bathroom before Malcolm joined me, hooked his arm around my waist, and lifted me off the floor.

"Hey," I protested.

"Yesterday, you stayed in there for four hours."

"It's a nice tub."

"No."

"You're mean."

"At least earn your bath first today. Your burns are healed enough it should be safe for you to try shifting to see if it helps your hair. If you insist on taking over my bathroom again, I'm just going to take my morning shower while you're in there. Consider yourself warned."

What kind of warning was that supposed to be? If all I had to do to get a good look at him naked was take a bubble bath, I could live with that. A good soak plus a show seemed like a good use of my time. "Put me down."

"Why?"

"So I can go play in a bubble bath, duh. Dumb question. If you're offering to put yourself on display, I'm accepting."

"And that backfired rather spectacularly."

"I'm a cat who sometimes wanders around masquerading as a human. What were you expecting?"

"Modesty."

"Really?" I snorted, and since Malcolm wasn't showing any sign of putting me down,

I wiggled to make myself more comfortable. "I'm plenty modest. You're the one threatening to come into the bathroom while I'm bathing and get naked in the shower. That's all on you. Just because I'm willing to accept your invitation and share your nice bathroom doesn't mean I'm not modest. You're the one who isn't modest. I'd already be in the tub, and you'd be barging in on *me*."

"You weren't supposed to be coherent enough to realize that. How are you feeling?"

"I'm not itching nearly as much now." I lifted my arms and pushed up the sleeves of my new pajamas, which were made of silk and so slick on my skin I considered never changing into real clothes ever again. "I seem to have skin. That's an improvement."

Malcolm chuckled. "I thought you'd be a lot paler. You've still got a nice tan despite the burns."

"Egyptian," I reminded him. "Despite appearances, I don't have a sunbathing hobby. How much work have you missed babysitting me?"

"Not much. I've been doing everything from here, and I'm off rotation at the firehouse for another two weeks while the police try to track down who hired the pyro. While he claims he was after you, we have no way of knowing if he was lying. It's a matter of public safety."

"Because someone might start setting fires to hurt you."

"I see most of the drugs have worn off. That's the most intelligent thing you've said and done this week."

Dangling from his arm made it difficult to glare at him, and I dug my fingernails into his wrist. "Put me down or make yourself useful and take me to the tub. For that, I am owed a bubble bath."

I really liked the way he laughed, although I wasn't a fan of the drop to the hardwood floor. Landing with a grunt, I got onto my hands and knees and headed for the sanctuary of his bathroom. He snagged my collar to stop me. Damn, silk was strong to be able to withstand the battle between us. The fabric choked me, and he stood firm without budging an inch.

"If I let you go in there now, you'll stay for hours."

"That's the idea."

"Are you aware breakfast exists and should be eaten before noon?"

Was he actually expecting me to agree with him? "No."

"That would explain why you haven't had breakfast once this week. You should try it sometime—like right now. I have a business proposition, and business propositions are nicer over breakfast."

"But my bath."

"You aren't going to die if you take your bath after breakfast."

"But my bath."

"Are you even awake?"

A yawn slipped out before I could stop it, and I flopped to the floor with a tired groan. "It's all your fault. You kept making me take those pills. They make me sleepy and stupid."

"You're not stupid, but you do need breakfast. Unless you start trying to scratch your skin off again, you won't get any pills at all today. Breakfast, business, then bath."

Why did the pretty men always have to be so bossy? Still, after making a wager with the devil, entertaining a business proposition from Malcolm would likely serve me better than stubbornly indulging in my bath before breakfast. "If I get sick because you insisted I eat breakfast before I bathe, you'll be forced to wait on me hand and foot."

"I've been doing that for the past week. I've even been a gentleman and resisted the urge to evict you from my bed every time you crawled in because you seem to believe I'm a living furnace existing solely for your comfort."

Either I could face him directly or give him the victory. Since surrender was not an option, I replied, "You're not?"

"I'm really not." His tone, stern with the

faintest hint of his amusement, promised some form of retribution for my bed-invading tendencies.

"I guess you're going to make me do this breakfast thing in the kitchen, aren't you?"

"That's the general idea."

With the help of the wall, I got to my feet, grumbling curses. In reality, our little war amused me, but I'd play up my disgruntlement to see what he did.

Malcolm laughed, put his hands on my shoulders, and turned me in the direction of his bedroom door. "The kitchen is that way, baldy."

Baldy? I hissed at that declaration of war. If he wanted to start lobbing well-aimed bombs my way, I wouldn't play fair. "It's on, sparky. You're going to regret that."

"You could always shift a few times and see if you upgrade to a fro. That hair of yours has to get frizzy. If I'm going to have to deal with you sneaking into my bed, I want long hair to play with on my pillow. That's a fair request, I think."

I admired his immediate assault in our newly fledged war. Two could play at that game, and if he thought he could make requests of me regarding *my* hair, I'd make demands of my own. Since he didn't sleep with his shirt on as it was, I'd have to target his next line of defense, his flannel pants. He didn't need them, and while I'd gotten several good looks at his bare chest, he defended his legs with admirable dedication. "If my long hair belongs on your pillow, your pants belong on the floor."

As my volley was best presented with a careless, disinterested attitude, I strolled for the kitchen, adding a little extra sway to my hips to make it clear I was the victor. Either way, I won.

I wanted my hair back to its original length, and if I was going to sleepwalk into his bed, I could live with more exposed skin to keep me warm. If he got to objectify me for my hair, I'd objectify him right out of his pants.

"Trying to get me out of my pants already? I find this potentially promising."

"If you found it promising, you wouldn't whine when I sleepwalk and end up curling up with the nearest warmest object," I countered, refusing to let him get the last word in—and win the first battle through hinting at what might result due to promising pantsless situations. I still had some of my morals intact, and technically he was still my client.

Invading his bed because he was warm didn't count, and neither did his lack of pants.

I could still win. Maybe. But how? That was the real question.

"You could convince me to change my mind once your hair grows back."

"I could also grow it back, turn it into rope, and tie you up so you don't become a menace."

"I'm not sure if you're trying to dissuade me or encourage me."

I wasn't sure, either. Fortunately, I had an easy way to avoid answering, and it involved breakfast and business. "If I can't take my bath, you need to get a move on with the breakfast, Malcolm. And breakfast better involve something nice, like bacon."

"As if I would dare to deprive you of bacon. I'm convinced you're the only woman who will stare at the refrigerator whimpering for bacon at two in the morning."

"It doesn't count if I don't remember it," I countered—and it was the truth, I didn't. Had I been in my right mind, I would have just fried the bacon myself. Then again, I rarely cooked and my attempts often ended in disaster.

"If only I didn't," he groused, snapping his fingers and pointing at one of the stools at his kitchen island. "Kitchen disasters sit there and don't touch anything. I've replaced enough appliances this week. I still haven't figured out how you killed my coffee maker twice."

"It doesn't count if I don't remember it." I

slid onto the stool and scowled so I wouldn't smile. A reputation as a kitchen destroyer was a step up from sleepwalking bed-invader. Malcolm would feed me to protect the rest of his appliances from destruction. "You could be saying that to try to get me to buy you new appliances."

"You've seen through my dastardly plan. Do you eat anything other than bacon?"

"I'm sure I could, but why would I want to?"

"You have issues, Kanika."

"I don't see the problem. My issues lead to bacon."

"I can't argue with that. Would you care for an omelette in addition to your bacon?"

"Will this omelette you speak of include bacon?"

"I suppose it could."

"Bacon sounds good."

Malcolm sighed and headed to the fridge, a nice stainless-steel model, the expensive kind I'd buy for myself if I ever settled down instead of wandering. He pulled out enough ingredients to feed at least three or four and went to work.

"What's this business you want to discuss?"

"Do you think shifting will restore your hair?"

"It's worth a try." While I wouldn't tell him

so, I'd rather avoid the devil's practitioner, too. I'd already gotten in deep enough with the Lord of Lies, and he somehow kept involving himself in my affairs—or tricking me into involving myself. Add in my wager, of which I'd already squandered a week, the last thing I wanted was to owe Satin an actual debt. "If shifting doesn't help, I can wear a wig. There's no need to worry about my hair."

"You liked it. That's reason enough for me to worry."

I regretted the day I'd done the devil a favor and agreed to Bubba Eugene's job. Had I met Malcolm in any other fashion, I would've been able to toss my dying morals aside. His looks put him in a class all of his own, but if anyone realized he was more than a pretty face in a perfect body, women around the world would hunt him down for a chance to be his one and only.

Either the curse was far more potent than I thought or Caitlin was the dumbest woman alive. I'd seen so much of America, but I'd met precious few people who spoke so selflessly.

He'd offered his home to me, dealt with me breaking his appliances while under the influence of drugs, and tolerated my sleep-walking with remarkable restraint and dignity. The devil had truly played me.

Ten little words had turned the wager into something far more serious. I owed Malcolm for his help, and that had factored into my decision to work with him. His generosity and good nature chipped away at me until I wanted to win the wager because he deserved happiness and the family I believed he wanted.

Damn it, I was doing it again. I'd end up draining the devil's bank account dry if it meant repaying my debt to Malcolm—a debt I never intended to let him know he was owed.

When I remained silent, he went back to cooking, frying bacon, cracking eggs, and doing all the things my aunt had done when I was a child, before I'd gotten old enough to realize the truth. My aunt had done it out of familial obligation.

Malcolm did it because he wanted to.

"One way or another, I'll take care of my hair," I promised.

"That leads me to the actual business, which is also part of the reason I'm worried about you and your hair. I need a favor."

Uh oh. Favors equaled unpaid work, which for a rare change I didn't mind at all. However, favors often meant personal business, business destined to lead me into even more trouble. "What sort of favor?"

"Well, it's one part favor, one part job. I'll pay you what you're worth and then some, but it's business of a personal nature."

"Just tell me."

"Bubba Eugene has been running his mouth to the rest of my family that you're staying with me. As a result, we've been invited to a charity event. Unfortunately, because no one actually believes I might be involved with an actual woman, they neglected to inform me of this until yesterday evening. The event is in New York tomorrow night."

The Stewarts hated Malcolm. Springing a charity event on someone with such little notice should've counted as a crime, and the ruthlessness of their tactic astounded me. There wasn't enough time to prepare.

A wealthy man might be able to pull it off, especially if he already owned a lot of suits. Me? All of the saris in the world wouldn't fit a charity event in an expensive city like New York.

"Your family hates you, don't they?" I groaned at my rudeness the instant the words left my mouth. "I'm sorry. I shouldn't have said that."

"It's true. Don't worry about it. It's not that they hate me. They really don't believe there's any chance of a woman in my life, so they don't believe I'll be inconvenienced. In fact, I don't think they expected me to accept the invitation for two at all. Therein lies the problem. It's a costume party for the rather wealthy at the American Museum of Natural History in New York, and all proceeds go to the museum. The favor is to please forgive me for accepting without conferring with you first."

"I definitely don't have suitable clothes. What's the theme?"

"I can take care of the clothes. Honestly, I'm hoping it'll give you a chance to get a feel for my family and gain their trust. If we're really lucky, we'll be able to figure out what they're up to. I wouldn't put this past them to use this event as a test to see what you're made of. The type of women they prefer wouldn't be caught dead without hair, and I have no doubt my cousin told them about the accident."

Despite my annoyance and misgivings about the situation, I laughed. "I'm not exactly thrilled about having my hair burned off. If needed, I'll wear a wig."

"You're willing to give this a shot?"

I could have refused him, but I'd look like a petty coward—and confirm his family's beliefs about Malcolm. No, I needed to play the game. If shifting failed to restore my hair to its former glory, I'd borrow a few tricks from my ancestors. "I am. The event's at the American Museum of Natural History?"

"Yes. It's one part exhibit viewing, one

part social gathering, one part charity auction."

I hated New York so, so much. The people I hated most lived there, and I did my best to forget about them and the reasons I'd left my aunt's home in the first place. Sighing, I nodded. "All right."

Malcolm echoed my sigh. "This is just another one of my cousin's stupid games. He probably had the extra tickets for months and decided to give them to me just to piss me off at the encouragement of Uncle Edwin. They do petty shit like this all the time."

"Let's exceed his expectations. What's the theme?"

"Historic figures." Malcolm plucked the bacon from the pan, set it on a paper towel, and grabbed the eggs. "It's a masquerade gala, and we'll be expected to pretend we're the figures we've chosen."

I hoped I wouldn't be eating egg shells in a few minutes, as pride and an ingrained dislike of wasting food demanded I pretend they weren't in the omelette. Wait. Historic figures? Masquerade gala?

I got to play pretend on someone else's dime? Hallelujah. "Most call that a costume party."

"Unfortunately."

Finally, finally, *finally* something had gone right in my life. Of all the jobs in the world, there was none I could do better. If Malcolm needed a historic figure, I could provide, and I'd be able to provide with ease. For the first time in my life, I could play the part of Bastet or Cleopatra without anyone judging me. I'd make Malcolm shine, and all I had to do was be myself and embrace the proud tradition of my Egyptian heritage.

I could also dance through the night as a Ruska Roma if I chose.

And, in a true miracle, I could even go as a sphinx. In any shape, I would be able to help Malcolm.

That left me with one serious problem: Malcolm. "Who are you going as?"

"I'm not sure yet."

Yep, we had a problem. Solving it would fall to me, I feared. But where to begin? I favored Bastet as my choice, for while I enjoyed the prospect of going as Cleopatra, I liked the idea of attending equipped with natural weapons. Add in Bastet's aloof, cat-like personality, and I'd be in the best position possible to mingle with sophisticates. "I think I'll go as Bastet."

"Interesting choice."

"As long as my fur has grown back, I won't need hair; I'll wear a headpiece, usekh, armbands, and a traditional attire. It won't take me long to put it together."

"I think you underestimate how long it takes to get Egyptian anything, Kanika."

"Just trust me. Anyway, if I go as Bastet, my hair isn't an issue at all."

"That's fair, and a good point. That just leaves my costume."

"If you're such a black sheep of the family, why not go as a Scottish lord or something along that line? Snub them through your costume choice."

"How exactly is doing that snubbing them?"

I laughed. "It's subtle, but you'd be waltzing in claiming you could be the white sheep just like they want but that you choose to be different. That, plus it'll make them ask questions. When they're the ones asking questions, you have the advantage and better control of the situation."

"I could also go planning to insult them all. If you're blurring the lines between fact and fiction, I can, too."

"Who would you go as for that?"

"King Arthur." Turning away from the stove to face me, he smirked. "I know just the person who can help me put together a costume today, too. I like it. Not only will I get to taunt my family, they won't be able to chastise me over it because I'll be playing to the theme and taking it seriously—at least on the surface."

Something about his playful smirk and the spring in his step as he went back to his breakfast-making duties promised the next two days would be a disaster in the making. "This is going to blow up in our faces, isn't it?"

"I certainly hope so, or I'll be bored out of my mind. I hate these events. I always feel like I'm the one up for auction."

"Maybe you should go as someone rather ugly; perhaps the Hunchback of Notre Dame?"

"I doubt that would work. I don't know a makeup artist who would be willing to turn my face into a disaster, and I don't think I have enough time to find one."

"True. It would take a lot of work to make you ugly."

"King Arthur should work. My family will hate it, the other attendees will love it, and that makes it a victory in my book."

"We're going to be a mismatched pair."

"Even better."

Had Malcolm lost his mind? Maybe my sleepwalking bed-invasion had broken something in his head. "I don't follow."

"It's symbolism. We're portraying independent, powerful figures—forces to be reckoned with when alone. Together? We'd count as a true threat. I think it's perfect."

So many regrets and worries, so little time. What could go wrong?

Ah, right. Everything. I was willing to bet what could go wrong would go wrong, it was only a matter of when. At least I'd be able to claim I wasn't a coward. "Then it's decided."

"You're not going to regret this."

Was he a mind reader? He startled a laugh out of me. "You're joking, right? I already do."

THIRTEEN

What the hell was I supposed to
do now?

WHAT COULD GO WRONG DID GO WRONG
the instant I attempted a shift. I managed to
shift, but I became a sphinx. Under normal
circumstances, I would've been thrilled with
my transformation, especially since my hair,
feathers, and fur were all intact. Exhaustion
smothered me, which I blamed on the drugs
still working their way out of my system.

Getting stuck, however, hadn't been part
of my plan.

Tapping my claws on the bathroom tiles, I
scowled at my reflection. A fortune in jewels
and precious metals decorated my hair,
weighing my head down. A silver usekh
worthy of a goddess, bejeweled in rubies,
lapis lazuli, and smoky stones, clung to my
throat and draped over my shoulders.

My inability to shift again shouldn't have
surprised me; I'd been stuck as a burned

human for over a week. I shouldn't have expected a different result. There was a silver lining, however. With Malcolm's help, I could pillage my jewelry for when I did manage to shift, hopefully before the gala.

I really hoped I did, or I'd have far too many problems for my liking. The rumor of a sphinx in New York might reach my family. My infrequent taunting of my aunt ensured that the woman knew I was alive somewhere, but if she learned what I was, I feared what she would do.

A sphinx would transform me into a desirable. If I never met any of my biological family ever again, I'd die a happy woman.

What the hell was I supposed to do now? I lashed my tail, rustled my wings and settled them over my back, and engaged in a staring contest with myself. Mirror-me won as usual, and I hissed my disgust over being trapped in my favorite body at the worst time.

Malcolm knocked on the bathroom door. "Everything okay?"

After over a week at his mercy and invading his bed due to sleepwalking episodes, what was one more embarrassment? I sighed. "I'm stuck."

Malcolm yanked open the door, caught sight of me, and his eyes widened. "Holy shit."

"It's really not what you think."

"You're a sphinx?"

"Okay, maybe it is what you think."

Malcolm straightened, opened his mouth, closed it again, and looked me over head to tail, spending the most time focusing on my wings. "Can you go to the charity gala like that? You're splendid."

Of all the things I expected, his admiration hadn't been one of them. "But why?"

"You're a mythos! I'll be honest, if I come with a mythos they believe is my girlfriend, I'll be the clear victor of this episode of our family feud. I won't even have to lift a finger. It's brilliant. No one wants to get into a fight with a mythos."

"I'm *a* sphinx, not *the* Sphinx, Malcolm. Sorry."

"You're still a mythos. This is so much better than I hoped. What are your abilities? Your diet?" A gleam lit his eyes. "Do you do riddles?"

"Riddles are Greek. I'm Egyptian. Egyptian sphinxes are guardians. Greek sphinxes will eat your kidneys for breakfast because they're in a bad mood. Egyptian sphinxes are good-natured. Greek? Not so much."

"That's fantastic. What is someone like you doing working as a mercenary?"

I considered biting him, but he'd fed me a great deal of bacon for breakfast, and I couldn't risk losing my bacon supply.

"Making a living. I don't know what you're thinking, but you have the wrong idea. Sure, I look like a sphinx, but all I can do is shift and summon clothes when I do. I don't have any other special abilities. I don't do riddles, nor do I eat people when they get them wrong."

"Some would say your ability to shift *is* special. Lycanthropes with three forms are prized. How many forms do you have? Four?"

"Five, and I have no control over which form I shift to. Until the car accident, I could shift reliably—by that, I mean I could always shift. It's a problem right now."

"If three for lycanthropes is considered spectacular, five forms are the definition of something special. Your papers say you're human?"

At the rate I was going, I wouldn't have any secrets left by lunch. I huffed, shook out my wings, and dropped to the floor to make myself as comfortable as I could on the tiles. "I'm typically categorized as a shapeshifter or a human."

"Interesting. Can you fly?"

"I can."

"Now that's really interesting. How long can you stay in that form?"

I almost didn't answer him, but after consideration, I shrugged. "However long I want I guess. I like shifting, so I tend to do it often."

Malcolm chuckled. "I would, too, if I were you. But this is excellent. I have an idea."

Ideas worried me, as they tended to cause me trouble in some form or another. "What idea?"

"You'll see soon enough, so don't worry about a thing."

INSTEAD OF TRUSTING Malcolm like a stupid fool, I should've worried, made plans, and done anything other than catch a catnap by the pretty fish pond in his back yard. Maybe if I'd used my head instead of succumbing to the temptation of a pleasant puddle of sunlight, he wouldn't have had a chance to put my own damned suppression bracelet on me.

I evaluated every mistake leading to the moment he turned the tables on me. Some of the blame went to the painkillers; I'd been sluggish through breakfast and could barely remember the dirty bit of business involving a costume party at a museum at some charity event I never would've attended without someone paying me to do it. The painkillers would take most of the blame, actually. They fogged my head and lowered my defenses almost as much as the luxury of Malcolm's home, especially his bed when he was in it.

The man was too handsome and warm for

my own good. My bed invasions alone justified part of his desire to get revenge. I'd started it, and I only had myself to blame for letting him steal pages from my book on kidnapping, coercion, and manipulation.

I deserved a little misery in the form of wearing my own suppression bracelet. There wouldn't be a next time, however. Lesson learned.

Malcolm Stewart was not to be underestimated again.

Movement caught my attention, and I glowered at my new worst enemy. "This is taking turnabout is fair play too far."

"Knowing what you are changes things."

New intel often did change things, as I learned on far too many occasions. "How?"

"You're right. My family's cursed, and unless the curse is broken, the line ends with me and my cousin. You can open doors for me—doors currently closed. That bracelet is my insurance policy. Please believe me when I tell you I don't enjoy this, but as long as you help me, I'll take it off—after the curse is broken."

I unsheathed my claws and dug them into his pretty grass, tearing at the dirt. "And here I thought you had a poor relationship with your family."

"I do, but that doesn't change anything.

They're my family. If I want a family of my own, I need to break the curse."

Everything circled back to my initial impression. For Malcolm, his dream was to have a family, and he longed for what he couldn't have. I wouldn't betray my suspicions yet. Lifting my left paw, I displayed the bracelet. "What good does this do for you?"

"There's someone I know with an interest in mythos—personal interest. She's a knowledge trader, and she specializes in curses. In exchange for a blood sample and a questioning session, she might be able to point me in the direction of someone who can break my family's curse—or at least help me identify it."

If his specialist was being honest, the first place she'd direct Malcolm was hell and its lord. Without any effort of my own, I'd found myself jammed between a rock and a hard place, and not even the nice, muscular type of hardness capable of getting a girl in a lot of trouble in a hurry.

Head to toe, Malcolm had more than his fair share of hard muscles, and I couldn't even blame drugged me for repeated bed invasions.

Still, I needed to sound offended. His ploy disgusted me, but it also amused and impressed me. Cat-like ruthlessness never failed to catch my attention, and he'd beaten me at my own game.

"You want to use me as a test subject." I even managed to make scorn drip out of my voice when I wanted to throw back my head and laugh.

The bastard had gotten me good, and damn it, I respected him for his cunning.

"No, not a test subject! It's for knowledge. If she wants more than a blood sample and asking you questions, she's going to owe you *and* me far more than some pointers about curse lore. No, under no circumstances will I allow anyone to use you as a test subject. You'll only be asked to donate a small sample of blood and tell her everything you can about your species. I'll be paying you for the inconvenience as well."

At the rate people kept wanting to pay me for things I really didn't want to do, retirement would be a realistic possibility. Had the devil guessed what Malcolm would do?

Probably.

I sighed. "You could've just asked for my help."

The smug bastard smiled. "I could have, but then I would've robbed us both of an interesting game. I want to see what you'll do."

Maybe the devil hadn't wanted to barter for my soul because he had foreseen how my life would become a living hell. Why bother

stealing my soul when he could torment me?
I'd have to thank him for limiting his evil to
while I still drew breath.

I almost felt sorry for Malcolm; I suspected his specialist friend knew more about
sphinxes than I did, including my potential
lifespan. Death seemed rather nice, as I'd escape all the nuisances in my life. No devil, no
evil aunt with ideas to sell me off to perverted
men, no obnoxious clients, and no men like
Malcolm.

Was an afterlife without pretty, stubborn,
and infuriating men like Malcolm a heaven or
a hell? I'd have to think about it. The cat in
me said hell. The sane, logical woman in me
said heaven.

As long as I wore the damned bracelet,
however, the cat side of me might enjoy certain luxuries. Malcolm might find himself
with an unwanted 'sleepwalking' bed invader
as punishment for daring to shackle *me*.
Stealing his warmth would only be the beginning of my revenge.

If he wanted to play, I'd play. "You think
this is a game?"

"Yes, I do. It's two birds with one stone,
really. It's serious, but it's a game as well. I
win either way. I have a chance to break my
family's curse while getting a good look of
what you're made of. You said it yourself. You

can only shift, so the bracelet shouldn't hurt you."

The man dared to use my own twisted logic on me, which vexed me almost as much as his smug smile. He'd pay for that, too.

Only one thing separated us in our way of thinking: I wouldn't have done it for my family. I'd been abandoned once, and when that hadn't been enough to erase me as the family shame, I'd been put up for sale like a brood-mare. No, if I were in his shoes, I'd need a different motivation. I could respect him for his desire, though.

Sometimes, late at night and after a few too many drinks, I thought about what it might be like to be a part of a good family—one of my choosing. I'd have to stop drifting, hang up my hat as a wandering mercenary, and settle down, but a girl could dream.

Still, I couldn't help but wonder about what he said. "Why do you care what I'll do?"

"Because I do."

I lashed my tail and shredded his grass some more. "What sort of dumb answer is that?"

"I find you interesting."

Boys and their toys. Why did I have to be the current toy of the hour? Ugh. I could make the most of the situation, and I'd be in a better position to win the devil's wager. Ah, good old silver linings in my storm clouds.

Whenever I looked hard enough, I could find one. "Fine. You should strip this crap out of my hair, take off my usekh, and let me shift back to human."

"But you're so pretty as a sphinx."

"I like having hands, Malcolm."

He sighed. "And your sworn word you'll help me break my family's curse?"

If only he knew about my wager with the devil. "I swear I'll do everything in my power to break your family's curse."

"Shall we take this inside, then?"

I snarled curses at him, took flight, and winged my way to his house. First, I'd get mad. Once I worked through my rage, I'd get even. I'd plan my first bed invasion for in a few days , after I recovered from the embarrassment of my drugged sleepwalking. Maybe I'd wait a few weeks. I had two months and three weeks to discover his family's secrets. A few weeks meant he wouldn't expect me slipping into his bed to steal his warmth and make him uncomfortable with my presence. Malcolm had said as much. He wanted to test me.

The game was on, and I wouldn't lose to him again.

I WOULD NEVER ADMIT to enjoying Malcolm

fussing with my hair. Hell would freeze over first, the heavens would burst into flames, and the devil and his estranged relatives would kiss and make up long before I confessed how much I enjoyed his attention. When I had asked him to strip the gold and jewels from my hair, I hadn't expected him to interpret my request as an excuse to brush out my fur, too.

I wished I could purr.

Malcolm dug his fingers deep into the fur between my wings and scratched. Had I been on my paws, I would've melted to the tiles. Later, I'd be grateful for my inability to purr, as I would've embarrassed myself even more.

"All right. Try to shift." Untangling his hand from my fur, he took a stepped back and spoke the word Hagnar had taught me, his smug smile fixed in place.

I looked forward to the day I changed his expression to one of shock and surprise. The temptation to deny him froze me in place for several breaths, but duty, determination, and practicality won the battle; I liked having hands, which would make my task much simpler. Snarling a few choice profanities, I transformed. It took longer than I liked and hurt far more than I expected. It was painful enough I whimpered before I could stop myself. Instead of human flesh, I embodied Bastet in her full glory, my fur glossy and thick. Lifting my hands, I touched my head, fearing the worst.

Hair. I had hair, and while it wasn't as long as I liked, resembling a mane more than anything else, I wouldn't be ashamed to go out in public. With the help of some extensions plus the silver, gold, and jewels I'd pilfered from my other form, I'd be able to trick most into believing I'd made a full recovery from my burning. As though my magic pandered to Malcolm's desires, I wore a white kalasiris overlaid with a blue, gold, and silver strands of beads. In modern society, gold surpassed silver, but in the old days, when the pharaohs had ruled Egypt, silver represented wealth and nobility.

The silver hooded cobra coiling around my upper arm alone would've marked me as a member of a wealthy family. The wrist cuffs, made of silver, carnelian, and lapis lazuli, branded me as nobility.

I found it ironic that I sought an end to a curse, a gypsy's art, but my magic insisted on embracing my Egyptian heritage.

Behind me, Malcolm spoke the word to suppress my magic. Curling my lip up in a snarl, I spun to face him. "Happy now?"

"You're beautiful."

Were compliments a man's base defense mechanism against an angry woman? It occurred to me that for many centuries in

Egypt, women often exposed their breasts, as practicality had ruled over modesty, a rather modern convention. Sucking in a breath, I checked my dress, then heaved a relieved sigh. My magic, fortunately, had accounted for more modern sensibilities, and while my kalasiris skirted the line of decency, it covered everything important.

"You're delusional." I picked up my usekh from the vanity and secured it around my throat. "Complimenting me isn't going to win you anything. I already agreed to help you, so you're wasting your breath."

He smiled. "You're just angry I bested you."

While true, I glowered at him. "You could've hired me."

"I could have, but then I'd worry someone might pay you more. That's the problem with mercenaries. Money comes above all else. Can you really blame me? This is too important to leave to chance."

I lifted my chin. "So, my species is the only reason why?"

"Of course not. You're skilled. You showed me that the night you got the jump on me and kidnapped me. There has to be a reason my cousin wanted you. If you're in my corner, I'll have the upper hand. Originally, I was going to have you look into my cousin and uncle, but when a chance to end my family's curse comes calling, I'm taking advantage of it. I'm sorry."

With him, family would always come first and meant more than anything else. I couldn't understand it. To me, family meant fear and nightmares, and while I held the hazy dream of having one founded on love, the terror of my youth remained.

To him, family meant so much more than blood.

To me, it meant slavery and nothing else.

"So, you have me. What are you planning to do with me now?"

His smile widened. "I'm taking you shopping. That outfit will be spectacular at the gala, but you're going to need more appropriate attire for the rest of my plans. If any of your other clothing fits, get changed. We have a lot to do and little time."

First he turned the tables on me, but then he decided to take me shopping? How ballsy could one man be?

I had the feeling I was about to find out.

FOURTEEN

I can buy my own clothes.

MALCOLM TOOK me to an expensive boutique and didn't care that I wore a pair of his sweats. Never in my life had I been so tempted to kill someone. Malcolm had absolutely no clue why waltzing into a store specializing in expensive women's apparel while wearing clothes he'd probably sweated in might upset me.

That I liked the idea of him hot and sweaty only pissed me off even more, and I hoped the heat of my rage lit his ass on fire. To add insult to injury, from the instant we'd gotten into his car, he'd made it clear he meant to pay the bill.

"I can buy my own clothes," I hissed, digging in my heels at the threshold into the store.

The pair of shoes in the window had red soles and cost several hundred dollars, and the infuriating man on a mission kept staring at them with an interested expression.

"Not only am I buying, I'm picking the clothes." To confirm my suspicions, he pointed at the pretty black and red shoes with a heel so high I could use them as lethal weapons. "I don't know what I'm buying, but it's going to look amazing with those heels."

"You're a cretin."

"I'm a cretin with a credit card and a love for your legs. A man gets this chance exactly once in his life, and I don't mean to squander it."

"You're also a lunatic."

He scowled at me. "Why would you say that?"

"Look at me!" I wailed, gesturing to the gray sweats he'd foisted on me the instant he'd realized I was either going as a full-blown Egyptian goddess or in a pair of shorts so short they didn't even classify as underwear.

He loved the shorts but had confiscated them for home-use only.

When we got back to his house, I'd be introducing my claws to his jeans. I'd objectify his fine ass in equal measure and give him a taste of his own medicine. While I was at it, I'd teach him it was never acceptable to tell me what I could and couldn't wear.

Even if it meant I got a free pair of black

heels with cute little red soles I could wear as lethal weapons attached to my feet. I narrowed my eyes, leaning towards the display for a closer look at the price tag.

I had missed a zero at my first glance at the shoes. If he wanted them, he'd have to spend over a thousand dollars for them. I hadn't had a pair of shoes with red soles before; my magic made shoes had matched my outfit, but they never had a *brand*—they just were.

"I am looking at you. You're beautiful, and you deserve to be dressed in clothes worthy of you."

He made it rather difficult to be offended when he dished out the compliments without any hint of hesitation; the ready, confident way he spoke rang of truth, and my unreasonable reactions to him only stoked my anger. Stealing my damned bracelets I'd used to kidnap him and using them on me was the final straw.

I'd pay him back for his cunning somehow. The dose of just desserts tasted sour, and not in the nice lemon meringue sort of way.

"You're going to be ravishing when I'm finished with you. Stop being such a scaredy cat and go into the store. You need the clothes to do the job for me, and I'm not going to allow you to cut into your wages to replace your clothes. I'm paying the expenses. Get used to it, Kanika. I take my business obligations seriously, and you're worth every penny."

"You're still a lunatic."

"I'm a lunatic with a credit card and no limits. March, ma'am. I still have to get my costume dealt with, you need clothes so you're not wearing my sweats, and I need to see your legs in those shoes."

"Is there a reason you're so fixated on my legs?"

"Those legs got me kidnapped."

He had a very good point. I'd unashamedly used my legs against him, although in reality, I'd been showcasing my ass. Huh. In a few ways, I was being the unreasonable party; I *had* lured him into a trap wearing scandalously short shorts while bending over to display the goods to lure him into parking and lowering his guard.

"Who knew? I'm quite the asshole." Admitting it made me feel much better—and it got me to step into the store.

A young woman stared from the counter, the only employee in the place, and her eyes widened. "Mr. Montgomery?"

Did *everyone* in Nashville know Malcolm?

"Hello, Patsy." Malcolm planted his hands on my shoulders and marched me to the counter. "This is Kanika, and I need your help finding her clothes as beautiful as she is."

I'd met enough men who looked me over like a piece of meat on the market to recognize when Patsy did it, and the brunette licked her lips like she'd just arrived at an all you can eat buffet. "You've given me a challenge, Mr. Montgomery."

Once I got out of the boutique, assuming I survived the experience, I would have to ask why everyone in Nashville called him Mr. Montgomery. "I'm not—"

Malcolm covered my mouth with his hand. "She'd like to try on the black cocktail dress in the window with the black and red shoes."

If he put me in all black, I'd end up looking like an angel of death. Taking hold of his wrist, pulled his hand away. "Black fur, black dress, black shoes? Am I auditioning for a gothic event?"

"I like the color black."

"Braindead male," I muttered. "If it keeps you quiet and entertained, I'll try on the dress."

"It'll keep me entertained, but I can't promise I'll be quiet."

Fuming over my transformation from mercenary to model, I went with Patsy, grumbling over the dress designed for a succubus, accommodating her wings, and her tail. Fortunately, the designer hadn't gone the low-back route, instead opting for a discreet slit and straps that worked with wings instead of accounting for them as a base necessity. If I shifted to my winged form, I'd appreciate that later. Patsy stuffed me into it, and the dress fit well enough I suspected someone—Malcolm—had been taking certain measurements.

I'd have to question him about that, too. Had he been undressing me with his eyes to get the estimate? If he had been, I'd toss basic decency to the four winds and enjoy the scenery a lot more openly than I had been in my effort to be civilized. With a few careful tugs, I situated the slick material and prepared to be objectified.

I stepped out of the dressing room with my ears flattened back, hissing at the object of my displeasure.

The object of my displeasure stared, blinked, and opened his mouth.

I waited, tapping my toes in the wickedly expensive shoes he'd forced on me. When I got tired of waiting, I turned around, and gave him a good show of my lashing tail to ensure he got the hint I wasn't happy with my new job as model.

Silence.

I turned once more, and Malcolm straightened, his gaze sliding over me, swallowing several times. "I'm buying you that dress. Next."

Patsy laughed and herded me back to the dressing rooms. "He's so shy. It's been a while since he's been here, but he was quieter. Last time he hardly said a word and tried to avoid looking at the woman he was with. She didn't seem to mind, since she was far more interested in her reflection and the price tag than what he was thinking. She wouldn't let him pay the bill, either. How odd."

"When was the last time he was in here?"

"Five or six years ago. I'd just started working here when he brought her in. I think she liked calling him by his middle name or something, too."

"Stewart?"

Patsy's expression brightened. "Yes. Mr. Montgomery didn't seem too keen about it, either. I thought it was weird when he asked me to pull out our succubi gowns in your sizes, but looking at you, it was a perfect choice. You could probably teach those demons a thing or two about turning heads. Your tail's a lot better suited for the dresses than theirs, I think. Shall we try something with more color?"

"Why not?" With Malcolm buying the clothes, the least I could do was help rid him of his money. By the time I finished waging war on his wallet, he'd regret making me model for him. I feigned enthusiasm for the task, cooling my temper enough that my intended victim hopefully wouldn't notice my irritation simmering beneath the surface.

Two hours and countless outfits later, my plan backfired. Malcolm didn't reject a single outfit, some even leaving him at a loss for words. When I finally escaped the boutique, I wore his sweats. If I ran for the hills, at least I'd be comfortable. Malcolm wouldn't want his clothes back, not after I'd cut a tail hole in them.

The thought of escaping tempted me, but I'd wagered with the devil. I couldn't leave with my dignity intact. I respected Malcolm's reasons, but I hated when someone *I* had initially outwitted caught me flatfooted and then had the audacity to be gentlemanly and generous afterwards.

How annoying. It made it difficult to remain cranky, so I focused on the one thing guaranteed to send me into a blind fury: my aunt and my unwanted suitors in New York.

"You're not going to cool off anytime soon, are you?"

I got into his car, buckled in, and grunted so I wouldn't tell a lie. He put two bags in the trunk, a small fraction of my new wardrobe. Sliding behind the wheel, he started the car and grinned at me. "Admit it, Kanika. You secretly enjoyed bleeding my wallet dry."

The man hadn't rejected a single outfit, not even the pink skirt, although I suspected the pink skirt's short length had contributed to his immediate acceptance of the purchase. I scowled and resorted to thinking about New York and the very slim possibility of running into someone I really didn't like to keep my temper sour for his enjoyment. "You weren't exactly happy over being kidnapped, either," I reminded him. With no idea how long I'd be in the car while dealing with Malcolm's costume, I kicked off my shoes so I could stretch my feet and unsheathe my cramped claws.

Bastet claws and shoes didn't mix, although I'd gotten used to dealing with the reality of human attire in a non-human body. At least my magic-made shoes accommodated my irregular foot shape unlike most brands. I supposed succubi had odd feet, too, since most of the shoes from the boutique fit tolerably well.

"Ah, but I was more furious at myself for being caught in the first place. Therein lies the difference. I'm going to handle my costume errand tonight after stores close; my friend is a night owl, and I already talked to him about what I needed while you were getting changed, so all I have to do is drive over late and pick it up. I'll come back to the house, then we'll leave for our flight in the morning. Our next stop is an electronics store. If you're going to be working for someone in my family, you'll need a work-specific laptop, a business-specific phone, and a good briefcase. Appearances matter to them."

"Yet your cousin goes by Bubba Eugene."

"I never said it made sense."

"True."

"So, outside of stellar kidnapping techniques, what are you good at?"

"I'm a decent shot," I confessed. "I'm comfortable with my aim and usually hit my mark."

"While important, that's not really a needed job skill in an office situation."

Shit. He needed office skills? What kind of office skills did he think I had? I could stack papers with the best of them, but if he wanted me to do something productive with them, I could file in alphabetical order. Since I doubted that's what he was looking for, I turned my head to stare out the window. "I've never had an office job before."

The reflection in my window betrayed Malcolm's wide-eyed glance in my direction, which he covered by backing out of his spot and hitting the road. "Never?"

"Sorry to disappoint you, but I don't have a high school diploma. I can use a computer." I shrugged. "I'm a drifter."

College required tens of thousands of dollars to spend on credits, a full-time job, a permanent residence, and a high school diploma. If I'd obeyed my aunt's wishes, I would've gotten all those things as a trophy wife with an education dictated by my unwanted husband's wishes.

I would've been lucky to be allowed an English degree. They wanted me for one reason only: bearing children.

My anger boiled, but I kept quiet, my teeth clenched, waiting for the condescension I'd come to expect from well-educated businessmen.

"Oh boy. This is going to be even more interesting than I thought. Buckle your seatbelt, baby. It's going to be a bumpy ride."

KEEPING quiet and fuming gave me an advantage over Malcolm; his ignorance became the foundation of my trickery, fooling him into believing I lacked intellect while goading him into making basic mistakes. Like so many, he believed my lack of a diploma reflected my knowledge of life, but unlike most, he took it as a challenge to be overcome, as though he could somehow change reality to make my past fit his standards. His determination annoyed me.

It also baffled me, as he seemed to take my lack of a formal education personally. I'd seen men on missions before, and Malcolm went from amused to flinty-eyed and determined.

I pitied how he'd been brainwashed into believing a college education and degree quantified someone's value. I'd enjoy teaching him the truth after I inflicted a little more monetary revenge on his wallet for his incorrect assumption. While he muttered curses and made plans for my blitzkrieg education, I admired the scenery.

If settling down ever became an option, I thought I'd like Nashville. It blended the urban charm of a city with the wildness I liked about forests and the untouched places of the world, somehow coexisting without destroying each other.

Old trees, planted long before the city's birth, grew from medians planned around them, which made the layout of the streets odd at best.

The trees ultimately made way for steel and concrete near the heart of the city, much to my disappointment, and the electronics store he took me to annoyed me with its cookie-cutter styling and lack of personality. Within, sane price tags and plentiful sales expanded my fiscal revenge to a blend of quantity and quality.

Without a single word to me, Malcolm

began his rampage in the computer section, muttering curses as he kidnapped a sales clerk and started pointing at a computer, a desktop costing more than I thought reasonable for a machine I couldn't lug around with me. I leaned against the metal shelving, an eyebrow arched as he dictated his first purchase to the poor clerk, who paled with every request.

A second clerk got assaulted with technical nonsense, and he ran off to obey Malcolm's wishes.

Malcolm glanced in my direction with narrowed eyes, pointed at a silvery laptop on display, and said, "The best model of that you have in stock."

The clerk beamed at that request, and the instant Malcolm's attention turned away from me, I slipped off to begin my share of the expedition. He wouldn't know what had hit him by the time I was done. I struggled to remain angry while I wanted to rub my hands together with glee over the trouble I could get myself into given an hour in the store.

I began in the software department, loading a cart with copies of every piece of software compatible with the system he'd selected. I also snagged an external disc drive, as I was aware the computer wouldn't have one in its sleek body. I could've downloaded the programs I needed, a financial tool and a spreadsheet, but if I went with the physical copies, I'd encourage his mistaken belief about my ignorance.

With the first phase of my conquest complete, I selected four different cameras, several bags, the smallest audio recording devices I could find, and was debating a tablet when Malcolm found me, glaring at my cart full of unrequested purchases.

"What are you doing?"

"Spending your money for daring to imply I'm stupid because I lack a degree." I pointed at the best tablet the store offered. "I want that one, and I want the art stylus to go with it. Case, too. It'll be useful if I need to record any minutes. And yes, I know what minutes are."

He poked through my cart, ignoring my demand, humming to himself. "Four cameras?"

"I liked them all and couldn't decide."

"I'm not sure I want to ask about the recorders."

"Revenge is a dish best served with full audio."

"Should I be concerned?"

I allowed myself a smile. "Probably. If you don't buy them for me, I'm buying them for myself."

"This must be what my father meant when he warned me about scorned women." Malcolm sighed and pointed at a smaller tablet. "You want that one, too. You might not have a lot of space at some meetings, especially if they're at a restaurant."

"Good thought. I'll take it." After another look around the store, I considered my options. "I also want a drone."

"A drone? You meant those mini helicopter things? Why?"

"Yes, those mini helicopter things are called drones. I enjoy confusing you with the bonus of making you ask questions. I also want a micro camera for my drone."

"Again, should I be concerned?"

"We already went over this. Probably. I think I have everything else I need from this store once I've selected my drone."

"Care to enlighten me on why I'm buying so much stuff? This isn't going to fit in my trunk, Kanika."

"That's your fault for having such a dainty car for such a big man like yourself. No space for stuff in addition to that ego of yours."

With a heavy sigh, Malcolm turned to his recruited store clerk, requested both tablets, and hung his head. "You're not going to let this go, are you?"

"Why would I do something like that?" I smiled my sweetest smile, showing off my sharp teeth. "Don't you have a lot to teach me?"

"Why do I have the feeling I've contracted a serious case of foot in mouth disease?"

"Maybe because you might not be as stupid as you look, pretty boy. You know how it is; all beauty, no brains." I huffed and marched to the aisle with the drones, and because I wanted to be an ass, I picked two just in case I needed to recruit Malcolm's help when I started my new career as a corporate spy.

ATTACKING Malcolm's wallet classified as rude and unprofessional, but I had always wanted a space to call my own. In my entire adult life, I'd never had a desk and chair picked out for me and me alone. What started as an off-handed comment about how nice Malcolm's home office was ended with his promise to take me to a furniture store so I could pick what I liked so I wouldn't hold his couch and coffee table hostage.

I liked his couch and coffee table, too, but I kept my mouth shut so he wouldn't interpret it as an excuse to get rid of them for something new.

"I don't suppose you care to explain why you tried to buy the entire electronics store, do you?"

"Spite."

"How charming."

While most of my purchases wouldn't be delivered until we returned from New York, I had enough to begin stripping away Malcolm's misconceptions. I grabbed the bag with my necessary software, laptop, and recording devices, beginning the tedious process of setting everything up so I could enlighten him on the errors of his ways. "I'll show you. Before I begin, I'm going to make it clear I'm pretty peeved you think I'm stupid just because I don't have fancy pieces of paper saying I paid a school to make me look smart."

Malcolm had the base decency to grimace at my accusation. "That wasn't fair to you. I apologize."

While petty, if he wanted me to accept his apology, he'd have to work a lot harder for it. I pulled out the receipt and pointed at the drone purchases before drawing his attention to my cameras and audio recorders. "I could probably rob a bank with these given some time and a few extra tools."

That caught his attention, and his eyes widened. "What? How?" Crossing his arms over his chest, he directed his glare to the cameras, particularly the one that had cost him over a thousand dollars. "You can't rob a bank with that stuff."

"Get your laptop," I ordered, snapping my

fingers and pointing at the coffee table. He looked like he wanted to argue, but he got up and headed to his home office, grumbling complaints from the moment he left until his return. I left him stewing, setting up my new machine. Once it began installing updates, I pulled out the external drive and unpacked my new software. "If you want to rob a bank, you want to do it digitally. Electronic records can be modified, systems hacked, and funds relocated. Of course, the banks don't want this to happen and take steps, but if you can get into the heart of their banking software, it can be done—and people have done it. Still do it. It has to be maintained to keep ahead of the developers trying to protect their systems against hackers."

"You mean to take advantage of security breaches?"

"Yes and no. Step one is to pick the target. Banks are pretty good at catching mass theft. What you want to do is pick a specific person with a lot of money, monitor their activities, and look at how they spend their money. That's what the financial software is for. Once a target has been selected, it's a matter of infiltrating the bank system, running a payment from my target to a disposable account, and transferring the funds off shore. You take a loss on the stolen money, but if you run it through enough accounts, it's hard to figure out where it has gone. Now, here's the trick. Log into one of your banking accounts—it can be any one, just make it small. Wouldn't want me to rob you blind, after all."

"You mean you haven't already?" Malcolm snorted a laugh, shook his head, and sat beside me, doing as I asked. "All right, this is a charity fund account; every year, I take everything I've put into this account and donate it to my charities of choice."

I admired his choice; if I robbed him blind, I wasn't hurting him, I'd be hurting charities. He scored a point for being clever, and I pointed at the link to show his transactions. "Click there."

Once he pulled up the list of transactions, I tapped the screen. "The goal is to wipe the transfer files from this listing and modify the records so that when someone does a data dump and checks the amounts, the incoming and outgoing funds match. A good accountant will catch it quickly, but if someone is only looking to see if the credits and expenditures match, they're not going to notice the theft. Depending on the wealth of the target, I'll hit a bunch of accounts, skimming from all of them to hide my activities. Of course, if I'm doing a big hit, I'll clean the bastard out, take his money, and run for it. The bank is liable for the theft, which makes it a victimless crime—if you don't consider the fat cats running the banks victims. I don't."

Malcolm narrowed his eyes and scrolled through his transactions, all of which were transfers into the account except for several large lump-sum payments issued in the previous year, matching his claim he did year-end charity contributions. "You can really do that?"

"I have." I shrugged. In reality, the client had paid me a pittance for the work compared to what I'd stolen, but I had liked the old man's story—and held a personal grudge against the victim.

The asshole target had been one of the slimy businessmen my aunt had wanted to ditch me with, and I'd enjoyed ruining him. He'd been one of the fringe candidates, relatively poor compared to the big three my aunt pursued for their money.

"How?"

"It's not hard if you know certain pieces of intel."

"I find that hard to believe. Bank security is tight."

I reminded myself Malcolm was right to doubt me; bank security *was* tight—but I had connections, connections like Hagnar—and a willingness to get my hands dirty. In reality, with the victim's username, password, and security question answers, draining someone's account dry took very little time, especially when the victim had no transfer limits to protect his money. "Maybe you're my first notable kidnapping, but you're not my first big job."

Of all the things I'd gotten recently, I liked my new phone, and I pulled it out and searched the internet for my biggest hit, a museum robbery. I held out the device to Malcolm. "This was my work."

Malcolm leaned over and peered at the screen, reading through the article. "You really think I'm going to believe you did this job?"

Forget my aunt and her band of evil bachelor slavers, Malcolm took the top prize for pissing me off. "Now you're just being insulting."

The bastard smirked, and I realized he'd done it on purpose to tweak my tail. "This robbery made national news."

Oh, how subtle his jab, with the perfect inflection in his voice to imply he expected better from me, as though I should have made *international* news instead. *Better?* I'd taken a priceless artifact someone had decided was only worth ten million from a museum and had gotten away with it. "Yes. The diadem was magical, too. I owed someone a favor."

"That's some hell of a favor. What does a

man have to do to get you indebted to him for that level of work?"

Was Malcolm still toying with me? I curled my lip and hissed at him, flattening my ears. "It's not happening again. I'm out of the museum robbing business. I came pretty close to spending a long time in jail over that heist. Also, should you speak a word of this to anyone, you won't have to worry about your family's curse because I'll cut you into small pieces and feed you to your fish."

His smirk broadened to a grin. "You're of no use to me in prison."

"I'm so glad we agree on that."

"Since I've already contracted an ever-worsening case of foot in mouth disease, what skills do you have that translates well to corporate work?"

"Auditing."

His smile vanished, replaced with a thoughtful expression. "Auditing?"

"You know, finding where people might be trying to hide money? I'm good at that."

"How'd you learn *that*? That's…"

Busted. I turned his smirk against him. "That's something people pay colleges a lot of money to learn?"

"You're going to make me lick your feet before you'll forgive me for being a foolish, prideful man, aren't you?"

I enjoyed the sound of victory, especially

when it came from Malcolm's lips. "I have a few grudges, and I swore if I ever got a chance to ruin their business affairs, I would, so I researched banking and auditing. I've gotten one of them, but I haven't had a chance to get the others. I still think about it sometimes."

"Had I known how perfect you are, I would've been the one hiring someone to kidnap *you*. So many birds with just one stone. What will it take to make you my partner and get your full loyalty and coop-eration?"

I snorted at his question, the man's au-dacity annoying yet amusing. He wanted *me* to be loyal and cooperative with *him*? As a partner? Had he lost his mind? "I think we've already burned that bridge, Malcolm. Be happy you have your mythos for your little curse specialist. I'm playing your game be-cause I was stupid and made too many mis-takes. Take what you can get and be happy with that."

I lied a little, but he'd never learn the truth. However much he pissed me off, I still enjoyed the game with him, but I couldn't let him learn that. He'd find some way to twist it to his advantage—and he might make me like it.

Under no circumstances could I let that happen.

My goals were clear. First, I would learn his family's secret, get paid, and be content I'd taken the high road, helping Malcolm despite my anger over being discounted due to my lack of formal education. The sooner I beat the devil at this own game, the sooner I'd be back on the road where I belonged, leaving Malcolm and too many regrets behind me.

I made a show of ignoring the man, pretending I cared about what was on my laptop. Once upon a time, I had lived to discover what lay beyond the next hill. I'd somehow lost the desire to get up and start walking again, and I wondered what that would mean for me in the future.

Every choice I ever made for myself involved putting one foot in front of the other. What was I supposed to do with myself if I *stayed*? No, I couldn't afford to think about it. Once I finished my job, the next hill to climb waited, and that was that.

FIFTEEN

If I'm not going to let a guard put
you on display in your panties, I'm
definitely not letting him display you
without them.

I FOUND it odd Malcolm's family flew in a
private jet to New York while we took a commercial flight. According to him, they'd left
even earlier than us, probably to take care of
some business in the city before the start of
the gala. Malcolm's costume took up two
suitcases, which were labeled in glowing
runes as property of an elf.

The airport employees were reluctant to
even touch the suitcases. Hopefully that
would deter people from opening them and
that they'd arrive safe and sound so the elf
wouldn't have to eat anyone. I'd heard elves
had a tendency to do just that when someone
screwed around with their property.

I'd never met an elf before, and I didn't
want to start with the one who owed Malcolm a favor. My costume caused problems,

as I was forced to wear it under a long coat with most of my jewelry in a bag doubling as a purse. The security guard narrowed his eyes at my bejeweled attire.

"Take off all your metal," he ordered.

To do what he wanted, I'd have to get completely undressed, as even my damned underwear had gold and silver beads. I opened my mouth to say something, and Malcolm held up his hand. I clacked my teeth together. The guard and Malcolm bent their heads together, and after a few minutes, the guard passed me through the detector to an x-ray machine. I kept a tight hold on my bag and grumbled over the crowd of people watching me.

Malcolm chuckled and patted my shoulder. "I wasn't going to let some lecherous guard put you on display in your panties."

"The panties have gold and silver, too."

His eyes widened. "If I'm not going to let a guard put you on display in your panties, I'm definitely not letting him display you without them."

"Good to know." I shot him a glare, huffed, and headed for the gate, my ears flattened at the subtle hint of jealousy in his tone. The damned man drove me to the brink of insanity. No matter how devilishly handsome the Scot was, if I kept him company for much longer, I'd end up accustomed to his displays of jealousy and offbeat sense of humor. Worse, I might grow to like it.

With his usual smirk in place, he lifted his arm enough I could see his bracelet. "How do you not have smoke rolling out of those pretty ears of yours yet?"

"Were you not invited to join the rest of your family on their cushy private flight?"

He laughed. "I told you they don't like me much. I booked commercial for their sake. Within an hour, you'd have bits of several Stewart men in your claws, ruin your lovely dress, and possibly damage your jewelry. This was the safer choice for everyone. It would've been a nightmare flight."

"As if this isn't," I muttered, queueing into the line to board. A hint of something rancid hung in the air. If I could've flattened my ears more, I would have, so I lashed my tail instead.

Malcolm grabbed the tufted end of my tail and held it still. "That should be classified as a lethal weapon. What's got you so worked up?"

How could I mention the smell without offending someone? I turned to him, leaned to his ear, and hissed, "Sensitive sense of smell."

"Pardon?"

"Something smells rancid," I complained, snatching my tail out of his hands.

"It's an airport. That happens with unfortunate frequency."

"I wouldn't know."

"Never flown before?"

I shrugged. "I suppose I must have when I first came to America."

"You're handling this really well for a first-time flyer, then. I really thought you'd done this before in light of how you handled security."

"I figured attacking the security guard would get me in trouble."

"You figured correctly."

Even I had to laugh at his wry tone of voice. We boarded, and I found the insides of the big plane far more cramped than I anticipated, requiring me to squeeze by people. When I found our row, I discovered we had a seat mate who'd already claimed the aisle for himself despite it belonging to my ticket. I tensed.

Malcolm gave me a gentle push towards the window. "Didn't want the window seat?"

"I hate the window," he replied. "Please, take it."

It wasn't until he stood and I wiggled around him that I realized he was some form of undead, and the rancid stench I'd smelled belonged to him.

Gross.

I shivered, took the window seat, and challenged Malcolm with bared teeth.

"Don't mind her. You know how cats get." Malcolm rolled his eyes and sat between us, bumping his foot against mine in warning. "Dead long?"

"Last week. Nice kitten. Where can I get one of those?"

"Trust me on this one. You don't want her. She's as high maintenance as they get. Damn lovely though, right?"

"You're a lucky, lucky man."

"I see dead people," I hissed, unsheathing my claws. "I bet I can cut you into small enough pieces to fit in my bag, Malcolm."

The corpse laughed, and decomposing flesh fell from his cheek. "Good luck with her, man. You're going to need it. Still, prettier than any picture I've ever seen. If I'd known lycanthropes could be so damned beautiful, I would've taken my chances with one in life. How'd you win a broad like her?"

"Right place at the right time," Malcolm replied.

Most people would have called an unexpected invitation to a kidnapping the wrong place at the wrong time, but I had to give the man credit. He sounded like he believed it, and if I hadn't known better, I would've been flattered. Since there was nothing new about men and backhanded compliments, I did as society demanded and played it polite.

I wouldn't thank either one of them, but I wouldn't tear Malcolm to shreds and stuff him in my bag—yet. It took a great deal of work to clean blood from between beads. Without Malcolm, I'd lose my wager with the devil, too.

Either clueless or sensing he'd barely escaped death, Malcolm ignored me in favor of our new travel companion. The rancid smell strengthened the longer I stayed in my seat, and my stomach turned knowing it came from a human—a recently expired one.

"How are you going to rot out?" Malcolm asked as though he met the walking dead every day.

I admired him for his flawless handling of a situation I found nauseating at best.

"I'm going in for mummification next week; too far gone for vampirism, and I didn't like the compensation package for becoming a ghoul. I'm lucky. I'll earn my freedom after a hundred years of service."

The stench forgotten, I gaped at the man, my eyes widening as my mind went blank at the thought of someone having the choice to become undead. Without glancing at me, Malcolm bumped his foot against mine.

I snapped my teeth together, and despite

his silent warning, I couldn't stop my fur from standing on end.

"Mummification? What will you be guarding?"

My admiration for Malcolm grew to full-fledged awe, as the man seemed utterly un-surprised by the mummy-to-be's confession.

"I'm hoping for a family vault. It should be interesting. There are several up for grabs among the mummification candidates."

"Well, good luck to you." Malcolm turned back to me, saw my expression, and laughed. "You look like you've never met a lingerer before."

"A lingerer," I echoed, leaning forward for a better look at the corpse with the aisle seat. In life, he'd been young—or I so thought. The green and black splotching on his face made it difficult to tell. "I'm Kanika, a freelancer."

"Got a company reference?"

"No. I run my own business, Whatever for Hire."

Malcolm groaned, settled back in his seat, and sighed as though the weight of the world burdened his shoulders. "That's such a ter-rible name."

I took a page out of his book and kicked his foot.

"I'm Zac. I died last week in a car crash. Makes me glad I cut a deal because I wasn't ready to go yet. Do you do security work?"

Zac's mention of cutting a deal piqued my interest. "I have. Did you make a deal with the devil?"

If he had, I'd be having a long talk with Satin about leaving the unliving roaming around stinking up airplanes I needed to use.

"If only I were so lucky. No, I was stupid. I cut a deal with a rival faction. You're interested in unlife?" Zac laughed, but the sound was so bitter I recoiled in my seat and leaned towards the window. "Trust me on this one— pick the devil if you can. You get what you pay for, beautiful. I wish I'd known that before I'd sealed my deal."

Malcolm grunted, and I couldn't tell if he was annoyed because of Zac's deal with a demonic or devilish entity or the offhanded compliment flung in my direction. Men. While I wasn't above drooling all over Malcolm and his chiseled body, I didn't call the Scot a stud, sexy, or any other true but objectifying cutesy name every other sentence.

In private, I might not be above testing his reactions.

"What do you mean by that? You didn't get a good deal?" The devil's deals were all about the details, and the Lord of Lies masterfully manipulated his victims into giving up far more than they anticipated, but he always, always delivered his end of the bargain to the letter. The spirit often got left behind, but that was what the devil did; he found every advantage in the details and profited from them.

Zac scowled, and another bit of his cheek rotted off. In the future, I'd think of those in his situation as rotters. If they were going to leave bits and pieces strewn around for others to find, there was no way I was prettying it up with a nonsensical, politically correct name.

I needed a shower already, and Malcolm was the one taking the hits—and the decaying bits of Zac—for the team.

"I dodged death in exchange for a hundred years of service. When I'm done, I'll have nothing to show for my work. I'm free labor. At least with the devil, I'd get a fair compensation. When I signed, I was told I'd have meaningful, paid work. Turns out the 'pay' is my room and board for the hundred years I'm in service. I'll start my free unlife broke, homeless, and out of touch from society. I'm not the only one who got offered a shit deal. It looked good on the surface, but after I thought about it, I realized it wasn't. I've lost my soul for a hundred years, and delays in paperwork cost me my choice of undead. My soul, even for a hundred years, is worth more than that. I should have become a vampire! I signed up to become a vampire. I bet the bastards deliberately lost the papers for three days so I'd be screwed out of my preference. I'll be a mummy—not bad as far as undead go, but it's not what I wanted."

The outburst startled me. I exchanged a long look with Malcolm, who had turned a suspicious shade of gray-green. I swallowed, wished I could cover my nose to avoid the rotter's smell, and asked, "You've lost your soul for a hundred years? But how can you survive without your soul?"

"I asked that, you know. I was told not to worry about it. I guess they just need a body for guard duty. Either that, or my soul isn't nearly as important as I thought. I guess I'll find out."

What *was* the value of a soul? Why bargain for only a hundred years? Curiosity once again got the better of me, but I knew who to ask—after I did a bit more digging of my own first. "Can you tell me who you cut a deal with?"

"Sure. I've got a business card. Not sure why such a pretty kitty like yourself would need to make any deals, but here." Zac pulled out a battered, stained wallet and offered me a thin card. "That's part of the deal, too. I have to send people their way. Too bad for them they didn't make me swear to say good things about their business."

"Indeed," I murmured, reaching across Malcolm to take the card, lowering my gaze to read it. Two things caught my attention. First, Wishing Well had skimped on their business cards. Second, they were located in Georgia.

Interesting. No wonder the devil was on the move; someone was edging in on his turf, and I was willing to wager he wasn't happy about it. I slipped the card into my wallet, aware of Zac and Malcolm watching me.

"You're really not thinking about making a deal, are you?" If Malcolm paled any more, I worried he wouldn't make it through the flight without getting sick, not that I'd blame him.

My stomach wasn't happy with me either.

"I'm going to look into it." While keeping an eye on Malcolm, I turned most of my attention back to Zac. "You made your deal before your accident?"

"Yes, two weeks before. Bad luck. A drunk driver hit my car. It caught on fire."

I sucked in a breath at the memory of flames eating away at me, and my throat constricted. "Your car caught on fire?"

Malcolm nudged me with his foot, a gentle pressure unlike his previous kicks.

"I got lucky. I suffocated. The fire department stopped my body from burning. There's fewer options if charred."

Malcolm breathed in slow and deep, and

his foot remained pressed to mine. "That's terrible."

"It is, isn't it? I guess it's a good thing I made a deal, else I'd just be dead instead of dead and on my way to a hundred years of servitude. I should be grateful."

I couldn't help but wonder if Zac would still be alive if he hadn't put his soul on the line in the first place.

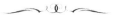

LA GUARDIA AIRPORT reeked of death. I made the mistake of breathing out of my mouth, and the taste of rot drove me to the nearest bathroom. I made it just in time only to discover two freshly dead women touching up their makeup and talking about the weather.

I gulped and sucked air so I wouldn't puke all over them and their designer shoes while they stared at me.

"You don't look so good, sweetie." In life— damn it, I'd be happy if I went through the rest of my life without ever having to think of someone like that ever again—the girl had had red hair, but most of it had fallen out. On my second look, I realized part of her skull was missing.

No one would really blame me if I fainted, would they? I swallowed several times to control my stomach and remembered to breathe out of my nose.

"Yeah, babe. You really don't look so hot," her friend added. "Do you have the flu? I thought I did, but it turned out to be food poisoning. I never thought I'd be one of the ones to die from food poisoning. Not a pleasant way to go, let me tell you. Take it from me. Go to the doctor. I'd probably still be alive if I had."

"T-thanks for the tip." My first steps wobbled, but I made it to the nearest stall without heaving, not that I had much in my stomach, a small blessing. "What are you in town for?"

The women laughed, and one of them said, "A vampire offered to turn me. I'm fresh enough."

Out of the corner of my eye, a flash of red caught my attention in time to get a good look at the red head flipping what remained of her hair over her shoulder. "I'm aiming to be a lich. Go big or go home, I say."

"Good luck with that," I squeaked, retreating into the stall. I turned, locked the door, and swallowed to keep control over my stomach. I wouldn't throw up, not with an audience.

Something wet squished to the floor, and I shuddered.

"I hate it when that happens," the vampire-to-be complained.

"I just don't have the heart for this anymore," her friend replied with laughter in her voice. "At least I didn't spill my guts this time. That's something, right?"

"Just don't hack out a lung again. That's gross."

I swallowed and fought a brutal war against my stomach until the pair left. I ended up on the floor, shaking and hugging my knees waiting for my nausea to ease.

It didn't, not really. Groaning, I got to my feet and emerged from the stall.

They had left a trail of black and red smears on the tile.

I had two realistic options. I could lock myself in a stall and refuse to leave, or I could retreat to Malcolm, kiss my dignity goodbye, find out if fainting from shock was possible, and hide for the rest of my life.

Either way, I couldn't avoid the stink. Shuddering, I sidestepped the mess, did my best to ignore the trail of spots leading to the door, and left the bathroom without throwing up.

Salvation stood in the main terminal along the wall, far enough from the crowd I could spot him around the other travelers. Unfortunately, the hallway had turned into a corpse convention. If I wanted to escape, I'd have to push through a maze of rotters.

Great. Fantastic. Not only would I have to

smell them, I'd have to touch them, too. I could handle it, or I could hide in the bathroom until they left and hope none of them needed to touch up their makeup. Narrowing my eyes, I considered the decaying gauntlet and calculated my odds of reaching Malcolm and the relative safety of the terminal.

It took me a moment to realize I no longer spotted my target, which dropped my odds to approximately zero. I'd hide in the bathroom, and if Malcolm wanted to find me, he'd have to come in after me, because there was no way in hell I was going to push my way through a bunch of rotters without a goal—or a living person witnessing me hit the floor in a faint.

A hand touched my shoulder, and a startled roar burst out of my throat, which ended in a shrill scream. My fur stood on end, and before I could launch myself towards safety, a strong arm wrapped around my waist and kept me from entering orbit or climbing the nearest wall.

"It's just me." Malcolm laughed in my ear. "I was worried. I bet you'd be green if you were in your human form."

"I didn't throw up," I hissed.

"That's impressive. I did."

Huh. I gave Malcolm a lot of points for making that confession. "If I get dead person on me, I will."

Malcolm's living warmth helped, and I swallowed several times and took a few deep breaths, which settled my nerves—and stomach—enough that I relaxed against him. He kept his hold around my waist.

Any other time, it would have bothered me, but he kept me on my feet, for which I was grateful.

"I've never seen so many undead in one place before, not even at night." Worry darkened his tone, and I wondered if I had moved closer to him or if he'd pulled me—or if we'd moved at the same time. "They're congregating. But why?"

"Are they like Zac?"

Without releasing me, he pulled out his wallet, flicked it open and showed me several stained cards. I took them and confirmed they were from Wishing Well. "Seems like it to me. All got similar deals, too—at least the few I spoke to."

A suspicion stirred, and the thought chilled me. "And they all died suspicious deaths?"

"Good guess. A lot of car wrecks."

"One food poisoning." Taking care to breathe out of my nose, I looked over the gathering. After my roar and scream, people should have taken notice of me.

No one gave either of us a second look.

"I've booked us into a hotel not far from here. We'll both feel better after a shower."

If he wanted me to make it to the gala, I'd need the hottest shower I'd ever taken in my life to cleanse me of the reek of death. "If I got anything on my dress, I'm screwed."

"We'll figure something out if you did." Malcolm slid his hand over my stomach before linking his arm with mine. "Let me handle this."

I found it intriguing he thought he could do something about the horde of undead jamming the hallway and spilling into the main terminal. What could—

Malcolm stepped forward and dragged me along with him, and the sea of bodies parted as though they feared the man. A few glanced in our direction but quickly turned away, shuffling to give Malcolm more space. Even those with their backs turned to us made way as soon as Malcolm got within five to ten feet of them.

Magic moved the dead; there was no other explanation for it. But what could frighten those who had already died? There was nothing angelic about Malcolm. Meeting Michael and Gabriel ensured I'd never forget what it was like to stand in the light of the high heavens.

No, the undead feared Malcolm, and I didn't understand why. I appreciated his ability, however. Within ten minutes, we escaped the airport, located a living cab driver, and left for our hotel. My stomach churned the entire time, but I made it to our room before surrendering to the inevitable.

"Sensitive sense of smell?" Malcolm asked through the door.

Damn it. I bet he'd heard every last sound of my misery, too. I gasped for air, bowed my head, and whispered, "I could taste it."

"Change of plan. Try shifting back to human. I can't guarantee we won't meet any more of them at the gala."

Malcolm sounded worried, and that made me hesitate instead of snarling at him for doubting my ability to compose myself in the face of decay.

While part of me resented him telling me what to do, I obeyed. It took several tries to become human, as my body seemed determined to remain as Bastet, and once I succeeded at becoming human, nervousness swept through me until I transformed again.

He wanted me human, but he was getting Bastet with wings instead, with a bonus pile of free clothing and accessories, an equal mix of Egyptian, Ruska Roma, and American—southern American, cowgirl style.

Magic truly worked in mysterious ways.

"Kanika? Are you all right?"

I dug through the pile of Egyptian-centric

apparel and picked a white silk kalasiris overlaid with a diamond pattern of silver chains,
onyx and ruby beads, and gold accents. It
barely conformed to modern standards, covering just enough of my breasts to classify as
public appropriate. In a departure from ancient Egyptian standards, a slit up the right
side offered me better mobility.

Instead of sandals, I wore red heels, something I liked a lot.

Malcolm tapped on the door. "Kanika?"

"I'm fine. I'm getting dressed."

"Do you need help?"

I curled my lip, not that he could witness
my displeasure at his question. "I can
handle it."

To a point I could—and did. When I only
had my hair left to do, I opened the bathroom
door and tossed my new clothes in the direction of the bed.

It occurred to me the room only had one
bed, one I'd have to share with Malcolm. I
wasn't sure what I thought about a mandated
bed invasion, but I could improvise. I liked
warm men.

Malcolm counted.

I thought about the bed for longer than
polite. Mistake or intentional? Either way, I'd
have to live with snuggling up and stealing
Malcolm's warmth, or I'd have to get another
room. Considering I wasn't about to waste a

lot of money for no good reason, I'd have to cope with the tragedy of sharing a bed with a gloriously warm male who had tolerated my drug-induced sleepwalking with patience and grace.

"I'm a blanket hog," I warned.

"I'm well aware of your blanket-thieving ways. It's a risk worth taking, as long as you don't try to kill me in my sleep. I'm expecting my uncle to snoop in my affairs, so we need to maintain appearances. He'll hire someone from the hotel to look into this room, confirm we're sharing it, and come to certain conclusions."

"That we're sleeping together."

"And not in the restful sense, either. My family expects me to behave a certain way. They'll bribe housecleaning to check for condoms, too—and evidence of birth control." Malcolm held his hands up in helpless surrender. "I'm using their misconceptions against them."

For someone who wanted to break his family's curse so much he'd cuffed me with my own suppression bracelet, Malcolm enjoyed screwing with them. "You claim you want to break your family's curse, but it sounds like you'd much rather feud with them."

"Why can't it be both? My desire to break our curse is entirely selfish. I want a family of my own, one that isn't stuck entangled in Stewart family affairs. That's why I have my own business, and that's why I do business as a Montgomery."

"And what about them inviting you to this gala?"

"I'm considered a viable gene donor again."

I grimaced, understanding a little too well what it was like to be on the receiving end of that sort of treatment. "I've walked in those shoes before. I'm sorry."

Malcolm tensed. "You have?"

He'd told me enough willingly, so I saw no reason to hide the truth. "My mother's Egyptian. My father's not. Gypsy, of the Ruska Roma bent, from what I've been told." My magic had done most of the telling, although Malcolm didn't need to know that. "I was shipped to America. Egypt doesn't issue birth certificates for illegitimate children. The United States government adopted me as a refugee, gave me a birth certificate, and granted me citizenship. That's why I don't have a last name. No one told the government officials what it was, just that my name was Kanika. I lived with my aunt until she tried to marry me off to the highest bidder. So, here I am, doing whatever people need so I can scrape by. Today, that involves helping you."

I glared at the bracelet around his wrist, but I found it hard to wake my anger. I was so tired of being angry all the time.

Malcolm remained silent.

Sighing, I shrugged. "You really could have just hired me, you know. I would've helped you."

"Even through a blood test and questioning?"

Laughter rolled out of me, surprising us both. "I've spent my entire adult life trying to convince people I'm actually a sphinx. Not even the CDC cares. They register me as a shapeshifter most of the time. DNA tests show enough human DNA they're willing to ignore the inhuman bits. I'm not worth studying."

"Most would be happy with that verdict."

My laughter died away. "It's all I have. And before you say a word, remember how you looked down at me because I never finished high school. I have a job to do, and right now, that job involves helping you. Try not to get in my way."

Malcolm nodded, and I thought I saw something akin to regret in his expression, especially in his eyes.

SIXTEEN

Elves aren't good enemies to have.

WITH A LITTLE HELP FROM MALCOLM, I finished my transformation into a winged
Bastet. It took us two hours to braid and be-
jewel my hair to match my accessories and
kalasiris, which left Malcolm scrambling to
get changed into his costume.

A king's circlet suited him, as did the polished suit of armor and crimson cloak. The
sword, however, made the man, and I gaped
at him in his full glory. Maybe I resembled a
goddess, but when he stepped out of the
bathroom, he carried the same gravitas as the
Lord of Lies.

Right down to the scabbard, which fea-
tured dueling dragons on a black field, he'd
become something far more than what he'd
been before stepping into the bathroom.

When he drew the blade, the metal sang. I
knew little of swords, but if I were to want

one, it'd be one like his, the long blade tapering to a point, a promise of death wrapped in silvered beauty. Instead of a straight groove down the center of the blade, runes decorated the weapon, Celtic in origin, although I couldn't decipher what they meant —if they meant anything at all.

"Excalibur isn't real, at least as far as I know, but if it were, it'd look like this. A plain enough blade, ironically, but clad in trappings fit for a king. This sword is named Heart Song, for the metal likes to sing, and it was quenched in the heart of the first man it killed, fresh from the forge, wielded by the man who'd made it. Its owner is a friend of mine—well, as much a friend as elves get. He owed me a favor, and elves hate to be beholden to anyone. When I told him about the gala, this is what he chose for me." Malcolm returned the weapon to its sheath, adjusting the belt on his hips so the pommel wouldn't jab him in the ribs.

For a sword with such a violent birth, the pommel stone seemed such a gentle, warm, and living blue. "Sapphire?"

"No. Diamond. The stone began its days clearer than the purest rain, but time and magic changed it—or perhaps its owner did. Elves are even more mysterious than magic."

I found that hard to believe, but I wouldn't

question Malcolm on it. "An elf." I considered the blade, and the weapon confirmed everything I had decided based on speculation and myth; elves were to be avoided and treated with wary regard. "Elves aren't good enemies to have."

"No, they're not. The only good enemy to an elf is a dead one."

Maybe I wouldn't ask anything else about the blue stone, but some questions I couldn't ignore. "How did you befriend an elf?"

"Very carefully."

"Define very carefully."

"It involved a fight, the destruction of my clothes, and more bruises than I care to think about. After I broke his nose, he dragged me to a bar. We got drunk, and—"

I decided I didn't want to know. "I'll take your word on it. What now?"

He chuckled. "We grab a quick bite to eat and head to the gala. Your job's simple. Socialize, keep an eye out, and play nice with the other Stewarts. You can get as rowdy as you want with me, but stick close. Few will want to annoy me too much, so they'll be nice to you to keep from pissing me off. Expect job offers. You can tell them you'll think about it, but don't accept or decline any of them. It'll drive them insane, especially when you refuse them all."

"I can do that. And if they ask about us?"

"Use your judgment. Stick to the truth, though; my family isn't above asking an angel to confirm your words. If they do and you tell them we're living together, it'll help out my cause. You're the first woman to share my home with me, so that'll get their attention."

Since we were living in his house together, and I'd even invaded his bed several times while drugged, not even an angel could truthfully deny my claim. I could even say we'd slept together, misleading them into believing sex was involved.

I'd never blame another woman for assuming a man like Malcolm plus a bed equaled sex. No matter how annoyed I got with him locking my own damned bracelet around my wrist, *I* thought about him and a bed for things other than a good night's sleep.

"And how will your family react to this?"

"They'll pry. That's their nature. We'll have to play it by ear, as it depends on who shows up. My uncle will want to know everything about you. My father will, too, but he'll be more interested in your personal life more than your professional one. My uncle's the opposite; he'll want to know about your professional life more than your personal one, especially since Bubba Eugene's already been gossiping about you."

"How many other relatives do you have?"

"I've got six other uncles, and most of my

great uncles are still around, too. I wouldn't be surprised if they all show up."

I couldn't bring myself to ask why Malcolm avoided mentioning his mother or any of his aunts. What happened to the Stewart women? Were all of his uncles from his father's side of the family? Malcolm's mother wasn't a Stewart, technically, but beyond his father attempting to marry out of the curse and failing, I realized I didn't know half the story.

Was the curse an issue of fertility, or was there something more nefarious behind their inability to sustain their family line? How old were his uncles for him to have so many despite the curse?

I wanted to know, but I couldn't force myself to ask—not directly. Not yet. "Anything else I should know?"

Malcolm's expression darkened, and he gripped the hilt of Heart Song so hard his knuckles whitened. "If Caitlin shows up, she'll start trouble."

One day soon I needed to find out if there was more to that story than broken trust and a threesome gone wrong. The man's eyes, shadowed from emotion, told me there was, but once again, I quelled my curiosity. "And if I start trouble back?"

"Everything I own I would lay at your feet

but for one chance to see her suffer as she made me suffer."

Yep, there was definitely more to the story than I knew. Revenge and anger I understood, and I stared into the stormy eyes of a scorned man. "I can't promise you that, Malcolm. If you truly want revenge, there's only one way to get it."

His eyes narrowed. "How?"

"Live happily ever after without her in your life. Love someone else. Move on. You won't need revenge at that point, because she'll no longer mean anything to you. When someone says her name, don't care. Since she won't mean anything to you, she can't hurt you." The truth hurt, as I needed to do the same in my life. I'd moved on in body, but I still resented my mother abandoning me for being inconvenient. My aunt's attempts to sell me didn't help, either. "It's easier said than done," I confessed.

"Any other pearls of wisdom you wish to impart?"

"Yeah. Don't make a deal with the devil. It'll bite you in the ass."

"Or with Wishing Well."

I grunted. "Deals are nothing but trouble."

The grin Malcolm flashed me sent shivers down my spine. "I like your sort of trouble, so keep dealing. I want to find out how deep this rabbit hole goes."

For some reason I couldn't identify, Malcolm's words unsettled me far more than the deals I had made with the Lord of Lies.

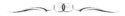

UNFORTUNATELY FOR US, the newly dead left the airport and converged on New York City, resulting in the brutal murders of our appetites. We fled to the American Museum of Natural History, hoping to avoid most of Wishing Well's clients. The stench of decay lingering warned me we weren't finished with walking dead quiet yet.

"There has to be hundreds of them," Malcolm complained as we climbed the steps and passed beneath the stone arch flanked by columns on our way to the main doors. "Why here? Why now?"

The next time I agreed to attend a party, I'd wear pants—pants with pockets. I wanted to know, too, so I held my hand out to Malcolm. "Phone, please."

Malcolm chuckled, retrieved my phone from the leather pouch hanging from his belt, and offered me the device. I took it, drew in a soothing breath, and considered my choices. If I had to dance to the devil's tune, I'd at least make him worth my hassle. I dialed his number while we waited in line for security to let us into the building.

The devil answered on the first ring. "Hi, cupcake. I was starting to think you didn't love me anymore."

Ugh. "Hey, Satin. I have a question for you."

"I'm honored. What do you need?"

"There's an incorporation named Wishing Well. Know anything about them?"

"I do. What's gotten your tail in a kink?"

"A lot of dead bodies."

"Ah. They've made their move, then. I was wondering when it would happen. How many have they ensnared thus far?"

"Hundreds." It worried me although it didn't surprise me that the devil knew of the company. "What's going on?"

"Same old game, new strategy. It's a matter of demons and devils, but some of the contestants are trying new tricks. Do yourself a favor: don't make any deals with them."

I snorted. "Wasn't planning to. I like my soul right where it's at. I've never seen dead people just keep going like this before. What's happening?"

At first, I thought the Lord of Lies wasn't going to tell me, but then he sighed. "They sold their souls, and the new owner isn't letting them move onto the next life, so their souls are animating their rotting bodies. Since they can't finish dying, they'll linger until a practitioner or certain undead, such as vampires, convert them into true undead. It's a rather nasty process, really. If they were following the rules, the souls would be retrieved from beyond death, thus converting the unoccupied body into an undead. Death has been temporarily circumvented."

I thought about it, humming at the idea of eternal unlife. It didn't take me long to figure out I'd rather just die. "And after their bargained time is up? What will happen to them then?"

"They'll find out that souls aren't so easy to return—and that there's a reason I have the reputation I do. My bargains are always good. Misleading at times, yes, but I fulfill them to the letter. It's child's play to take a soul, but another matter entirely to restore it to its rightful place. No, those lost souls will remain lost, even if those behind Wishing Well have their way, which they won't. They're fools, and they're not even clever enough to realize they've done nothing but secure their failure."

"Why do you say that? What are they after?"

"For some reason, a group of them seem to think if they succeed, they'll rise to become my heirs." The exasperation in the devil's voice made me laugh. "They're idiots. I'm a true immortal; my portfolio will never change hands, but there's a certain hierarchy among devils and demons. I'm at the top. As I've decided to pick an heir, some interpreted this to mean I'm entertaining applications. I'm not. So, they meddle in my affairs and annoy me without any hope of success."

Despite answering my questions, the devil left me wondering about far too many things. I couldn't understand why anyone would want to be the Prince of Lies or whatever the hell they'd call someone destined to rule in Mephistopheles's wake should someone—preferably me—wipe him from existence.

The devil snickered, and I suspected the smug bastard overheard my thoughts.

"Indeed," he confirmed. "Go ahead, cupcake. Ask your questions before curiosity gets the better of you."

"Are the undead the reason you're visiting Georgia?"

"Not entirely, but in part."

"There's a lot of dead people, Satin. I think they were murdered. Why? Why try to gather so many souls at once? What's the benefit?"

I wanted to ask why no one valued human life, but I already understood; greed and selfishness kept people apathetic to the plight of others—and greed and selfishness led straight to bad bargains with people wanting to go toe-to-toe with the devil himself.

"Those are better questions. Souls are timeless, but they aren't without limit. Magic can be harvested from a soul. Two souls can meld and make new life. It takes time for the seed of life to grow into a new soul, especially in humans. That's why human infants are so fragile. Their bodies and their souls grow together. I'll even give you a tip: the children who seem wise for their age *are*. They're old souls given a new breath of life, wiped clean and given a chance to live again. They're wise beyond their years because their souls have already grown."

"So that's how it works for a reincarnated soul? Their souls are old but their bodies haven't caught up yet?"

"And now you're asking even better questions. Excellent. Few can reincarnate a soul. I'm one of them—and the only one willing to bargain to make it happen. It's otherwise the whim—or punishment—of God. Well, a god. Anubis can reincarnate a soul, as can Ma'at."

The fact that both other divines he mentioned were Egyptian intrigued me. "What about Bastet?"

"She's known to meddle from time to time. But, here's the catch: a life for a life. That's the price of a soul. That's also why there aren't any ways to truly bring back the dead. It's difficult enough to replant a spent seed of life. A soul burdened with the weight of memories and years? No, no one can do it. Not me, not any of my angelic brethren, no one. It is the one law of the universe without exception. The only way to bring a soul back to life is to wipe it clean and begin anew."

"Then what's the point?"

Satin drew in a breath and heaved a pained sigh, the sound so human it stunned me. "No matter how hard we divines try, the soul remembers with time, usually as dreams. I've learned to stop questioning it. The universe works in mysterious ways, but I have a few theories. My favorite is that no matter how thoroughly I bleach a soul so it can be reborn, it is the seed of life itself that remembers, and that's a gift from the universe itself."

"What will happen to them because of their bargains with Wishing Well?"

"They'll die their true deaths or be locked in limbo. It's best if they die, but I expect the worst. In limbo, they might have a chance to be given their soul's earned rest, but I expect they'll be extinguished beyond anyone's salvation, not even mine. Ma'at won't weigh them, the high heavens won't even notice they never reached the gates for judgment, and while I'm aware of the passage and loss of souls, a bargain made is a bargain kept, and they'll be beyond my reach."

"You can't save them?"

"No, cupcake. I can't. Bargains are unbreakable oaths. But, I'll leave you with this: there are ways a bargain can be manipulated, changed, and essentially broken. I can't do that for Wishing Well's victims. An enterprising individual might be able to do something, however. Should Wishing Well be found to violate their end of the bargain, there's no oath that prevents me from taking over responsibility for a soul."

Interesting. "Let's assume someone were to discover a violation of a Wishing Well bargain. What would happen?"

"It would depend on the bargain made."

I never thought I'd be happy to have taken the time to talk with a corpse. "Let's say someone became a mummy who agreed to work as security for a hundred years, with their soul sold for that period of time."

"A mummy? Someone's meddling with dangerous magic. Mummies are no different from vampires. The soul is lost. That's an invalid bargain. The original soul *can't* be returned to its body. A new soul has taken its place."

"Could two souls occupy the same body?"

The devil hummed. "Occupy, yes. Control, no. One soul would be a prisoner. That's a very dangerous loophole."

If Satin kept being so damned helpful, I might have to like the insufferable bastard. "Why is that dangerous?"

Fingers brushing my arm startled me into squeaking and whirling, my eyes wide. Malcolm nodded behind me, and I realized I'd created a traffic jam near the doors thanks to my conversation with the devil. Blushing, I took my ticket from him, gave it to the doorman, and scampered inside and out of the way.

The Lord of Lies waited until I found a safe spot before he cleared his throat to recapture my attention. "One body, one soul. That's nature's intent. Two souls within one body is unbalanced, chaos without order to control it—or give it purpose. Order without chaos is an equal crime in the eyes of the universe. That is why I am what I am, and that is why I rule over the universe's many hells—and why the high heavens are in eternal conflict with me. Together, we are balance."

"What will happen to those souls?"

"They'll fight for dominance. If I were someone determined to attempt to circumvent the rules of reincarnation, I might try that method. It wouldn't work, but few understand the universal laws."

I thought about it, determining he spoke the truth. While I thought I grasped the basic idea, I suspected I truly knew nothing about the universe and its many rules. "What would happen if I bargained for eternal life?"

"That's a secret. I'll tell you this much, however. All things die eventually."

"Even you?"

"It's not called the end of days for nothing, cupcake." The devil hung up, and for a while, I stared at the far wall without seeing anything at all.

Malcolm's hand clasped my wrist over the suppressor bracelet, giving a gentle tug. "Kanika? What was that all about?"

Pinning my ears back, I handed Malcolm my phone for safe keeping. "Do you ever feel like you've bitten off more than you can chew?"

"Often. Why?"

"I have a really bad feeling about Wishing Well and those people who died. It's not right. I don't know what to do about it, or even if I can or should do anything."

"Do you need to do anything about it?"

I grimaced. "Am I obligated to? No. Should I? Yes. Will I? If I can."

"Why?"

Why, indeed. I straightened, perked my ears forward, and met his gaze. "Because it's the right thing to do. If *my* soul were stolen from me, I would hope someone would do the same for me."

"But they bargained willingly."

"If they were murdered for their soul, it's no longer a fair bargain."

"That's a fair point. So. Where do we begin?"

"We?" I blurted.

"We. It's important to you, so it's important to me, too."

We had lost our minds. There was no other explanation. I forced a grim smile. "Thank you."

SEVENTEEN

You're definitely the black sheep of
the family, King Arthur.

UNLIKE ANY OTHER party I'd ever attended,
the guests had free rein to explore the museum without escort. Guards kept a careful
watch at the doors and checked everyone entering or leaving the building, but they ignored the exhibits, trusting in little signs to
keep people from breaking something. As
warned, everyone showed up in costume, and
the Stewart family proved easy to find; they
wore kilts with matching patterns in blue,
green, and brown.

"You're definitely the black sheep of the
family, King Arthur," I muttered, shaking my
head.

The Stewarts weren't the only Scots in at-
tendance, if the different colors and patterns
of the kilts designated families like I thought
they did.

Malcolm nodded, and the corners of his

mouth twitched. "Caitlin's family are the ones in the black, yellow, and red tartans. The women will likely be wearing period gowns in their clan colors."

I hoped something would go right this evening, although I had my doubts. "She's probably here?"

"Probably." With a faraway look in his eyes, Malcolm turned from the gathering of Scottish men, facing me. I doubted he saw me at all. "She'll probably bring her latest suitor of the hour for a chat to remind me why I shouldn't have left."

"She sounds charming." I flattened my ears, fighting to keep my tail still rather than lashing it. I gave her the record-holding spot for pissing me off in a hurry.

"Sex is a weapon in her hands, and she knows how to use it."

I wasn't above going home with random men, strutting my stuff to catch their attention, but I had standards. While I wouldn't judge someone for exploring more than I liked, I also drew the line at doing more than showing off in tight clothes to stoke a man's interest. Whatever Caitlin had done to Malcolm, I suspected it went beyond a threesome with two men and declining to participate, putting him in an awkward position.

In his shoes, I'd be pissed, too.

"She's pissed at you because you have limits," I speculated.

"Right."

I marveled how one word could convey so much disgust, and I suspected he targeted himself as much as the woman who'd ruined him.

Until he clammed up, I'd dig for answers to help me get a better feel for the woman—and best decide how to rub her nose in the mud. "Since you're one of these picky Stewart men, it goes beyond someone doing something shitty to you. People believe she was—is—it for you?"

"Correct." Wrinkling his nose, Malcolm strode across the lobby, leaving me to follow, and halted at the main museum map. When I joined him, he pointed at the Hall of Ocean Life. The museum was much larger than I anticipated, and when we finally reached the exhibit, I gawked at the monstrous blue whale hanging from the ceiling.

I spluttered, pointing at the model. "That's crazy."

"Life-sized model of a female blue whale. Impressive, isn't she?"

"Very." I sighed, wishing I had the sort of eloquence capable of making difficult questions come out better. "Do you still love her?"

"No, I don't."

I believed him, if only because there was

far too much anger and loathing in his tone and expression to have room for something as gentle as love. "So why do you let her bother you?"

"She's the heiress of a large clan, which would elevate my family's standing. My father and uncle believe the curse will be broken if I marry out of the clan, preserving the bloodline even if I lose my clan name. The Stewart family would gain any of our sons, and the Murray family would keep the girls."

"What does that even accomplish? Wouldn't that mean your family would end up in the same exact position? That's not breaking the curse, that's continuing it, isn't it?"

He shrugged, and I flinched at his worn, tired expression. "Desperate times, desperate measures. That's how I was born—my father married into a different clan. Turns out there were complications. My mother can't have another child."

"And your mother took the Stewart name?"

"No. That's why they think it'll work if I marry Caitlin and take her name."

Not only had she pushed him on a sexual front, his own family wanted the pairing to break the curse? That they had pressured him despite knowing he needed someone loyal to him and only him turned my annoyance into full-fledged rage. "But you need someone who is loyal to you. You resent that she's not, don't you?"

He sighed and nodded. "Exactly."

Between Caitlin and his family, I wanted to pick up a new side business. No one would notice a few disappearances in a family already slated to be wiped out due to a curse, would they? Maybe I could revisit my kidnapping scheme, claim Malcolm as mine, and run off with him. It would take work, but perhaps I could coerce the devil into a different wager to clear out the family curse— on Malcolm and his descendants, rather than the whole lot of them.

Most predators didn't bother me, but the more I heard about Caitlin and the other members of the Stewart family, the less I liked them. "They expect you to marry her, someone you dislike due to her behavior, which implies she's prone to cheating, which means you're being pressured into marrying someone you can't love."

"Stewarts don't marry for love. We marry for survival."

I wanted to punch whomever had fed him that line and made him believe it. My aunt had tried to sell me a similar bad deal, but I'd emerged aware of what she'd done.

Judging from his tone, Malcolm believed if he didn't, his family wouldn't survive.

"I see."

"It doesn't help she views me as her rightful property."

No wonder he wanted some revenge. I had run away to avoid that fate. I spent a few minutes thinking through my options while staring up at the blue whale. One idea intrigued me, and I bet I could hit two birds with one stone. "I can't promise you any revenge, but I might be able to redirect her attention for a while."

"How?"

I smiled. If Caitlin wanted to treat men like property, I'd bring the cat fight to her. "When you spot her, let me know. I'll take care of the rest."

Hopefully, Malcolm would forgive me later. Even if he didn't, I could his ire.

"What are you planning?"

"Trouble." While I had no problems with carrying out my plans while dressed as Bastet, Cleopatra would suit my needs far better—and *she* had the right reputation for what I wanted to do. "I'll need to be human for this. Know a quiet spot I can shift?"

Malcolm nodded. "Follow me."

MALCOLM GUIDED me to an exhibit dedicated to gemstones, and it amazed me the other attendees ignored the treasures it held. Not even the guards cared about our presence in the room, and I found a shadowy corner to transform while he stood guard. I expected trouble with my clothes and shape; sometimes my magic wouldn't change what I wore, leaving me in baggy clothing at risk of falling off.

My unreliable magic decided to cooperate, and I became Cleopatra in truth. My hair, scraggly and abused from my burning, had grown out to adhere to ancient customs, decked out in the silver and gemstone trappings worthy of a pharaoh. My clothes fit better, and my magic stripped all the gold from my kalasiris, exchanging it for silver, too.

I lifted my hands to my head, sucking in a breath when I touched the cold metal of a crown. I frowned, leaned over, and peered at my reflection in the polished glass.

In ancient times, pharaohs wore the cobra crown of gold and blue to war. The khepresh made sense; in a way, I meant to wage war, and I appreciated my magic's honesty. Unlike the traditional khepresh, my cobra rose from the golden base in silver, and lapis lazuli inlays decorated the cobra's hood and eyes.

It weighed far less than the sweeping, monstrous crown representative of Egypt's might. I smiled, for I wore a war crown suiting modern times, reflecting my reality and my heritage in a perfect meld of old and new. Unless I did some research, I wouldn't be able to fully untangle what was modern, but I decided it didn't matter. Past and present mixed together made me who I was, and I enjoyed when my magic acknowledged the reality of my situation.

Straightening, I took a few moments to smooth my kalasiris. "I'm ready."

Malcolm's gaze swept over me. "You're radiant."

"That's a different crown," I quipped, struggling to hide my smile. I failed. "This one isn't nearly as nice."

"Oh?"

"You'll see," I promised.

My altruistic streak landed me into too much trouble, but if I could help Malcolm at little cost to myself, I would. As long as I had a say in the matter, he'd be free to choose who he loved, the curse be damned.

No one deserved to be chained into a loveless marriage, not even him. I'd use my talent at burning bridges for his benefit, and I'd enjoy every minute of it.

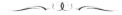

WE EXPLORED THE MUSEUM, and I took childish delight in the exhibits ranging from the deepest oceans to petrified forests. A little bit of everything graced the museum's hallowed halls, and in a detour from the natural, one gallery focused on ancient Egypt and her pharaohs. King Tutankhamun's mummy took the front row seat, and the Gilded Lady accompanied him in all her glory. While far more gruesome than his royal companions, Ginger also took a place of honor in the display.

Ginger interested me the most, as he lacked the trappings of the rich and famous, and was believed to be one of the first known cases of mummification, although I wondered if his remarkable state had been an accident.

"They're spectacular, aren't they?" Malcolm leaned forward to get a better look at the world's oldest Egyptian mummy. "Do you know why he doesn't have a death mask?"

"He wasn't from a higher caste, I presume."

"What about you? If you were mummified per Egyptian tradition, how would you be buried?"

I pointed at Ginger. "Lowest of the low. Bastards like me aren't even recognized as people in Egypt; illegitimate children aren't issued birth certificates. So, I'd be interred like Ginger. Though, to be honest, I have no idea how Egyptians are buried nowadays."

"Charming." Malcolm straightened, leaned towards me, and whispered, "There's a gentleman to the right who keeps staring at you. He's made two phone calls, watching you the entire time. Know him? He's wearing a red and gray suit, looks like he came dressed as a prohibition mobster."

I glanced out of the corner of my eye.

With a touch of gray in his black hair and a dark tan betraying his Middle Eastern heritage, Isaac Asfour was one of the three businessmen I'd fled from as a teen. Then, he'd been thirty-two and openly lecherous enough to frighten me—and make it clear what he wanted in a young wife.

My blood ran cold in my veins. "I know him."

"And? Who is he?"

I swallowed. The shaking started in my hands, crept up my arms, and worked through me until my entire body trembled. "He's one of the three men my aunt considered betrothing me to in exchange for money. Isaac Asfour, a local businessman."

"Seems like I'm not the only one with marriage woes."

If I shook any harder, everyone in the museum would notice something was amiss, and I sucked in breaths through my clenched teeth until I could speak without my voice wavering. "He's the reason I left home."

I wouldn't call it running away. I'd salvage that much of my dignity and pride.

Malcolm eased closer to me, turning his attention back to Ginger, although his body tensed. "What sort of business does he run?"

I shrugged and leaned forward with him, feigning interest in the mummy, too. "I haven't kept track of him, but back then, he dealt with stocks and real estate. I don't know the specifics, but my aunt liked him because he was talking about paying up to a million for me."

Huffing, Malcolm shook his head. "What a cheapskate. You're worth far more than that. Does he know what you are?"

"No. I hadn't had my first shift yet."

"Well, he can't touch you with me around. Just stay close. If he tries anything, I'll take care of him." Malcolm eased his arm around me, placing his palm on the small of my back. In a louder voice, he said, "Shall we take a closer look at King Tut?"

We already had, but I didn't mind a repeat, especially if it meant I got some distance from Asfour. "Sure."

While we browsed the exhibit, Asfour watched me, just like Malcolm had claimed, and the feel of the man's attention pricked the back of my neck. It took all my will to keep from bolting for the door and running for the next state.

"He's definitely following you." Malcolm scowled, and he drummed his fingers against my back. "Do you trust me to take care of him? You'll have to play along."

"I'm asking you to trust me about Caitlin," I reminded him.

"True. I need two things from you to make this work."

"What?" I'd take off my clothes and jump Malcolm with an audience if it meant Asfour would go away and leave me alone for the rest of eternity.

Malcolm didn't need to know that.

"That devil friend of yours—the teleporter. Can you convince him to do you a favor?"

I winced. "He doesn't do favors. He bargains."

"I'll pay him, but I'd like him to show up and play pretend for a few minutes."

When Malcolm learned what he was asking me, he'd kill me for bargaining with the devil again. "Play pretend as what?"

"Your brother."

I lifted my brows. "My brother?"

"I know how men like Asfour tick. They're territorial until a bigger shark claims the turf. If you can claim kinship with a devil, he won't make any moves until he investigates the situation—and find out why he hadn't been told you have a devil for a relative. It'd buy you time, and once we're out of here, he'll have to face me on my turf."

The implication Asfour would hunt for me after the gala worried me even more than his close proximity. "You assume he'll make a move."

"He's looking at you like you're a brood-mare in season—one that he owns. He'll make a move."

I swallowed several times so I wouldn't throw up. "All right. And the second thing you need?"

"Don't question me when I make my move. Just go with it, no matter how angry I make you."

Damn it. He played my game against me with equal finesse. If my living nightmare wasn't stalking me through the museum, I would've stopped to enjoy his ploy.

"Give me my phone."

Malcolm retrieved my cell from his pouch and handed it to me. Calling would expose his idea too soon, so I sent the devil several texts explaining the situation and asked how much cash he'd charge to play along.

My phone rang moments after I sent the last message. "Kanika."

"If the pest is nearby, say okay and listen," the Lord of Lies ordered.

"Okay."

"I can be at the American Museum of National History in five minutes, but it won't be as your brother. The price is for you to accept the role of my choosing without question."

"What is it about men demanding I don't ask questions?" I muttered beneath my breath.

Apparently, I hadn't muttered quietly enough, as the devil laughed. "Smart women with smarter mouths are the most dangerous of creatures. Do we have a deal?"

I hoped whispering would be enough to keep Asfour unaware of Malcolm's plan. "What about the cash?"

"Oh, fine. He'll owe me five dollars for my assistance."

"I'm going to regret this, aren't I?"

"Probably. Lure the man to the most crowded part of the museum and wait for me there. Remember, five minutes."

Why couldn't I do anything the normal way? Making yet another deal with the devil classified me as a desperate idiot. Still, if I had to choose between Isaac Asfour and eternal damnation, I only had one thing to say: Hail Satin, Lord of Hell.

The choice was a no-brainer for me. Death and the devil over Asfour without question.

"Okay," I confirmed.

"Bargain made. I'll see you soon, cupcake.

I'll bring the wife along for the fun." Satin hung up.

Why me? I sighed and gave Malcolm my phone. "You owe him five."

"Hundred? Thousand? Hundred thousand? Million? Billion's pushing it, but I'll deal if necessary. Five what?"

My train of thought crashed into a brick wall, and it took me a shamefully long time to recover. Malcolm would deal with paying five *billion* to help *me*? "Five dollars," I choked out.

Malcolm blinked. "That's it?"

"That's it, that's all." I gulped. "We're to go to the most crowded place in the museum and lure him there."

"The Grand Gallery. People like the cafe and the exhibit, plus it has plenty of space." With his hand still on my back, he guided me through the exhibits, taking a single look to confirm Asfour followed us. "He's really only charging me five dollars?"

"I'm paying most of the bargain," I confessed.

"What's his price?"

"I'm not allowed to question the role he picks. He didn't like the brother idea. He's also bringing his wife."

"He's married? Huh. That's unusual for a devil. Marriage is more up a demon's alley. You're just full of surprises, aren't you?"

So was he. I'd have to do some digging to

find out how he'd learned so much about
devils and demons, since nothing I'd seen of
him implied he did more than work with
them sometimes.

We entered the Grand Gallery, and Malcolm sucked in a breath. "There's Caitlin;
she's wearing the yellow dress with the black
feather headpiece."

I spotted his former lover near the canoe
serving as the exhibit's centerpiece. With
copper hair, blue eyes, and porcelain skin
splashed with freckles, she seemed like the
sort of woman who made demands and got
her way while men worshipped the ground
she walked on. Even when imitating Bastet
on my best day, I couldn't compare.

I didn't even come close.

I had one thing on her, though. A few
sandwiches and a couple of chocolate cakes
would do her a world of good. I could count
her ribs through her dress, and I wondered
how Malcolm hadn't broken her in half. I
took a step away from him, turning until his
hand rested on my hip. "We need to have a
talk about your taste in women. That can't be
healthy. How could you touch her without
breaking her in half?"

"Very carefully. The only number she likes
is zero. She also hates wearing the same thing
twice. That said, she can be nice."

A nice woman didn't emotionally abuse

her lover and torment him, but I'd fight that battle with him another day. I had a better one to fight, one that would compromise some of my morals. "For the record, I'm rather durable."

Malcolm's startled laugh captured the attention of everyone in the room. Turning to face us, Caitlin targeted a glare at him, then her eyes widened in recognition. "Malcolm? You actually came?"

In any other environment, her deliberate refusal to acknowledge me would've counted as rude, especially when her former lover had his hand resting on my hip with no sign of moving anytime soon. I was almost tempted to shift my weight so he'd put his hand somewhere a bit softer and a lot less appropriate. She'd learn her mistake soon.

She approached, and I waited until she was close before I graced Malcolm with my best smile.

"Darling," I murmured, lifting my hand and pressing my palm against the breastplate of his armor. "Is she the woman I need to thank?"

Malcolm could play ball, and so could I, and I meant to push hard until his ex figured out she wasn't included in our party of two.

His eyes widened, but he recovered and smiled back at me. I gave him full points for his acting skills—and the heat in his eyes promised trouble for someone, probably me. "Kanika, this is Caitlin Murray, the heiress of Clan Murray. It's been a while, Caitlin."

"Too long," my new rival replied, her gaze flicking in my direction before gluing back on Malcolm. "Have you finally come to your senses?"

I held my breath, hoping he'd take hold of the opportunity I'd built for him.

"You might say that."

I chuckled at the subtle way he misled his former lover. "You must come to these parties often, Caitlin."

Caitlin's gaze dipped to where my hand rested over Malcolm's heart. *Mine*, my touch declared, and the woman's expression soured. "Who are you again? I'm sorry. I've never seen you before, and as you say, I do come to these parties often."

Had I cared about the opinions of the rich and famous, her words would've hurt. Since I couldn't care less, I grinned and prepared to return fire. "Oh, I'm sure you know how it is. It's so much work running a business. Right, Malcolm?"

"Very much so. We've been busy, Caitlin. I'm pleased you noticed our absence."

The plural reference worked like a charm; Caitlin's eyes narrowed, and she turned her glare to me. "This man is mine."

Malcolm stiffened, and I relaxed, leaning

towards him, drumming my fingers against his breastplate. "Oh? I don't think he got the memo, dear." I widened my eyes, feigning some realization or another. "That reminds me, Malcolm. Will we be back home in time for my desk? I'd like to get my home office set up so I can stop leaving my work in our bedroom."

Had I not witnessed it with my own eyes, I never would've believed Caitlin was capable of paling.

Malcolm chuckled, a deep, sensual sound I found far too intriguing for my own good. "We'll be back in time."

"Good. I hate keeping you awake on nights I have to work late."

"You know how much I don't like it when you're not close to me."

Too bad we were a farce, as I liked the idea of someone wanting me around like that. I returned my attention to my intended target. "How could you let such a fine man go, Caitlin? Seriously, thank you. He's such a gentleman."

"Him, a gentleman?" Scorn darkened the woman's tone, and her expression twisted into something so ugly it amazed me I'd ever thought of her as pretty. "Cute, Malcolm. This must be your pathetic attempt to pay me back for last time. Fine. I apologize. That's what you want, isn't it?"

"He better be a gentleman to my little girl," the Lord of Lies and Master of Hell declared from behind me. "As if I would allow just any man to wed *my* daughter and heir."

Oh hell no. My mouth dropped open, and a strangled squeak emerged.

"Tsk, tsk, cupcake," Satin warned, patting my shoulder. "You promised."

Oh my holy god, what had I done? I snapped my teeth together so I wouldn't scream at having been so thoroughly caught in a trap of my own making—and giving the devil the leeway to make his move without worrying about me protesting his sick and demented choice of roles in my life. "Oh, it's you."

"It's me," the devil replied, striding forward.

With all pretenses of humanity abandoned, Mephistopheles loomed over everyone at ten feet tall, a nightmare given flesh, black beauty married to lethality. If I squinted and tilted my head, he resembled an oversized, muscular human with leathery wings tipped with dark feathers.

Flames licked from his horns and sheathed his body, serving as clothes. Instead of feet, the sharpened points of his cloven hooves dug into his floor, his weight cracking the tiles.

A succubus stood at his side. She wore a

kalasiris a lot like mine, although the silk of hers was darker than the night, a perfect match for her husband.

"Now, what's this nonsense, son?" The devil's gaze landed on Malcolm, and his eyes gleamed with a golden light. "Seems like you have some explaining to do."

Malcolm stood firm in the presence of the devil, and I admired his lack of fear. With a faint smile, he reached into his pouch, pulled out a five dollar bill, and held it out. "Caitlin doesn't quite understand what ex means, sir."

Satin claimed the bill and offered it to his wife. "They have those disgustingly sweet coffees you so love here, my dear."

With a soft laugh, the succubus claimed the money. "And miss all the fun? Now you're the one spouting nonsense. I'll get one before we head home."

While Malcolm had stood firm before Mephistopheles, Caitlin flinched when the devil's gaze landed on her. "I recommend you invest in a dictionary. Ex means if you come between my heir and the man she's hunting, I'll enjoy exterminating you like the bug you are. Also, while you're looking up new words, I recommend you learn the definition of food. It's important for you mortals."

Ouch. I cracked my elbow into the devil's ribs, relieved when the flames didn't burn me.

"Body shaming is rude. Aren't you supposed to be the Lord of *Lies*?"

The devil snorted and shot a glare at me. Miraculously, I survived his wrath. "I can't let any of my incubi play with her if she doesn't put on a few pounds and build some muscle. She'd break. Then my incubi would feel guilty and come crying to me, and I can't stand when they whine because their latest toy broke. It's for her own good. She's half a pound away from hospitalization. I was being nice. You always complain when I'm not nice, but when I'm nice, you complain."

I inhaled, lifted my hand, and pinched the bridge of my nose, well aware I couldn't protest his choice of roles and the absurd idea he'd act like I was his *daughter*. "I can't take you out in public, can I? Why are you here?"

"Someone upset you." Lucifer lifted a hoof and stomped hard enough the tile disintegrated into powder, revealing newly cracked concrete beneath. Glowing red lines filled the gaps, and the stench of brimstone hung in the air. "I don't like it when someone bothers you, cupcake."

"Cupcake?" Malcolm whispered in my ear.

I stepped on his foot, forcing a smile so the devil wouldn't decide Malcolm had bothered me. "Everything's just fine."

"Good. If anyone bothers you, do let me know. I'll deal with it."

Satin shifted his weight and tapped his hoof to the tiles, smashing another one. I wanted to claim I could fight my own battles, but after witnessing the floor's fate, I kept my smile plastered on my face. "I'm sure I can handle it myself."

"Oh, I know you can, but when I leave you alone for too long, you tend to cause excessive property damage I have to pay for. Be considerate."

Great. Everyone was going to believe I was his daughter *and* a walking catastrophe. "You exaggerate."

"Like hell I do. Try not to destroy the entire museum tonight."

I gave up. What else could go wrong? "I'll try not to."

"Good girl." Satin turned to his wife, and his tail coiling with hers. "Come along, dear. Let's go get that awful coffee you so love."

The succubus winked at me. "Try not to die tonight. I think I'm going to like you a lot. You're tough. Also, put a leash on that man of yours. It'd be a pity if he got away."

The pair headed to the cafe while everyone else in the room gaped at me.

Somehow, despite all odds, Caitlin paled even more. "You're the heir of the *devil*? The chosen Heir of Hell?"

Damn it, I really had been tricked. I couldn't even protest thanks to accepting that stupid bargain without thinking it through. I'd lived so long without a mother or a father it never occurred to me someone might want to claim the role as theirs. "So it seems."

Malcolm cleared his throat. "If you'll excuse us, Caitlin?"

"O-of course." Malcolm's ex spun and hurried to the relative safety of her clan.

"Since when were you the devil's heir?"

I made a show of retrieving my phone from his pouch and checking the time. "Ten minutes ago, when I bargained and promised I wouldn't question his choice of roles."

Malcolm smacked his forehead. "What were you thinking striking a deal with the devil?"

"I don't know," I wailed before banging my head into his armored chest. My khepresh fell off, but Malcolm caught it. "I'm so stupid."

"Or brilliant. I'm not sure which. Mr. Asfour would have to be insane to threaten Satan's daughter."

"He's not actually my father. He's a bored menace who thinks it is funny to fuck with my affairs."

"It doesn't matter. He says he is, and no one questions the devil, not about something like this."

"Why not?" I knew why; the devil had told me himself. My heart skipped several beats as realization struck me.

I had signed mystery papers witnessed by two angels, both of whom had seemed pleased with the arrangement I'd made with the devil, their brother. The hotel employee had mentioned the Mephistopheles *family* account. What had I done?

No, I knew exactly what I'd done. I had blind signed my way into one hell of a situation, authorizing Satan to do whatever he wanted, which included adopt me—and potentially bequeath a last name on me, one I'd unknowingly picked. I dialed the devil's number and heard a phone ring across the Grand Gallery.

"Yes, cupcake?"

"You made me sign adoption papers?" I hissed. I wanted to shriek, but I controlled myself, barely.

"I knew you were a smart little girl. You figured it out. Have fun on your date. Don't worry, we won't wait up for you."

He hung up, and I whimpered.

"You look like you need a drink." Malcolm took my phone out of my hand. "Let's find my family, let them see I showed up, and get out of here. We'll make a new plan later—one we don't screw up by making deals with the devil."

"Good idea. Next time, I go with my first plan," I swore.

"Which was?"

I looked him in the eyes and replied, "An investigation of your mouth with my tongue so thorough it needs to be censored."

"You have my attention."

Men. I threw my hands in the air and walked off to locate the rest of the Stewart family.

EIGHTEEN

Slavery isn't legal here.

THE DEVIL'S appearance did nothing to deter Asfour from stalking me through the museum, and while everyone else gave me a wide berth, he drew closer and closer until I wanted to hide behind Malcolm to wait for him to leave. Maniacal determination lit my former suitor's eyes and promised a great deal of trouble for someone—me.

We found the Stewart family in the exhibit with the blue whale, and the instant Malcolm took more than three steps from my side, Asfour made his move, cornering me near one of the exhibits. "Kanika. For a moment, I believed my eyes had deceived me. How did a nameless like you get an invitation to a party like this?"

If I had to play the devil's game, I'd take advantage of it while I could. "Mephistopheles," I corrected, easing my way along the glass display of sea fossils. "I thought it was obvious I'm with someone—someone I live with. What do you want, Mr. Asfour?"

I feared I knew exactly what he wanted, but I hoped he wouldn't pursue it, or pursue me. They were one and the same.

"My property."

Next time, I wouldn't do something as stupid as tell the devil I could handle my own problems. Next time, I'd call him and let him deal with my living nightmare while I made a strategic retreat. With Malcolm dealing with his family, a task equally unpleasant as me dealing with my problems, I couldn't justify dragging him over to serve as my security blanket. "Your property?"

"You. I was promised your—"

"No. I really couldn't care less what asinine agreement you reached with my mother's sister. Slavery isn't legal here, and even if you two attempted to coerce me into an unwanted marriage, I would have immediately filed for a divorce." And attempted to strangle the life out of his perverted body long before he forced me into a bed. "Do yourself a favor, Mr. Asfour. Walk away. I won't be honoring any illegal business deals you've made with my aunt."

Asfour's expression darkened. "You won't speak to me like that again. I have a contract. You belong to me."

"You have a contract I didn't sign, which

means it isn't legal. I know my rights, Mr. Asfour, and I'll request an angel to verify my
statements."

"You wouldn't dare."

How could someone so stupid have so
much power over me? I wanted to hiss at
him, but I settled with a soft huff. "You're an
idiot if you believe that. I have a rather bad
habit of testing my luck. To keep your lecherous hands off me, I'd summon the devil by
misspelling his name in blood. Preferably
yours, but mine'll do."

The asshole laughed at me. "And you
think that man is better? Do you really? I can
—and will—give you everything you could
ever want. I've been looking for you for a
long time. If you think I'm just going to let
you walk away now, you underestimate me.
You belong to me."

No wonder my magic had called forth a
war crown. I needed it. "I don't belong to
you."

He leaned close, and his breath reeked of
alcohol. "According to the papers I signed and
the money I paid, you most certainly do belong to me. We can do this one of two ways.
You can come quietly with me, or my associate will eliminate that man you came
with. One gesture from me, and he is dead.
Have I made myself clear?"

I believed him—in that I believed he'd try

to kill Malcolm for no other reason than associating with me. Clenching my teeth until my jaw ached, I thought it through. The devil had warned me of trouble; he had asked me to avoid destroying the entire museum. Without any actual weapons, I'd be at a disadvantage. If I shifted so I could use my claws and teeth, Asfour would likely desire me even more.

Damn it.

Running and screaming like I'd contracted the plague wouldn't work, so I went with my second plan. Threats probably wouldn't work, either, but I'd try. "If you even think about hurting him, I'll spend my last breath destroying you. Anything in my power, I'll do. I'll even bargain with the Lord of Hell should you try. If you do, you better make certain I'm dead, too. Have I made myself clear?"

"I warned you." Asfour lifted his hand, and if I hadn't known his intent, I would've believed he waved to someone.

I whirled towards Malcolm.

Even when suppressed, gunfire could deafen at close range. My ears rang, and terror choked me. People screamed, reacting to the sound. I doubted any of them noticed Malcolm jerk and fall against his cousin, who caught him with a vehement curse.

Pandemonium swept through the crowd,

and the wise fled while I stood rooted in place, my attention locked on Malcolm, his cousin, and the red drops splashing to the floor at their feet. For a few breathless moments, I thought he'd stay standing, but then Bubba Eugene knelt and took Malcolm with him, and more blood fell, staining both men.

Asfour grabbed my arm and yanked me towards the hallway. The first step jarred me back to my senses, and the trembling fear burned away in the face of my fury. I burned to my bones, my blood boiling while my breath seared my lungs.

I pulled free, turned, and moved, my arm and hand acting without any thought from me. His throat seemed so soft and yielding in my grip. When I squeezed, the give of his flesh in my hold tempted me into adding more pressure.

"What have you done?" I spoke, but I barely recognized my own voice it was so calm and quiet, reasonable despite the tempest raging beneath my skin.

"I told you," he wheezed. "You belong to me. Release me. Now."

I laughed, tightening my grip until he gagged and batted at my wrist, his fingers digging into me in his effort to break free of my hold. If I gave him a chance, he'd overpower me.

As an unarmed woman, if it came down to

a battle of strength, I would lose. I could do nothing in my thin, human shell. But if I shifted, I would win, overpowering him and inspiring the fear he'd inspired in me. It didn't matter if he learned what I was.

Because he'd wanted me, he'd hurt Malcolm. My form no longer mattered. All of them had claws, strength, and teeth surpassing a human's. My magic had spoken; I needed a khepresh, and I would do my cobra crown justice. I had given my sworn word with my threat, and he would pay.

If my magic abandoned me and left me naked, I would bite and claw my way to victory. Tension enveloped my chest, and the suppressor bracelet heated around my wrist.

My anger blossomed and ignited into a conflagration, and the pressure in my chest intensified, rose, filled my throat, and erupted from my lips as a roar.

I had no memory of shifting, but black fur covered my hand, and my claws pieced the tender flesh of his throat. "What have you done?"

Asfour's eyes bulged, and he struggled to speak. A better woman would've loosened her hold. I tightened mine, and his hands fell away from my wrist. He flung an arm in the air.

I expected treachery from him; I'd seen him for what he was even as a child, but I hadn't expected him to give up his property without a fight. The bullet punched into my back before I registered the gunfire. The pain I anticipated didn't come, and I would make use of my window of opportunity. I would tear him to pieces before his cowardice leeched away my life.

No, I would do worse than merely kill him. Branding his face with my claws would come first, so whenever he caught a glimpse of his reflection, he would remember me.

My first slash tore him from temple to jaw on his right side, each claw tearing a jagged line through his skin, too deep for even magic to prevent them from scarring. He screamed, the shrill and pained cry of prey. With a twist of my wrist and another swipe, I carved four grooves across his nose.

Oh, how he bled. Asfour staggered, recoiled, and fell to his knees. "M-monster!"

I spared a moment to glance at Malcolm. Bubba Eugene had him on the floor, and he remained still. Blood stained the floor, though not as much as I thought there should be. Malcolm didn't move, and Bubba Eugene's wide eyes and touch to his cousin's throat, searching for a pulse, told me all I needed to know.

Revenge for the living, revenge for the dead, they were the same.

Asfour would suffer, and if he lived, I

hoped his scars would haunt him as he had haunted me.

"Yes," I snarled. A single step closed the distance between us, and I lashed out, marking the left side of his face the same what I'd marked his right.

A rasped growl behind me distracted me from my prey, and I answered with a snarl of my own, straightening and twisting around, Asfour's blood dripping from my claws.

The golden death mask of King Tutankhamun glinted in the museum's overhead lights, and the hoods of his crown's cobras glowed crimson. The mummy clutched a woman's throat, lifting her up, and her skin blackened where his wrappings touched her flesh.

A gun fell, bounced off her shoe, and discharged with a bang.

Ginger scampered across the room on all fours and crouched at my feet. The hollow sockets of his eyes burned with a golden luminescence. A whimper behind me reminded me of Asfour's presence.

"I'm not finished with you yet," I stated, my voice as dead as the risen mummies. Facing him, I stepped forward, knelt, and slashed open his suit, cutting red lines down his chest. "Tell me of the contract."

"You're mine. Mine! Obey me, as is your place."

I dealt with a fanatical madman, and I bared my teeth, hissed, and swiped with my claws again, adding more scratches to his collection. "I'm my own. You'll speak, Isaac Asfour. Tell me about the contract."

A woman shrieked, then her cry cut off in a gurgle. The thump of a body striking the floor cooled my fury enough to hold my temper in check. I didn't strangle Asfour.

I wanted to.

An eye for an eye balanced the scales, and for the moment, we stood even.

"A million," he gaped. "I paid a million for you, to your blood. It binds us, you and I."

Footsteps drew close, and the shriveled remains of King Tutankhamun flanked me. Ginger shoved his head and golden hair beneath my hand, shifting and squirming until I gripped his shoulder. The mummy radiated living warmth.

"We're not bound." I lifted my hand and beheld a true Pharaoh of Egypt, ancient long before the birth of Christ. Respect would've been wise and prudent, but I had greater concerns. Mummies protected, and there was only one I wished I could safeguard from harm. "Protect my fallen."

Magic worked in mysterious ways, and King Tutankhamun bowed his head and glided to Malcolm. The Stewart men wisely scattered before the mummy, leaving Mal-

colm alone on the floor. I wouldn't blame
them for abandoning him, not in the face of
the living dead—the dead who heeded my
words without question.

"Ginger."

The mummy leaned against my leg and
rasped something in ancient Egyptian, two
words I didn't know yet understood all the
same. He named me his queen, a pharaoh in
my own right, although I didn't understand
why. I supposed it had something to do with
my crown, my khepresh, and my declaration
of war.

"Take this filthy man out of my sight." I
wanted to kill Asfour, but I restrained myself.
It took several long, tense moments before I
could force myself to restrain the mummy,
too. "Don't kill him. He should live a long life,
remembering the mistake he made today." I
lowered my voice to a whisper. "If Malcolm
dies from your machinations, you and your
descendants will regret it until the end of
days."

Ginger pounced, and Asfour screamed,
flailing to escape the mummy. At first, I
thought them equals in strength, but then
Ginger fisted his desiccated hand and
clubbed Asfour upside the head. The man fell
limp to the floor.

I gave the mummy space, my teeth
clenched so hard my jaw ached.

Grabbing Asfour's foot, Ginger dragged him across the museum in a haphazard zig-zag. The first time the mummy collided with an exhibit, I grimaced. The second time, the display toppled, and I sighed. I watched until the pair disappeared through the doorway leading to the next gallery.

I turned to King Tutankhamun. "Does he live?"

The pharaoh bowed, and the glow surrounding his death mask faded. Unlike Ginger, he didn't speak, and I wondered about that. The mummy bowed again and stepped away from Malcolm. Every eye in the room watched me. Many had stayed, more than I'd expected. I spotted Caitlin with Malcolm's clan, her mouth hanging open.

I ignored them and strode to the man who'd been shot because of me, kneeling at his side. Blood stained the floor, although not as much as I feared. I wiped Asfour's blood away on my kalasiris so I wouldn't touch Malcolm with it. Most of the crimson came from his nose, which puzzled me. With a shaking hand, I checked his throat for a pulse.

He lived, and my breath left me in a sigh. Slicing through the drawstrings of his pouch, I retrieved my phone. My first call requested an ambulance.

My second summoned the devil, and he didn't leave me waiting for long. In his silent way, King Tutankhamun bowed to the Lord of Hell.

"I left you alone for an hour. Now look at this place." Satin snorted flames. "What do you require?"

I pointed at Malcolm. "Take care of him. You're paying the bill."

"I am?"

Hissing, I flattened my ears and bared my teeth. "You are."

The devil threw back his head and laughed. "Why not? Very well. Any other demands?"

"I want names. All involved with his shooting this night. I want their names, so I might make it clear they've chosen poorly."

"That's within your power to learn, don't fear. It'll be a satisfying hunt for you, cupcake. Give it a few minutes. The bloodlust will fade—as long as no one else decides to act like prey. Also, you might want to get that looked at." The devil took his turn pointing, and I frowned, following his finger to my chest—no, shoulder, which had a rather bloody hole through it.

"That's going to hurt later," I predicted.

"Indeed." The devil sighed. "How troublesome. I suppose I better stick around, just in case someone else gets a stupid idea. Right, Caitlin Murray?"

Malcolm's former lover froze, her eyes widening. "R-right."

"Good girl. Run along. And Caitlin? However tempting, I wouldn't touch that gun if I were you. I'd really hate to wreck that pretty face. My claws are sharper than my heir's, and they're much longer, too."

The woman fled, and the devil cackled, a bloodcurdling laugh. "Well, I guess that's a wrap."

I scowled. "I'll say."

"You really should put a bandage on that wound, dear. Bind it nice and tight before you bleed out. I'd hate to tell your mummy you died."

My cheek twitched. Maybe if I kept quiet, he'd stop.

"It's my dry sense of humor, isn't it?"

King Tutankhamun groaned and shambled in the direction of his exhibit, and I swore I heard the mummy cursing in ancient Egyptian.

"Someone must have slipped him decoffinated coffee when he got up today. So grumpy. Relax, Tutankhamun. No need to be so wound up."

No one would blame me if I tried to kill the devil, would they? King Tutankhamun wisely kept walking away.

"He has a rather stiff sense of humor,

doesn't he? I bet he just doesn't have the guts to face me."

Death would be a far better fate than enduring another one of the devil's puns. "What did I do to deserve this punishment?"

Damn it, he had me doing it, too. I bowed my head, sighed, and regretted everything.

"Don't feel bad, cupcake. They're groaners."

I WENT from fine to whimpering in the blink of an eye as I made friends with the floor. One uncontrolled shift later, I bled as a human rather than a bipedal feline with a mummy problem.

Well, I still had the mummy problem. Ginger crouched beside me, staring at me with his hollow sockets. The golden light had dimmed, leaving two faint, shimmering orbs in place of his eyes.

"You've made a friend." Satin knelt beside me and placed his clawed hand on my shoulder, applying pressure to my gunshot wound. "Since you dodged death by fire, you had to test your luck against metal?"

"Sure. How's Malcolm?"

"Better off than you are, cupcake. Turns out that armor he's wearing packs a layer of kevlar beneath the metal plating. He cracked his nose on his cousin when he got the breath knocked out of him. The fall stunned him, then he stayed down with a little help from his clan—safer for him that way. I don't think anyone expected Asfour would try to kill you, too. That's what makes mortals so much fun. They're unpredictable. I expected chaos and destruction, not a bloodbath."

Talking helped distract me from the intensifying throb in my shoulder. "How much did you know?"

"Know? Nothing. It's against the rules to peek into matters like this—it's also not worth the headache. I guessed, I lurked, and I listened. I'm naughty like that, listening in on private conversations. You let him off lightly. I'm so curious to learn how potent your curses will become. Now, that leads me to my one problem with this situation. You called an ambulance for him when you're the one who needs it. I suppose I'll have to interfere."

"Interfere?"

"Like this." The Lord of Lies lifted his hand and stabbed his finger into my shoulder. Blue flames shrouded his arm and pierced my skin. I yelped at the shock of heat, which cooled to numbing ice. "A fringe benefit of my origin. I'm sure you won't mind most of the consequences. You won't bleed to death, which is important. Don't worry. You'll stop glowing in a few hours."

I turned my head to get a better look. My blood burned, and blue flames danced over my skin. "The last time this happened, I lost all my hair. I don't want to lose my hair again, it just grew back," I wailed.

"Hellfire blended with a bit of heavenly light. Those pesky angels upstairs hate when I do this. It reminds them I have the same tricks they do without nearly as many of their rules and scruples. Of course, I never work for free, but this time, you were working in my name. Consider it compensation for your efforts. I do tend to do things that benefit me in some fashion or another, and it'd be annoying if I lost my heir on her first public appearance, especially after such a lovely display. To wake King Tutankhamun in his full glory surpassed most of my expectations. I look forward to watching you grow—and seeing what you're capable of when your anger doesn't consume you."

Ginger hissed at the devil, and golden dust spilled from the gaps in his wrappings, swirling around him without touching the floor. The mummy opened his mouth, and emerald scarabs skittered out. They congregated around Ginger's throat and clustered over his heart. "Ginger stay. Zezemonekh stay."

The devil snickered. "King Tutankhamun

likely finds it offensive a mummy of non-royal heritage dares to be his equal."

Ginger lifted his hands, and dust and sand coiled around his throat. The orbs in the mummy's empty sockets flashed, blinding in its intensity. When I could see again, a gold and emerald usekh covered his shoulders and hugged his neck, and a triad of scarabs rested over his heart. Ancient linens brightened to pristine white, reformed as though new, and golden hair braided into tiny strands fell to his jaw, each tipped with a silver bead and a teardrop emerald.

"Then again, he probably didn't want to end up your servant."

I must have fallen unconscious and dreamed; that seemed more likely than the Lord of Hell sticking his finger through my shoulder and igniting my blood so it burned blue. Ginger spitting scarabs and rejuvenating to a mummy in full glory had to be a figment of my imagination right along with King Tutankhamun's appearance.

Maybe I had lost my mind earlier than I thought. I couldn't be the devil's heir. I must have made the whole thing up. Oh! Maybe I had fainted in the airport, overwhelmed by the wretched stench of the recently dead.

"If that makes you feel better." Satin patted my shoulder, which hurt like hell.

"I'd feel better if you stopped doing that."

A siren wailed in the distance, and the devil rose to his hooves. "You. Bring the paramedics here. You, deal with the police. Tell them the name of that miserable human who caused this trouble."

"Isaac Asfour," I provided.

"Isaac Asfour. Do make sure the clansman goes to the hospital. Try not to ruin that armor getting him out of it. Its owner tends to carve out pounds of flesh in payment for damage to his property. Oh, cupcake? I'll hold onto your male's sword. It wouldn't do if *that* fell into the wrong hands. Try not to wreck the hospital. It'll be annoying enough making a suitable contribution to the museum to convince them to look the other way."

"Sure." I could humor my twisted psyche. How hard could it be to avoid wrecking a hospital? I'd probably wake up in the airport terminal gagging over the reek of week-old corpses.

"Good girl. I'll check in with you later."

"Please don't," I begged.

The devil laughed and disappeared.

NINETEEN

He's harmless.

IT WAS difficult to deny reality when it hurt so much. Add in the trip to the hospital, the brace and cast to immobilize my shoulder, and the staggering stack of paperwork, and I couldn't pass off my situation as a really bad dream. To make matters even more complicated, Ginger refused to leave my side. The mummy shed piles of golden sand wherever he went, much to the nurses' dismay.

"Miss, could you please ask your friend to wait outside? Please?" Nurse Abigail sighed, looking up from my medical chart. "We'll be at this all night otherwise."

While I thought Ginger wasn't bothering anyone and behaving himself despite his tendency to shed sand, I regarded the mummy with a weary sigh. What was she expecting me to do? 'Stay' had gotten him to lurk in a corner, and he'd chased the ambulance, running on all fours like a demented, linen-wrapped dog.

Maybe I could relocate my mummy problem for a while. If Nurse Abigail wanted anything else from me, she'd be disappointed. "Ginger, could you find Malcolm and guard him, please?"

The mummy hissed. "Future King?"

Oh dear. If Malcolm found out, he'd probably get upset with me. It wasn't really lying, was it? Given half a chance and the removal of my self-imposed rule about sleeping with or dating clients, I'd pounce. I could express my desire to get the unobtainable to an old dead guy wrapped in rags and get away with it. Maybe. "That's the idea."

Ginger rose to his full height and strode across the room, moving with the same grace and dignity as King Tutankhamun. The sand slithered after him, leaving no evidence of the mummy's presence in the room. Startled cries in the hallway amused me enough I grinned.

"What was that?" the nurse grumbled.

"His name is Ginger. He's the first Egyptian mummy; he used to be on display at a museum until he woke up." Nurse Abigail didn't need to know I'd been the one to wake Ginger, although the specifics of how I'd done it remained a mystery. "He's harmless."

I was such a liar.

"He's an actual mummy? Now I've seen everything. Anyway, back to you. You got lucky; the bullet clipped the bone and cracked it, but otherwise, it punched through fairly clean. As long as you take your medication as prescribed and do physical therapy as ordered, you won't experience much if any impairment."

"Huh. I thought the doctors gave the verdicts. Cool. I got the super nurse." I wrinkled my nose and glared at the bulky cast and rod assembly keeping my shoulder immobile. "How long do I have to wear this thing for?"

"That depends on your health insurance; if you qualify, a bone-trauma specialist can mend the bone. The treatment takes several hours and is very expensive. There are few mages in the medical field who can do that level of work. If you don't qualify, expect at least four weeks. That's considered a normal recovery time for an injury of this nature."

The thought of four weeks in a cast made me shiver. To make things worse, I wouldn't be able to shift until the cast was gone. For whatever reason, my magic could handle clothing and basic restraints, including handcuffs, but casts and broken bones caused problems. Broken bones I could shift through, but I didn't heal faster. It actually slowed my recovery; the last time I'd broken something and shifted, it had cost me at least a week.

It also hurt so much I could barely do it. If I wore a cast, the pain became so intense I couldn't shift at all.

I loathed the idea of spending four weeks stuck in my human form. Sighing, I poked the unwieldy monstrosity. "That's going to be so gross when it comes off."

"It won't be too bad. A shower will fix you up good as new. The itching'll be what gets to you. Normally, we would have handled your insurance first, but we try to address gunshot wounds immediately. Let's begin. Give me your full name, please."

Why couldn't my entire day just have been a bad nightmare? When I told the nurse my new last name, she'd have me committed—or accuse me of lying. "Kanika Mephistopheles."

Nurse Abigail's eyes widened, and she gaped at me. "Pardon?"

I spelled it for her, and since I was doomed to answer a lot of questions anyway, I gave her the devil's phone number and policy number. "Please don't misspell it on any of the forms; he hates that. You'll also have to call him, I'm sorry. It's part of the policy agreement. And yes, the number on file works, and yes, that is actually the policy number."

The woman took it better than I thought; she wrote down my answers, stuck to asking for information, and while she seemed curi-

ous, she didn't pry into my private affairs. It
took an hour to sort through the paperwork,
and by the time we finished, I stifled yawn
after yawn. Nurse Abigail spoke to the devil
on the room's sole phone, and he manifested
in the room in a cloud of steam and brimstone, disguised as an incubus in a suit.

I hated the smell of brimstone. It burned
my nose and made my eyes water.

"This is easier than dealing with the
phone," the devil announced, sticking his cell
in his pocket. "You look tired, Kanika. Maybe
that cast will keep you out of trouble for a
few days. Where's that man of yours?"

Poor Malcolm. "He's not my property."

"Sure he is. He was yours the instant you
bent over the engine of an SUV, slapped a
mystical ball and chain around his wrist, and
took him to your lair."

My lair? Since when did I have a lair?
When I wasn't quite so tired, I'd have to teach
the devil about the concept of professionalism, morals, and an appropriate sense of humor. I couldn't really argue about the bent
over the engine part of his speech, as I'd done
just that to get Malcolm to pull over. Oh well.
"Good question. I asked Ginger to keep an
eye on him."

"Perhaps you should inform Ginger he
can return to his slumber."

"Couldn't he if he wanted, like King Tutankhamun?"

"Well, yes. He could."

"Ginger has free will?"

"Yes."

I dismissed his complaint with a wave of my hand. "If Ginger wants to go back to sleep, he can. Ask him what he wants to do. I'm not his master." Turning my attention to the nurse, I plastered my best smile on my face. "Can I leave now?"

"In the morning," she replied, checking the display of her phone. "It's too late to discharge you unless you have an official nocturnal rating, which you don't. We start processing discharges at eight for diurnals."

The devil checked his watch. "Two hours, cupcake. You'll survive for that long. While we're waiting, I'd like to speak to her surgeon, please. I'd also like a copy of her medical records; you'll find the authorization forms within the insurance policy. Kanika, I'll be back in time for your discharge, so don't think you can run off without me. Try not to wreck the hospital."

"Why do you think I'm going to wreck the hospital?"

"Where to begin? I'll start with the rental car and the museum. What can go wrong does go wrong with you, and when they go wrong, they go really wrong. No trouble. Wait here quietly."

How rude. I huffed, turned my head so I wouldn't have to look at the damned devil, and gave him my best dose of the silent treatment. Neither the rental nor the museum were my fault. How could he hold those incidents against me?

"Please come with me, Mr. Mephistopheles."

"No trouble," Satin ordered before following the nurse out of the room.

What sort of trouble did he expect me to get up to in a hospital? Then again, boredom tended to make me do things I regretted later. Within ten minutes, left alone with nothing to do, my appetite and curiosity got the better of me. Exploring the hospital in search of something to eat was *not* causing trouble. That I needed to find Malcolm first to reclaim my wallet meant nothing.

I was in a hospital. Hospitals were safe, quiet places of healing. How much trouble could I get into?

Stupid Satin, toying with me because he could.

ROAMING around wearing a hospital gown drew a lot of attention. The nurses I met scowled at my cast, smoothed their expressions, and questioned me. When I told them I was going to be discharged at eight, they smiled and returned to their work.

I explored the entire floor without finding Malcolm or Ginger, much to my disappointment. Instead, I found Isaac Asfour, and his smile chilled and annoyed me.

"Well, well, well," he murmured, looking me over. Unlike me, he wore a suit—a different suit from the one he'd been wearing at the museum. "It seems the tables have turned in my favor."

Wow. Had Asfour always been so stupid? I suspected so, since a much younger version of me had run away to escape him. "You just can't take no for an answer, can you?"

"Why should I? You're even more valuable than I had ever hoped. You know what they say. Great risk brings great reward, and I've already killed the man who thought he could interfere. You look half dead. Don't worry about a thing. I'll take you home and care for you. You're worth everything to me alive, but if you fight me, healthy is optional."

I considered the ramifications of murder. Could I pull it off in a hospital, or would the staff stop me before I managed to strangle the life out of him? The cast would make killing him a challenge, although I enjoyed the idea of taking my time with his demise. "You have got to be the dumbest man I've met in my entire life. Go away, please. Your stupidity might be contagious. Also, if you even think about touching me, I'll scream. If I scream, it'll catch everyone's attention. After I'm done screaming, I'll take you to court, request an angel, and make it my life's mission to ruin you beyond redemption. I won't stop there, either. I think I'll like making your life as miserable as I can possibly make it. Let me use small words so you can understand. No. I won't cooperate with you. Leave, Asfour."

"I can't do that."

"There are millions of single women. Find one who won't mind your idiocy."

He barked a laugh. "I already paid for you. Why should I waste my investment?"

Between Asfour and the devil, I had a stinker of a headache. I was willing to bet Satin knew Asfour was around, which explained why he thought I might wreck the building and otherwise cause trouble. With that in mind, his insistence I sit tight and wait made a great deal of sense.

Go figure. The devil was capable of giving sound advice. I sighed and shook my head.

Why did so many men—of most species— have to be entitled morons?

"Cooperate, Kanika. It's for your own good."

"No. Leave me alone." I did the only thing

I could without lowering myself to public displays of violence. I spun on my heel, staggered from the cast unbalancing me, and walked away.

He followed me. Surprise, surprise. His shoes tapped the tiles, and I fantasized about spinning and smashing my fist into his jaw. Hitting first would make me the guilty party, so if I wanted to get the best revenge possible, I needed to wait until he made his move.

"No," I repeated.

How many times would I need to tell him before he'd actually listen? "Are you incapable of understanding multisyllabic words? No. Leave me alone. I'll begin with a restraining order. Should that not dissuade you, I'll make it my life mission to make sure everything you touch fails. If you walk away and never look back, I might not view you as an enemy. If you stay, I'll dedicate myself to ensuring you'll never be able to go out in public without being mocked. Your former associates will laugh when they hear your name." I sidestepped and turned so I could meet his gaze. "Are we clear?"

"What makes you think you're capable of doing what you say?"

Bastard. "I'm willing to make deals with the devil. You tell me."

"That was a cute trick, calling a devil to pretend he's the Lord of Hell. You'll have to tell me how you pulled that off—and give me the secret to conjuring those mummies. They gave me rot."

"What a pity there's a cure for that. You're delusional. Too bad there isn't a cure for that."

"Enough talk. I spent a great deal of money to have you, and I will." He reached for me, his expression turning coldly neutral.

Screw it. I'd pay any fines for rearranging his face, and spending a few days in jail beat the alternative. The cast hampered me, but I put all my weight behind my fist, connecting with his nose. "I said don't touch me."

Blood sprayed, and Asfour cried out, clutching at his face. "You whore!"

"Why is it men like you always call women whores when they don't get their way?" Shaking my hand, I took a step back. My knuckles hurt, and I hoped I hadn't broken a finger punching the idiot. "I warned you to leave me alone. You only have yourself to blame."

Asfour reached into his pocket and pulled out a black device. At first, I thought it was an oversized cell phone, but then I recognized the twin prongs.

Taser.

I drew in a breath to scream and yanked my fist back to give him a second taste of my knuckles.

The weapon discharged, and I swore to

never again would I underestimate a stun gun. Agony rippled through me, and I collapsed to the floor in a convulsing heap.

ONLY AN IDIOT ATTACKED someone in a hospital, which made me equally guilty as Asfour, thus deserving the smack down the staff would dish out the instant they got a hold of me. The stun gun hurt like hell, but I clung to consciousness, although my twitching body refused to obey me. Asfour crowed his laughter, kicked me in the ribs, and reached down to snatch a handful of my hair.

I'd been to enough hospitals to recognize there were few things as stupid underestimating doctors or nurses. Those who could heal learned the finer points of tearing someone apart, and when predatory centaurs were as likely to work in a hospital as a mundane human, there was usually someone around capable of breaking up a fight.

A lion roared, and a flash of tawny fur drew my attention to the centaur moments before he reared up and batted Asfour off his feet with a single swat of his plate-sized paw.

Blood dripped from the lion's claws and splattered to the floor.

To round out the hospital's contribution to the brawl, a pair of pixies, each no taller than six inches, dove into the fray, dodging the lion. They spun and fluttered their wings, and glittery dust billowed in my face.

I held my breath, aware the instant I breathed in any of the dust, I'd be a goner. If I could avoid most of it, I'd be able to function.

Pixie dust wasn't my friend, and I avoided the damned stuff like it was the plague. Apprehension bloomed into full-fledged fear. My lungs burned, and another convulsion tore through me. I gasped, and a sweet scent filled my nose.

A tingle spread from my nose and mouth, and my muscles relaxed, soothing away the shaking the stun gun induced. Within ten minutes, I'd be lucky if I remembered my own name.

Damn it, I hated pixie dust. If I wanted my head in the clouds, I'd fly.

"That's enough," the lion centaur snarled, swiping the stun gun out of Asfour's hand and sending it clattering across the floor. The prongs tore out of my side, and I yelped at the unexpected pain. I shuddered but couldn't force my body to do what I wanted, which involved getting as far from Asfour as I could before the pixie dust sucked me under.

The lion smashed the stun gun with his paw. "How dare you bring violence to my hospital!"

Asfour babbled something about how he

needed to teach his property to behave.

I'd make him pay for that later.

"Wrong answer." With his tail lashing, the centaur pinned Asfour to the floor with his front paws. "Chains for this one. Send for a trauma specialist to do a full set of tests on the woman. File an official complaint and make this male responsible for all payments for her care. Once she's under observation, send for the police. I'll file the assault and harassment charges personally."

A nurse hurried off to obey the lion's orders. Someone else spritzed neutralizer in my face and everywhere the pixies had dusted, ensuring no one else would be contaminated. Once the dust no longer glittered and pink residue coated my skin and hospital gown, the centaur helped me to sit up, careful of my cast.

The numbness spread, sinking deep to my bones. "Not his," I slurred.

When the pixie dust stole away my will, I wanted someone to know I wanted nothing to do with Asfour.

"I heard you warning him to leave you alone. Don't try to stand. You took quite the jolt."

Did the centaur really think I could even try to stand? I giggled. "Did I wreck anything?"

"Only his nose."

Another giggle built in my chest and slipped out. "Doesn't count. Only not allowed to wreck the hospital. Damned nice pixies. Stupid dust." I tried to think, but someone had stuffed fluffy warm cottony balls in my head. "I should need wings to fly," I complained.

"Oh dear. You haven't had much exposure to dust, have you?"

"Sus..." my tongue tied, and I blew raspberries in my effort to regain control of it. "Not good."

"You're susceptible?"

"That word!" I chirped.

"I see. How are you feeling?"

Was he serious? I laughed. "Just swell."

"And your shoulder?"

My shoulder? I had two of them, and I liked them. They made my arms work. The lion centaur nodded towards the cast. "Oh, that shoulder?"

"Yes. That one. How is it feeling?"

Huh. It did hurt when I paid it too much attention. "It's a bit ouch. I forgot. Not cool. It's ouch."

"I'll make sure your file mentions you're susceptible to pixie dust." The lion centaur sighed, twisted around, and flagged a pair of nurses who brought a gurney with them. "Run a scan to find out if our patient has a pain inhibiting reaction to pixie dust. If so, dose her with our best grade dust instead of traditional painkillers."

I scowled at the gurney. "I can walk."

"You probably can, but this is more fun."

"I thought doctors hated fun."

"I rather like fun, actually. If you're good, I'll ask one of the floor nurses, Carl, to pop a few wheelies for you on your way out when you're in the wheelchair."

I'd never done a wheelie before, not even when I'd done my few stints in a wheelchair leaving other hospitals. While I thought the concerns of liability were taken to the extremes, wheelies did seem entertaining. "Okay. I've never done one before."

"If you're here for long, maybe if you're really good, I'll have Carl take you up to the physical therapy floor for a wheelchair race."

"That sounds irresponsible."

"It helps keep patient morale up. Don't worry, we're careful, and those too sick or injured to participate get to watch."

"You have got to be yanking my chain. Not nice."

The centaur laughed, helped me to my feet with the aid of one of the nurses, and convinced me to sit on the gurney. "Only a little. Sometimes we do have wheelchair races, but the racers are physical therapy patients. That shoulder will need therapy unless you qualify for a magical reconstruction of your shoulder. Even then, you'll have to work the muscles to help them heal. It's possible you might get to participate in one."

Huh. I'd finally met a doctor without an allergy to fun and with a surviving sense of humor. "Are all doctors so weird?"

"Not at all. You just go with the nurses. They'll take care of everything. You don't have to worry about that other patient. He won't bother you again."

"Isaac Asfour," I spat.

"Just relax, Miss Mephistopheles. You'll be back on your feet in no time."

How nice. The doctor knew my name. Relaxing seemed like a good idea, especially since I wasn't twitching anymore. The gurney was also much more comfortable than it looked despite my cast getting in the way.

One of the nurses tricked me into lying down, and once I stretched out, sleep appealed far more than anything else. Who needed to walk when naps were an option? Naps were the ultimate form of relaxation, so I indulged. If anyone scolded me, I'd blame the doctor, which was several steps up from having to blame the devil. Old dogs—and cats—could learn new tricks, although it occurred to me staying out of trouble in the first place would do me a lot of good in the long run.

Oh well.

TWENTY

I hadn't even let the poor man get to
a bed before using him.

I DEVELOPED a love-hate relationship with
pixie dust. I loved the disconnect, which offered refuge from my shoulder. While I was
aware it hurt, the pain didn't matter. I floated,
lost in the moment. On the other hand, I recognized I tended to do whatever anyone
wanted, often obeying before realizing something had been asked of me.

Time also had a tendency to sneak off
without my permission, and when I finally
managed to reestablish a connection with reality, my cast was gone. I liked that.

What I didn't like nor understand was
how Malcolm had been reduced to serving as
a living bed. Why was he sprawled beneath
me on the couch while I used his shoulder as
a pillow? I blamed the drugs. Drugs, including pixie dust, turned me into a bed-in-

vading monster. Technically, I hadn't even let the poor man get to a bed before using him.

Had I been in control, I would've at least let him go to bed first.

Then again, did it even matter? He kept me toasty warm, nothing hurt, and I was a little dazed and a lot sleepy. Was moving necessary? Malcolm slept beneath me, his breaths slow and even. He didn't snore. Not snoring rose to a whole new level of importance in my basic requirements for a relationship.

Careful to avoid using my left shoulder, I used my right arm to lurch upright. While I managed to sit up, Malcolm hooked his foot around my leg, which did a good job of trapping me on the couch with him. I supposed it counted as fair payback, although I wished I remembered invading his personal space in the first place.

I twisted around for a better look, tugging to pull free. The bastard tightened his hold. I scowled. What the hell? I gave a jerk to free my leg, wrinkling my nose at my odd captivity.

Malcolm proved a rather persistent foe in his sleep, and he captured my other foot with his to prevent my escape.

"Go back to sleep," Malcolm muttered. "It's not time to get up yet. The alarm hasn't gone off."

Alarm? What alarm? I yawned, abandoning my effort to reclaim my legs in favor of getting a feel for my surroundings. Light streamed in through a picture window, the gauzy curtains doing nothing to keep the sun outside where it belonged. I eliminated a home as our locale; the layout reminded me of a long-stay hotel, but a good one with a dedicated living room. "Where are we?"

Malcolm cracked open an eye. "Don't remember?"

I shook my head. After struggling with it, I shrugged and dredged up the last thing I could recall. "I got shot at the museum. I don't remember anything after that."

"We're in Rochester, Minnesota. They've had you pretty heavily drugged after you broke your hand breaking Asfour's face."

"I broke his face?" Damn, I wished I remembered that.

"His nose and cheek bone. Well done. The doctors did warn me you might have recollection issues. Pixie dust is not your friend."

"It's really not."

He chuckled. "You were feeling no pain, which was good, since the doctors didn't need to give you any actual painkillers. Unfortunately, the average zombie has more common sense and willpower than you do while under the influence. The hospital in New York used the good stuff on you, and let's just say you've been in orbit ever since. It worked out since your hand and shoulder needed some reconstruction work. Also, I was right. I need your health insurance."

I gawked at him, not sure where to begin. Why were we in Minnesota neared the top of my list, although the whole waking up on the couch using Malcolm as a bed issue took the first place spot.

Laughing, Malcolm untangled his legs from mine and sat up, reaching for his phone, which was on the nearby coffee table. "Ah. Your timing isn't bad. It's eight, and I'd set the alarm for nine. You have an appointment for eleven at the clinic; if the bones are fused and the infection's gone, we'll be able to head home today. I've decided we're driving, as I've had my fill of corpses on planes."

"There's more of them?"

"Not like that day in New York, but yes. From what I can tell, there's a hundred or so new bodies turning up every day. The devil doesn't seem worried."

Mindful of my shoulder, I stretched and yawned. While sore, it didn't hurt anymore. "What happened with the mummies?"

"After you confronted Asfour in the hospital, I managed to convince Ginger to return to the museum to keep King Tutankhamun company. They've taken to scaring the piss out of visitors. Neither went back to sleep, but they seem content enough guarding the museum."

There went my hopes the incident with the mummies had been part of a really bad dream. "And Asfour?"

"Will be leaving you alone if he knows what's good for him. He's already facing charges for attempted child slavery, child endangerment, and attempted kidnapping. Your aunt was brought in for questioning, and as a result, the police got a warrant to locate the contract, which has been confiscated as evidence. They didn't even try to hide their tracks."

Great. Malcolm had all the sordid details about one of my dirty secrets—far more than I wanted anyone to know. "I'll deal with him."

"You're stubborn."

"I'm a drifter. We're stubborn by default. We have to be."

"You're also part cat. You really can't help it, can you?"

I huffed, tucked my feet under me, and turned my head, studying the far and rather blank wall. "What else did I miss?"

"Nothing significant. I worked, you slept when you weren't eating everything in sight, and I took you to your appointments. You had a devilish visitor several times, and a pair of angels popped in to question you about your aunt and her attempts to sell you to the highest bidder."

Damn it. I bet the angels were actually archangels, and that Gabriel and Michael would report every last word to the devil. "How much did I tell them?"

Malcolm sighed. "A lot. Sorry. Whenever anyone asked you a question, you gave very thorough answers without us having to lift a finger. I really recommend you avoid pixie dust in the future, though. You were quite happy, but you were also a handful."

"I don't use it intentionally. I don't use any type of medication, only when prescribed."

"Which explains your reaction to it. Anyway, it's going to get ugly, especially for your aunt. And here I thought *my* family had issues. Turns out your family believes Egyptian laws apply to someone without Egyptian citizenship living abroad. Your aunt also assumed you weren't a naturalized American citizen, which you are. Their plan would have worked if you had an Egyptian birth certificate. It seems your mother attempted to have one issued for you, but it was denied as the United States had claimed official responsibility for you when you were a baby. Since you're a United States citizen, the request was denied in our courts."

And with those few words, I realized Malcolm knew more about my family and life than I did. Shit. "You've been busy. And just how did you find *that* out?"

"Well, you've been drugged with pixie dust for a while. While there's nothing wrong with a light dusting to make a bad day easier, just be careful next time you have some—and warn me first. You like to cuddle."

I liked to *what*? My cheeks burned. "What?"

"There's a reason the bed in this room hasn't seen any use, and it's because every time I sat down, you pounced so you could take a nap."

I whirled to face him, my eyes wide. "I didn't!"

Smirking, Malcolm reached over and pressed his finger to my nose. "I think you like me."

Even better. I'd assaulted and harassed the man while high on wing glitter. "Should I start groveling for forgiveness now or later?"

"Not necessary. I have no problems with being the object of your affections. I'm grateful you've spent most of your time as a human, however. Your claws are sharp when you knead, and you roar when startled. You're pleasant company, so you won't hear any complaints from me. Well, except for that one conference call I was on that became rather interesting. A car alarm went off outside. You about jumped out of your skin."

Uh oh. "I'm so sorry. What did I do?"

"You tried to crawl into my shirt while I was wearing it."

As I could see myself doing just that when startled, I groaned and covered my face with my hands. "I'm so sorry."

"I found it rather amusing, especially since I'd been on a video call. Once the alarm stopped, you went right back to sleep. Yes, with your head hidden in my shirt."

Malcolm seemed to be enjoying himself far too much. "What else did I do?"

"Not much. The hardest part was making sure you didn't wander off. No matter what you were told to do, you'd do it, so I had to keep a close eye on you. In good news, you stayed out of trouble. That said, we need to test to see if it's worn off. I think it has since you're coherent, but better safe than sorry."

As a fan of personal freedom, I wanted to make certain I had full control of myself, too. "All right. How do we test?"

"I'll tell you to do something. If you stay put and disobey me, you're clear. I'm going to even give you an order you won't like as a way to help make sure you won't do anything you don't want to."

"If I end up obeying you, I may be forced to kill you."

"It's a risk I'm willing to take."

"Sounds like a plan, then." I hoped I wouldn't regret my consent in a few moments.

"Good. Get naked."

I blinked. I blinked again, and my mouth dropped open. "What?"

"You're wearing clothes. Naked is the state when you're no longer wearing clothes. Take your clothes off."

Malcolm must have lost his mind. Granted, if I could reasonably run into a situation where we both happened to have no clothes on without compromising my already compromised morals, I wouldn't mind it at all. In fact, I was certain I'd enjoy it a lot. "Why would I do that?"

"The pixie dust has worn off. See? It's easy to tell. If you were influenced, you'd be stripping for me right now."

While he presented a good argument, I still frowned. "And if it had?"

"I would've told you to go to the bathroom first and take a shower, which has been the routine for the past four days. I prefer my woman willing and in full control of her faculties."

Malcolm was a clever bastard, I had to

give him that. "Dare I ask how many strip shows you've gotten?"

"Disappointingly, none."

I found that even more interesting than his use of nudity to test the pixie dust's control over me—especially for a man supposedly fixated on his ex, even if revenge and hatred motivated him. "I see."

"Pixie dust is an interesting substance. It often brings out the best and the worst in people. Most want to please others in any way possible. That's why it's regulated like it is. You're different."

"I am?"

"You followed orders since you didn't have a choice, compelled to do things directly asked of you, but you didn't go out of your way to make me happy. That's what's so annoying about pixie dust usage. Most people try to make everyone around them happy, too. No, all you wanted was to be near people, usually me. I think you like me."

Malcolm sounded way too happy about that for my peace of mind. Had he forgotten I'd been hired to kidnap him? I lifted my left wrist to show him the bracelet, but it was gone. I shook my hand at him. "What the hell?"

"I took it off. I didn't want it interfering with the doctors. Since you've brought it up, I have a question about it."

I scowled. "What? That thing cost me a lot of money, Malcolm."

"When you put that thing on me, were you aware I could have killed you if I decided to try to bust through it?"

Uh oh. All the happiness in Malcolm's tone vanished, leaving him colder than ice. "I knew."

"And the empathic link?"

"I knew." I stretched out my legs and propped my feet up on the coffee table. "It's not a big deal. I didn't pick up a lot from you, just a lot of anger."

"At first. Were you aware that the longer they're worn, the stronger the link becomes? Where the hell did you get them? That's high class magic. I had my suspicions in the museum when you decided to go all out on that asshole." Malcolm plunked his feet beside mine. "You're damned lucky I opened the bracelet. You're even luckier I'd done some homework and testing. You've got the talent but little power, so I fed you some of mine through the master bracelet. I bet you had no idea you could do that, did you? What I don't know is if the link is permanent, especially since we've both worn the controlling bracelet. I wasn't able to find out in my research."

Shit. "I'm not sure if you're trying to be overgenerous or not," I confessed. "Or you're just deluded. First, I'm not talented. I can shift. That's it."

Well, I could awaken mummies, but if Malcolm forgot about that, I wasn't going to remind him. Unless I could do it intentionally, I considered that whole nightmare a fluke.

"Kanika." Malcolm leaned his head back and closed his eyes. "You lost your temper and raised two mummies. Those mummies are now terrorizing a museum because they're bored."

"That's not my fault."

"It is, because you're the only person the mummies even think about listening to. While you don't remember this, you spoke to both of them on the phone and asked them to limit their pranks to startling people rather than reorganizing the exhibits in the middle of the night. King Tutankhamun demanded all his worldly treasures, and museums around the world are scrambling to comply, afraid he'll take the pranks and chaos to them. It's a disaster, and you made it happen."

If he thought I was going to accept responsibility for being shot, he was out of his mind. "It's Asfour's fault. It's also your cousin's fault. If he hadn't come across as scum, I wouldn't have needed to look into ways to protect you from him. I would've just dumped you in a pond across the country, taken the money, and run. But no, he gave me a bad vibe, and I have a weak spot for kittens and puppies."

He grinned. "Wouldn't that make it my fault?"

"Sure, you can take some of the blame for this. You're the one who decided to pose shirtless with cute animals. He's obviously jealous of your bare chest."

"Or he's planning something. He's been spending a lot of time with Caitlin, and she's always planning something. She's really not happy with either one of us right now."

"Oh, nice. Yet another person who has just cause to get rid of me. Just what I needed. What other bad news do you have for me?"

"Obviously, you are no longer influenced by the pixie dust. It also seems your sarcasm is alive and well. Caitlin's not stupid enough to do anything to you, not directly. When Satan himself says not to do something, she's smart enough to listen. I'm probably her target. I have a few ideas I want to run by you. It'll benefit us both, plus we might be able to put an end to this bullshit."

So much bullshit, so little time. "Which bullshit are you referring to?"

"All of it."

"That's a lot of bullshit, Malcolm. Be reasonable. Prioritize the bullshit. I really don't want to drown in bullshit, which is exactly what will happen if we're not careful." I sighed. "There's really that much of it."

"I'm willing to prioritize the bullshit. Problem one is Isaac Asfour, your aunt, and the other businessmen who showed interest in you. We need to figure out why you're worth so much to them. On the surface, your aunt doesn't exactly have an impressive portfolio. I have no idea what she can offer a man like Asfour. That leaves you or your parents."

"I've never met either one of them, nor do I know anything about them."

"Your mother's the more likely candidate; she married into wealth after your birth. It's unknown if your step father knows about you."

"Maybe you should live my life for me since you seem to know more about it than I do."

"Relax, Kanika. I've had several days to look into your situation. Add in your willingness to answer my questions, and it was child's play to profile you. Your research into me was far more impressive, especially when you told me how you worked around my cousin's misinformation. I did question you about that. I'm not sorry. Well, I'm sorry about your memory lapse. I promise to be upfront and honest about what happened while you were under the influence."

If I went back to bed, could I restart my

day? Since everything else had gone wrong already, I decided to take a plunge into the deep end to find out just how badly I'd behaved while high on pixie dust. "Did I sleep with you?"

Malcolm slapped his forehead. "No!"

Well, shit. High, drugged me hadn't jumped him? How disappointing. I could've lived with myself if I'd jumped him. Him jumping me would've been another story—or not. No, definitely not. He could've jumped me, and I would've been just fine with that.

Why couldn't I just ditch the pesky morals already?

I sighed. "Did I try to sleep with you?"

"You slept on me often, but you only tried to relieve me of my pants twice. The first time, you sprawled over me, declared my pants were in the way, and passed out about ten seconds later. The second time, you stole my pants while I was showering and decided to wear them, so I wore my bathrobe for the rest of the evening. Don't worry. Your dignity and self-respect are intact."

"Apparently, I'm an idiot when under the influence of pixie dust."

"But you were a very happy idiot. That counts for something. You also sleepwalk. I'm beginning to believe you need supervision even on non-prescription painkillers."

A change of subject was definitely in order. "I need a bath."

"Breakfast, too."

I hissed at him, lurched to my feet, and staggered to the bathroom to make my escape. "Fast food breakfast."

Instead of being properly cowed by my snarling, he laughed. "As you wish."

TWENTY-ONE

Maybe that'll teach him not to
involve me in his scheming.

THE EXAM TESTED my patience and took four hours, but when I finished, I was given the all clear to leave. An hour of the session involved a lengthy explanation of my operations and recovery. I couldn't remember any of it, but it had taken two practitioners four sessions to repair the damage. I peeked at the invoice to discover the devil owed the hospital thirty thousand after insurance coverage.

I laughed all the way to the rental, and when I spotted Satin leaning against the car, I fell against Malcolm, tears of mirth streaming from my eyes. "T-thirty thousand."

"At least you're almost coherent. Almost. It's not that funny."

"Yes, it is. Maybe that'll teach him not to involve me in his scheming."

"That's a fair point."

Satin sighed and stood straight. "You're so

mean to me, cupcake. How was your appointment?"

"I escaped, and I don't have to come back. I need another exam in a month, but any doctor with an x-ray machine will do."

"Going back to Tennessee?"

"Yes," Malcolm answered.

"I have a proposition for you, Mr. Stew—"

"Don't do it," I blurted.

Malcolm laughed. "You want her in Georgia, and you want me with her."

"Have I mentioned you two are the ruiners of my fun?"

I crossed my arms, ignoring the devil so I could give Malcolm my undivided attention. "Why would you think that?"

"Because he made a show at the museum and publicly claimed you as his heir. He's working on something in Georgia, so it makes sense he wants you there. It consolidates his position—and it puts you close to him if someone decides to target you. It's a good move on his part."

Oh. Right. I flushed at my oversight. "And why would he want *you* there? And I don't see what good that will do him."

"It must be residual pixie dust still in your system. It makes you a bit thoughtless. I'm sure you'll remember your strengths later. You do have them. Try squinting when you look in the mirror. It might help."

The damned bastard dared to smirk at me. His pretty face, excessive generosity, and nasty mouth made him the ideal candidate for revenge—or a good prank. A good-natured prank would keep me amused while I came up with a better way to punish him. "It's not my fault pixie dust is awful."

"I didn't mind, although I do appreciate your improved conversation skills. You're more interesting when you're sparring with me rather than catnapping the day away."

I crossed my arms and scowled. "Why am I not surprised. No. Going to Georgia will ruin your work even more. Haven't you been disrupted enough because of me? No, no, no. You're going back to Tennessee where you belong."

The bastard's smirk blossomed into laughter. "You're so prickly today. Don't worry. Arrangements can be made. I've made good progress catching up, and relocating to Georgia for a while won't do much harm at all. I'll take the opportunity to expand my operations into Georgia. I expect this to become a lucrative venture if I play my cards right."

Satin lashed his tail, and he matched Malcolm's smirk. "I recommend real estate, Mr. Stewart. The new lost souls are learning their unlife doesn't come with free rent or escape from the burdens of mortal existence. Employers are learning they have a new source of cheap, inexhaustible labor."

"Potentially profitable for the depraved." Malcolm unlocked the rental and shook his head. "I'll consider it, but I have reservations."

"Edwin Stewart has opened a factory in Savannah. He'll need more property to continue his efforts. You might be able to convince him you're there on his business. He'll have interest in my heir, too. If he believes you're there for his sake, he may lower his guard."

Malcolm hesitated long enough I feared he'd be sucked into the devil's trap, but I kept my mouth shut. It wasn't my place to tell him what business to avoid. Maybe I didn't like it, but it wasn't *my* choice.

Damn it.

"I'm possibly interested. What's your proposal?"

"Several things. I want you to buy all the real estate you can in Savannah and cater to the new undead. When you draft their leases, I have a few lines I want added to the contracts. These will put me in a favorable position. In some ways, it will benefit the new dead as well. I'll acquire a slight advantage over several adversaries annoying me. I'm willing to pay you a management fee of ten percent over your active mortgages monthly for a period of thirty years. Upon expiration of our contract, I will purchase the properties from you at their market value at the time of sale."

"I'll need a copy of the contracts. I'll also need at least one angel to confirm the details. I'll also require a detailed list of management responsibilities. I'll be including a stipulation that you'll pay fifty percent of all employee salaries for those hired to assist with this project. That'll include all levels of employees from janitors, landscapers, and maintenance workers to landlord-level managers."

"Done."

"I'm taking Kanika home. Contact me in a week. Until then, we have no bargain. This way, I won't be lying when I negotiate with Uncle Edwin."

"Deal. I'll see you in a week, then. Oh, and in the interest of establishing a cordial relationship, I'll gift you with some free advice. Don't drive to Tennessee. You'll be much happier if you fly, but I recommend avoiding commercial for a while. You'll find there's a rather disconcerting number of passengers who have passed their expiration dates."

THE NEXT TIME the devil gave free advice, I'd listen. No matter how stubbornly Malcolm fought against the extra expense, I wouldn't let him win. I'd tie him up and drag him onto the chartered flight I hired. Never again would he convince me to go with what he wanted.

Never again.

I sat in the back row with a pair of rotters while a stewardess snagged Malcolm and gave him a free upgrade to first class. In a moment of pure stupidity and pride, I'd refused his offer to take his seat.

Not only would I refuse to go with what he wanted, I'd accept his generous offers without guilt or question. Next time, I'd be greedy and let him suffer.

In the ten minutes after boarding, my seat mates had shed bits of flesh, most of which landed on me. Had I not been in human form, my flight would've ended before takeoff. Green and black mottled the little skin they had left, which wasn't enough for my comfort.

"Putrefaction is nasty business," the rotter with the window seat said, and then he laughed. A piece of his cheek plopped onto the armrest between us.

Maybe if I stared at the seat in front of me, I would make it through the flight without getting sick or fainting. Fainting seemed wise; if I fainted before takeoff, could I escape the flight altogether? I sucked in a deep breath and held it. I could handle an hour and a half crammed between two undead without throwing up *or* being rude to them. When we landed in Chicago, I'd have three hours to recover before the two-hour flight to Nashville. I remembered to avoid breathing through my mouth and exhaled.

Clasping my hands together on my lap, I spent a few more moments composing myself before I asked, "Are you transitioning?"

"I waited too long, so I can't become a vampire. Maybe I'll apply for mummification. It's a real pisser, though. Vampires are turned in pairs, and I lost my spot thinking about it for too long."

Great. The rotter was a talker, and he seemed eager for a conversation. I swallowed several times. Could I survive the hour and a half? I hoped so. If not, I hoped ghosts were real, as I had plans to haunt Malcolm for subjecting me to a commercial flight. "I'm sorry to hear that. Why a mummy?"

At least I had one useful bit of information; I hadn't known Wishing Well was creating vampires in pairs.

"Their goddess is a hot number, and I'd like to get her out of those wrappings of hers."

"Mummy goddess? Which mummy goddess?" I frowned, as the Egyptians believed in two goddesses who protected those who had already passed on, Nephthys and Isis. "Nephthys?"

"Who?"

I closed my eyes and sighed. "Nephthys, the Lady of the House, protector of mummies, guardian of Osiris and Set."

"Oh! You're a chaperone?"

I peeked through my lashes. The rotters leaned towards me, staring without blinking, their eyes milky from death. "Sorry. I'm just a traveler with an interest in Egyptian deities."

"You should become a chaperone. You don't run and scream like most. It pays well. I've heard you can bag a hundred a day accompanying new dead like us."

While I wanted to shudder and gag at even the thought of going out of my way to keep the newly dead company, I feigned interest. If I learned something, the flight wouldn't be a total loss—or quite so unbearable. "Expenses paid?"

Both men pulled out stained business cards from their pockets. Each gave me a stack, stuck together and barely legible, but I recognized Wishing Well's logo. Surprise, surprise. I bet the employment contract included a generous offer of unlife and an assassination, too.

"Don't know; only the living can be hired as chaperones. This flight has two. Airports now require one chaperone per five new dead. Helps keeps problems to a minimum, you know."

"Good to know. Who's your chaperone?"

The rotters pointed at a woman in the row in front of us and across the aisle. Her suit made me think she was either a lawyer or a businesswoman rather than an undead babysitter. Squirming in my seat, I pulled out my phone and snapped a picture of her. I also took pictures of my seat mates. "I'll think about it."

"You should. Wishing Well will change the world, lady. Image it. No one will worry about death ever again, for we'll all become immortal."

THE LIVING, the dead, and those in between converged in Chicago, and a miasma of decay hung in the air, invisible yet cold and clammy on my skin. While some travelers wrinkled their noses at the smell, only I seemed chilled and disconcerted by the presence of so many unliving. To escape the rank odor clinging to me, I went in search of a gift store, discovering clothing boutiques, perfume-infested tourist traps, and restaurants. A leather coat in the window caught my eye and lured me into the store, and the clerk's professional refusal to acknowledge the stench wafting off me made me stay.

With my clothes hiding in a suitcase somewhere, buying something was the only way I'd be able to make it to Tennessee without snapping or throwing up on someone, probably Malcolm, unless he escaped with the other rich, beautiful people again. I couldn't blame him; he'd offered me the better seat.

When I got a few minutes, I'd take my pride out back and give it a beating it would never forget.

After spending enough money I flinched while paying the bill, the clerk quietly offered to dispose of my stained outfit so I wouldn't contaminate my clean clothes or bag. Forty minutes later, I left the store wearing brand new clothes, strappy heels with enough bling to make me happy and show off my legs, and a skirt short enough to feel scandalous without displaying too much unintentionally. Humming my satisfaction, I strolled around the airport in search of Malcolm.

I found Satin instead.

I put my hands on my hips and scowled at the devil. "You're a stalker, aren't you?"

"When the mood strikes me. Nice jacket. How much did that cost me? I won't ask about the rest of that outfit; I've learned the hard way the less material is used, the more expensive it becomes."

"Way too much. What do you want?"

"Can't I visit my little cupcake?"

"No. Not in an airport, and especially not when you saw me this morning."

"I come bearing gifts."

"Are they gifts I'll actually like?"

"It's a gift of a plane charter for you and your Stewart, which will leave in an hour, one without any undead on board. In addition, you'll enjoy dinner in the air—and not your usual flight fare. I'm certain this trip hasn't done your appetite any favors. I'm also including this packet of papers for you to read. You'll find it interesting. Finally, I come with a warning. Asfour is out of the hospital, and I wouldn't put it past him to make a bargain to get what he wants."

Uh oh. I clenched my teeth and growled. "A bargain you might grant with the right terms?"

"No. A bargain I won't grant because you'll enter a bargain with me to prevent it." The devil's smile frightened me almost as much as his pleased tone. "We can do this the hard way or the easy way, but we are doing this, cupcake."

"Hasn't anyone told you the height of stupidity is making a deal with the devil? I lose IQ points every time I talk to you."

"Don't be nasty. Not all my deals only benefit me, just most of them. This one benefits us both. You'll bar me from making bargains unfavorable to you. I'll have your promise to come to at least one family dinner a year with your Stewart male. I'll be nice and limit this to thirty years to coincide with his business agreement with me."

"You can make bargains with anyone you want, but if you even consider bargaining me off to anyone, not only will I never attend one of your so-called family dinners, but I will amuse myself until my dying day trying to kill you."

"You drive a hard bargain." The Lord of Lies met my gaze with a slight narrowing of his eyes.

Alarm bells went off in my head, and I remembered the cardinal rule of lying: always look your victim in the eyes without wavering. When I considered the possibilities, I bottomed out with the worst possible option. "Did you already bargain me off to someone?"

The devil had the decency to look chagrined. "Maybe."

"What have you done, Lucy?" I snarled.

"It's entirely beneficial for you. I couldn't help it. It was too good of a deal to pass up. Beneficial bargains shouldn't count."

I thought long and hard about wrapping

my hands around Satin's throat and wringing the life out of him. "Define beneficial."

"Doesn't harm you and results in a profit for you. I solemnly swear none of my bargains involve completing any betrothals arranged by your biological family."

Why me? I suspected I was a reincarnated soul who'd done something particularly heinous to deserve the devil's personal attention. "My soul is off limits."

"You'd be useless as my heir if I took your soul. Your soul's safe. I would prefer if you didn't do something foolish like bargain it away. I'd have to hunt it down and give it back, and altruism gives me ulcers."

"I rather like my soul where it's at."

"Good girl. I won't even make you come to the main house for dinner. Unless you'd like a few dates with Asf—"

"No."

"I didn't think so. So, do we have a bargain?"

"This is coercion," I grumbled.

"I know. It's great. I have to teach you the ropes anyway. The best way to learn is through experience. So far, you have done fairly well protecting yourself, except for that one time. Never sign papers I drew up without reading them very carefully. You might end up adopted. At least you can spell your new last name, right?"

"Does that make you Mephistopheles Mephistopheles? If so, you have an awful name."

"An unexpected backfiring. Your mother finds my current situation endlessly amusing. Oh, when you visit us, bring her an iced coffee. She really enjoys them."

"Sure." All things considered, bringing an iced coffee to a succubus seemed reasonable enough. "You really got us a charter?"

"And dinner. That's important. You need to eat more, cupcake."

"Fine. If this bargain backfires on me, Lucy, I will make it my eternal mission to kill you."

"Bargain made. Your Stewart male is at the gate and rather grumpy that he lost track of you. Take his ticket, give it to the woman at the gate, and tell her to reassign the seats. A stranded couple will really appreciate your seats."

"At no expense to them. *You* will pay all the fees."

"Very well."

"Give me everything."

The devil gave me a sleek black briefcase and an envelope. "Keep the briefcase; it'll be useful later."

"I'll keep that in mind."

"You should. That's something devils have in common with angels: we never do something without reason. Have a good flight, dear."

The devil vanished in a cloud of yellow smoke. Brimstone smelled better than decomposing bodies, and that realization startled a laugh out of me.

Who knew?

TWENTY-TWO

Miracles could happen.

I FOUND Malcolm at the food court, and he glared at me. Ignoring his displeasure, I snatched the boarding passes out of his hand, spun around, and beelined for the nearest boarding gate. After a short but sweet discussion with the airport employee, she promised to transfer the tickets to a pair of needy travelers on the devil's dime.

While I felt bad about subjecting them to the funk of rotting corpses, I wanted to enjoy a flight without battling nausea the entire time.

Malcolm crossed his arms, posing to make every last one of his muscles bulge. "Why did you do that?"

After I got him on the plane, I'd have to recommend he be tested for testosterone poisoning. "We have a charter flight, and we're leaving now. March, Malcolm. I've been promised an undead-free trip, and so help me, if you interfere, I will kill you."

He raised his hands in surrender. "Okay. Lead the way."

Amazing. Miracles could happen. I checked the charter package for our gate information and pointed Malcolm in the appropriate direction.

When we arrived but before I had a chance to pull out our boarding passes, the stewardess smiled and intercepted us. "Please follow me, Miss Mephistopheles, Mr. Stewart. As soon as you're settled, we'll be ready for takeoff."

I followed her, and Malcolm tailed me, muttering curses low enough I doubted he meant for me to hear them. Between his disgruntlement over his plans being thwarted and my escape from the stench of undeath, I liked the way my day was turning out.

A few hours without worrying about corpses seemed like heaven to me.

Unfortunately, hell waited on board, and the Lord of Lies lounged in a leather armchair at a table for four, and judging from the place settings, he meant for me to cozy up with Malcolm on the other side of the table. "Damn it, Satin!"

"Fancy meeting you here, Kanika. What a surprise. Dinner will be served as soon as we reach altitude. Sit, children. Make yourselves comfortable."

Malcolm laughed, patted my shoulder, and gave me a push towards the table. "You should have insisted on a devil-free flight."

"You're right. I should have." Accepting the inevitable, I sat across from the Lord of Hell, hoping to mitigate some of his influence on Malcolm. "I'm going to make this clear now. This fulfills my requirement to have dinner with you for the next year."

"Very well, cupcake, but only this once."

I considered the concession my victory and made myself as comfortable as I could with both the devil and Malcolm watching me. "What do you want?"

"I thought it wise to accompany you to prevent any incidents. You have enemies now, cupcake, and they aren't all of my making. You're not used to attention of this caliber, so it falls to me to make sure you live long enough to learn the ropes. Of course, the wise ones want you alive as leverage against me. I'll be impressing upon certain individuals that attacking my heir will endanger their lives—and compromise their souls. I'll enjoy tormenting any naughty beings I catch who believe they can get away with hurting you. It'll keep me from getting bored. I do hate being bored."

Malcolm sat beside me, leaned over, and

whispered, "Under no circumstances should Satan be allowed to become bored."

"Thank you, Sir Obvious. When he's bored, he bothers me."

The devil ignored our murmuring, although he grinned, making it perfectly clear he'd heard us. "I have information for you, Mr. Stewart, and I wish to strike a bargain for it."

Sucking in a breath, I glanced at Malcolm, who shot me a glare. "For the record, this is entirely your fault," he muttered.

It probably was. I winced. "I'm sorry."

Malcolm nudged my foot with his before turning his glare to the devil. "All right, Mephistopheles. What do you want?"

"It's a two-part bargain." The Lord of Lies pulled out a thin, long box and set it on the table. "The information I have deals with your clan's recent activities. You'll find it useful. In exchange, I'll require you to wear this."

Within the box, 'this' proved to be a bracelet the match for mine, and I tensed. "I won't allow it."

"Don't worry, cupcake. I don't have any designs on your Stewart. I won't be wearing the master bracelet. You will be."

I'd be wearing it? I lifted my hand to stare at the one I wore, then I graced Malcolm with my sweetest smile. "I've changed my mind. Please, continue."

Malcolm scowled, and Satin laughed. "I thought you'd like that. It seemed fair."

I waved away the devil's complaint. "I get it next week."

"This will resolve the issue your Stewart has been attempting to counter without your knowledge. It's rather sweet. He's so awkward. Of course, the curse *is* hampering his ability to handle the situation like a normal adult, but intent matters. He's made more headway against the curse's nature than most. So, this will require him to willingly submit to you, and you'll have to willingly accept his submission and submit to him as well. It'll be easiest on you, as you've already agreed of your own volition to wear the bracelet."

I frowned. "What issue?"

"Mephistopheles, is it really necessary to go into the details?" Malcolm asked in a strained voice.

"Yes, it is. I'm assuming the original set was sold without declaration of some of the more nefarious consequences, so it's mandatory my little cupcake knows exactly what she's gone and gotten herself into."

One day, I really would kill the devil, and I'd list his absurd nickname for me as the top reason. "I already know he could kill me if he tried to forcefully use his magic, and that I would begin sensing his emotions."

"That's better than I expected, to be honest. The problem is this. The bracelets forge a connection between the master and servant bracelets. The sensing of emotions is the first sign the bond is taking hold. That bond can be quite difficult to break, dependent on the nature of the relationship between the wearers." The Lord of Lies picked up the pair of bracelets, holding them up and looking them over. "Your nature would ensure a bond on your end, and Stewarts like yours have an unfortunate tendency to obsess over their chosen female. Your Stewart is rather peculiar, as you are not the first female to catch his attention."

"Caitlin," I snarled.

"Yes. I do hope she made herself a sandwich. It'd be a pity if she ended up in the hospital. I intend on sending incubi in need of a reward her way, especially ones who are ready to have children. A few children might settle her down a bit—and ruin her plans of clan domination."

Malcolm grimaced. "And the worst part is, she wouldn't even say no to a fling with an incubus or three."

"Three?" I squeaked.

"She'd take as many as she could get her hands on. That's her nature." Malcolm shrugged. "Had I realized that was her nature earlier, I would've avoided her altogether."

"It's part curse, part nature for him, cupcake. You'll find your Stewart will be loyal to a fault. It's a birth defect, I'm certain of it. I'd never deliberately design a being with morals the match of a stuffy angel."

I took the high road and decided against reminding the devil he actually liked angels, especially his brothers. "So, how does this work? What happens if we're both wearing master bracelets?" The plane's jets rumbled to life, and I tensed at the vibrations. "What's the point of suppressing each other at the same time?"

"You wear them with the bonds open, silly girl." Satin tilted his head back and laughed. "Buckle up, children. I'm a bit more durable than you two are. It's always wise to take precautions."

I buckled in just in case the devil wasn't screwing with us. The liftoff happened without incident, and the Lord of Lies laughed at my relieved sigh. "You're such a jerk, Lucy."

"I am. Now, Mr. Stewart, do you agree to my terms?"

Malcolm shook his head. "Not until I hear the rest of your bargain. I'll decide then."

"Take note, Kanika. Had he agreed now, he'd be bound to both parts of our bargain. *Always* find out the entirety of the deal before you agree to anything."

"Noted." I nudged Malcolm's foot with mine. "How'd you know that, anyway?"

"I've bargained with devils and demons before. It's not unusual to run into both types in the business world. The bargains in business are strictly material wealth, however—no risk of souls. It's taboo to involve spiritual matters in base business dealings. The last time a devil tried it, he was run out of the industry completely; no one would do business *or* bargain with him. He had to go to Europe. I probably won't even be alive when the embargo on that idiot's lifted."

Huh. Later, I'd have to ask how often he dealt with the forces of hell, and if he had any ideas on how to mitigate my devil problem. "Okay. What's the second part of the bargain, then?"

Malcolm jabbed me with his foot, and I twisted mine and stepped on his toes with my heel. We engaged in a short but fierce battle beneath the table, which he won by virtue of having bigger feet. I wrinkled my nose, as he held my feet hostage with this shoes, careful not to put too much weight on my toes.

The devil arched a brow at us, turning to Malcolm. "I'll give you all the information I have on the Stewart clan; this will include developing situations and current news, history, and interesting rumors that might have substance. I'll also make it clear if the information is reliable or not when I give it to you. In exchange, you'll vow to withhold from entering into any bargains with another clan."

"Define clan," Malcolm ordered.

"Anyone other than me and my chosen negotiator. For the purpose of this agreement, this means you can only bargain with me or Kanika. I may, at my choosing, decide when she will negotiate on my behalf. Furthermore, I ban any transference of your soul in any form. By entering this agreement, you'll agree that I have overriding ownership of your soul. I'll swear you'll retain full will and freedom, and that upon your physical death, your soul will be accounted for per the actions of your uncursed life; all actions of your cursed life will be cleansed. In short, should you not regain ownership of your soul prior to your death, your soul shall be declared suitable for admittance into the heavens."

On the surface, it was a good deal for Malcolm, and I could see him thinking about it, his eyes narrowed and his expression thoughtful. "How will I know when I'm uncursed?"

No matter what, I wouldn't flinch at the question—or the meaning behind it. The instant he was uncursed, I knew what Malcolm would want. He'd want to find—or make—that perfect family for the house he'd built despite knowing he might never get what his heart desired.

My role in his life would be long over at that point, no matter what bargains we made, how I involved myself with the Stewart family affairs, and how much I loathed the barriers that would continue to divide us. I pressed my lips together so I wouldn't say a word, and I waited.

"As part of this agreement, the time you learn of your uncursing will be decided by me, and it will only become valid when I notify you in the presence of an angel."

Malcolm scowled. "And if I should die before notification?"

"Your soul will be cleansed, and you may enter the heavens should you choose."

"How does this benefit you?" His scowl eased to a more thoughtful frown. "Too much of this benefits me."

"Until your death, your soul belongs to me and is tallied in my book. In the eyes of the heavens and its angels, you're my servant. The condition of your soul's purification and free will will allow you to potentially serve as a negotiator between the heavens and my hells. This would grant you a rather high position in my army."

I clenched my teeth until my jaw ached before growling, "Don't—"

"Kanika, it's my soul." Malcolm relaxed

into his chair, although he still kept my feet pinned with his. "How would this change my status within my clan?"

"It doesn't, not unless you choose to change your status."

"What is that supposed to mean? How might my status change?"

The devil laughed. "You'd become the head of your clan; your rank within my armies would give you a more devilish nature, which would mean you would outrank any other Stewart male, living or dead. Despite the addition of a few devilish perks, I would continue to safeguard your soul and protect it from lasting harm. Still, it'd behoove you to maintain some balance on your own. It'll make the cleansing of your soul easier on you upon your death."

Malcolm fell quiet, and while we waited for him to speak, the stewardess brought covered dishes, revealing plates of salad garnished with grilled fish. Deep down, I wanted to tell Malcolm no, to reconsider his considering, but I kept quiet.

He was right. It was his soul, and I couldn't make the decision for him.

"No undeath," Malcolm stated when the stewardess left.

"Upon your death, your soul will be shepherded properly. You won't be turned."

I sighed and picked at my salad, nibbling

on a piece of tomato, staring at my plate so I wouldn't glare at the devil. If I discovered Satin played the bargain wrong, that Malcolm's soul was at risk, I had one card I could play, one I bet the devil desired.

It would ruin me for the rest of eternity. I could exchange my soul for Malcolm's. My scales wouldn't balance, not with how I'd led my life, but it would be a small price to pay. I already had a one-way trip to the hells booked. If I could make the price of passage worthwhile, I could live with that.

I'd already made myself into the devil's heir, poised to lose everything. Would Malcolm realize the truth? It wasn't his soul they bargained for, but for mine.

"Indeed," the Lord of Lies murmured, his expression pleased. "How clever. You'll keep that thought to yourself."

I grumbled curses and stabbed at my salad, pushing it around my plate rather than eating it. "Fine."

Malcolm considered me, his lips curving into a smile. "So there is a trick."

"Indeed, there is. I *am* the devil, after all. The Lord of Lies. The Betrayer. The Trickster. Can you figure out the secret of my bargain, Malcolm Findlay Stewart? And if you do, what do you plan to do about it?"

"There are several possibilities," Malcolm admitted.

"There usually are, but one's more important than the rest," the devil conceded.

No kidding. I sighed.

"If I agree until my death, you could prolong my life until you're satisfied—potentially indefinitely."

"I'm rather fond of that option."

I hadn't even considered it; an extended lifespan didn't seem like a bad deal to me, although it *would* prolong my suffering when it came to the devil.

"You could decide against notifying me my curse had been broken."

Satin pouted. "That's not fair. You weren't supposed to figure that one out yet."

I added another tally to the list of things I hadn't figured out, although once again, I couldn't see any bad points about it. If Satin refused to notify Malcolm the curse had been broken, Malcolm's soul would be safe. No matter what he did in his life, his soul would be cleansed.

It seemed like too good of a deal to me, and I couldn't figure out what the disadvantage was.

Malcolm released my feet, and I peeked under the table to discover he was stretching out to make himself more comfortable. "If my soul belongs to you, and I'm wearing a master bracelet, you might manipulate me into doing something to Kanika, to which I say no."

"At no time will I force or manipulate you into cutting off Kanika's magic. I fully intend on cultivating you as a channel for her talents, but when you give her your power it will be by your choice. I may ask it of you, but it'll be your choice."

"You could lock me in stasis until the end of days."

The devil snorted. "I could, but you're more useful to me conscious."

"What am I missing?" Malcolm picked up his fork, and like me, he prodded at his salad rather than eating it. "There's something else."

"Take your time." Satin smiled, smug and satisfied.

It occurred to me Malcolm had come close to the truth, but he hadn't taken the thought far enough. I supposed it made sense. To him, his soul held the most value. It made sense he wouldn't worry for mine.

"Don't underestimate him," the devil whispered in my ear. *"You don't know his thoughts or his heart."*

Satin's lips didn't move, nor did Malcolm seem to hear the devil's words, so I kept my mouth shut and waited.

For several minutes, Malcolm tortured his salad and shredded his fish. "I have a condition."

"Speak."

"My soul can't be bargained for, used as an

incentive for any purpose, or held hostage for another's."

"Must you ruin all my fun?"

Malcolm glanced at me out of the corner of his eye. "Yes. I won't let you use me to hurt her."

Huh. Turned out the devil was right. I set my fork down, leaned back in my chair, and wondered at that.

"Hurting her would defeat my purpose."

"That leads to another problem. I could end up in the heavens, and she'd be trapped in hell with you for all eternity. That's unacceptable."

"You know, strangely enough, I do have the ability to ensure the final destinations of two souls, in this life and the next—and the next, and the next, and the next, for however long I see fit. That, however, would cost you."

I twitched. "Malcolm, it's worth pointing out two archangels have confirmed my soul is at no risk from Satin Blabbermouth Liar Mc-Smarty Pants."

"You're ruining my fun, too," the devil complained.

"Then you shouldn't be trying to bargain away my soul to someone else," I hissed.

"No bargaining *my* soul to someone else, either."

"But what if I want to sell your soul to

Kanika? My little cupcake doesn't have any extra souls yet. You could be her first."

"Not at the price of hers."

Satin pouted. "How unfair. Very well. I accept your condition. I won't use your soul to secure Kanika's."

"You won't use it, period."

"Absolutely no fun!"

"That's my condition."

"I accept. Bargain made?"

"Bargain made," Malcolm agreed.

"Mark my words, little boy. You're going to live a long time because of this, and I'll enjoy tormenting you until the end of days."

I sighed, expecting nothing else from the Lord of Lies, the most wicked being known to man—or any species with any intellect at all.

TWENTY-THREE

Explain, but not so smugly.

I GAVE the devil and Malcolm a hefty dose of the silent treatment, which lasted the entirety of the flight. When Michael and Gabriel met us at the Nashville airport, I snarled my frustration.

"I haven't had this much fun in decades," Gabriel declared, fluttering his wings. "How has my esteemed brother bothered you this time, Kanika?"

"He conned Malcolm out of his soul. What else?"

The archangels were quiet for a moment before their laughter chimed, soft and soothing. Gabriel dismissed my anger with a wave of his perfect hand. "The devil lost that bargain, dear niece. We'll laugh at him for you, if you'd like. He so dislikes protectorates; that's part of what drove him from the high heavens in the first place."

I shifted my ire to Michael. "Explain, but not so smugly."

"Mephistopheles has forgone any claim to your male's soul, and at the conclusion of his protectorate, the soul will be purified. It's simple. Upon death, your male will have the choice of his final destination—or choose to reincarnate should he desire. There's no doubt of who lost this bargain, and it wasn't your male."

"I was going to claim both their souls if my meddlesome child hadn't blabbed she has a balanced soul."

The archangels laughed, and Michael clapped Malcolm's shoulder hard enough to stagger him. "I like you, boy. You watch yourself with my brother, you hear? He can't take your soul, but he can annoy you to death."

"Or turn you inside out if you look at his heir the wrong way," Gabriel added.

"Has everyone heard about that?" Flexing my hands, I took deep breaths until I regained control of my temper. "No turning Malcolm inside out, no killing him, and no torture of any sort, Satin."

"How about a little misery?"

"No."

"I suppose it's for the best. I do need him around if I want little grandchildren to spoil and corrupt."

Grandchildren?

My eyes widened, my face flushed, and under no circumstances would I look at Malcolm. "What grandchildren?"

"When a girl likes a boy and invades his bed and takes off his—"

I lunged at the devil, wrapped my hands around his throat, and did my best to rid the Earth of the Lord of Lies.

WE LOST two hours to the devil and his brothers, who abandoned their dignity and gossiped in a huddle, giggling the entire time. When I tried to leave, Satin snagged me by the collar and dragged me to his side.

"I'm not finished with you yet," he declared.

"You wouldn't let me kill you, now you want something? Ugh. What do you want now?"

"I'm putting you in charge of getting a head count of Wishing Well victims. Make a list of undead types they're offering. If possible, tally by type. Also, find out where their nodes are."

I sucked in a breath, remembering the glowing, hovering stone over Hagnar's home. "Nodes?"

"Concentrations of power. A magical hot spot is the likeliest candidate for what they want to do. Michael and Gabriel will be looking for loopholes in the meantime."

That the forces of heaven and hell joined sides worried me; if the Lord of Lies allied with his enemies, how powerful did they expect Wishing Well to become? Something didn't add up. I expected the Lord of Lies to twist and hide the truth, but the archangels kept quiet. Neither wanted to give me the full details, which meant I'd need to be extra diligent to prevent the immortals from putting me in an even worse position. Once I ditched the divines, I needed to talk to Malcolm.

I sighed. "Fine. I'll look into it."

"Good girl. Off you go. I'll see you and your Stewart male next week to finalize his bargain."

Escaping the devil's hold, I ran for freedom, grabbing Malcolm's hand so he wouldn't get lost—or stupidly stick around. The car rental stand would get us away from the airport and the pervasive stench of the dead. Once on the road, I'd be in a better position to make plans of my own.

Malcolm freed his hand from mine and walked at my side. "That was unnerving. An alliance of devils and angels mean trouble, the kind capable of destroying worlds. This goes beyond the battle between good and evil."

"What do you know?"

"Probably not much more than you do. Until now, the devil hasn't really concentrated his power. The selection of an heir allows him to do a full restructuring of his armies—and take better control of the demons. You technically count as a demon now, which means he's consolidating power through you. Demons tend to resent devils, as devils have a more direct conduit to the top."

Nothing sounded good to me about his declaration. "Great. Just fucking great. What am I going to do with a bunch of demons?"

"Point them at the enemy, sit back, and watch the carnage. Devils are strong, but demons are more varied and come in higher numbers. The sides balance out—if the demons decide to fight together. They usually don't."

"You know a lot about demons."

"I know some. I've done a lot of business with demons. What's our game plan?"

With a week until Malcolm officially accepted another deal with the devil, I needed to solidify my position—and try to learn more about the Stewart family so I could steal their secrets. I frowned.

In my wager with the devil, I hadn't promised how I got the information, only that I learned it. Nothing stopped me from blatantly asking someone about it. Once I learned the truth, I'd decide how to deal with the Lord of Lies—and find out how much trouble I'd gotten myself into. "We should scout the Georgia situation before you finalize your bargain. They're definitely up to something."

"They always are. Devils and angels are opposite sides of the same coin. The heavens have lower numbers, but they're all like the devil, at least in some ways. Two archangels working together *might* beat him. Maybe. And even if they did win, he'd just come back later."

"If demons are devils born on Earth, what are the equivalent of angels born on Earth?"

"I don't think there are any. If anything, I'd say humans are it. That might explain the constant fight over souls."

In my entire life, I'd never bothered to think about the situation much. "So, the devil is keeping the hosts of heaven at bay as much as the hosts of heaven keep the devil at bay."

"Extremes on either side aren't good for the whole. If heaven were to win, there'd be no freedom for mortal man."

"And what would happen if the devil won?"

"No idea. I expect chaos."

"Chaos isn't good *or* evil, though."

"Good and evil are relative. Good according to whom?" Malcolm shrugged as he
approached the rental counter to get a car.
"We'll go to Georgia and snoop around. I'll
call in some people. I'll find a place for us to
rent while we're there. It could be a waste of
time, but my problems aren't as important
—*my* soul is safe."

The reminder annoyed a growl out of me.
"Will a week be long enough to evaluate the
situation?"

"We'll find out."

IF THE DEVIL really wanted to track my activities, I had no doubt he could. That didn't
stop Malcolm from wanting to make it difficult on Satin, so I ended up with one of Malcolm's bank cards. I thought the precaution
was excessive, but if using one of his cards
made Malcolm happy, I'd shut up and deal
with it.

We took a rental to Georgia in case another pyro got any ideas. With both of us
wearing suppressors, left open at Malcolm's
insistence, I doubted we'd have quite the
same problems if one did attempt something.

Malcolm claimed he could handle a pyro,
and I believed him.

Eight hours later, we arrived in Savannah,

Georgia, and the stench of decay and brimstone clashing with the sea did me in. Not only did my stomach betray me, my head spun and my legs refused to do their job.

Only Malcolm's intervention kept me from melting to the sidewalk.

"You need to shift," he growled, helping me back into the car.

"So I can taste it, too? Great, just great."

"I was more thinking you'd have an easier time resisting the devilish forces. You're not going to make a very good Heir of Hell if you throw up whenever there's a devilish congregation."

"Why aren't you sick?" I complained, shuddering at the thought of staying in the city any longer than necessary. "Not fair."

"I'm just a bit more tolerant. Just shift, Kanika. I'll find us a hotel nearby; the place I was originally thinking of staying will probably have even stronger devilish influences. You'll feel better in a few hours."

"Or die from the stench."

"You're not going to die from the smell. Just shift already."

I grumbled curses, slammed the door, and hunkered in my seat while my stomach staged a rebellion. Transforming hurt more than normal, and to add insult to injury, wings and the sporty rental didn't mix, nor did I appreciate the short skirt, coin belt, and stomach-baring halter top my magic deemed appropriate for the situation.

Asshole magic.

The knee-high leather boots, however, I'd keep.

Malcolm circled the car, slid behind the wheel, and chuckled while looking me over. "I'm so glad we're going to a hotel."

"Why?"

"I'll explain when we get there."

I blamed my feline nature for my curiosity. Malcolm spent a few minutes on his phone before starting the engine. While the rank odor permeating everything still bothered me, shifting had helped. I considered it a miracle when I regained control over my stomach. By the time we arrived ten minutes later, I could breathe without wanting to cut off my nose or vomit.

Unlike his previous attempt at checking into a hotel, his credit card was accepted without question.

One day, I'd ask why Malcolm liked the top floor so much. A pair of incubi joined us in the elevator, and they looked me over like I was dessert. My fur stood on end, and I flattened my ears, bared my teeth, and growled a warning.

No only worked on incubi if spoken early enough.

"She's off limits," Malcolm snapped, his tone colder than I'd ever heard him.

"Says who?"

I unsheathed my claws and hissed, "Me, asshole. You come between me and a shower, and they'll be calling you Satan's gelding. Got it?"

"Feisty," the sex demon purred.

"Feisty with sharp claws, pointy teeth, and no desire to play with incubi today. No. If I find out you influenced either one of us, I'll hunt you down and use you as an example."

Both incubi grinned, and they took their time looking me over again. The one who thought I was feisty leaned towards me, licking his lips. "But you're dressed for a good time."

"Not with you, I'm not."

"Don't be such a prude."

"I'm not a prude. I'm just not interested in a threesome or a foursome. Not my style. If you want to hook up with a succubus or two, I might be able to help you." I paused, considering the many ways I could use a pair of incubi to do my dirty work. "It'll cost you, though."

That caught their attention. "You know a succubus?"

I sighed and rolled my eyes. Incubi had two modes of operation; they wanted sex, or they wanted productive sex. "I know someone who can help you out. What are you actually after? A quick fix, or are you after something a bit more?"

"More," they whispered.

Lovely. The incubi wanted babies. I pulled out my phone and called my least favorite phone number in the universe.

"It's like you can't go a day without my affections, cupcake."

"Do you know a couple of succubi looking for a pair of incubi? If I have to decline their invitation again, I'm shipping them to you in pieces. I think they're looking to make a few little incubi babies."

"I might. Where do you want them? When?"

"Twelve hours, Malcolm's house. And no, you can't go with them."

"Spoilsport. What do I get out of this?"

I clacked my teeth and hissed, "I don't ship you two incubi in a box, asshole."

"You're cruel."

"If you talk back, I'll send them to you via ground transit without refrigeration."

"My, my. You're so cranky today, cupcake. Very well. I'll have two succubi at your Stewart's home in twelve hours. You get a passing grade for your negotiations this time. When—"

I hung up on the devil. "Malcolm, give them your address, a set of your keys, and directions on how to get into your place. As for you two, you're going to stay at his house with your succubi, you're going to take care of the property, and otherwise house sit for a week. You'll steal nothing. You'll fix or replace anything that breaks, and otherwise make yourselves useful for the duration of your stay. In addition, you will recruit your succubi and help me with a research project. I want you to compile a list of all accidental deaths for the past two months. I also want a list of any orphaned children and information on where they're located, if available. I'm sure a handsome pair of sex demons like you can get me the info I need."

Malcolm's mouth dropped open, but he did as I ordered.

"You are feisty," the incubus murmured, taking Malcolm's keys. "How on Earth did *you* win her?"

I smiled my sweetest smile. "He hasn't."

Not yet at least, but if I didn't do something soon about him, he might—to hell with my morals.

THE INCUBI WHINED about having to change their schedules; both worked at a devil-run brothel catering to humanoids, and the devil in charge refused to permit breeding, not

even with a succubi. No wonder their desper-
ation levels had peaked off the charts.

While they left me alone, Malcolm fidgeted, and I expected to be warding off his
advances, knocking him out, or indulging in
something I really shouldn't: him. No one
would care what I did—or didn't—do with
him. Well, the devil might, but he could kiss
my ass if he didn't like it.

I sighed. Work and pleasure weren't supposed to mix.

"Why don't we take a walk to the beach,"
Malcolm suggested through clenched teeth
once the sex demons had finally left.

Yep, the incubi had definitely gotten to
him. "How far is it to the water?"

"Quarter mile; it's a bit off the beaten
path. We're skirting the better beaches here."

"Been to Savannah before?"

"A few times. There are a few good restaurants nearby, too."

"I should shift then, unless you like wet
fur." Fortunately, cats didn't get the equivalent of gross wet dog smell, but it would take
forever to get the salt and sand out of my fur.

"That… might be wise." Malcolm swallowed, and he shifted his weight from foot to
foot before marching down the hall towards
our room. "If being human doesn't make you
ill again."

"I should be hunting them down and filleting them," I growled.

"It wasn't intentional. It's not their fault I'm a male. It's their nature."

"All right, then, Mr. Demon Expert. Why am I fine then?"

"You're stubborn, you threatened to castrate them, and you arranged succubi for them. You're their best friend right now."

"Valid points." I followed him to the door, waited for him to let us in, and turned to engage the deadbolt. Maybe the incubi hadn't gotten to me, but Malcolm doing his best to be virtuous in the face of two sex demons certainly did. "I'm not sure the beach is a wise idea."

"Why not?"

I smiled. "If I decide to take your clothes off, I don't want anyone photographing the goods." I faced him, and before I could take another breath, he pounced, pinning me to the door with his body.

"If?" Malcolm captured my hands in his, weaving our fingers together. All I needed to do to break free was unsheathe my claws, but I kept still and waited. "What do I need to do to turn that if to a when?"

Wings against a wall hurt, so I shifted hoping for anything with two legs and no wings. I'd never shifted with someone so close before. When the flash of pain eased, I was human.

Along the way, I'd lost my new clothes but somehow managed to keep the boots. Nice. I could live with that.

"Is that an invitation?" he growled, pulling my arms higher over my head and securing my wrists in one of his hands. "Tell me yes."

"And if I tell you no?"

"I'm a patient man. I'll wait until you say yes—or nibble on you until you can't resist me anymore. I'll improvise."

Patient and willing to fight an incubus's influence intrigued me almost as much as his hold on me along with the way he ducked his head, his breath warming my throat. "And if I say yes?"

"I'm the jealous kind, and I play for keeps."

The cat in me loved the challenge in his voice while the human in me demanded the loyalty he offered. The rest, a mish-mash of both, wanted him to put his money where his mouth was and scratch every last one of my itches. I didn't even need a bed. The wall would do nicely. "Tell me more."

"I haven't been with anyone in a few years," he growled, and true to his promise, he nibbled on my neck.

Holy hell. If he did that again, I'd end up trying to bite his clothes off. "I obviously can't take so much repressed masculinity outside."

"No, you can't."

I wanted another nibble, but Malcolm teased me with a kiss instead. "Why me?"

The infuriating man dared to laugh, and he worked his leg between mine, nudging my feet apart. I shifted my weight, and he took advantage of the opportunity to slide his hand along the length of my leg to my knee. A moment later, he forced me to stand on one foot, trapping me so securely I'd have to shift to escape him.

Yep, I was a goner. He just hadn't figured it out yet.

He chuckled. "Do you want the polite answer?"

Hell no. I wanted whatever motivated him to stop teasing me. "You can start with polite, I suppose."

"The first time I saw you, I thought you were an angel, but then I learned you were a demon in disguise, my heaven and hell in living perfection. Then you were hurt because of me, but you refused to be a helpless victim. You're smart, you're wary, and those shorts you sometimes wear should be illegal in all fifty states. When you kept sneaking into bed with me because you were cold, I kept turning the thermostat down to lure you back. By the time you woke those mummies because I'd been shot, I had already figured out you were it for me. The longer I'm with you, the less I like the idea of letting you leave my sight. I'll fight the devil for you if I must."

"How about a pair of archangels?"

"Them, too."

"I guess it's a good thing you're a picky Stewart man. I don't share."

"How tragic for me." Malcolm took another nibble. "I could do this all night, you know."

I growled. "Typical man, all talk. Why do men always promise all night and last ten minutes? Don't make promises no man can keep."

"Challenge accepted."

I didn't get the chance to even laugh before he let go of his restraint and gave me a very thorough demonstration of what Caitlin had foolishly given up.

I SWORE NEVER to challenge Malcolm when it came to sex ever again. When I'd said all night, I hadn't meant the entire night plus the majority of the next day. He took what he wanted, how he wanted it, when he wanted it, and long after I forgot most of my vocabulary, he did it all over again.

Maybe I should have asked him to stop

after reducing me to a limp mess of quivering muscles. On second thought, could I afford to spare the breath? Probably not. After years of repressed sexuality, I considered myself lucky Malcolm rewarded me with tidbits of food when he wasn't busy living up to his promise.

No, if I let him continue, he might kill me. Then again, if I were going to die, there were worse ways to go. "I surrender."

Malcolm gave a low, throaty chuckle. "Too late. I've already conquered every last inch of you."

No kidding. "What happens now that you've conquered me?"

"I marry you so no one, such as that Asfour fellow, gets any ideas. I vote we quietly elope so we have the appropriate legal documentation to prevent any unwelcome advances. After, we have a disgustingly elaborate wedding to snub the various assholes in our lives."

"But what about the curse?"

"It is what it is. If we can't have children together should we want them, I'll cope. I'd rather have you."

Having seen his home and the wistful family picture it painted, it hurt even thinking he'd let it go for me. He had no way of knowing what I'd already wagered. For the rest of my life, I'd remember his willingness to sacrifice so much. I'd also wonder how

Caitlin could walk away from him—or treat him like property.

I blamed the curse, although I suspected she held equal guilt. Still, there was a simple solution to his problem. No, our problem. "Curse, schmurse. Should push come to shove and we want children, we'll adopt an entire brood of them."

Malcolm grunted, trailing his finger up and down the length of my arm. "Adoption hadn't occurred to me before."

"There are plenty of little brats running around who need asshole parents who won't take their shit or sell them out."

"You've decided we're asshole parents already, have you?"

I rolled over, groaned at my stiffening muscles, and poked his chest. "You're an asshole. I'm an asshole. That, by default, makes us asshole parents."

"I prefer to think of myself as manly."

I laughed. "That you are."

"We should elope, then we should fake a honeymoon."

Why the hell not? "How big will the real wedding be?"

"I think that'll depend on if you-know-who figures out about it before we publicly tie the knot."

"Good point. How do we elope?"

"Tomorrow morning, we'll deal with it. Tonight, we're busy."

"We are?"

Malcolm pounced with a mock growl. "You're still capable of talking. I haven't worn you out entirely."

Holy hell. What had I gotten myself into, and did I even want to escape?

TWENTY-FOUR

If Caitlin comes anywhere near my
man, I'll murder her at my
convenience.

MY PHONE RANG, and I groaned, reached for
it, and ended up with a handful of naked male
chest. "Make the noise stop."

With one of his sensuous chuckles, Malcolm tucked me close to his side, then he said,
"Kanika's phone, Malcolm speaking."

I supposed answering the call made the
noise stop. Grunting, I snuggled close to steal
his warmth. Before him, I'd been a 'hit the
floor running at dawn' girl, happy to have a
man scratch my itch and leaving before either
one of us could become attached.

I'd have to file some sort of complaint
later; how dare he sneak his way under my
skin before luring me between the sheets?

"No, she's not dead. What gave you that
dumbass idea? Do you really think I'd allow
anyone to touch her after that stunt in New
York? No, I don't want to talk to Caitlin. I

don't care what she told you. No, as in never applies. Really. What do you want from Kanika at seven in the morning?"

Some asshole had called me at seven? I lifted my hand and waggled my fingers. "Phone."

It took two tries to get the wretched device situated where it belonged. "I don't know who the fuck I'm talking to, but I don't care. If Caitlin comes anywhere near my man, I'll murder her at my convenience, which will be when I'm not busy sleeping with him. Understood?"

"Good morning, Kanika," Bubba Eugene replied. "Are you just saying that to throw her off his trail?"

"Oh, no. I never tell someone I'll kill them unless I mean it. What do you want?" I snarled.

"I wanted to ask you about that devil at the gala."

"His name is Satan. He's not 'that' devil. He's *the* devil. He's the real deal. I watched him turn a minotaur inside out once. What do you want to know?"

"What's someone like *you* doing with the devil?"

I deliberately misinterpreted his comment and replied, "You're confused. The only man I'm with is named Malcolm. What you saw in New York is exactly what reality is."

"Shit."

"Since you've bothered me about the devil at seven in the morning, tell me this: what does Caitlin want?"

Bubba Eugene sighed. "What Caitlin always wants: Malcolm."

"Then maybe she shouldn't have cheated on him. Tough shit for her. He's mine."

"She disagrees."

"Do I really need to repeat myself? Apparently, I do. Tough shit for her. He's mine, and I don't share."

Malcolm dropped kisses along my neck and chuckled. "You're so grouchy before you've been fed."

I needed to put a few warning labels around Malcolm's neck—and get him to stop before his cousin heard some wildly inappropriate behavior from us. "Stop that, Malcolm. I'm on the phone."

His growl sounded a lot like a purr. "But I don't want to."

"Wait," Bubba Eugene blurted. "Is he sleeping with you? He actually let you sleep with him?"

I swatted at Malcolm until he relented, although his pout almost did me in. "He's not sleeping with me right now. And what do you mean by let me? He pinned me to the door and made me beg for it. Go away. It seems I've been booked for a morning seduction, and you're interrupting us." I hung up. "Obviously, I've learned your ulterior motive, Mr. Stewart. You need me to marry you to protect you from Caitlin. I have reviewed your application for a protectorate marriage and find the terms acceptable."

Married to me was a lot better than letting her stalk him for the rest of his life when he obviously didn't want her. Also, married to me meant I'd never have to let him go, and it wasn't really violating all my morals if I married him, was it? "I need a shower, then I need to look into this eloping business so she can't sink her claws into you."

He pouted some more. "But what about the morning seduction?"

If I didn't leash him, we'd never leave the hotel room. "Elope first, then breakfast, then work, then seduction, in that order."

"I don't like that order."

How dare he make sulking so damned attractive? "You'll live." Leaning over him, I smiled and kissed his brow. "I'm going to make her regret that she thought she could hurt you like that."

"You're making it very difficult to skip the morning seduction."

"Leash the libido until tonight, Mr. Stewart. At the rate you're going, I'm starting to believe you're an incubus in disguise."

He laughed. "I'm not, sorry to disappoint. I have no incubus genes."

I thought about it. "You're right. It's obvious you can't be an incubus. They have nothing on you—and yes, I've been with one. You're superior. Don't let it go to your head too much. Let's go take care of that paperwork so we're both free of our past mistakes."

Marriage to Malcolm Stewart might be a mistake, but at least it would be a mistake of my choosing, one I could live with.

"You had no choice in what Asfour tried to do to you, Kanika. My mistakes with Caitlin were all my own."

While I thought wallowing was beneath him, I patted his chest and gave him another kiss. "Think about it this way. If it weren't for her, you wouldn't have met me."

His eyes widened. "I hadn't thought of that."

"Take a page out of my book, Mr. Stewart. Thank her the next time you see her. If she had loved you, she wouldn't have treated you like she did."

"And what about you?"

I'd never told anyone I'd loved them before. Some days, I didn't think myself capable of the emotion. Still, I had an answer for him, although I doubted he'd appreciate it. "I figure love isn't a destination. It's a journey." I hesitated, as my next words would condemn me, although I wasn't sure what the outcome of my condemnation would be. "I'm picking you as my best bet on making it work. Any man willing to put his soul on the line for eternity is worth fighting for, even if the trip gets bumpy on the way. I don't believe in love at first sight. Hell, I'm not sure I even believe in love, period. But, I do believe when two people want something bad enough, good things can happen."

I left him to think about it, aware of his gaze on me when I headed into the bathroom for a much-needed soak. There'd be time for regret and worry later, after I put my money where my mouth was.

With luck, I wouldn't learn first-hand if it was better to love and lose than to never have loved at all.

I HAD ALWAYS BELIEVED marriage to be a complex, annoying affair involving a great deal of paperwork. Within ten minutes of arriving at the courthouse, we had a document declaring our legal status as husband and wife. The name change form threw me for a loop, but Malcolm claimed the sheet for himself.

"A lot of women change their names, but I've been trying to escape mine most of my life, so if you don't mind, I think I'll steal yours."

"If you spell it wrong, he might show up."

Malcolm's mouth twitched into a smile. "Spell it for me, please."

We truly had too much in common. It took less than five minutes to claim him, name and all, as mine. "If I had to choose, I'd take Mephistopheles, too. Your family is infested with assholes."

"While I wish I could argue, I can't. In the next few weeks, there'll be a lot of paperwork we need to fill out. I'll set you up with a DBA so we can continue my Montgomery operations; some of my clients wouldn't like invoking the devil's name as part of daily business. It'll also give us some privacy."

"You won't hear a single complaint out of me."

"I'm also assuming you'll want to continue your mercenary work."

I shrugged. "Probably, although I suppose I won't be drifting much anymore."

"If you get the urge to roam, I can take my work with me."

I truly didn't deserve Malcolm's selflessness. "I can work around that." I gestured at the certificate and the accompanying paperwork. "Is this really it?"

"That's it. You're officially my life."

"I think you mean wife, Malcolm."

His smile, which was far too genuine to ever count as a smirk or anything other than heartfelt, promised I was wrong although he didn't correct me. I definitely hadn't done anything to deserve that from anyone. I flushed, locking my gaze onto the paperwork declaring our legal partnership.

The realization Asfour could have done the same robbed me of breath, and my blood drained out of my head and pooled in my feet. A courthouse and twenty minutes—or a licensed minister and several witnesses—could have made me a man's property. If the witnesses colluded and claimed I had signed willingly, everything would have been different. I gulped. "What happens if we want a divorce?"

Malcolm sucked in a breath, and then he narrowed his eyes. "Are you thinking about Asfour?"

I jerked my head in a nod.

"I've looked into it already, for the same reasons you're thinking of. I wanted to know what I was getting into if I caved and married Caitlin. Six months to a year of separation before finalization is required, and if he had a prenuptial, which he would have, he'd likely include clauses to make divorce difficult to process—and leave you without anything when it was said and done."

I swallowed. "Okay."

"You're fine, Kanika. Even if he attempts to draw up a fraudulent marriage contract, you're safe. It won't stick. All you need to do is request an angel to confirm you hadn't married him. You can also confirm that you were forced to run away from home to protect yourself. That would allow you to pursue damages against him. Confirming your willing marriage to me will also solidify your position, too."

Scowling, I planted my hands on my hips. "As what? A gold digger?"

In the gold digging department, I'd made off with the motherlode marrying Malcolm Stewart.

Instead of being insulted as I expected, he laughed. "Hardly. I'm fairly certain your adoptive father is far wealthier than I am. That makes me the gold digger."

"Oh." I supposed it technically did.

I'd have to spend some time mulling over that sharp left turn in my life.

"Fortunately for both of us, I'm far more interested in the woman than the money. In the interest of disclosure, Caitlin did want to do this exact same thing to me so I couldn't escape her, and she had come armed with a prenup, one that benefitted only her."

"For the record, this is a completely fucked up situation."

"It's unfortunately common. It's a bit of a

trend. Couples get a court marriage, give it a year or two to see if their relationship is going to work, *then* they spend the ridiculous amount of money on a proper wedding. So, we're doing things the wise and cautious way, although our lack of a prenuptial will likely have some turning their noses up at us."

"Huh. I had no idea."

After getting into an argument with the clerk over it, Malcolm filled out the name change form, received a confirmation so he could update his driver's license and other paperwork, and guided me out of the courthouse. "I'd like to start the actual wedding plans sooner than later. While the Stewart clan will not be invited, I have a lot of business colleagues and friends who I'd like to have at our wedding. I know you're not going to have a large guest list, but I know some people who would love to become friends with you for no reason other than you're different, interesting, smart as hell, and honest to a fault."

"What a ringing endorsement."

Malcolm smiled. "To me, there's none better."

If he kept sweet-talking me like he was, I'd have to reconsider the order for the rest of my day and bump the seduction up a few places on my to-do list. Then again, I was wise to save the best for last.

"I'm all right with starting any planning needed after we've dealt with the Wishing Well situation."

"Agreed. The intel on Savannah being a hot-bed of death seems spot on, and the brimstone levels here are smothering. Regular humans might end up incapacitated. Demons and devils call it smothered, angels tend to call it suppression."

"What do you mean?"

"They'll be like you, sick from the smell and devilish influences. It's usually not an issue since devils rarely congregate. Demons don't inspire the same sort of reaction."

Huh. I'd have to find out how Malcolm had come across such good information later. "Is there some reason the humans haven't moved away?"

"Yes. They can't at this stage. If you put enough devils in the same place, their miasma makes humans incapable of exercising their free will. Those who could leave have. Angels can counter it, and the higher-level devils can redirect or contain their miasma. That's why you didn't notice anything with the devil. He was actively working to contain his miasma. Won't stop the brimstone stench, but I bet he could if he wanted to. He is the devil, after all."

I frowned at the thought of what could happen in a populace lacking their free will.

"If Wishing Well is here, would they be able to take advantage of that miasma to make bargains?"

"I don't know for certain, but I'd guess so."

While disappointed, both with his lack of certainty and the possibility Wishing Well was taking advantage of the miasma to coerce people out of their souls, I considered my options. Only one route would get me the answers I needed without fail. Grabbing my phone, I called the devil.

"It's like you only call me when you want something, cupcake."

"Like? It's true. I have a couple of questions for you."

"Shoot."

"How many devils would it take to overwhelm a city's population?"

"Depends on the devil, cupcake. If it's me, one. In a worst-case scenario, it would take the three devils beneath me working together to pull it off, depending on the population in question. If you're looking at the lesser devils of average strength, you're looking at closer to a hundred."

"How likely is it your top three devils would gang up together to do it?"

"Did my naughty little girl go to Georgia?"

I rolled my eyes. "Maybe."

"Atlanta, Savannah, or Augusta? All three have miasma fields at current."

"Savannah."

"Seventy-five are mine, but they're weak—too weak for the level in the area."

"How many aren't yours?"

"Two."

That didn't sound good at all. "Two of your top devils have gone rogue in Savannah? Come on, Satin. Don't tell me you coerced me into this shit job to clean up your damned mess."

"They're angling for your job, cupcake. That's what devils do. Until they violate a bargain, they're as innocent as devils get, and I have to follow the rules."

I sighed. Of course the devil had to follow the rules. The devil may have left the heavens to bat on the side of evil, but evil was relative, and at heart, however twisted it was, Satin had been born an angel.

Sometimes, when I looked for it, it showed.

My first step would be finding out how I could resolve the internal problems before eliminating Wishing Well. "Can devils be killed?"

"Of course. They aren't me. It's so tiresome reclaiming a devil's seed and regrowing it. I suppose I'll do it if I must. You're really going to go kill my devils, aren't you?"

Between Malcolm and Satin, did I even need to have children? I figured children had nothing on their ability to whine. "If you didn't want to regrow their seeds, you shouldn't have let them do whatever they want then, Satin. You reap what you sow, and it's not *my* fault *you* got lazy."

"You're so very cruel."

"I'm sure you'll survive. So. These two devils can be killed, correct?"

"They'll provide a challenge for you and your Stewart male, I'm sure. When you do kill them, if you're going to mail them to me, at least use a refrigerated truck. Rotting devils have a rather strong and unique aroma."

"That's disgusting."

"It's also true. Anyway, don't worry yourself too much about the humans. They're remarkably resilient, and they'll go back to normal within a week of the miasma field dissipating."

"Unless Wishing Well bargains for their souls while they're under its influence," I snapped.

"Ah, but the miasma suppresses ambition, cupcake. It's a chicken and egg situation. Wishing Well might be able to talk a few of them into making a bad decision, they might get a few extra souls, but it won't work well for them. The bargains made will lack strength, and if they don't fulfill those bargains, I'm free to act."

However much I disliked it, I understood the tactic. "You're setting them up."

"That's the idea. I also have no proof they're the devils behind Wishing Well. They're using vessels, which is making it difficult to confirm guilt."

I hated being so damned ignorant about devils and demons, especially when I was stuck neck deep in their affairs. "Vessels?"

"Anyone who makes bargains on behalf of a devil is a vessel. The vessel is in a contract with the devil. While demons often serve as vessels, humans can become vessels as well. They're using vessels to cover their tracks. It's rather clever, really. Since *I* follow the rules, they have a few more options open to them. It's a raw deal, but I have to work around it."

"You're the universe's most lawful bad guy, aren't you?"

"Why does everyone think I'm the bad guy? Just because I turn people I don't like inside out sometimes doesn't mean I'm bad. Well, I do trick people into making unfavorable bargains for their souls. I suppose that is a little bad. It's tough being me."

I bet it was. Shaking my head over Satin's antics, I asked, "If I were to ask for angels, how many would it take to counter the miasma in Savannah?"

"Why would you want to? I brought in extra devils to make certain the miasma fields were strong enough to prevent Wishing Well from making good bargains. All removing the miasma field will do is put more souls at risk. If you bring in angels, Wishing Well will regain their ability to bargain with mortals."

"There's something to be said for free will. If our goal is to help the victims after the bargains have been made, then we need to catch Wishing Well in the act."

Satin sighed. "I chose a troublesome child. Your concern for your fellow mortals is disgustingly endearing, but it's more complicated than catching them in the act. If they can make new bargains, the numbers of undead will rise. That's not a problem easily solved. If the miasma fields fail, Wishing Well will be able to create tens upon thousands of new undead—and stronger undead. Undead happen, but it's like angels, devils, and demons; there's a rhyme and reason to it. That's no longer the case."

"What sort of bargain would be needed to help Wishing Well's victims?"

The long moment of silence didn't bode well for the men and women murdered for their souls. "The ones who could do it don't bargain, cupcake. Sorry."

"Angels, then?"

"Correct."

"Do those brothers of yours have a phone number or some civilized way to reach them?" I snarled. After browbeating the devil, how hard could it be to knock some sense into a pair of archangels?

"I'll have them call you."

"Can't they just drop in?"

"Sure, they could, but your Stewart male won't like it."

I frowned. "Will it kill him?"

"No, of course not."

"He's a big, manly man. I'm sure he can handle himself."

"Go somewhere private. I'll ask if they're free, and if so, I'll tell them to find you in twenty minutes."

"Call me back if they're not free."

"Will do." The devil hung up.

"You're planning something," my new husband accused. "What are you planning? When you plan things, disasters happen."

I couldn't blame him, since lately, that did tend to be the result. "I'm not planning anything yet. I need to ask two angels a question."

"Why angels? They're so…"

"Creepy?"

"World-endingly dangerous."

Why me? "Do I need to send you to our room until I'm done talking to them?"

"There's no chance in hell am I leaving you alone with a bunch of damned angels."

However amusing it might be to argue the finer points of angels, their inability to be damned and retain their rank as an angel, and Malcolm's possessiveness, I settled with rolling my eyes and laughing. "You're just going to have to play nice with the angels. We need to find a private place to meet them in twenty minutes."

"I know just the place. Follow me."

TWENTY-FIVE

I had found someone who viewed his
cup as half full with a twist.

SCRAGGLY GRASS ENCROACHED on the pristine sands far enough away from the popular
beaches to offer the illusion of privacy—and
escape the stench of decay and brimstone for
a while. Malcolm smiled and pointed at the
ridge above us. "The foot path is on the other
side, and few like this spot. It's just not as
pretty as near the pier or boardwalk."

People were strange. I appreciated the
wild, untouched ocean and the natural jetty
blocking my view of civilization. "It's plenty
pretty."

"There's a nice rock that way some couples enjoy if they don't mind possibly putting
on a show." Staring off into the distance, Malcolm sighed. "That's how I found out what
sort of woman Caitlin really was."

I grimaced. "This isn't a place you like,
is it?"

"This is one of my favorite places in the world. She never found out that was the night I learned the truth about her. No, I'm grateful for this quiet stretch of beach. I wouldn't have said no the first time she tried to rope me into marrying her if not for that rock. I found freedom here."

Huh. Obviously, I had found someone who viewed his cup as half full with a twist. "And a hefty amount of resentment to go with it. How do you know I'm not the same way?"

On second thought, I probably should have asked that question *before* marrying him.

Malcolm lifted his arm and displayed his master bracelet. "This helped. Mostly, I watched you. While you were recovering in Minnesota, I talked to you. Now, that's an unfair advantage since you don't remember it, but to be fair, I hoped you would. When I was shot and fed my magic to you, I felt it all. You really don't do things in half measure, do you? You're a lot like the devil, you know."

"I am not!"

He grinned. "But you are. When you give your word, you mean it. That's what I first admired about you."

"And here I thought it was my legs and ass."

"Those are two very potent weapons in your arsenal. And I don't just like them, I love them. Yes, your legs and ass caught my attention, but *you* held it. You were so determined to protect me from my family, fearing treachery you couldn't confirm. Some men don't like that, but I do. It says a lot about your character."

"So does ambushing you using my legs and ass as bait, shooting you with a dart, and kidnapping you. Now look at me."

"I am. I'm rather pleased I convinced you to marry me. I was starting to get desperate." Malcolm rested his hands on my hips and pulled me close. "I took advantage of the opportunity. I should feel guilty, but I don't."

"How was it taking advantage? I agreed to keep Caitlin away from you, you agreed to keep Asfour away from me."

"While I fully intend on keeping Asfour as far away from you as possible, that was not my main motivation. I'm selfish, and I wanted you for myself." Malcolm smirked and drummed his fingers against my hips. "Maybe you don't believe in love at first sight, but I do. I'll wait however long it takes for you to feel the same way, so take your time. I'm also a firm believer of lust at first sight, too. It's fair to say I fell for you twice in one moment."

When I got some one-on-one time with the devil, I needed to ask him about the nature of Malcolm's curse, because I had no idea how he was being affected by it. If the curse began and ended with no children, I didn't care. Why would I?

His sincerity wasn't faked. I had more than my fair share of insecurities, but I had faith in him, and not because he was a so-called picky Stewart. Malcolm saw me as more than a skirt to chase, although he cheerfully admitted he liked the package, especially the legs and ass that had led to his downfall. The novelty would wear off one day, although I hoped he wouldn't change.

I respected him more and more each day. Hell, I had no idea what love actually was when I thought about it.

No one had loved me before.

"I might not be good at this whole wife thing," I warned.

"Just be yourself. That's all I want. I even took your advice. I married who *I* wanted, not who my family wanted. I probably won't be any good at the whole husband thing, either. We'll take it day by day. Sound good?"

"Sounds good."

"We'll be fine," he promised.

It amazed me how easy it was to believe he was right.

MICHAEL AND GABRIEL showed up in a flash of silver light, startling a yelp out of Malcolm while I hissed my displeasure. The archangels laughed, and an invisible weight lifted from my shoulders.

"Thanks for coming." I breathed in the salty air, grateful the two archangels somehow blocked Savannah's stench. "I know you don't do bargains, but I want to ask for your help."

Gabriel sank down where the sand and surf met, sticking his feet in the water. "Our brother can be quite prideful. He could ask for our help if he really wants. He did when he tricked you into signing those papers. You've been busy. How can we serve?"

"I'm worried about Wishing Well's victims. We met a few on the way to New York, and I suspect they were murdered after making their bargains."

"That's a potentially dangerous claim, Kanika," the archangel warned.

"I know. I don't know if I can prove it, but it's suspicious. Then you have this congregation of the newly dead, plus there's two higher-level devils the devil isn't counting as his."

"A worrisome issue, yes. Our brother's hands are tied."

I waggled my fingers at the archangel. "Mine aren't."

"It's rather refreshing to have a free agent with morals around. I'm not sure what we can do to help you, though. Your thoughts, Michael?"

"I see no obvious ways we can lend you aid," Michael confirmed.

"Can you at least hear me out?"

"Of course. We're here in an official capacity. *He* has noticed the problem. Our brother's lucky. The current holder of the portfolio is a family man. That matters, especially when the prayers of the living are so burdened with grief. That'll wear off in a few decades, I'm sure. For now, his nature works in your favor."

"Does Satin know that?"

"No."

I shook my finger at Michael. "Naughty, tricksy archangel. All right. Satin thinks if I ask you two to mitigate the miasma, Wishing Well will have better footing in their bargaining. Satin also thinks the devils involved are using vessels to make the bargains, so he's unable to do anything about the situation. Is this correct?"

"You're correct."

I nodded, sighed, and hoped I wasn't about to get myself into even more trouble. "I'm not bound by those rules. Correct?"

"That's correct."

"Do you know what'll happen if Wishing Well goes unchecked?"

The archangels fidgeted. Gabriel wiggled

his toes in the surf and splashed at the water when the waves broke high enough on the shore for him to reach. I waited.

Gabriel cracked first, snapping his wings out and grunting his displeasure. "Yes. *He* told us."

"Enlighten me, Archangel Gabriel."

The instant the words left my mouth, I realized I'd given one of *His* archangels a rather direct order. I tensed, waiting for lightening to streak out of the clear skies and strike me dead.

"Very well. You'll die during the conflict, and when your powers are needed, you'll be but a memory. Because of your death, others will die. At first, everything will seem normal, but within five years of Earth's time, the first consequences of your death will become apparent. No new children will be born. The dead will walk, the living will die, but their souls will remain trapped in the mortal coil. No new seeds of life will be planted. It begins."

The cold neutrality of Gabriel's voice terrified me. "It?"

"The end of days, at least for this Earth."

Holy hell. "All because I die?" I squeaked.

"You began as nothing. You have become something. In that one moment, for Earth, you will become everything. Earth's history is full of little moments like that, but yours is a little more important than others—for this moment."

"Isn't there some paradox rule about if the maker of history knows what they'll do in advance, they'll fuck it up?"

The archangels laughed, and their good humor in the face of Earth's destruction—the end of bloody days—annoyed a hiss out of me.

Michael patted the top of my head. "Don't worry, little niece. You can't, as you say, fuck it up, fortunately for us all. Your father never cheats. This is a critical part of his existence."

"He's the Lord of Lies—"

"No, Kanika. *Your* father. The one who planted the seed of *your* life. *He* never cheats. My brother cheats whenever the rules let him. That's his nature. But for my brother, one rule remains unbroken. He never, ever violates the universal laws."

"Back up. What does my birth father have to do with anything?" I shrugged. "I know nothing about him beyond the fact he's the one responsible for my affinity with sari and coin belts."

"This is when our discussion will become inevitably uncomfortable for your husband. Clever of you, by the way, stealing the devil's new daughter right out from beneath his nose. Well done."

Malcolm straightened, and he smirked,

and something about his eyes made me believe the Michael's compliment meant far more than he wanted anyone to realize. "Opportunity knocked."

"We're both very impressed you haven't run away from us yet, too."

That wiped Malcolm's smirk off his face, much to my disappointment. "I'm not a coward."

"No, you're a demon who has lived most of your life hiding the true strength of your powers so you won't be used by those you fear."

I stiffened. Malcolm was a demon? It explained a few things about his behavior in bed, but I had trouble believing it. It also explained how he knew so much about demons and devils. "In-ter-est-ing."

"Kanika, I—"

"Not human either." I feigned a faint, sprawling onto the sun-warmed sand. "Oh, no. I married a demon."

The archangels snickered.

"Can't you see there's a damsel in distress here?" I complained.

Their snickers blossomed into chiming laughter.

"How rude," I muttered, hopping to my feet and brushing the sand off my clothes. "I've been adopted by the devil, Malcolm. I'm a sphinx. Unless you're one of those demons who eat their wives, I don't see the issue. If you *are*, I have a problem with that. I am *not* dinner."

"You married a pervert," Gabriel informed me.

"I had that figured out around the same time he did a full demonstration of his ridiculous endurance."

"He might slow down after a few hundred years, but I wouldn't count on it."

Holy hell. My eyes widened, and I looked Malcolm over. "I take it he's a long-lived species, then."

"Demons typically are. Depending on how well he matures before the magic fades, he'll likely take a long nap until the next emergence, assuming the end of days does not begin prematurely. I expect your father will meddle to ensure that happens."

"Which one?" I grumbled.

"Both. Can I be the one to tell your male he unwittingly signed up for a very long life? It's also worth mentioning he was ah, how do you modern mortals phrase it? Ah, yes. Screwed. He was screwed the instant he bargained with our brother. You were set up."

Malcolm grinned and dipped in a bow. "I know. I wanted to see what Kanika would do. I'm particularly fond of her latest nickname for him. Ask me what it is. You know you want to."

The archangels giggled, and Gabriel took the bait. "What is it?"

"Satin Blabbermouth McSmarty Liar Pants."

I smacked my forehead. A pop and a hint of brimstone marked the devil's arrival. "You can't wrap him in satin and light him on fire."

"Why must you insist on ruining my fun?"

"I like this one so you're not allowed."

The devil lashed his tail. "I'm so glad I got an invite to this party. I would've been so sad if I'd missed it all."

I glared at Malcolm. "Good job. Next time, just think it. He only shows up if summoned by written or spoken word. He might listen in on what you're thinking, though—if he thinks you have some juicy secret he wants to know."

Malcolm smirked at the devil, and the devil snapped his wings out, stomped a hoof, and breathed blue flame, which came within a hair's width of scalding my husband. "Please stop thinking about that. It's rather uncomfortable."

Gabriel snickered and kicked at the water. "Did I mention your male is rather perverted?"

"You had, but thank you. If you stopped listening in, you wouldn't be subjected to his perversion."

"Ooh," the archangels and the devil replied.

I smacked my forehead again, successfully giving myself a headache. "I'm surrounded by idiots. So, step one: I can't die due to ignoring Wishing Well. Correct?"

"Correct," Michael confirmed. "Surviving is rather important at this stage."

"You're cheating," the devil growled.

"If you can't keep a lid on being a goody-goody, I'll uninvite you," I warned.

"But they're *cheating*."

Malcolm pinched the bridge of his nose as if he was warding away a growing headache, too. "There's so much wrong with this I'm not sure where to begin. This isn't going as expected."

"I'll uninvite you, too. You and Satin can go cry in a beer if you can't behave like adults. We're not cheating. We're cleverly interpreting the rules in ways that benefit me. Now, shush. So, Michael. What's the best way to resolve our issue with Wishing Well?"

"Kill the vessels, take claim over the bargained souls, and release the bargained souls to the afterlife. If you can kill the vessels, it'll take time for the devils responsible to find replacements. Alternatively, you can kill the devils and demons involved, invalidate the bargains, and take over—and rewrite—the contracts. You could just kill everyone in-volved. That would work, too."

Obviously, I couldn't afford to let Michael be in charge of making the plans. His method involved a lot more killing than I was com-fortable with. "Gabriel?"

"I volunteer to help with the killing."

My mouth dropped open. "What is wrong with you two?"

"We oppose an unscheduled end of days," they choroused.

"We can't just kill everybody."

"It's just one city," Michael complained.

"No."

"It would solve the problem, guaranteed. And it would smell a lot better here when we're finished."

"It would be three cities, actually," the devil pointed out.

Michael shrugged. "It'd still smell a lot better when we're finished."

I stomped my foot. "No."

Playing in the surf, Gabriel flopped onto his back, and I could feel him staring at me despite his lack of a head. "You're making this unnecessarily difficult."

"We are *not* slaughtering hundreds of thousands—"

"Millions," the devil corrected.

I hissed at Satin and kicked sand in his direction. "We are *not* slaughtering millions of people to make this easy. No. No, no, no. No means no. No doesn't mean argue with me. It means *no*."

"Why not?" the archangels demanded.

"You're supposed to be the good guys. No. There will be no indiscriminate slaughtering of entire cities."

Michael sighed and closed his wings, huffing his displeasure. "Why did you pick this one again, brother? She's most stubborn. Listen, little niece. It's the most efficient solution. They have a protectorate of undead out of control. Destroying them would ensure Earth's survival."

"At least until the scheduled end of days," I muttered.

"Correct. Nothing lasts forever, not even us."

Nothing was ever easy, and I wanted to dig a hole in the sand and stick my head in it. "What sort of protectorate are you talking about?"

"Mummies, zombies, and similar."

"I like mummies. They have more common sense than most sentients combined," I declared, pulling out my phone and dialing the number for the Museum of Natural History. When someone answered, I said, "I need to speak to Ginger, please. It's Kanika calling."

"Ginger?" Michael hummed. "How interesting."

I was put on hold, and several minutes later, I heard a click and the rasp of breath. "My queen?"

"I need a favor, Ginger."

"Anything."

While I wanted a clear answer on why mummies breathed, I set aside my curiosity and focused on the more important things, including preventing a premature end of days. "Join me in Savannah, Georgia, and ask King Tutankhamun if he would also grace us with his presence. If you have other friends who might be bored, they are welcome to join us as well. There are some upstarts here I need to deal with." I considered Ginger's rather violent way of handling Asfour and played my more vicious card. "Apparently, if I ignore them, I'll die."

"Yes, my queen. I come soon," Ginger hissed. "No. We come. Bring friends. Find Queen."

The phone clattered to the floor, and I hung up so I wouldn't have to listen to the museum employees whine about their exhibits talking back to them again. "Ginger will see if King Tutankhamun will join us, and he's looking to bring some friends with him as well."

Gabriel chuckled. "Were you aware you

were speaking in a very, very old form of Egyptian?"

Huh? "I was?"

"That definitely wasn't English," Malcolm confirmed.

"Cool." I added speaking dead languages to my list of things to research when I had some time, preferably after the world wasn't about to go to hell without the benefit of a hand basket. "Anyway, I'll ask the mummies for their help once they arrive."

Gabriel twisted and pointed at the devil. "You neglected to tell us she could already raise mummies. And you say we cheat!"

"You could peek into the past if you desire. You didn't ask. I can't tell all my secrets, little brother. Anyway, she had help. Her Stewart channeled power for her. While a sphinx, she lacks strength. It's well enough. If she had strength, she'd be cursing souls whenever she got annoyed. I wisely tricked them into wearing suppression bracelets to keep her from accidentally raising any more mummies. They should be locked by now."

I tensed. "Locked? What do you mean by locked?" Lifting my hand, I glared at the bracelet. "Satin! What have you done?"

"They're special made. Go ahead. Try to take them off."

I tried to take both of mine off to discover the clasps wouldn't budge. Malcolm tried, too, and when he failed, he shrugged. "In my defense, I had no idea they could lock, Kanika."

A growl slipped out, and I locked my gaze on the devil's throat. Malcolm wrapped his arms around my waist, pulling until my back rested flush against his chest. I reached for my adoptive father, hissing curses at him. "Mephistopheles!"

"I neglected to give you some important information, yes, but it's entirely your fault. You didn't ask me the right questions. I do that a lot. It's a bad habit. Oh, that does remind me. Malcolm, do regulate any magic you give her very carefully. It's bad enough she woke two powerful mummies. If you're not careful—" The devil blinked. "Oh. I suppose that could work, too."

Gabriel fluttered his wings, and when the angel laughed, it was a harrowing, wicked sound. "It could. It hasn't been done like that before. That's the problem with crossbreeds. They change the rules."

"Dangerous," Michael muttered. "We might end up destroying the city anyway. It would be more efficient to just do it ourselves."

"No," I blurted, not even sure what I was arguing against anymore. "I don't know what you're talking about, but no. And we're not blowing up the city because it's easy."

Michael heaved a sigh. "Why did you teach her that word?"

"She came with it, I'm afraid. Why not, Kanika?"

"Are you children? Indiscriminate murder is bad."

Malcolm whispered in my ear, "It's like having kids, but they're bloodthirsty kids who could end the world. Please don't adopt any of these three. They might kill us in our sleep."

"I'm going to agree with you on this one."

The devil stomped a hoof, and the sands steamed. "Why are you two talking about children when we're trying to plan mass murder?"

"No means no. There'll be no indiscriminate mass murders. Don't be such a child. Discriminate murders of responsible demons, devils, and vessels only. Am I understood?"

If the archangels had faces, I was certain they'd be pouting. Michael's shoulders slumped. "But you wanted us to help. We're helping."

I needed a stiff drink and a break from reality. "Malcolm?"

He hugged me closer. "Yes?"

"The next time I think about asking angels for help, distract me."

"And how would you like me to distract you?"

"Another marathon session might work. If I still think I need an angel's help after, discuss it with me."

"Please think about asking angels for help often."

I truly was surrounded by idiots, and I had married one of them. Wonderful. "All right, Michael, Gabriel. How can you help *without* reducing Savannah, Atlanta, and Augusta to smoldering piles of rubble?"

The archangels took their time thinking about it, and right when I was ready to start kicking them, Gabriel sighed. "If we declare you adjudicates in this matter, we can grant you our favor."

Michael snorted. "The city might end up reduced to rubble anyway."

"Do I want to know what it means to be an adjudicate?" I probably didn't, and my worries were confirmed when the archangels snickered. "Belay that. Satin? How about you?"

"What about me?"

I pointed at myself and Malcolm. "If I'm working with two archangels to put an end to this situation, I may as well make you do your fair share of the work, especially if it takes both of them to match you. That way, everything's all nice and balanced, just like you sticklers like. That's what this is about, right?

No new life and no one dying equals no more Earth. Therefore, you should help."

"*I* should help? Me?"

"I'm already paying for it by putting up with your shit, Satin. I'll consider us even for making me watch you turn a minotaur inside out."

Gabriel laughed. "You truly picked a ruthless child as your heir."

"And since I'm a sentimental old idiot, I promised to keep their souls together. Don't tell the man upstairs. He'll never let me live this down."

Michael snorted. "I'm sure *He* already knows." Stepping towards me and reaching out, the archangel pressed his finger to my nose. "I'll make you my representative in this matter. Remember this, my little niece. I'm the one who trumpets in the end of days, and for however long you're burdened with my power, it is your responsibility as well. With one hand, I heal and bring life. With the other, I destroy. Choose wisely."

"Am I the only one here who finds it ironic I'm not even Christian?" I complained.

The archangel laughed, then Michael's finger pressed to my nose flared with heat and seared away my thoughts until nothing but light remained.

TWENTY-SIX

I thought my scream was a
completely justified reaction.

WATER FLOWED AROUND ME, and I jolted to
full awareness. I had no memory of entering
the ocean, but I spit out water along with vehement curses. I liked baths. I liked looking at
ponds. I enjoyed listening to the surf on the
sand.

Under no circumstances did I want anything to do with water deep enough to
drown me.

I couldn't swim.

All things considered, I thought my
scream was a completely justified reaction.

Unfortunately, the blue-gray beast with a
mouth full of pointy teeth didn't agree with
my assessment of the situation. I got a good
look down its throat and added a check to my
brand new 'oh hell no!' list.

A wave slammed into me from behind,
and I collided with a muscular chest and a

pair of spindly, knobby legs. My arms ignored my brain's insistence pointy teeth equaled a messy death. I clutched for anything I could grab to keep from drowning. My fingers closed around silky hairs, and I fisted my hands as tightly as I could.

It took a shameful length of time to realize I could just stand. While I remembered I had legs, the beast with pointy teeth stood still and waited. My second embarrassment followed quickly on the heels of the first.

I clung to a horse's proudly arched neck. I could deal with a horse, but why did the horse have pointy teeth? Since when did horses eat meat? I didn't want to be eaten by a horse *or* drown. If I had my way, I'd never get anywhere near the water ever again.

Cats and water just didn't mix.

I was certain of one thing. Nothing made sense anymore, and I mourned for the loss of my quiet, sane life.

"Stupid demon!" the melodic voice of an archangel called from the safety of shore.

Coward archangel, hiding where it was safe.

I whimpered, closed my eyes, and hoped the nightmare would end sooner than later.

"Your species lures people into the water to drown them, not to play bodyguard. You're doing this all wrong," the archangel complained.

If I made it to shore alive, I'd make it my life's mission to kill the archangel for giving the pointy-teethed horse ideas about eating me.

Satin cackled, a rather unpleasant, grating sound. "No, he's doing it quite right, actually. They breed in the water, too. Once we go away, he'll shift and seduce her to make little baby demons. We should leave them alone so he can get to the seducing in peace. We didn't hurt her, Malcolm. She's mortal, so the influx of divinity stunned her. There's no need to be a mule over this. It didn't hurt you, either."

The horse snorted and flattened his ears.

"Malcolm?" I squeaked, cracking open an eye. "You're a demon horse?"

The demon horse's eyes glowed sea green, and he squealed a protest.

"He's a kelpie, Kanika," the devil corrected. "Thanks to you fainting, he abandoned his humanity and dragged you into the water. It's a typical kelpie response when threatened, as they're stronger in the water. Sea water is his prime element, so he's quite at home there. He's much weaker in fresh water—keep that to yourself, cupcake. The rest of his clan is attuned to fresh water."

Well, that explained a few things, including why Caitlin would have her tryst near the ocean—and Bubba Eugene's insistence I leave Malcolm in fresh water. Had he been a fresh water demon horse like the rest of his clan, he would've liked being tossed into a lake. I still had my doubts about Bubba Eugene's sincerity, but if he believed Malcolm preferred fresh water, the contract made sense.

"Were you going to eat me, Malcolm?" I hissed.

The demon horse with pointy teeth whipped his head side to side.

Some things had to be addressed above all others, and my inability to swim took the top prize. "I can't swim, so there will be no sea nookie in our near future, sir. Do we have an understanding?"

He shook his head again with equal enthusiasm.

"I said no!"

The devil cackled. "He'll literally trap you in the surf until he gets what he wants. He can't help his nature. Don't worry too much, cupcake. He'll come back to his senses soon. Just think about it this way: he's cursed, so all you two will get is some exercise."

I really need to kill the devil very soon. "Malcolm, so help me, I will shift and castrate you if you even think about sea surf nookie before I learn how to swim. Let me out of the water. Now."

Malcolm hung his head and his ears drooped.

"I might consider letting you teach me how to swim after we deal with Wishing Well," I offered as a compromise.

My very own woman-eating demon horse flicked an ear forward and pawed at the water with a hoof.

"Seduction is on the list after lunch and work. We already missed breakfast. Please don't be a stupid idiot today."

Sighing, Malcolm chomped on my hair, turned, and dragged me out of the ocean.

The devil lashed his tail and snorted flame. "I underestimated his control it seems. I question his choice of biting her hair, however."

Gabriel's laughter chimed. "Well, she isn't going to escape him like that. Do you need help finding your humanity? It's always difficult for demons in their element. There's no shame in it if you do."

Once I stood on the shore without any help, Malcolm shifted from stallion to man, and unlike my magic, he returned to his human form fully nude. Water dripped off him, and I licked my lips, reconsidering my original refusal.

I needed to find him some clothes before I pounced him. "Where are his clothes?"

"They had an accident," the devil replied.

Malcolm staggered a step, sighed, and

slumped to the sand. I blinked. "Was he supposed to do that?"

The devil snorted. "Most call that a faint. That's what you did, which triggered his shift. I suspect adrenaline alone kept him conscious." Crouching beside Malcolm, Satin chuckled and checked my husband's pulse. "He'll be fine. Gabriel? You're better at taking someone with you without injuring your passenger. Can you take him to his hotel room?"

"I can, yes."

No one moved, and the devil scowled, twitching his tail. "Will you?"

"Maybe. Say the magic word."

"Do I have to?"

"Yes."

Angels were assholes, although I found the devil's brothers amusing.

"We try," they replied.

I laughed.

"What's the magic word?"

"Fine. Will you please take my demon to his hotel room?"

"Of course. I'm glad to help. Michael, please escort our lovely niece to their room. Remember, don't discriminately murder the whole city. She'll get mad at us."

"How about a part of it?"

"No," I snapped, glaring at the archangels.

Gabriel knelt beside Malcolm, grabbing hold of his wrist. "Take your time, little niece.

He'll be a while waking up. Lucifer and I will tend to him as needed, never fear."

I worried anyway, but I nodded and replied, "Thank you."

The devil, archangel, and Malcolm vanished in a flash of golden light, and I really hoped Malcolm would be all right in the custody of two of Earth's most dangerous troublemakers.

Michael fluttered his banded wings and stretched. "Now we can attend to business. First, you must eat. Then, we hunt."

"Why do I have a bad feeling about this?"

"That's because you've been paying attention. Time's wasting, and I have a lot more of it than you do."

"Michael, Archangel of Burn."

"Indeed."

IF I MADE a list of my recent mistakes, I would begin with leaving Malcolm in the care of the devil and an archangel. Two against one wasn't fair to begin with, and I doubted my new husband and partner-in-crime could keep the pair out of trouble. Leaving several potential enemies alive took second place. Third went to exploring the dead-infested city of Savannah. It took less than an hour for me to realize the brutal truth.

Few living remained.

"Where have they gone?" I whispered, swallowing so I wouldn't throw up again.

"The wise moved while they still could, those who couldn't afford to move bargained. The rest just haven't been killed yet."

"Are you seriously implying I'm the only run of the mill mortal here who hasn't bargained their soul away to Wishing Well yet?"

"Your husband hasn't, but in a word, yes." Michael pointed at a decaying apartment building down the street. "Tonight, they'll be burned in their sleep. The arsonist has already set a small explosive to rupture a gas pipe. If all goes to Wishing Well's plan, they'll be killed from the resulting fumes. Should that not work, they'll set the building on fire. It won't go well. The arsonist set the charges too close to faulty wiring. It'll spark."

"It's not cheating if it's the past?"

"Correct. You could find this out for yourself, too, if you thought to look. As you were wise enough to ask for our help, I am helping. So, knowing what you know now, what will you do?"

"Can we remove the devices?"

"We could, but it would only change the time of their deaths."

"And everyone in the building bargained?"

"They signed and updated their leases. The bargain was made within their lease. Unintentional bargaining, but they signed, so it's technically valid. Always read the fine print."

"That's disgusting."

"It's binding. They signed."

"And they can't revoke their agreement?"

"They could cancel their leases and lose their homes."

My eyes widened. "Satin wanted Malcolm to buy real estate here."

"My brother is as cunning as he is secretly altruistic. A new lease would invalidate the old one, if signed in time."

"But these people will die before Malcolm can make any property purchases." Dread cramped my stomach. "What can we do? If they die now..."

"They'll become new undead like most of this city. If I were to destroy the three cities now, the deaths would only number in the low thousands. Those behind Wishing Well would die with them."

Damn it. The low thousands were still too many innocent lives lost. "What would happen if I killed those behind Wishing Well?"

"You would become the owner of the bargained souls, and you would be responsible for them." Michael shrugged and stretched his wings. "For a time, you would on equal footing with your fathers."

"Fathers. Both of them."

"Your birth father is old, and old things have power. His is a subtle power, much like yours, but his has the strength yours lacks. Your father's father was the child of a god when gods openly walked the Earth to forge their myths. Your father's father was, in all ways, a mortal man. Your father is burdened with his heritage. Yours is a different path."

"Could you possibly be more vague?"

"It would be a challenge."

"Has anyone ever told you you're an asshole?"

"From time to time."

"You're an asshole."

"I find your honesty refreshing, but your foolish desire to save those paying the price for their wickedness is obnoxious."

"Poor inconvenienced uncle archangel, he can't just blow up three cities currently vexing him. Isn't *your* father all about forgiving sins?"

"Kanika, the Sphinx of Stubbornness."

"I didn't say we couldn't kill people, Michael. I just said we couldn't kill *everyone*." I wrinkled my nose. "And looking for a place to live and not reading the fine print is hardly worth losing their soul over. Do you know, for a fact, the fine print wasn't hidden? I've seen *that* trick before."

"You mean with magic."

"Yes, just like you hid the fine print when I got adopted by the damned devil!"

"It hadn't occurred to me to check. That *would* be a direct violation of the most holy of rules."

"Check with mortal eyes, as *they* would have seen the lease."

"I can do this. Don't wander." Michael vanished in a flash of silver light.

Me, wander? Did the apartment building right down the street count? I sure hoped not. I giggled and not wandered to the last place a sane woman would go, a building with a bomb primed to blow a gas line.

If I died, it'd be my own damned fault.

ON THE OUTSIDE, the apartment building deserved condemnation, and I could easily imagine a scumbag landlord selling the souls of the tenants for a chance to raze the damned thing to the ground. I expected the cost to restore the structure to a habitable state to be astronomical.

If I were to buy it, my first act would be to move everyone to a better place and level it. I suspected that was the landlord's goal, but to do so in such a way he wouldn't lose money on the job. How would Malcolm handle the situation? I'd have to ask him once I finished poking my nose where it didn't belong. After a quick check over my shoulder to be certain I was alone, I hoped for my tiny but fierce warrior form and shifted.

Luck was with me, and I stretched, swishing my tufted tail before stalking around the building. If anyone spotted me, I'd draw attention, but my sleek feline body, small size, and dark fur would hide me from most. I prowled around the foundation, peeking into holes in the brick, mortar, and concrete. Bars covered most of the windows, too many cracked and broken for my liking.

Most of the ground floor apartments were empty, which supported my theory about a scumbag landlord looking to ditch a losing proposition. Around the back, weeds engulfed the yard and strangled the hedges, hiding the windows from casual observers.

Tucked behind the thickest mess of undergrowth, a broken window and bent bars offered me the perfect way inside. Unable to resist the urge, I jumped inside, landing on rotting floorboards several feet below.

Dust clung to my fur, and I hissed over the decrepit state of the interior. Worse, I understood why someone would choose to live in squalor. Before the devil's interference, I might've been a tenant in a similar building, struggling to survive, discounted and looked down on for barely scraping by.

I could put every person in the building in a hotel for months and not miss the money. The thought halted me in my tracks. If I wrote a contract stating *I* became their landlord, would it release their souls?

Reality bit me in the ass. It wouldn't matter if they died before I could do anything about their situation. Why did I always seem to get into shitty situations without easy, ethical answers? Things would be far less annoying if I just let the archangels have their way.

Oh well.

Like the window, the apartment's interior had seen better days; holes in the walls revealed moldy studs and a noticeable lack of insulation. Dust caked everything, and the floor was littered with the evidence animals found the place inviting.

Gross.

I poked my head into every hole I could, shifting several times to access the higher places. I did the majority of my search as a human. Hands helped, especially when I needed to open doors. While someone had broken into the apartment, they hadn't left the bomb in the walls. I cracked open the hallway door, and the stench of decay hit hard, souring my stomach.

Two bodies, the kind that didn't get back up and walk after death, decomposed just outside the door. I couldn't tell what had killed them, and I didn't want to touch them to find out.

Double gross.

A dry wind washed over the back of my neck, bringing with it heat and the scent of a sun-scorched desert. I tensed, tore my gaze from the corpses, and turned.

King Tutankhamun's death mask glowed with a golden light. "You have called. We have answered. What would you have us do?"

I had no idea how the mummies had gotten to Georgia from New York so fast, but I decided against questioning it. Ginger crouched at my feet, and a dark, skittering wave erupted from beneath his wrappings. The emerald carapaces of scarabs glinted in the unnatural light, converging around my feet.

No matter how badly I wanted to, I wouldn't scream. I inhaled, held my breath, and waited for the urge to subside. "I need to kill some people, and possibly some devils and demons, too. They're tricking people into giving up their souls. They intend to murder the living tenants of this building."

"You mean to protect them." King Tutankhamun bowed. "Very well. Ten living beings reside in this space."

It could go either way if he counted me, too. "If I can, I will. An archangel told me they planted some sort of bomb to rupture a gas line and kill the residents tonight."

"And you believe this archangel?" If King Tutankhamun had eyebrows, I bet his would've been taking a hike to his hairline.

"Can archangels lie?" I countered.

"We can't," Michael answered from behind me. "I thought I said not to wander."

"I didn't wander. I deliberately meandered."

The mummies' laughter rasped.

"Your guess was correct. The devils obscured the contracts, deceiving the victims. Their souls have been recategorized as wrongfully threatened."

I thought of the worst scenario and considered it the likeliest possibility. "But the bargain holds if they die?"

"Yes."

"Nuking the city with archangel power would be bad, correct?"

"My brother must have picked you to annoy me."

"He's an ass like that, so probably. Can you write up some contracts for me?"

"I could, I suppose. Why?"

"I'm going to fight fire with fire. The devil gave me money. I'm going to buy out their contracts."

"You're going to what?"

"I'm going to buy out their contracts. I'm

going to have you write a contract that releases their souls from the bargain. I'll pay for
hotels for them for two months and relocate
them to a safe city."

"Boston is safe."

"Boston, then. Two months, give them a
hundred dollars a day to spend on food, necessities, and clothes. Stipulate those capable
of work must look for a new job."

"And if they're uneducated?"

"I'll figure it out after you get them to
Boston safely."

"Me?"

"You wanted to kill them, so you get to
help them move. They're your responsibility
now."

By the time I finished with Michael, he'd
name me the Sphinx of Delegation, and I'd
love every minute of it.

"You're making this complicated."

I smiled. "You'll love the next part, then."

"You want me to identify everyone who
was likewise tricked and arrange their relocation."

Mind readers simplified so much. "Yes.
While you're doing that, I'm going to recruit
some mummies."

"Do you even know how?"

"Not a clue in hell. I'm making this up as I
go. Chop, chop. You have souls to save,
Michael. I have a bomb to find."

"Second door on the right in the utility closet. It will detonate in three hours. I recommend tossing it into the ocean."

"And kill the fish?"

If Michael had a head, I was certain he'd be glaring at me. "You are an insufferably caring human. The alternative is yourself. I suggest you send one of your—"

"Ocean!" Ginger squealed, galloping through the doorway and down the hall on all fours. The swarm of scarabs followed, and when they finished surging over the rotting bodies, they left two skeletons in their wake.

"He might have been dropped on his head as a baby," I muttered.

King Tutankhamun snickered. "He's senile."

I opted against reminding the mummy he was far beyond his prime. "Can you handle evacuating the living from the city, Michael?"

"It won't be easy."

"Recruit a few more angels. If you need more money, the devil's paying. He's already coerced Malcolm into handling real estate acquisitions, likely aware these people would need new homes after Wishing Well is destroyed. If he whines, just tell him I'm being nice to him because I'm making you angels do the footwork."

The Archangel of Destruction, Healing,

and the Herald of the End of Days sighed. "Very well."

Ginger bounded down the hallway with a black-taped bundle in his mouth, his scarabs chasing after him.

"You have disturbing friends, little niece."

"Says the headless herald of death, doom, and burns."

"Try not to die. Replacing you would be very inconvenient."

It truly sucked being me sometimes. "And trigger and unscheduled end of days," I reminded him.

"Try not to let it go to your head."

HOW WAS I supposed to steal control over a bunch of mummies? Long after Ginger had run off with the bomb and Michael had gone to do my bidding, I wondered what I could actually accomplish to help the people of Savannah, Atlanta, and Augusta. I regretted having sent Michael off, although I doubted he would share the secrets of the universe with me. At a loss of what to do, I shifted.

My magic's choice of form and attire chilled me.

A full, traditional war khepresh strained my neck with its weight, and I wore a simple linen kalasiris, one ideal for moving. Keeping with ancient traditions, it barely covered my breasts, and if I needed to fight, I expected my clothes would be the first casualty.

Oh well. At least I had a badass crown.

While I wasn't certain how I'd accomplish it, my next trick involved tricking the devil into exposing the culprits, their vessels, and anyone else involved with the murders of so many. I would enjoy killing them. I'd show them I wasn't as nice or merciful as some liked to believe.

I'd draw out their deaths and make them suffer before tossing their souls to the devil for an eternity of misery and suffering.

At the rate I was going, I'd be as bad as an archangel by the end of the day. Since I wouldn't indiscriminately murder anyone, I decided my next stop would be the hotel.

King Tutankhamun followed me, and he worried me almost as much as the archangels hell-bent on destruction. If I wanted to murder a few devils and their vessels myself, I needed to deal with the mummy in such a way I didn't sting his pride and make him turn on me.

Kings needed something to rule, which gave me the perfect idea on how to get him out of my fur for a while. "How would you like to potentially lead a potential horde of mummies?"

"I would enjoy it."

"I have a few ground rules."

"Speak."

"I got married this morning, and instead of spending time with Malcolm, I'm doing this shit. Despite being married in an impromptu eloping, this pisses me off. So, if any mummies refuse to cooperate with you, deal with them. Turn them into rags, scatter their dust, shove their scarabs up their asses for all I care. Give those who have bargained with Wishing Well two choices."

"What choices?"

"They join us, or they die."

"I can do that. I will enjoy it."

"Good. Try not to pick a fight with Ginger, no matter how senile he may be. He's still our friend. Are any of your other allies coming?"

"The Lady brings them. She's slower to awaken, but you'll find her an acceptable companion. Allow me to deliver you to your king, then I will sound the war cry. Our enemies will regret their choice to defy us this day."

I regretted my choices, too. Only an idiot would unleash the forces of the heavens, hell, and ancient Egypt on a city for the sake of the dead and dying. Not only did I need a raise, I needed a vacation—or a really long honeymoon. I could live with that.

TWENTY-SEVEN

Do you think he has any idea how
creepy that is?

SINCE MALCOLM HAD the room keys, I needed to knock to get inside. My husband answered, grabbed me, and put his mouth to good use. A leash might control him—or keep him close so I could enjoy more of his kisses.

When he finally pulled away, I panted to catch my breath. "Are you going to do that every time I leave you unattended?"

"Probably." He pulled me into the room. "Hello, King Tutankhamun."

"The gods be with you, King Malcolm. I leave your queen in your care. I've work to do." The mummy inclined his head and left, sand swirling in his wake.

"Do you think he has any idea how creepy that is?"

"Do you think he cares?"

"Probably not." I peeked around Malcolm to find the devil and his brother playing cards on the bed. "Playtime's over, boys. Gabriel, please help Michael evacuate those with bargained souls from the city—and pass the word he's to coordinate the same efforts in Atlanta and Augusta as well. I'm taking responsibility for them. We may have found a loophole."

"I'm aware. I've been monitoring the situation. You'll save some this way. Not all, but some."

"Would you archangels quit raining on my parade? Satin, I'm only charging you at cost for this. In exchange, you'll give me the names of the devils, demons, and other sentients involved with Wishing Well's activities. Categorize them by role and guilt."

"How involved? There are investors."

"If they're aware of people being murdered for their souls, I want to know. They're as guilty as the actual murderers if they're knowingly funding the deaths."

"The truth may hurt."

Malcolm sighed. "I'm not involved, but I'm willing to bet my family is, and I have my suspicions about who hired the pyro."

"Your speculations are correct," Gabriel stated. "Kanika, I will spare your kelpie the discomfort of trying to tell you this truth. Your mother picked the pyro to maximize your chances of survival."

My mother? I frowned.

"He means my wife," Satin clarified. "The culprit made a bargain with my wife, which needed to be fulfilled, but she did so to favor you as much as she could, which I found out later. It works well, as it gives me proof of guilt."

I turned to Malcolm, put my hands on my hips, and demanded, "Who?"

"Caitlin. My uncle knew, and I suspect he fed Bubba Eugene a bucket of lies to recruit his help—or not. It could go either way with that lot. If the target was me, all they'd have to do is get a picture—or follow me, identify you and your rental, and turn the pyro loose. The pyro could then claim he was after you when I was the actual target. It falls in line with how my clan likes to do business—and with how Caitlin likes to do business."

My Malcolm was truly a black sheep among his family, and I didn't want him any other way. "What good does killing you do if they wanted you as a breeding male?"

The devil snorted flame. "The goal was to force his demonic powers awake. If your male died, it's no real loss. Caitlin would have then attempted to breed with a different Stewart. It's clan politics, stupid ones, too. If they thought it through, they would've realized he's a saltwater kelpie rather than a fresh-water one. They underestimated your surviv-ability. They also underestimated what would happen upon success. Their idea worked. It backfired, but it worked."

I was quickly coming to the conclusion I would never understand devils and demons. "I'm not sure I understand."

"He's a kelpie. Traditionally, they have two uses for—"

"There's no need to tell her this," Malcolm snapped.

Satin growled, and flames sheathed his body. "I think otherwise."

The two glared at each other.

"They're idiots," Gabriel confessed. "Most males are when they're fighting over a female. Just ignore them."

"Since you seem like the only reasonable adult here, how did their plan backfire?"

"Kelpies typically eat or breed with humans. Breeding with humans ensures a stronger bloodline."

"Damn it, Gabriel!" Malcolm hissed.

"And?" I tapped my toe. "That doesn't explain how their plan backfired."

"Following the awakening of his demonic nature, which had already been on the rise before the incident with the pyro, he picked you over her. He won't breed with her, which was the goal. He'll also hound you for his little foals until the day you die," the archangel replied. "Kelpie stallions of his nature have a tendency to fixate. They are extremists, kelpies. Either they'll breed with anything that moves, or they'll bond with a single female for life."

"I don't see the issue with this situation. Why are they being babies about it?"

"My brother doesn't appreciate some kelpie stud treating his little cupcake like a broodmare," Gabriel replied.

Huh. That made a startling amount of sense. "I suppose your brother will just have to mind his own business. Does this mean I can kill Caitlin now?"

"She'll certainly try to kill you. She's angry you took what she believes is hers by right. Kelpies can be rather idiotic."

Malcolm sighed. "I'd argue, but I really can't. He's right."

How was it I seemed like the only sane one in the room? I truly needed that raise and a vacation. "Gabriel, please go help Michael. Satin, I want that list. While you're doing that, Malcolm and I will come up with a basic plan."

Satin scowled at me. "How can you come up with a plan without any targets."

I smiled my sweetest smile. "I plan on planning the many ways I can kill Caitlin."

"You're being rather possessive today, cupcake."

"Get out and don't bother me until you have my list!" I roared.

The devil and archangel fled.

"Should I be concerned?"

I hissed at him. "I'm done working for now. What comes after work?"

"Seduction," he answered.

"Time for you to get to work, Malcolm."

"It's good to be the king."

MAGIC WORKED IN MYSTERIOUS WAYS, as Malcolm discovered he could, with enough effort on his part, make me purr. I also clawed and bit, which he didn't seem to mind.

Several hours later, the devil returned, and he wasn't alone. I couldn't see *Him* but feeling his presence in the room was enough to give me goosebumps. Malcolm paled and tensed.

I was grateful we'd managed to get dressed before their arrival.

"Michael has confirmed your suspicions and reported to the heavens. It has been reviewed, the past has been read, witnessed, and recorded. The Book of Names will be amended, and those tricked will be purged," The Almighty declared.

His voice pieced through my head and gave me a headache I'd never forget. "Purged?" I demanded.

"Erased from this world, purified, and

given three choices," Satin explained. "Forgive my daughter. She's sensitive about souls. It's her nature."

"Sphinxes have, since the beginning of all things, existed to vex me," *He* replied, his tone amused. "Continue, my fallen son."

The devil scowled. "Those purged will be given three choices. They may be reborn as new seeds, they may go to heaven, or they may serve me as a devil or demon. Their souls must not remain on the mortal coil unless they're born anew. The heavens and my hells are joining forces, and we march to reclaim the dead that are rightfully ours."

The devil refused to look at either me or Malcolm, and I got the feeling *He* matched the fallen angel's behavior. I frowned, crossed my arms, and lifted my chin. "What aren't you telling me?"

Malcolm captured my hand in his and ran his fingers over the lines on my palm, and I almost regretted having shifted to human. I liked when he stroked my fur. "They'll erase my clan for their involvement. They're demons; their souls are the devil's domain, and they've violated a universal law. The heavens and hells have a set host; that number never changes. For a new demon to be born, a devil must either be destroyed and leave the hell's power sphere or another demon must die. If there are no seeds of life available, demons will have purely mortal children. That's why neither God nor Satan can win their war; the battle is symbolic. They're balanced, and they must remain so."

Satin grunted but remained silent. *He* spoke, saying, "This remains the truth until the end of days, which is when the balance is broken, the world is destroyed, and it begins with new seeds of life. Two of those seeds are always the same."

I found it interesting the circle of life ruled over all things, even the gods. "Good and evil?" I guessed.

"Yes," Satin said. "For such objective things, they're absolutes as well."

What had I done to deserve the devil's attention? I blamed my bargaining father—my biological one, who had obviously interfered in my affairs without bothering to make an appearance. I owed dear old dad a knuckle sandwich if I ever met him. "Since I'm not insane like the rest of you, what's the most direct method of resolving this?"

"Assassination," the incarnations of good and evil replied.

When *He* voted on death without reservation or hesitancy, I worried—and it reminded me that the Christian faith had a long, bloody history. "You want me to do the divine equivalent of a nuke, don't you?"

"I know you're against the idea, but it

would be the most merciful choice," the devil admitted. "Within ten minutes, it would be all over. We'll have a great deal of work to do and many loose ends to clean up, but if you want the best way to end this, the kindest way is the Deus ex Machina."

The God of the Machine. I grimaced at the reminder Earth was just a living machine with a set destiny, running until the tank emptied and the whole thing stuttered to a halt. Choices drove us and forged us, but it all ended the same.

Life on *my* Earth would inevitably come to an end, then it would begin again with two little seeds.

All we did was change the date.

I had—maybe—saved those I could. I'd seen too many dead because they had wanted better lives for themselves. I understood why Michael had burdened me with his purpose.

It wasn't actual power, but the right to make a choice—one only I could make, a choice arbitrarily granted by the devil and The Almighty. I understood why I'd been told it didn't matter if I knew I had a moment where the weight of the world rested entirely on my shoulders.

With one hand, I could destroy. With the other, I could heal and bring life.

My next words would change everything. The khepresh I'd worn hadn't been for a lit-

eral war, but a figurative one. I could allow
my thirst for revenge to guide my hand, but
my satisfaction would be short lived.

"We're born without a choice in our birth.
If no one chooses to become part of your
hosts, everything remains balanced, correct?"

"Correct," *They* replied, and in that moment, I felt the echo of *Their* power, the one
that forged worlds and destroyed them.

"Replant their seeds of life. Let them live
again. If the devil loses a few demons, new
ones will be born."

He made a thoughtful sound. "And his
devils?"

"You're God. Can't you make him some
new ones?"

Malcolm sighed and shook his head.
"That's not going to fly, Kanika."

"I can," *He* replied.

"But will you?"

Silence.

I sighed. "It's either the end of days now,
or the end of days later. Decide. I'll just die
along with everyone else, but that's part of
being mortal. No matter what choice you
make, I still die. But the real question here is
this: do you love Earth and its creatures more
than you love your fight with the devil?"

He echoed my sigh. "You had to pick the
girl with the guts to stand up to me to be your
child, didn't you?"

"You're joking. I picked her because she has the courage to stand up to *me*. You're an angel in comparison."

"Literally."

I cleared my throat. "Well? Will you?"

"I will. Never let it be said I'm not a caring god. Our war will happen, Lucifer, but it won't be this day. When this is over, our numbers will remain balanced."

"Just not today," the devil agreed.

"It shall be done," *He* confirmed. "I have sent my angels to fulfill the promises my archangels made to you, Kanika Mephistopheles. In five minutes, the cities will be cleared of most innocent life. Then, the purge begins. Mortals, give me a token of their sin so I might wipe it from this world forever."

Malcolm headed to the room's desk and picked up the Wishing Well business cards we'd gathered, most stained with the blood of the dead. "Will these do?"

"Indeed," *He* confirmed. "Know this. Should I do this, there is no turning back. Not even I can undo what will be done, and you will carry the weight of these souls forever on your shoulders."

"What weight?" I held my hands out, palms up. "There will be death, but there will be life. They will not lose their souls. In this life, they are lost, but they will be born again.

They have a second chance. I didn't decide to murder these people for their souls. They're already dead. All I'm doing is giving them another chance. I'd hope someone would do the same for me."

Malcolm would; he'd already proven that.

"So be it. It will be done. May it be witnessed I have not broken my promise to the world of men."

"Witnessed," the devil announced.

He left, and I breathed easier without *His* presence in the room. Sighing, the devil shook his head. "Your clan and Caitlin will be the final obstacle, Malcolm."

Malcolm canted his head and arched a brow. "They hurt Kanika. They die."

If I rolled my eyes any harder, I'd hurt myself. "That's a dumb reason to kill them."

"It's the only reason I need."

"Give it up, cupcake. He's a kelpie, and he's chosen you—and don't you even try to claim you didn't choose him back. He's a demon. Let him reclaim his clan and pride without standing in his way."

Men. I gave up. "Fine, but if you get hurt being manly, Malcolm, I'll be pissed."

"Back atcha, dahlin'," he drawled.

I UNDERSTOOD why so many feared the end

of days. When *He* moved, no trumpets signaled his destruction, nor did light bathe Savannah. To all appearances, nothing had changed, but everything had changed, and the newly dead littered the streets, felled with no warning.

Nothing betrayed the workings of *Him* and his angels.

No one would know why so many had died, some victims, some murderers, and some bringing their deaths upon themselves through their greed. No one would learn, not unless we told them.

I wouldn't. Some things were better left secret.

Malcolm wrapped his arm around my shoulders and held me close while we stared out over the street from the hotel lobby. Even the staff had died, and I tried to remember the reasons I had done what I had done.

One day, they would live again, new seeds planted and brought back to life, their souls safe. It was a burden I could live with.

Malcolm sighed. "Who is going to take care of the bodies?"

Ew. Considering how many there were, I certainly didn't want the job, although I supposed the work belonged to me. How could I deal with so many corpses?

Had I been wise, I would have asked *Him* and his angels to take care of the mess, but I supposed dealing with the aftermath was only fair. Short of razing the entire city to the ground, what could I do? It would take thousands of workers to clear so many bodies, and I couldn't imagine the logistics of trying to bury so many dead at one time.

In such a short period of time, Wishing Well had done so much damage to so many. Buildings could be rebuilt. An entire city could be rebuilt.

Spending the devil's money, Malcolm could rebuild it, and I knew just the man who could raze an entire city—or three.

I leaned against Malcolm. "I know a guy with a dragon. Maybe the dragon can burn the whole place to the ground. Then you can rebuild everything from scratch."

Would fire be enough to erase the crimes committed where the city stood?

"You know a guy with a *dragon*?"

"Well, yeah."

"Kanika, do you realize the dragons haven't emerged yet?"

"So?"

"It's a *dragon*."

"Are you scared of dragons?"

Malcolm hung his head. "Why not? It's only a dragon. Go on. Go ask about your dragon. Do you even care you just suggested feeding a bunch of people to a dragon?"

"It can eat Caitlin, too, if it can find her."

"Sold. Where's your dragon?"

"Tennessee. I'll need to talk to the guy who sold me the bracelet." I had a sneaking suspicion Satin had supplied the damned thing to Hagnar, but I'd keep my peace about that. The results worked for me.

"I think I need to become friends with him."

"If I meet with him in person, I'm leaving you in the car."

"That's not fair."

"Deal with it." I sighed, shaking my head over the pointless, wasted deaths. I wondered how many had died because of my single choice. Maybe one day I'd ask. For the moment, I'd quietly live with my regrets, of which there were many.

I could only hope meeting with Hagnar wouldn't add to them.

TWENTY-EIGHT

He has a taste for everything.

THANKS TO SO MANY DEAD, we couldn't drive out of Savannah, so I called Hagnar's shop.

He answered on the third ring. "The rumor mill says you're neck deep in trouble, Kanika."

"Exchange trouble for bodies, and you'd be right. I have a question for you. Can you wake the sleeper in your basement?"

"Why would I *want* to? Do you have any idea how much food I'd need to feed that one?"

"If it likes its meat a bit ripe, I know a few places." I hated myself for the wording, but it was the truth. "Does it have a taste for human?"

"He has a taste for everything. He eats ash, Kanika."

"There's three dead cities in Georgia. All I ask is to try to leave as many buildings intact as you can, but if your dragon has a taste for condemned buildings, by all means, he can have them." Someone scratched at the lobby door, and I turned in time to watch Malcolm open the door to let in three ancient mummies. "It's the devil's work."

"You got involved with that nonsense? I'm surprised you of all people would do that."

"Heir of Hell and all that nonsense," I admitted. "The rumor mill is right. I'm in way over my head."

"Sounds like it."

"So, can you wake it?"

"Why do you always come to me with odd jobs?"

"Because I'm an idiot who picked a terrible business name."

Hagnar laughed. "For you, I will, but I bear no responsibility for what happens afterwards."

"Understood. Also, just a tip. That node of yours? You better make it disappear—or hide it really well. There are those who know they exist."

"For that tip alone, I charge you nothing for my help. Who knows?"

"It doesn't matter. If they aren't dead already, they're going to die."

"And for that, I owe you a favor. Just tell me one thing. How did you, of all people, end up in the middle of this mess?"

"I wasn't joking. Heir of Hell and all that shit. That's how."

Hagnar whistled. "Now *that's* a shit job."

Glancing at Malcolm out of the corner of my eye, I smiled. "It has its benefits."

SINCE WE COULDN'T LEAVE Savannah, I herded Malcolm, Ginger, the Gilded Lady, and King Tutankhamun to the beach. The mummies grumbled at me over the ruination of their fun. I couldn't blame them. I had wrecked my own plans. Who expected a multi-city armageddon? Not me. Before I'd agreed to kidnap Malcolm, scraping to get by fell in line with my expectations, and I had expected to struggle.

Only one loose end remained: Caitlin and the Stewart clan.

How had things gotten so strange—and how had they circled right back to the beginning? I sighed and stared out over the ocean.

"Why are we here?" Malcolm asked.

"Ocean nookie after ex killing." I shrugged. "Call her and have her bring your clan with her."

"There's two of us and at least ten of them, Kanika. The ocean doesn't make me invincible, and I don't know the finer points of fighting as a kelpie."

I pointed at the three mummies. "They got robbed of their undead army of mummies. I was thinking we'd just watch and let them work out their irritation on Caitlin and the Stewart clan."

"It's still a bad idea."

"Who needs to die, my queen?" King Tutankhamun demanded.

I stuck my tongue out at Malcolm. "The rest of Malcolm's clan and that bitch of an ex, Caitlin."

"The sands are ours, my queen."

I spotted a bright green scarab burrowing where the surf and sand met. "Right. Just lure them here, Malcolm."

"This is a terrible idea." Sighing, Malcolm pulled out his phone and checked the display. "I'm still amazed I have a signal. I don't want to talk to Caitlin. Can't we skip to the ocean nookie? I'm game for the ocean nookie."

Of course he was. He was a kelpie. I'd make him teach me how to swim first, but I planned to enjoy my reward for learning a new skill. "No. Call her."

He sighed and dialed. "Caitlin, I need to meet—" With wide eyes, he pulled the phone away from his ear, glanced at the screen, and returned it to his ear. "All right. Five minutes on the beach, then."

"What did she say?"

"I don't think *He's* as honest as we

thought, or he has a very twisted sense of justice."

"What? What happened?"

"*He* decided the Stewart clan had outlived their usefulness as demons and turned them into angels. *He* didn't kill them. *He* took them and made them *His* own."

My eyes widened, too. "Why would *He* do that?"

"All *He* said was that their numbers would be equal and that *He'd* replace the devils—and make the devil new ones. Conversions count, I suppose. It'll piss the devil off, too."

"But why leave Caitlin?" I growled.

Malcolm pocketed his phone, laughing softly. "*He* likely doesn't want the devil's cupcake aiming for the heavens. I have it on good authority she can be vicious."

Hissing, I flexed my hands and mimicked claws. "I'll show you vicious."

"Please do."

I sighed. "I can't blame *Him* for not wanting me gunning for him. I'm a walking disaster."

"It's okay. I still love you anyway." Malcolm grinned at me. "Were you serious about the ocean nookie?"

"You'll have to wait to find out."

"Damn it."

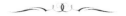

CAITLIN SHOWED UP ALONE. Since I'd last seen her, her hair had turned white. She kidded to a halt and glared at me. "Why are *you* here?"

I almost felt bad that the last moments of the woman's life would be spent having a fight with me. "There's no way I'd let you near *my* kelpie. No, I'm here as an observer. I don't want you to miss your date with the grave. You chose to align yourself with Wishing Well."

"They promised me Malcolm."

I shook my head, and I pitied her for her obsession over a man who'd never love her because of who she was and what she'd done to him. "That's one bargain that's never getting fulfilled. Sorry. I feel like I should give you a chance to try to redeem yourself, but—"

"I've done nothing wrong."

Wow. I'd finally met someone who was a bigger asshole than the devil himself. "You're really quite the bitch, aren't you?"

"How dare you!"

The longer I dragged it out, the more I might hurt Malcolm, who had already lost his entire family in one fell swoop. Sighing, I turned my back on her, stepped to Malcolm, and took his hand in mine. "She's yours, King Tutankhamun. Try to save a little something for your friends."

"How long might I play with her, my queen?"

"For however long you want. Share with Ginger and the Gilded Lady—and whomever else might be lurking in the sands."

"Yes, my queen."

The sands erupted, and a swarm of scarabs engulfed Caitlin. Only her screams convinced me she lived beneath the covering of insects. The three mummies stepped forward as one, claimed the kelpie, and dragged her away.

"And people say the devil's mean, but you're something else," Malcolm murmured, giving my hand a squeeze.

"Is that a bad thing?"

"I've never been so turned on in my life."

A startled laugh burst out of me. "You're so weird."

"I'm a kelpie in my element, and you just gave the demon of my nightmares to vengeful mummies. Nothing I could do compares to a mummy's curse, and she has the ire of three of them. There's no better gift anyone could give me. I'm free."

He'd already been free the moment he had married me, but I'd let him have his moment and enjoy his relief without undermining him. "So, is it better than ocean nookie?"

"I'll have to do some very intense studying to find out."

I could live with that. "Don't we need a control if we're going to be properly studying this? It's for the sake of science."

"We have a control already, the night I claimed you as mine."

My eyes widened. Did he truly expect to do better? According to his smirk, he most certainly did.

Holy hell and amen.

HAGNAR'S DRAGON came with the dawn, and it burned Savannah to the ground, and once the city smoldered, it ate.

And ate. And ate. And ate.

It was even larger than I believed possible, and I wondered what sort of magic had shrunk it to fit within Hagnar's caverns. It dwarfed the first building it incinerated, gulping down the ashes while they still glowed red. With every bite, its scales brightened, the black paling to an iridescent rainbow.

From the safety of shore, we watched it devour the boardwalk, leaving behind soot stains on the sand and erasing evidence civilization had ever existed within the city.

"I'm sorry about your father," I whispered, watching the dragon take to the skies and breathe flame so it might continue to feed. "It's my fault your family died."

"They didn't die. They're serving a new purpose now. And anyway, who said my father was turned into an angel?"

I held my breath and waited, not certain if I dared to hope for the impossible while wondering if Malcolm had wanted them out of his life or not.

"He's a MacGregor now, Kanika." Malcolm pulled out his phone and turned the display to me, showing several texts labeled as coming from his father. "Sure, my parents can be jerks. They are kelpies after all, but as far as kelpies go, they're nice enough demons. They'll adore you. My mother adores cats. You may want to stay human and neglect to show her your fur coat. She'll never let you out of her sight ever again if she learns you're also a cat."

I'd take his advice; I'd already had enough trouble from one cat lover as it was. Without Miss Angorra and Mr. Mistoffelees, I wouldn't have made a deal with the devil in the first place. I took a moment to compose myself. "Your parents are fine?"

"They're fine."

"Huh. That explains why you're in such a good mood for someone who was offered ocean nookie but declined it because he is incapable of teaching a cat how to swim."

"I don't want you to drown while I'm seducing you."

"Shallow water nookie was an option!"

"Next time—after you learn how to swim."

"You are such an incredible jerk, Malcolm."

He smirked at me, linked his arm with mine, and pulled me away from the water. "I'm starting to think you want the ocean nookie even more than I do."

"Jerk, jerk, jerk, jerk, jerk," I muttered.

"That I am. The water can wait. Don't worry, I'll make it up to you as soon as I get you home."

I bet he would.

THE DRAGON'S rampage lit the entirety of Savannah on fire, leaving our stretch of beach as the only safe haven. While the city burned, the mummies found a way to avoid the flames. Burrowing where the sea and sand met, they left a trench which the waves filled with water. I leaned over, narrowing my eyes where the trench turned into a tunnel heading inland.

Malcolm joined me, clucking his tongue. "I almost feel sorry for her."

"Why?"

"I would've just killed her. Those mummies will make her suffer for a long time. For some reason, I don't think mercy is in their dictionary, Kanika."

He was probably right. "Maybe I should have set some limits."

"And pissed off three ancient mummies itching for a fight because you stole their thunder? No. Caitlin reaped what she sowed, and she deserves everything those mummies put her through."

Once again, he was probably right. "This is such a mess."

"The news reports are going to be interesting in the morning, that much is for certain. My employees are going to find out Savannah was wiped out and flip."

"Maybe you should call someone and tell them you weren't eaten by a dragon."

"If I call them, I'll have to explain I need to update my DBA accounts, then they'll start asking questions, then they'll demand evidence there's actually a woman in my life, and then they'll start hunting you in packs, and I don't feel like sharing you with anyone yet." Malcolm scowled.

"Why do I have a feeling they actually believe you ran away from work?"

"I didn't run away. I did take a few days off to scout the situation here in Savannah."

"And served as my accomplice in blowing it to—"

Something exploded in the heart of the city, and with a headache-inducing shriek, the dragon rose into the sky before swooping down and breathing flames on what hadn't already been turned to ash. I sighed, hung my head, and wondered if I'd be held responsible for the destruction.

For some reason, I doubted Satin would foot the bill without one hell of a fight.

"I'm pleased to announce that there will be a lot of viable land for construction in the very near future, and there will be limited demolition and removal costs. If I get yelled at, you'll have to make me feel better later." Malcolm pulled out his phone, grumbled a few curses, and dialed a number. "It's Malcolm. I'm going to need you to do a check into real estate insurance companies in Savannah, Atlanta, and Augusta—"

The dragon breathed more flame, something else exploded, and a fine powdery ash rained down on us.

"I'm fine, really. As I was saying, I need to see if there are any insurance companies heavily working in those cities who are staging a buyout. I want a good rate for the policies—and the companies, if possible. I'll also need sufficient employees to handle claims. There'll be a lot of them."

A third explosion shook the ground, and

even the waves recoiled from the dragon's re-
lentless hunger.

"Yes, I'm still fine. I'm pretty sure my
rental isn't, though. No, I'm not worried. It's
just a dragon."

"Just a dragon?" a woman screeched on the
other end of the line.

Malcolm scowled and pointed his phone
at me. "See? You're getting me in trouble. I
told you I'd get in trouble if I called."

Since he'd put the phone in my easy reach,
I snatched it out of his hand, put it to my ear,
and said, "I'm so sorry for him, ma'am. He's
an idiot."

I grinned at the stunned silence.

The woman cleared her throat. "Excuse
me, ma'am, but who are you?"

"Kanika. I'm Malcolm's guardian so he
doesn't get eaten by a dragon. Honestly, I
think I deserve a raise."

While my husband wrinkled his nose at me
and grunted his displeasure, the woman
laughed. "I'm Sophie, Mr. Malcolm's secretary."

"If he's anywhere near as insufferable at
work as he is at home, you probably deserve a
raise, too."

I wasn't sure what to make of Sophie's silence, and just as I was beginning to believe
the line had gone dead, Malcolm's secretary
chuckled. "I was wondering when he'd finally

get around to taking a new woman home with him. How long do you plan on sticking around, Miss Kanika?"

Maybe giving Caitlin to the mummies hadn't been punishment enough. "My adoptive father would probably kill him if I let him go, so I think I'm stuck with him."

"Stuck?" Malcolm crossed his arms, his eyes narrowed. "You think?"

"Dare I ask?" His secretary sounded worried.

"Don't worry about it. Malcolm's going to be busy for a few days, as we're stuck in Savannah until the dragon either gets bored and leaves or finishes devouring what's left of the city." I shrugged despite knowing the woman couldn't see me. "He's going to be busy."

"Doing *what*?" Sophie screeched. I held Malcolm's phone away from my ear as the woman launched into a shrill tirade on where Malcolm should have been, what he needed to be doing, and how it wasn't wise for anyone's health to stay near a city being consumed by a dragon.

"I told you calling was a bad idea," he muttered.

I roared, and Sophie's rant ended in a startled squeak. "That's better. I'll make sure he's returned to you in pristine condition, Miss Sophie."

"Who the hell do you think you are?"

Malcolm's expression turned cold and hard, and I laughed. "His wife."

I enjoyed the stunned silence and hung up before she could recover. Sighing, Malcolm took his phone back. "You're a terrible person sometimes, Kanika."

"Only sometimes? Have you already forgotten I kidnapped you for the equivalent of pocket change to a rich guy like you?"

"I'm tempted to hire you to kidnap me every time we need a vacation."

"Or we could just go on a vacation."

"And miss the chance to see you bent over an engine again?"

Malcolm's phone rang, and he answered, "Sorry about that, Sophie. I've reclaimed my phone from the troublemaker. I'm going to send you some requests tomorrow for paperwork I'll need filed in addition to the real estate insurance company scouting. I'm also looking to buy out any promising lots in the cities I mentioned earlier; I'm in a new partnership deal that should open up a lot of opportunities for the company in the next few years, so we need to make a land grab now while the properties are hot."

I groaned and shook my head in disgust.

Malcolm frowned. "What?"

Pointing at the burning city of Savannah, I glared and waited for him to figure it out.

"Crap. Sorry. I'll call you back later, Sophie. My wife's looking a wee bit miffed with me." He disconnected the call and held his hands up in surrender. "It wasn't on purpose!"

"And you called me a terrible person."

"Would renegotiating the terms of some shoreline shenanigans absolve me of my sins?"

"Shenanigans? Is that what we're calling it now? What happened to ocean nookie?"

"Shoreline shenanigans has a much better ring to it."

"What happened to no shoreline shenanigans without learning how to swim first?"

"It's your fault you're so pretty when you get hissy at me."

"You need your head examined, Malcolm."

"Does that mean no shoreline shenanigans?"

Making him wait for an answer put me in the terrible person category, but I enjoyed his fidgeting too much for my own good. "Well, it's not like we can go anywhere or do anything for a while, so we may as well fill—"

Malcolm pounced.

TWENTY-NINE

Are you aware you have an
attachment?

AT THE RATE Malcolm kept destroying his
clothes shifting from man to a headstrong,
stubborn, obnoxious stallion determined to
drive me into the water, I'd go broke buying
him clothes. At least fortune smiled on me;
the dragon hadn't completely annihilated the
boardwalk, so I was able to pilfer something
for him to wear when he got around to
shifting back to human.

I wasn't holding my breath, which factored into my current status as the victor of
our odd dispute. He'd knocked me into the
surf once, and after I spent ten minutes
choking and coughing, he'd settled with
feigned attempts to herd me into the sea.

We needed to have a long talk about his
idiocy when sporting hooves. During the discussion, I wouldn't tell him how pretty he
was, his gray coat toned with blue with the

faintest sheen of green. I definitely wouldn't inform him I intended to drag him to the beach every chance I got so I could admire the scenery, which would include him. Man or beast, I won either way.

Malcolm took hold of the back of my shirt in his teeth and followed me while I carried his newly pilfered clothes under an arm. "What do you think you're doing?"

He snorted at me, bumping my back with his nose. As I wasn't fluent in demon horse, I sighed over my own idiocy for even attempting to talk sense into him. Aware he'd shove me back in the ocean if I gave him the opportunity, I angled away from the shore.

A figure stepped over the grassy bank above and waved. "Are you aware you have an attachment?"

The attachment snorted his displeasure, released my shirt, and draped his head over my shoulder, blowing more air while he flattened his ears and bared his teeth. I lifted my hand and rubbed Malcolm's nose. "He gets a little jealous sometimes."

"Kelpies usually do. Where on Earth did you find one?"

"I kidnapped him and made him take me home with him. I felt sorry for him, so I decided to keep him."

"You lead a very strange life, Kanika."

"Says the man who has a pet dragon."

"I wouldn't call him my pet."

"Are you his pet, then?"

"That's fairly accurate. I consider myself fortunate he allowed me to ride rather than carrying me here by my britches. He expresses his gratitude for his meal."

"Meals. He has two more cities to visit. I hope he's hungry."

Hagnar blanched. "Indeed."

For once in my life, I had won the advantage over the black market operator. I considered the bracelets Malcolm and I wore, and I wondered if Hagnar had any idea he'd been played by the devil, too. "Where'd you get the suppression bracelets you sold me?"

"I'd rather not talk business in front of an outsider."

"The outsider is the devil's son-in-law. I'm sure he won't bother your operations much. That, plus he'll probably end up funding some of my shopping trips."

"A buyer sold them to me a week before your job popped up."

"Satin, you piece of shit!" I yowled, stomping my foot in the sand.

The devil appeared with a flash of light and brought the stench of brimstone with him, and as though sensing he'd have an audience, he'd come in his full glory, sheathed in flame instead of clothing. "You called, cupcake?"

"You, sir, are a jerk." I wondered if shoving him into the ocean would do any good, but considering Savannah had already been razed, I wasn't eager to kill anything else, not even some poor fish. "You knew about the contract, didn't you?"

"I may have greased some wheels to make certain you were the one approached for the job, and as I knew your friend here was your most reliable contact for illegal goods, I thought I'd make myself useful. I gave him a very good deal on the bracelet."

To his credit, Hagnar didn't even flinch when the devil appeared, although he did sigh. "What trouble have you gotten me into now, Kanika?"

"You're the pet of a dragon. You got yourself into plenty of trouble without my help."

Hagnar eyed the devil. "Was waking the dragon your plan all along?"

Satin smiled, and then he disappeared in a flash of silver light.

"I'm going to take that as a yes," the black market operator murmured. "I don't know what he was working for, but I think he came out the victor of that round. The mold's been broken. He's claimed himself an heir, choosing a daughter instead of the son everyone expected. He has secured this era of magic, too. I shouldn't be surprised that the magic won't fade from the world again, not for a long time."

I pressed my back against Malcolm's warm chest, stroking his nose. "I'm not sure what you mean. Can't you just give me a straight answer for once?"

Laughing, he shook his head. "I should refuse on principle since you're not paying me."

"You'll enjoy spending my money again soon enough, I'm sure."

"I expect so. You're going to be doing the devil's dirty work for him. You'll need my services, and often."

"Give me a straight and true answer."

"The dragons only awaken when there's enough magic in the world to sustain them. They know. They always do. And when the magic begins to fade from the world, they'll be the first to return to their slumber. Watch the dragons, if you can find them, and heed my words, Kanika. This is only the beginning."

The beginning of what, I wasn't certain, although the world wasn't going to end, not yet. I'd ensured that much, although I remained baffled over what my role had been in the end game. One moment defined me, and I'd likely never learn which moment had done the trick.

Malcolm snorted and rubbed his head

against my chest.

"Three days," Hagnar announced.

"Three days?"

"That's how long it'll take for him to raze all three cities. After, I expect he'll go back to sleep for a while. A week, two weeks, maybe more. If we're lucky, we'll count his slumber in years." Hagnar narrowed his eyes, his gaze fixed where the dragon swooped, blew flame, and disappeared into the smoke. "We may all regret this."

I could imagine why. If a single dragon could devour three cities in three days, I didn't want to know what else one could do. "You may be right, but I think it's preferable to the premature end of days."

He hummed. "Yes, I suppose you're right. But all things come to an end. It's just a matter of when."

Malcolm stretched out his head and snapped his teeth at Hagnar, who lifted his hands in surrender.

"I think your kelpie disagrees with me. I recommend you leave before the dragon forgets humans aren't food. He always has a wretched appetite when he first gets up. He'll remember soon enough humans have other purposes."

After my lessons on kelpies, I had a few ideas what other uses dragons might have for humans, but I decided I just didn't want to know how it worked. If kelpies could wander around as humans, then I saw no reason dragons couldn't. Who was I to judge?

I was a sphinx, and I'd married a man-eating horse.

"How do you propose that?"

Hagnar pointed at Malcolm. "Ride him. He won't mind. Just stick near the shore until you're well away from the city. Go on home, Kanika, wherever that is."

It occurred to me, that thanks to Malcolm, I did have a home, although it currently suffered from an infestation of rowdy succubi and incubi. "I think we'll take a vacation somewhere quiet. Hey, do you happen to have any devil repellent?"

"Salt," the black market operator replied. "It sometimes helps. But with the sort of devil problem you have, I recommend surrender. You've already lost that war."

So I had, but I didn't mind.

Malcolm was worth it.

Owl Be Yours is the next book in the Magical Romantic Comedy (with a body count) series. These stories, with the exception of Burn, Baby, Burn (sequel to Playing with Fire,) can be read in any order.

About R.J. Blain

Want to hear from the author when a new book releases? You can sign up at her website (thesneakykittycritic.com). Please note this newsletter is operated by the Furred & Frond Management. Expect to be sassed by a cat. (With guest features of other animals, including dogs.)

A complete list of books written by RJ and her various pen names is available at https://books2read.com/rl/The-Fantasy-Worlds-of-RJ-Blain.

RJ BLAIN suffers from a Moleskine journal obsession, a pen fixation, and a terrible tendency to pun without warning.

When she isn't playing pretend, she likes to think she's a cartographer and a sumi-e painter.

In her spare time, she daydreams about being

a spy. Should that fail, her contingency plan involves tying her best of enemies to spinning wheels and quoting James Bond villains until she is satisfied.

RJ also writes as Susan Copperfield and Bernadette Franklin. Visit RJ and her pets (the Management) at thesneakykittycritic.com.

Follow RJ & her alter egos on Bookbub:
RJ Blain
Susan Copperfield
Bernadette Franklin